"Stop me if you mean to do so," Will whispered.

Amy's breathing grew faster, but she said nothing.

"You have until the count of three," he said.

Oh, dear God, I don't think I can deny him . . .

"One," he said, his voice rumbling.

He is a devil and cannot be trusted.

"Two."

You're ruined already.

"Three," he said in a rough tone.

Kiss me before I lose my courage.

He trailed his lips lightly over her mouth. The kiss was butterfly gentle and fleeting. No man had ever kissed her before. The sound of his lips meeting hers mesmerized her. He applied a little more pressure and reached round her, pulling her closer until her breasts were nestled against his rock-hard chest. There was something very exhilarating about being in a man's arms.

Of course, she must stop him, but he drew his tongue over the seam of her mouth. Her lips parted involuntarily, and then he swept his tongue inside.

Only the devil would kiss like this . . .

HOW TO MARRY A DUKE

"In her lively debut novel, Vicky Dreiling has penned a fresh, engaging take on Regency matchmaking that brims with clever wit and repartee. I found myself smiling and laughing out loud on numerous occasions. Here's hoping for more of this promising new author's historical romances!"

—Nicole Jordan, *New York Times* bestselling author

"An enchanting debut, full of humor and heart!"

—Madeline Hunter, *New York Times* bestselling author

"Vicky Dreiling delivers a tale chock-full of warmth, wit, and tenderness. She's sure to please readers everywhere!"

—Samantha James, *New York Times* bestselling author

"Sexy, fresh, and witty...A delicious read! Better than chocolate! Vicky Dreiling is an author to watch!"

—Sophie Jordan, *New York Times* bestselling author

"A terrific romp of a read!...Vicky is a bright new voice in romance."

—Sarah MacLean, *New York Times* bestselling author

How to Ravish a Rake

How to Ravish a Rake

VICKY DREILING

FOREVER

NEW YORK   BOSTON

Copyright © 2012 by Vicky Dreiling
Excerpt from *How to Marry a Duke* Copyright © 2011 by Vicky Dreiling
Excerpt from *How to Seduce a Scoundrel* Copyright © 2011 by Vicky Dreiling

Forever
Hachette Book Group
237 Park Avenue
New York, NY 10017

www.HachetteBookGroup.com

Printed in the United States of America

First Edition: April 2012

10 9 8 7 6 5 4 3 2 1

Forever is an imprint of Grand Central Publishing.
The Forever name and logo are trademarks of Hachette Book Group, Inc.

The Hachette Speakers Bureau provides a wide range of authors for speaking events. To find out more, go to www.hachettespeakersbureau .com or call (866) 376-6591.

The publisher is not responsible for websites (or their content) that are not owned by the publisher.

*To my talented and insightful editor,
Michele Bidelspach, because you loved Amy
from the beginning. I'm one lucky author to
have you for an editor. Thank you for
everything. xoxoxo*

Acknowledgments

Merci beaucoup to my very talented agent, Lucienne Diver, for all the guidance, explanations, speedy replies, professionalism—and the fun, too! I am so very fortunate to have such a smart and talented agent. Thank you doesn't even begin to cover it, but I look forward to many more successful years working with you. P.S. I sincerely hope the next time we meet for lunch that you don't get squirted by a greasy chicken. ☺

Thanks also to Deidre Knight for all the support and tweets. Many thanks to Elaine Spencer for your timely responses. Additional thanks go to all the talented staff at The Knight Agency.

Many thanks to everyone at Forever Romance. Shout-outs go to Brianne Beers for arranging the wonderful blog tour, Lauren Plude for guest hosting #mancandymonday ☺, the Art Department for the fabulous covers (I'm a fan girl!), and Jillian Sanders for providing promotional opportunities. Picture me with a big thumbs-up to all the fabulous editorial staff at Forever Romance for your out-of-the-box ideas. You guys rock!

A huge thank-you to my beta readers, Jamie Lynn

Murawski and Katie Rodriguez. Also, many thanks to Jamie, Katie, and Rita for the fun Vokle interview.

Appreciation goes to my talented web designer, Shelley, at Web Crafters, and her assistant, Peggy.

Hugs to my supportive family: Mom, Daniel, Regina, Amber, and Jonathan.

A nod to my son's squeaking cat, Foxy, who is the role model for Poppet.

Most of all, my thanks and appreciation to all of my readers. May the Magic Romance Fairies be with you!

How to Ravish a Rake

Chapter One

London, 1818

This season would likely be her last.

The orchestra played a lively tune as Amy Hardwick followed her friend Georgette through the Beresfords' packed ballroom. The lively tempo pulsed through her veins, and she walked along to the energetic beat of the music. The heat in the crowded room accentuated the fruity aroma of numerous potted orange trees. Garlands of ivy adorned two cream-colored Ionic pillars and the gilded ormolu marble mantel as well. Everywhere Amy looked ladies in filmy white gowns flitted about the room like butterflies.

To her, the spring season represented a beginning and a last chance to blossom—to thrive—to be merry and carefree. A chance to break free of her doubts and feelings of inferiority. A chance to dance, flirt, and laugh without reservation. A chance to be the woman she'd always dreamed of being.

She dodged a footman in a powdered wig carrying a tray of bottles and hurried to catch up to her friend. "Lady Beresford must be thrilled. Her ball is a veritable squeeze," Amy said, raising her voice.

Georgette drew closer and pitched her voice a bit louder. "We're too close to the orchestra to talk. Let us find our friends."

As they wended their way past numerous groups of people, Amy recalled the first time she'd entered this ballroom when she was seventeen. On that evening, she'd spun girlish dreams of being the belle of the ball, but she'd been intimidated because she knew no one there. In comparison to all the ladies dressed in sophisticated gowns, she'd felt like a country mouse. Her simple white gown had hung sacklike on her spare frame, because she'd been too nervous to eat properly for a fortnight prior to her debut. She'd sat on the wallflower row, watching all the gaiety and keeping hope alive, but not a single gentleman had requested her hand for a country dance.

Only once in the intervening years had anyone asked.

Five unsuccessful seasons later, she'd set her expectations much lower. Plain, shy ladies like her didn't attract the notice of gentlemen. But this year, she meant to shed her wallflower reputation.

Amy lifted her chin and straightened her posture, even though she imagined doing so made her look like a giraffe. She glanced down at Georgette, wishing she could be as petite and dainty.

"Oh, look, there is Sally with some of the other ladies," Georgette said. "They are coming this way."

Amy recognized them. Sally, Catherine, Charlotte, and Priscilla all wore excited expressions. No doubt they intended to impart gossip. Catherine and Charlotte were particularly fond of tittle-tattle.

Sally reached them first. Her expression looked awed as her gaze swept over Amy's white gown. "You look like a goddess."

Warmth suffused Amy's face at Sally's absurd exaggeration. Amy expected the topic to turn away from her, but Charlotte fingered the white fabric of Amy's skirt. "It is crepe," she said with a touch of admiration in her voice. "The emerald ribbons flowing over your shoulders are so striking."

"Turn round," Catherine said. "Slowly, if you please."

Georgette grinned and twirled her finger, indicating Amy should comply. With a deep breath, Amy slowly turned—to the accompaniment of gasps.

"It is beyond beautiful," Charlotte said in a breathless voice.

"The red silk roses are impressive," Catherine said. "How very clever to feature them on the back of the gown. Everywhere you walk, others will be compelled to follow you with their eyes."

Amy lowered her lashes and murmured her thanks. While she was a bit abashed, she was also secretly pleased by their praise.

"You must tell us who your modiste is," Priscilla said. "I simply must have something equally lovely."

"I agree," Catherine said. "Your gown is bound to be all the rage."

Georgette gave Amy a speaking look. "Will you tell or shall I?"

Once again, Amy blushed. "I confess I drew the design for a local modiste back home." On a whim, she had bought fabric and trims in London at the end of last spring, because she couldn't resist them.

The other ladies, with the exception of Georgette, stared at her. Was it because she'd revealed her dress was not made by one of the foremost dressmakers in London?

"You drew the design?" Charlotte said in a shocked voice.

Amy nodded. "I've always enjoyed drawing. It is a pleasurable way to pass the time."

Catherine's jaw dropped. "Georgette, does Amy have any idea how talented she is?"

"No, she is too modest about her accomplishments," Georgette said. "Her talents go beyond mere drawing. Amy has an eye for fabrics and trims, too. I would never have thought to put the trim on the back of my gown."

At one time, Amy had possessed little knowledge of fashion, but two years ago, she'd befriended Georgette and Julianne and had asked them for advice. While shopping with them last spring, she had taken suggestions from a premiere modiste in London. She'd asked Madame DuPont questions about the fabrics and trims. The modiste had taken Amy under her wing and showed her which colors enhanced her appearance. She'd also demonstrated with pins how the perfect fit in both the gown and stays made a critical difference in how the gown draped her figure. When Amy had viewed herself in the long mirror, she'd gasped at her reflection. The beautiful gown had transformed her from a badly dressed wallflower to an elegantly dressed lady. In that moment, she'd seen the potential to change the way she viewed herself and the way others perceived her. While she'd always believed that inner beauty trumped everything, she'd learned first-hand that everyone, particularly women, were judged by their appearances.

"But where did this talent come from?" Sally asked.

"I studied the latest styles in *La Belle Assemblée,* and then I started to envision walking gowns and ball gowns as well. One day last summer, I drew what popped into my head for amusement."

"Oh, my, that is truly amazing," Charlotte said. "Did you have a drawing instructor when you were younger?"

She nodded. "My governess encouraged me." After seeing Amy's drawings and watercolors, her parents had praised her accomplishments. While Amy enjoyed their compliments, she'd taken them in stride since they could hardly be objective.

While perusing fashion plates, she'd realized her designs were unique. A few weeks prior to leaving for London with Georgette, she'd commissioned a local dress-maker to make up a few of her designs, according to her specifications. The dressmaker had been impressed and had told Amy she had a singular talent.

Of course, her mother had expressed delight, but when Amy had shown her designs to Georgette earlier today, her friend had literally gasped. Amy would never forget Georgette's words. *Your designs put every fashion plate I've ever viewed to shame.* Then her friend had begged her to design a special ball gown for her.

"Amy, I would love to see your sketches one day, if you are willing to share them," Sally said.

"Of course," she said. "I value your opinion."

Georgette's cheeks dimpled as she whispered to Amy. "I knew you would be popular this year."

Amy thought her friend's words rather overblown, but she was pleased that others had admired her gown. She would never be beautiful, but she could dress elegantly.

Catherine looked out at the crowd and gasped. "The devil is here."

Amy exchanged a knowing look with Georgette. The scandal sheets had saddled Mr. William Darcett with that moniker. By all accounts, he had earned his notorious reputation. Amy did her best to maintain a serene expression, but she did not welcome the news that Devil Darcett was present. She'd met him at her friend Julianne's wedding last summer and preferred to forget that mortifying encounter.

Charlotte clasped her hands to her heart and sighed. "He is so beautiful I think I shall swoon."

Amy rolled her eyes. Why did women make cakes of themselves over rakes?

"I am determined to flirt with him," Catherine said.

Priscilla smiled slyly. "Not if I get there first." She lifted her skirts and walked away. The other ladies laughed and followed in her wake.

When Sally hesitated, Amy made an exasperated sound. "Sally, do not be one of the herd. Charlotte and the others will make fools of themselves ogling him, but you have better sense."

Sally pouted and then laughed. "You must admit he is gorgeous."

"He is well known for his high-stakes gambling and wild parties," Georgette said. "But Amy, you cannot disagree that he is uncommonly handsome."

"His looks are unimportant," Amy said. "He is an indolent rogue who spends all of his time engaged in vice and depravity."

Sally beckoned them closer. "I heard he can charm a lady out of her petticoats in five minutes flat," she said under her breath.

"Ladies of questionable virtue, you mean," Amy said.

Sally lifted on her toes and surveyed the room. "Julianne is coming this way."

Julianne looked as slender as always, though she had given birth to her first child only two months ago. When she arrived, Amy kissed the air by her cheeks. "You look radiant."

"Thank you, but look at you, Amy. Everyone is talking about your elegant gown," Julianne said. "I love it." She leaned closer and whispered. "This will be your year."

Amy met her gaze and dared to hope her friend's words would come true. "I've missed you."

Julianne smiled. "I've missed all of you as well. We had such fun last season. My husband has never let me forget all of the trouble I caused. He is still suspicious of all of you and believes you influenced me—especially you, Amy."

"Me?" She laughed. "I always tried to caution all of you."

Julianne grinned. "He is convinced that you instigated the worst schemes. He believes you hid it all behind your quiet façade."

Georgette grinned. "Amy, you often have this look in your eyes, as if the cogs and wheels are spinning like a roulette wheel."

"I do not," she said.

Sally shook her head. "It's true, Amy. While everyone else is chattering like monkeys, you look as if you're plotting something."

"I'm not plotting; I'm thinking."

"Now there is a euphemism if I ever heard one," Georgette said.

Julianne and Sally burst out laughing.

"Amy, you had better prepare yourself, because everyone wants the name of your modiste," Julianne said. "Charlotte told me you had a local seamstress make up your dress from a drawing you made."

"It's true," Amy said.

Julianne smiled. "I think you should show your sketches to Madame DuPont. She would be very impressed. Perhaps she would even make up one or two. We could hold a little gathering of ladies at Ashdown House and display your sketches."

"That is a wonderful idea," Georgette said. "Would you considerate it, Amy?"

Excitement raced through Amy. She was proud of her designs, and tonight she'd received confirmation of her talent. The idea of other ladies admiring and perhaps even wearing her creations made her pulse quicken. All the years she'd spent sitting on the wallflower row, she'd felt inferior to the prettier belles. She'd felt she could never measure up to them, but she was confident of her gown designs and wanted to share them with others. "Yes," she said a little breathlessly. "I would love it above anything if Madame DuPont is amenable."

"If the rest of your sketches are as unique as the gown you're wearing, I know she will be interested," Julianne said. "In one night, you have become the fashion darling of society."

"Her designs are truly exceptional," Georgette said.

"Then it is settled. Let us call at Madame DuPont's shop on Thursday," Julianne said. "Amy, be sure to bring your sketches. Now I must return to my husband. We cannot stay long, because I must return home to nurse Emma."

"I cannot wait to see your daughter," Amy said. "I'm sure she's beautiful."

Julianne laughed. "According to my husband, she's the most beautiful bald-headed lady in London."

After Julianne left, Amy meant to suggest they take a turn about the ballroom, but Lord Beaufort and Mr. Portfrey approached. Instinctively, Amy lowered her lashes. Her heart beat a little faster as she desperately tried to think of something interesting to say, but her brain froze as it always did when she felt pressed to respond.

"Miss Shepherd, if you are not presently engaged, would you honor me with the next dance?" Mr. Portfrey asked.

"Thank you, I will," Sally said.

By now, Amy's heart was pounding. She knew what was coming and tried to force herself to raise her eyes, but she couldn't make herself do it. She feared her anxiety would show on her face.

"Lady Georgette," Lord Beaufort said. "Will you consent to partner with me?"

Amy's face burned. All of her hopes that this season would be different shattered like broken glass. She found herself wishing that she'd stayed home. Why had she thought anything would change?

"Oh, I thank you, Lord Beaufort, but perhaps we could talk instead." Georgette sounded flustered.

Georgette meant well, but Lord Beaufort undoubtedly knew the reason for Georgette's request, and that only made the humiliation worse. Amy couldn't bear it. With every ounce of strength she possessed, she forced herself to lift her chin. She did her best to pretend nonchalance, but she could not control the blush that undoubtedly made her face blotchier. "Please go ahead. There is s-someone I wish to see," she said.

Before Georgette could reply, Amy bobbed a quick curtsy and walked away. She applied her fan as she skirted the perimeter of the ballroom. All the while, she darted glances into the crowd, hoping to see someone she knew. At that moment, she felt as awkward as she had at seventeen.

She kept walking through the packed room. As she neared the chairs where the dowagers sat gossiping, Amy saw the familiar faces of her oldest friends. Eugenia, Bernice, and Cecile watched the dancers with undisguised yearning. Amy knew all too well how they felt.

She remembered how they had shared amusing observations of the ton. They had laughed and called themselves the invisible belles.

Temptation gripped her. She wanted to see her friends. She wanted to sit in a safe place where no one would slight her or pass her up for prettier girls. She wanted to sit in a place where she felt she belonged.

She took a step in that direction, and fear clawed at her lungs. If she ventured to the wallflower row, she knew she would never be brave enough to leave again.

With a deep breath, Amy turned and made herself stroll away. Regardless of how difficult it was for her, she was determined to overcome the curse of being shy. Yet, as she surveyed the crowd, the idea of approaching a group intimidated her. She'd always found it difficult to converse in large groups, but when she grew anxious, she found it almost impossible to think, let alone converse.

All she needed was a few quiet moments to regain her composure. She thought of going to the ladies' retiring room, but she didn't want to face a crowd of ladies there. Instead, she would find her way to the garden for a bit of air. The breeze would cool her heated face quickly.

After she left the ballroom, she walked through a crowd on the landing. As she approached the stairs, she noted a tall gentleman with black, tousled hair speaking to a "lady" with painted cheeks. Something about him seemed familiar. When the man leaned back against the stairwell rail, Amy winced. It was Devil Darcett.

He was the last man she wanted to encounter tonight.

She scurried down the stairs before he caught sight of her. Upon reaching the marble floor, she turned right and treaded along an unlit, deserted corridor, hoping to find her way out to the garden. She trailed her hand along the wall to feel her way in the darkness. Then she came upon a door that was slightly ajar. The dim room beckoned her. She looked left and right, but no one was about. Promising herself she would stay only a short while, she slipped inside, closed the door, and waited for her eyes to adjust. Although the objects in the shrouded room remained indistinct, she could make out tall shelves along one wall. Obviously, this was Lord Beresford's library.

She padded across the plush carpet and collapsed on a sofa. Amy clasped her hand to her bosom as she waited for her heartbeat to slow. Thank goodness Devil Darcett had not seen her. She knew he would relentlessly tease her, the same way he'd done last year.

Amy blew out her breath, relieved to have escaped his notice. She wondered how long she should remain here before returning to the ballroom. Of course, she wouldn't have to worry if she hadn't left. She ought to have forced herself to stay, but she'd felt so uncomfortable. No matter how hard she tried, she could not be at ease with approaching a group and joining the conversation. She became tongue-tied when others spoke all at once. Often, she spent hours in her room, because she needed to be alone in order to think.

Now she had nothing else to do except twiddle her thumbs in a dark library. She sighed, wondering if she'd made a mistake by coming to London. Amy's parents had offered to bring her. She knew they did not share her fondness for the city, but her father had insisted she deserved to have another season in London. Amy had thought of all the years she'd failed miserably. Her wonderful parents would do anything for her, but she couldn't bear to disappoint them again. They would not view it that way at all, because they loved her, but she couldn't stand to fail them.

She'd told them she had no wish to go and had informed her friends. Then one day, she'd received a letter from Georgette, begging her to spend the Season with her. Georgette had said she had looked forward to seeing her all winter and would be miserable without her. In truth, Amy had missed Georgette and Julianne very much. She had read their letters again and again, always recalling their adventures of the last two years. After a great deal of thought, Amy had decided to accept Georgette's invitation, but a complication had arisen in the month prior to her journey to London, one that still unsettled Amy.

A light tap startled her out of her ruminations. When the door opened, she cringed. To her utter horror, a man walked inside and shut the door. In the darkness, she couldn't see his features.

"Alicia? I thought you were going to the retiring room first," he said as he shut the door.

Oh, dear God. She knew that voice. It was the devil himself. He'd come here for an assignation. "Wrong woman," she said.

His low chuckle irritated her.

He strode across the carpet, sat beside her, and stretched out his long legs. "Red? This is an unexpected pleasure."

Drat it all. He'd recognized her voice. "My name is Miss Hardwick, and the pleasure is all yours, I assure you. Now if you will excuse me, I must leave."

"Not so fast. Why are you hiding in here?"

He'd caught her off guard. "I'm not hiding."

He leaned closer to her, threatening her peace of mind. The scent of him, something she could not identify, curled inside her like a dangerous elixir. He was close enough that she could hear the sound of his breathing. His face was in shadows, but she sensed he was watching her as if he were the predator and she his prey.

"You're either hiding or you're waiting for someone. Which is it?" he asked.

She owed him no explanation. "My reason for coming here is none of your concern."

"I promise not to reveal your secret," he said, chuckling.

"You may go to the devil," she said.

"You do have a temper, don't you? I'm only teasing," he said.

"I got my fill of your teasing at your brother's wedding," she muttered.

"Are you still miffed? It's been nearly a year."

Her mother had warned her about the consequences of having a long memory, but Amy was in no mood to forgive the rogue who had embarrassed her. "You spilled punch all over me."

"Yes, I got you wet," he said, chuckling in a wicked manner.

She would never forget how the cool punch had pooled inside her bodice. Everyone had stared. "If you were a gentleman, you would not mention that incident."

"Ah, but I'm the devil, and as I recall, *you* bumped into *me*." He paused and added, "I did try to apologize for the mishap."

"You made a jest of it," she said.

"I thought it would put you at ease if we both laughed about it," he said.

At the time, she'd thought he meant to poke fun at her, but that did not matter. She could not stay alone in a dark room with a rake. "I would say it has been delightful, but I don't like to lie. Now, you will excuse me," she said.

When she rose, he stood as well. She was tall, but he was half a head taller, and for reasons that made no sense, that intimidated her.

She lifted her skirt and took a step back. He stepped forward.

She stepped sideways in an effort to evade him.

He followed.

She couldn't help laughing. "Stop that."

His wicked chuckle reverberated all along her spine.

She'd thought herself impervious to rogues, but despite her poor opinion of him, he'd managed to make her laugh with his antics. "You are determined to bedevil me."

"I think you like it," he said, his voice a little husky.

A warning clanged in her head. He had no doubt learned his seduction techniques from Satan's mistresses. "Mr. Darcett, I must leave now."

"Yes, I can see that I'm too much temptation for you."

She scoffed.

"It was a jest, Miss Hardwick."

She thought better of answering him, because it would only delay her escape. Amy turned, took one step, and halted at the sound of a rap on the door.

He grabbed her hand and pulled her behind the sofa. Then he crouched beside her. Amy's legs trembled, but she mustn't move or her rustling skirts would give away their hiding place.

A feminine voice called out, "Will?" After a moment of silence, she added, "Are you here?"

Amy's heart beat madly. She squeezed her eyes shut and prayed for deliverance. If they were discovered alone in the dark, she would be ruined.

Footsteps padded across the carpet. "Will?"

The *tick, tick, tick* of the clock seemed to go on forever, though only a moment could have passed.

"That sorry rake," the woman muttered.

Amy squelched the hysterical urge to laugh, even though there was nothing funny about her predicament. Oh, Lord, please let the woman leave.

The woman's skirts swished as her footsteps retreated. Then mercifully the door slammed.

The devil rose and offered his hand. She took it gratefully, because her legs felt a bit wobbly.

"Well, that was a lark," he drawled.

She stared at him. Though his expression was hidden in the dark, she heard amusement in his voice. "Do you realize what would have happened if we'd been caught?"

"I suspect Alicia would have grabbed the nearest makeshift weapon and thrown it at my head."

How could he be so cavalier about a near disaster? "You do realize the servants would have come running to investigate the disturbance. You may think it funny, but, unlike you, I value my reputation."

He chuckled. "Actually, I'm rather fond of mine."

"Is everything a joke to you?" Why had she bothered to ask when she knew the answer?

"It was rather exciting there for a bit. But if we had been caught by the servants, I would have bribed them," he said.

"The first time we met, I formed a low opinion of you. I regret to inform you that you have just sunk even further in my estimation."

"I'm sorry to hear it, but I would have done whatever was necessary to get us out of hot suds. If it had come to that, I imagine you wouldn't have been so quick to object."

She refused to admit it. "Good-bye, Mr. Darcett."

As she marched toward the door, he said, "You intrigue me, Red."

She halted at the door and looked over her shoulder. "You delivered that line as badly as the worst actors at Drury Lane." Then she opened the door and sashayed out of the library with a smug smile. Tonight, she'd taken him down a peg or two.

By Jove, she'd dealt him a verbal hit.

He closed the library door, because he didn't want to risk following too closely behind her.

Curiosity had gotten the better of him. He still didn't know for certain why she'd chosen to hide in the library, but it didn't signify. She was a virtuous lady, and he ought to have escorted her to the door the moment he'd recognized her voice. He'd rather enjoyed sparring with her, but he'd detained her a bit too long. There would have been hell to pay if they'd been caught.

He knew the rules, and respected them out of self-preservation. Virtuous ladies were off-limits. He'd always kept his distance from marriage bait, though quite a few had taken to following him around. They were titillated by his reputation and the danger he represented.

He hadn't lied when he'd told her she intrigued him. Earlier, he'd watched her enter the ballroom in that remarkable ball gown with the green ribbons. Ordinarily, he paid scant attention to women's clothing, unless he was trying to strip it off. But she'd drawn everyone's attention, including his.

When he'd first met her at his brother's wedding, she'd walked past just as he was turning with that cup of punch. She had not accepted his apology and definitely had not appreciated his attempt to make light of the matter. Tonight, he'd thought to charm her and then attempt to apologize again, but she'd made her low opinion of him quite clear.

Ah, well, it didn't signify. With a shrug, he took a step and noticed something on the carpet. He bent to retrieve it and strode through the corridor. When he reached the great hall, he saw it was a red silk rose. He pocketed the silk rose with the intention of returning it to her, but he glanced up at the crowd on the landing and spotted Alicia scowling at him. He decided to leave this tepid ball for a far more interesting entertainment. His friends had told him about a party given by the demimonde. He might as well live up to his devilish reputation.

Later that night

"Miss, one of the silk roses is missing from the gown," Lizzy, the maid, said.

Amy's night rail and robe swirled round her ankles as she walked over to examine the gown.

"I thought they were all secure," Lizzy said in an anxious voice. "Perhaps you could find another to replace it."

"It's not your fault, Lizzy. I'll probably have to replace all of the roses as I doubt I can find a perfect match."

"Then you could wear it again," Lizzy said. "It is such a beautiful gown."

Amy doubted she would ever want to wear the gown again, because it would remind her of her failure tonight. "Will you braid my hair?"

"Yes, of course," Lizzy said.

When Lizzy finished, Amy thanked her. Her hair had grown well past her shoulders in the last two years. She wondered if a shorter style would be more becoming. "I'm considering cutting my hair short."

Lizzy shook her head. "I know it's the fashion, but keep it long for your future husband. Gentlemen prefer it."

Amy thought about Mr. Crawford, the vicar back home. He was the first man to express real interest in her, and that thought alone made her lungs feel constricted. She didn't want to think about the end of the Season and the choice she would undoubtedly have to make. Her stomach clenched. She had so many doubts about him. How could she turn down the only proposal she was likely to ever get?

Her nerves rattled. She didn't want to think about her last conversation with him or her parents' unspoken hopes. They had made their approval clear. Her father had said Mr. Crawford was a good man who cared about his parishioners. Her mother had said a man of his stature would surely seek a wife soon. Amy had said nothing at all, because she hadn't wanted to disappoint them.

"Is something wrong, Miss?" Lizzy asked.

"Oh, no. Thank you, Lizzy." She appreciated Lizzy's concern, but this was not a topic to discuss with anyone except her closest friend. Amy had a terrible dilemma. In her heart, she knew what was right, but she had to think of her parents, too.

After Lizzy departed, Amy sighed. Mr. Crawford had not wanted her to leave. She'd told him that she wanted this last chance to spend the Season with Georgette. He'd looked unhappy, and then he'd said he understood. At that moment, she'd wished that he would have made demands or questioned her feelings for him, so that she would feel justified in turning him down, if he proposed. But she knew he meant to do so when she returned.

God help her. She did not want to marry a man who said they were both practical people and well suited.

She knew her parents had expectations, and that kept her awake at night. After so many disappointing seasons, she felt guilty. Amy wanted to please them. She wanted to make them happy, but marrying to secure her future would make her unhappy. The worst part was that she'd not told her parents about her misgivings. She'd waited until the last minute to speak to Mr. Crawford. When her mother and father discovered the truth, they would worry.

They would be far more worried if they knew what had transpired tonight.

She'd vowed to change, but once again, she'd failed.

She'd let her humiliation overcome her and had gone to hide in that library. Her momentary victory over that confident rake had dissipated the minute she'd returned to the ballroom. She'd been on her guard the whole time, certain he would beleaguer her. She'd not seen him again, but her anxiety had spoiled the rest of the ball for her. Once again, she wondered if she'd made a mistake in coming to London.

A soft knock at the door startled her. Georgette poked her head in the door. "I'm glad you're awake." Her nightgown billowed round her slim figure as she padded to the night table and set her candle on it. "Shall we sit on the bed?"

They sat cross-legged on the mattress. The sheets smelled sunshine fresh, so at odds with Amy's gloomy mood.

"We did not have a chance to talk last night, because we arrived so late," Georgette said. "And today, we were busy unpacking and getting ready for the ball. I had only a quick glimpse of your sketches, but I'll view them tomorrow when the light is better."

The candlelight cast shadows over Georgette's face. "I wish you hadn't left the ballroom."

Amy didn't want to talk about her reason for leaving, because it still stung. "Did you enjoy dancing with Beaufort?"

"Well enough. He's witty and handsome."

"What is wrong, Georgette?" Amy asked.

"He is so determined," she said.

"What do you mean?"

"He persuaded me to take a drive in the park twice this week. Tonight, he wanted to know which entertainments I plan to attend this week."

"It sounds as if he's smitten," Amy said. "Do you not return his feelings?"

"I like him, but he is so persistent. A gentleman should not rush a lady. Of course, Mama has taken notice and approves." She scoffed. "Because he will inherit an earldom," Georgette said, imitating her mother's haughty voice.

Georgette's mother was a forceful woman. Amy didn't envy Georgette on that account. "Is your mama insisting you marry this year?"

"Yes, she believes it is past time I wed. She cannot bear that other belles have married when I have not. I thought she would relent when my brother married last fall, but she is even more determined. She is constantly comparing me to Suzanne."

Lord Ramsey, Georgette's eldest brother, had given up his rakehell ways upon falling headlong in love with Lady Suzanne, now Lady Ramsey.

"Thank goodness my papa stands up for me," Georgette said. "I won't marry until I cannot eat a bite and swoon at the mere thought of my beloved."

Amy laughed. "Where did you get such silly notions of falling in love?"

Georgette grinned. "Well, that's the way Suzanne described her feelings for my brother. But then, she's a silly goose, and I am far too reasonable for such nonsense. I shall probably end up a spinster with a dozen cats."

Amy suspected that Georgette wanted to cling to her girlhood as long as possible. "Georgette, I believe he has developed tender feelings for you. You have known him since last year."

She hesitated. "We both know he first fell in love with Julianne."

"People are often crossed in love. His past feelings do not signify. What matters is how he feels now and how you feel about him."

"I like him very much, and sometimes I feel a rush of excitement when I'm with him. We had a lovely time at his parents' house party last winter."

"What is troubling you?"

"I only need more time to sort out my feelings."

Amy wouldn't press Georgette. She would work out her feelings in her own good time.

"Enough about me," Georgette said. "I suspect you have something to tell me."

"You know me well," Amy said. "I have inadvertently encouraged a gentleman, and I'm so torn."

"It is the vicar, Mr. Crawford," Georgette said. "You mentioned him only in passing in your letters, so I did not think much about it. Then I saw him at your home. He looked unhappy, and I knew something had transpired."

Amy sighed. "He didn't want me to leave."

"We have always entrusted our secrets to each other. Your silence on this subject worries me," Georgette said.

"When I first wrote to you, I didn't realize Mr. Crawford's interest in me amounted to anything more than friendly regard." He'd approved when he'd seen her taking food baskets to the sick and elderly in the neighborhood, and he'd called her thoughtful when he found her setting flowers on the graves at the churchyard.

"You did not tell me that he has been courting you." Georgette sounded a bit offended.

"I wasn't sure what to make of his attentions or I would have written to you about it. He started calling on my father regularly. Then one day he asked me to walk with him. It became a habit, and I didn't comprehend the significance at first."

"What are your feelings for him?" Georgette asked.

"Mr. Crawford is a good man. He has devoted himself to the church. Everyone in the neighborhood admires him."

"I asked about *your* feelings," Georgette said.

"I think he is a steady man with flaws like all of us." He could provide her with a home, children, and security. But there were little things that troubled her. He often asked if he could make a suggestion. While he spoke in gentle tones, his suggestions were actually criticisms. When she'd showed him her sketchbook, he'd frowned and asked if her time might be better spent on charitable activities. Once when they were walking, he'd observed her new bonnet and asked her if it wasn't too ostentatious for the country. He'd spoiled her pleasure in it, and she'd never worn it again in his presence.

"Amy, you are troubled," Georgette said.

"He takes his position as a vicar very seriously. I believe he expects me to give up ostentatious bonnets and my drawing."

"What?" Georgette said in an outraged tone. "No, you will not give up your designs. You are talented, and he has no right to prevent it."

"He means well. I know he is mindful that some of the parishioners are poor, and he worries that frivolous expenditures would send the wrong message." On the day he'd criticized her pretty bonnet she'd tried to gather the courage to tell him that he was impertinent and had no right to tell her what to do. Then he'd apologized for making her sad. He'd smiled a little and told her that he understood that young ladies liked to indulge in their pastimes.

Mr. Crawford had expressed confidence that once she married, she would give up her girlish ways.

"You have always devoted yourself to charitable activities at home," Georgette said. "It has never interfered with your drawing."

Amy said nothing. His insinuation that he intended to propose had alarmed her. Panic had gripped her so hard that she'd barely been able to breathe. But she'd held all of her vexation inside, because she'd not known what to do.

"I detect no tender feelings on your part," Georgette said. "Am I mistaken?"

"No. I tried to brush away my doubts. My parents have said nothing specific, but I know they are in favor of the match."

"Amy, are your parents trying to persuade you to marry him?"

"They would never force me to wed anyone." But the day she'd told her mother that Georgette had invited her to spend the Season with her in London, her mother had frowned. Then she'd asked Amy if she thought it wise to leave "just now." Her mother's question had left no doubt in Amy's mind that her parents held hopes that Mr. Crawford would offer to marry her.

"You look very glum," Georgette said.

"He believes we are both practical people and well suited." She suspected he was primarily interested in her marriage portion. Her father was not an aristocrat, but he was a wealthy man. "Mr. Crawford said he would wait for me, but I refused to make a commitment, because I was confused." He had regarded her with a patronizing smile and said he felt certain she would come to her senses after a week or two in London. Then he'd repeated his intention to wait for her, despite her objection. She'd felt awful.

"You cannot marry him," Georgette said. "You cannot."

Amy met Georgette's gaze. "He may be my last chance to marry."

"No," Georgette said, raising her voice. "You deserve better, Amy. I know you want to marry for love."

"I may not have a choice." After uttering the words, she felt defeated.

Georgette leaned forward. "You will not settle for a marriage to a man who does not cherish and love you. Amy, you will be miserable. I won't let you give up so easily."

You are my dear friend, but you cannot possibly understand, because you are beautiful and vivacious. And you will never have to make the painful choice I have to make.

"You made no commitment to him, so you are free to court others," Georgette said.

Foolishly, she'd hoped that would happen, but tonight, she'd faced the truth. No pretty ball gown would transform her into an English rose.

"Something else is vexing you," Georgette said. "I can sense it."

"I found out belatedly that Mr. Crawford asked my father's permission to correspond with me. Now I am obliged to answer his letters." Her parents had beamed, leaving no doubt in her mind that they were pleased.

"Why did you not tell them that you had made no commitment?" Georgette said.

"They looked so happy. I felt awful and guilty."

"You cannot marry him to please your parents," Georgette said. "You must think of yourself first."

Amy set her feet on the bed and wrapped her arms round her shins. "Mr. Crawford is the first man to seriously express interest in me."

Georgette smoothed the covers. "Amy, you have so many doubts about him. I understand your concerns, but you do not give yourself enough credit."

She did have doubts, but it changed nothing

"You have this season," Georgette said. "I hope you fall madly in love with one of the gentlemen in London."

"No one will even dance with me." Only once in five years had anyone asked, and Amy knew Julianne had arranged it.

"I think you're inadvertently signaling that you do not wish to dance," Georgette said. "When the gentlemen approached us tonight, you lowered your eyes."

"It is an ingrained habit." In truth, she'd known neither of them would ask, because no one ever did.

"You think your shyness is impossible to overcome, but I don't believe it," Georgette said. "If you will only allow the world to see the real you, my wonderful friend, you will be so much happier."

"It doesn't come naturally to me," she said.

"You only want practice." Georgette hesitated. "Of course, you wish others to see you as friendly."

Amy stared at her friend. Her pulse sped up. "Do others think I am aloof?"

Georgette focused on smoothing her nightgown. "No, absolutely not."

Amy knew then that it was true. She blinked back threatening tears. It had never occurred to her that others would misinterpret her shyness.

Georgette touched her hand. "I know how clever and

witty you are. Break free of your protective cocoon and let others see the Amy I know."

Her throat clogged. Fearing her voice would break, she merely nodded.

"This year will be different. I promise," Georgette said with such emphasis that it was as if she believed saying the words would make them true.

Amy didn't believe her, but she vowed to try harder. In truth, she had nothing left to lose. It was her last season, and she knew she would always regret it if she did not make an effort to come out of her shell.

Chapter Two

ir, you are wanted in the gold salon."

Will opened his bleary eyes just as his valet drew back the drapes. Sunlight flooded the room. "Argh," he yelped, shading his eyes.

"I beg your pardon, sir," Jenkins, the valet, said, his voice devoid of any sympathy.

In all fairness, sympathy was not part of Jenkins's job. Nevertheless, Will's mood was not improved by the sudden onslaught of sunlight. His eyes felt as if they were full of sand, and his head pounded. The sour taste on his tongue made him suspect he'd drunk one too many bottles of claret, but his recollection of last night was hazy at best. He vaguely recalled stumbling out of a hackney and lurching to the front door. Obviously, he'd managed to drag himself upstairs and into bed.

He squinted at the bedside clock. "It's bloody ten o'clock. Jenkins, shut the drapes."

"Sir, his lordship instructed me to wake you," Jenkins said. "You are expected for a family meeting."

Will groaned. Not another one. What now? Was his grandmamma suffering from faux heart palpitations again? Or was that her mysterious sinking spells? Or had Peter, his eldest nephew, pissed on Mama's hothouse roses for the third time this week? Will loved his family, but they were driving him mad.

Over the past four years, he'd traveled on the Continent and had almost forgotten what it was like to deal with his relatives. He'd actually thought he could escape them in this monstrosity of a house, but no, that was impossible, especially with his busybody sisters and their annoying husbands invading the drawing room three to four times a week. Without fail, there was some new *crisis* the entire family must discuss in endless detail.

He briefly considered sending word to his brother that he was too ill to attend, but if he did, they would send for a sawbones. Then *he* would become the latest problem. Visions of his mother trying to feed him broth and toast were enough to prod him to sit up. He glanced down at himself, belatedly realizing that he'd slept in his shirt and trousers. After rummaging among the tangled sheets, he found his wrinkled cravat.

Jenkins's mouth puckered in obvious disgust. Then he took the mangled neck cloth from Will's outstretched hand and held it as if it were a dead rodent.

Will scrubbed his hand over his bristled jaw. He'd not spent much time at Ashdown House since returning to England. After his brother's wedding last year, he'd attended one house party after another with his bachelor friends. He'd spent Christmas with his family, but after the holidays, he'd escaped once again and spent the winter carousing at his friend Bellingham's hunting box.

Upon returning home a fortnight ago, he'd found himself cooped up indoors far too often. His family expected him to attend balls, Venetian breakfasts, and dinner parties. They insisted he twiddle his thumbs in his mother's drawing room on her "at home" days while his mother's friends, all dragons, paraded inside. One day after a long night of revels, he'd nodded off next to Grandmamma on the sofa, a faux pas that had not amused his mother and sisters.

Weariness from a night of carousing overcame him. He flopped onto his stomach and pulled a pillow over his head. He dreamed a woman with long red hair cascading over her breasts crooked her finger at him. He tried to kiss her, but she turned and fled into darkness, leaving him frustrated.

Someone shook his shoulder. With a gasp, he jerked up to find his brother staring at him. "Deuce take you," he muttered.

Hawk waved his hand. "Egad, you smell like a brew house, and you slept in your clothes."

"I took my boots off."

Hawk regarded him with a wry expression. "I commend you."

"Ha-ha." Will massaged his aching temples. "Seriously, why should I attend this family meeting? It's bound to be something ridiculous again."

Hawk set his fist on his hip. "Actually, the meeting concerns you."

Will regarded his brother with suspicion. "What about me?"

"We'll discuss it in the drawing room. Everyone is already gathered. Make yourself presentable and report downstairs in twenty minutes, tops."

Will pulled a face. "I'm not in any condition to face them, you know."

"You'll manage, I'm sure." Then Hawk quit the room.

When Will walked into the drawing room fifteen minutes later, Montague, his eldest sister's husband, regarded him with disdain. "It took you long enough."

Will thought of several choice responses, none of them polite. In deference to the ladies present, he kept his reply between his teeth and sat on the green sofa next to his snoring grandmamma. She had agreed to stay for a short time in Richmond. Every day, she said she would return to Bath soon. He hoped she would remain, because he worried about her health, even though Aunt Hester thought she made up her various ailments for attention.

"William, your eyes are red," Mama cried. "Are you ill?"

Aunt Hester adjusted the tall feathers on her ugly purple turban and snorted. "Louisa, that boy has been pulling the wool over your eyes for years. The only thing he suffers from is the bottle ache."

Montague snapped his newspaper shut. "Little wonder the papers call him the devil."

"I'd no idea you were fond of the scandal sheets," Will drawled.

Hawk held up his hand. "Let us leave off the quarreling. We are family and should not take that for granted," he said, cutting his gaze meaningfully to Grandmamma.

Will glanced at his grandmother's slightly parted lips. During his absence from England, she had grown frail.

She walked with a cane now and needed assistance on the stairs. She missed her friends in Bath, but he didn't like to think of her living so far away, with only a companion to look after her.

Hawk stood beside his wife, Julianne, and smiled at their infant daughter. Then he gazed at Will. "I'm glad that you had your adventures, but you were sorely missed. We're all glad you are home for good."

Will frowned. Home for good? He drew in a breath to tell his brother that he had no intention of remaining home for much longer, but his mother's voice forestalled him.

"I am grateful that you are back in the bosom of our family," Mama said. "I worried every single day that you would meet with harm. Did I not, Patience?" she said to her eldest daughter.

"Yes, you did, Mama." Patience patted the dowager countess's hand. "As a mother, I can only imagine how difficult it must have been to have your son away so often."

They were slathering the guilt on a bit thick, but then his female relatives specialized in exaggerating their feelings, with the exception of Aunt Hester, who spoke plainly and regularly shocked his mother and sisters. Thank God for her.

"Will, we are glad to see you settled now," Harmony, the middle sister, said.

Hope, his youngest sister, regarded him with a sly expression. "Not entirely settled, but I will gladly assist you with that matter."

Will rubbed his aching temple. "What matter?"

Lord Kenwick, Harmony's husband, snorted. "They mean to see you leg-shackled."

Will reared back. Damn. His sisters thought matrimony the pinnacle of a man's existence.

Aunt Hester rummaged in her reticule, produced a vial, and nudged Harmony. "Pass the vinaigrette to your brother. He looks ready to swoon."

"Hope, we will not press him to marry," Hawk said. "He's only five and twenty."

"Six and twenty as of last week," Will drawled.

The dowager countess cried out, "I forgot his birthday. What kind of mother forgets her son?"

"Mama, you must not blame yourself," Patience said. "Will has been gone so much of the time that it was all too easy to forget."

Will rolled his eyes. So now it was his fault that they had forgotten his birthday.

"You must not feel guilty, Mama," Hope said. "None of us remembered, either."

Hawk winced. "Will, I'm sorry."

"It doesn't signify." As the youngest of the brood, he'd grown accustomed when he was a child to everyone forgetting about him and had learned to appreciate his freedom. Of course, they'd remembered him when they caught him getting into mischief, but he'd gotten away with far more than they knew.

"How could I forget?" The dowager countess sniffed and dabbed a handkerchief at her teary eyes. "He is my babe."

Aunt Hester lifted her quizzing glass to inspect Will. "He's a prodigious big one. It's a wonder you birthed him."

Naturally that set off a hue and cry.

His sisters apologized profusely and swore they would make it up to him.

"I don't care about my blasted birthday," he said. "If it makes you feel better, I celebrated with friends."

"We all know you're accomplished at celebrating," Montague muttered.

Will's head throbbed. "Could we possibly get to the point?" he said a bit too sharply.

They all gaped at him.

"Since you insist, I will," Patience said in her pompous elder sister voice. "Imagine our dear mother's embarrassment upon learning that you have taken up with that disreputable Mrs. Fleur, if that is even her real name."

He was tempted to tell them they need no longer worry about Alicia, but he thought better of mentioning it. "My private life is none of your affair," he said.

"It is hardly private," Hope said. "You are accounted the worst libertine in England."

He rolled his eyes. As soon as this foolish meeting ended, he intended to pack his trunks and leave.

Grandmamma awoke with a start. She looked about her with a confused expression.

Will patted her hand and gave her a reassuring smile.

"Did I miss something?" she hollered. Due to her diminished hearing, Grandmamma had a tendency to shout.

"Not a thing," Will said, raising his voice so that she could hear him.

"William," the dowager countess said. "How can you say such a thing? You are not taking the family meeting seriously."

He lifted his palms. "You're glad I'm home, but you don't like my reputation. Now that we've established those facts, perhaps we can disperse."

Hawk gave him a warning look. "There is another matter."

Will groaned. How long would this blasted meeting last?

"Now that you're home for good, you need an occupation," Hawk said.

Will held his hand up. "Wait. I never said—"

Grandmamma tugged on his arm. "What did he say?" she shouted.

He raised his voice. "I need an occupation."

Grandmamma clasped her hands and bellowed, "The church would be perfect."

Hester scowled at her sister. "Maribelle, the parishioners would revolt. The papers have named him the devil."

"That isn't very nice," Grandmamma hollered. "You go first."

"Go where?" Hester called out.

"To the devil," Grandmamma shouted.

Will held his fist to his mouth in an attempt to hide his laughter, but his shoulders shook. Meanwhile, baby Emma Rose chose that moment to squall.

"Oh, she's hungry," Julianne said. "I must take her to the nursery."

Hawk helped her to rise and kissed her cheek. He kept his gaze on his wife until she disappeared. Then he returned his attention to Will. "I have a proposition that I think will suit you."

Clearly his brother did not understand. All of his relatives assumed he meant to stay home, but if he'd had any misgivings about leaving before, this ludicrous meeting had abolished them. No matter how much he loved his family, he simply could not continue to live with them.

"My steward is retiring. Someone must take over his duties." Hawk folded his arms over his chest. "What do you say?"

Everyone, even Montague, beamed at him. Will's cravat felt like a tourniquet. Their expectations pressed upon him like a thousand-pound boulder. For a moment, he felt trapped, pinned down by the weight of their hopes, but it was his life, not theirs. "I appreciate your generous offer, but I'm a rambler. It's not in my nature to stay in one place for any length of time. I'm planning another trip to the Continent."

His brothers-in-law exchanged knowing looks. His sisters were trying to comfort his mother, who was mopping up tears again. Even Hester regarded him with disappointment. Only Grandmamma smiled at him, and that made him feel worse, because he knew she hadn't heard what he'd said.

Hawk released a sigh. "The issues won't be resolved at this meeting. I will keep everyone informed, but for now, I know you all have other business awaiting you."

Montague stood. "If you want my opinion..."

Hawk lifted his hand. "Thank you, but I'll handle the matter. William, let us repair to my study."

Will walked about the study and sent the standing globe for a spin as he passed by. "Sorry for the misunderstanding, but you know I'm not one to put down roots." He turned round and smiled at his brother. "This time, I'm planning to venture to Switzerland."

When Hawk remained silent, Will added something he hoped would placate his brother and the other members of the family. "Perhaps in a few years, I'll be ready to settle down in one place."

"Be seated."

He gritted his teeth and took a chair in front of his brother's desk.

Hawk fiddled with the beads of an abacus. "You do realize you've dealt a severe disappointment to our family."

"They'll grow accustomed to my absence soon enough. It's not as if I've spent much time at Ashdown House."

"I heard a great deal of grumbling over your frequent absences," Hawk said. "I promised our mother I would speak to you about a career. Your intention to travel to the Continent for an extended period leaves me with the devil of a dilemma."

He lifted his palms. "How so? I'm the one leaving, not you."

Hawk met his gaze. "Without your quarterly allowance, you'll not have the means to undertake another journey."

Will's heart beat faster. "What?"

"I'm responsible for the dispensation of your quarterly funds. If I withhold them, you will no doubt resent me. That's understandable. On the other hand, if I fund your journey, I will disappoint our mother and likely alienate the rest of the family. They already believe I was too lenient about your extended travels."

"Ridiculous," Will muttered.

"You traveled for four years. That's far longer than most young men on their grand tours. Since your return, you have spent very little time with our family. If I provide the funds for another journey, they will rightly feel that I have paved the way for you, thereby giving my tacit approval." He moved two beads over and then met his brother's gaze squarely. "Tell me, Will. What would you do if you were in my situation?"

The question startled him. "How am I to answer? You know my wishes. They'll not change because others disapprove."

"Perhaps that will give you some understanding of my predicament," Hawk said. "No matter what I decide, someone will be unhappy. And I'll be honest. I think it is in your best interest that I don't fund this journey. Right now, your life consists of nothing but revelry, and I blame myself for it. I'd hoped when you returned to England that you would give up the carousing. But it has gotten worse. Last night, you were so drunk that you slept in your clothes. You regularly come home in the wee hours of the morning and disturb the servants. It's not fair to them, Will. They work hard, but you don't seem to notice or care. Then I realized you would never give up your carousing unless I insisted you take up a career."

"You were no saint," Will said.

"I made plenty of mistakes, and I regret them. But I never completely abandoned our family, and I took my responsibilities in Parliament seriously."

"I won't allow the family to dictate what I do." Anger rose up inside him, but he knew better than to let it show. His brother would respect only rational responses.

"They don't think of it that way, and neither should you," Hawk said. "When you stated your intention to leave, our family members felt as if you were abandoning them again."

"Rubbish. I'm not abandoning anyone."

"If they didn't care about you, they wouldn't give a rat's arse if you disappeared forever. But they missed you. *I* missed you."

"I'll send letters regularly."

"Given your previous history, I've my doubts on that score. The only time you wrote was when you needed funds." Hawk frowned. "I am to blame for not calling you home sooner. You've become almost a stranger to us."

"For God's sake, Hawk. I enjoyed my journeys."

"You grew too attached to traveling."

Will inhaled deeply and let his breath out slowly. "You don't understand. There's a whole world out there that I want to explore while I'm still young enough to enjoy it."

"I allowed your traveling to go on too long. You were very persuasive, and I had the responsibility of our sisters. It was easier to let you continue to travel."

"I saw far more of the world than most people ever will in a lifetime. There's no reason for your regrets," Will said.

Hawk shook his head. "You've had too much freedom and insufficient responsibility."

"I'm responsible for myself," he said, unable to keep the edge from his voice.

"Sometimes, you have to sacrifice for others," Hawk said. "And this is one of those times."

"What are you saying?" Denial rose within him, but he knew.

"I can't fund your journey without creating a lasting rift in our family. No one, least of all our mother, will accept it. I've only recently made amends with the family. And I have Julianne, our daughter, and our son to think of as well."

"Let's compromise," Will said. "Give me six months to purge the wanderlust out of my blood."

Hawk folded his hands on the polished mahogany surface. "I'm sorry, Will, but I can't do it."

"I can't sit at a desk all day. I'll go mad."

"Some of your duties will involve inspecting the property for needed repairs, new construction, and ensuring there is sufficient drainage. You'll also be responsible for the rent collection."

"I'm unaccustomed to living my life in a cage."

"Will, this is hardly a cage."

"It will feel like one to me. Everyone in the family constantly noses into everyone else's affairs. I'll be a lunatic within a month."

"That brings to mind another issue. For the sake of our female relatives, be more discreet with your liaisons. You need to take their tender sensibilities into consideration."

Will glared at Hawk. "That is precisely why I stay away. There is no privacy. Everyone meddles in my life."

Hawk met his gaze. "You have a family who loves you. Does that mean nothing to you?"

"Of course, I care, but I've every right to live my life on my terms. That is not negotiable."

"You've lived independently too long and have forgotten that you should take your family's needs into consideration."

Deuce take it. He couldn't believe this was happening.

"Take the steward position for one year," Hawk said. "Set aside a portion of your earnings each quarter. In a year's time, you should have sufficient means to fund another journey. Since it will be money you've earned, there can be no question about your right to do with it as you wish."

Will was breathing harder and trying to control the resentment building inside him. "In other words, I've no choice."

"It's only for a year, Will."

A muscle in his cheek twitched. The next twelve months would feel like a prison sentence. His family would mark every move he made and constantly question him about his whereabouts. They would expect him to attend their dinner parties and make appearances at balls. If he didn't show, someone would be sure to chide him. When he was younger, they had pushed and prodded him to conform to their expectations—when they remembered his existence. Now, they were doing it again, and this time, they would win. How could he bear a year of their constant interference?

Hawk sighed. "I will ask the others to respect your privacy, but if you continue with your flagrant liaisons and wild parties, they will object."

Will scowled. "In other words, I must surrender my autonomy to please them."

"That's an exaggeration, and you know it. All I ask is that you use discretion and attend some of the family events, without having to be prodded. You make the decision about which events are important. Some will not be up for discussion. You need to attend church with the family."

He pulled a face. "Right. I can see it in the scandal sheets now. The devil went to church."

Hawk's shoulders shook with laughter. "Just placate our mother and sisters. Attend a ball or two with them. Dine with the family a little more often. Take our mother to a play. You would make her very happy."

No matter what Hawk said, Will knew nothing would change.

Hawk stood, walked around the desk, and leaned against it. "I know this is not what you wanted, but the time will pass quickly."

He had no choice in the matter, but his brother had tried to compromise. Will knew it was a generous offer. "Thank you for your offer of employment, especially since I have a sad lack of experience."

"You'll catch on quickly," Hawk said.

Will did not doubt his ability. He had a keen memory and had always learned faster than his peers. But he'd be bored silly working on account books. More important, he knew his family would poke into his affairs, the way they had done today. They wanted to coerce him to settle in England and have a family. He had no intention of marrying and tying himself to his intrusive relatives.

"You're disappointed, but I honestly believe the experience will be a good one for you," Hawk said.

Though he felt trapped, Will saw the concern etched on his brother's face and sought to reassure him. "I'm sure you're right."

"The time will pass quickly. You'll see. I've got to travel to Devonshire and meet with my man of business there. When I return in a fortnight, we will discuss your duties in more detail."

Will nodded and strode out the door, determined to find a way to escape his family's stranglehold.

The Albany, later that evening, Harry Fordham's rooms

Will poured a brandy, set the decanter aside, and downed his drink in one swallow. Then he poured another and sprawled in a shabby chair. He was determined to drown his frustration.

"Most unfortunate about your brother, Darcett." Harry Fordham stumbled while attempting to stir the coals. The poker fell with a decided clang on the marble.

Andrew Carrington, the Earl of Bellingham, retrieved the poker and set it aside. Then he replaced the screen. "Steady, old boy."

Fordham lurched over to the cast-off green sofa his mother had given him and sprawled lengthwise on it. A curly blond lock fell over his forehead. "Why is the room spinning?"

"Because you're corn, pickled and salted," Bell said.

"I'm jush grieving for Darcett," he muttered. "It's hell being a younger son. I should know."

Will snorted and took a drink. "Until today, I rather liked being the spare. No obligations, no wife, no brats."

"No money," Fordham mumbled. His empty glass dangled from his hand. "I need another drink."

Bell scoffed. "You're three sheets to the wind."

"Not foxed." Fordham's glass rolled onto the carpet. Within minutes, he was snuffling.

Bell lifted the decanter and eyed Will. "One more?"

Will crossed the room with his glass.

Bell topped it up. "This isn't the outcome you wanted, but your brother provided you with a means to earn the funds."

Will downed the brandy and set the glass aside with a thunk. "Yes, but that means living with my meddling family. Everyone is trying to coerce me into settling down. There is no privacy. Nothing I do pleases them, because I refuse to conform. If anything goes awry, they call a family meeting. Hell, today, one of my sisters offered to find me a bride."

Something flickered in Bell's eyes. Then he looked away.

"Sorry, I wasn't thinking," Will said.

"Don't." Bell returned his attention to Will. "It's been four years. Life goes on."

Will poured another brandy, remembering the haunted look in Bell's eyes after he'd lost all his family—mother, father, and younger brother—to consumption. The night after the funeral, Will had taken him to Fordham's rooms. They had plied him with brandy, hoping Bell would pass out. None of them said a word. In the wee hours of the morning, Bell had broken down and wept. It was an awful thing to witness. He'd thanked God when the three of them had left for their scheduled grand tour shortly thereafter.

A year later, long after Fordham's family had called him home, Bell had admitted he'd considered blowing his brains out. To this day, Bell's confession shook Will.

Bell regarded him with an assessing expression. "Do me a favor. Don't think about it."

"Right." He drank his brandy to cover his thoughts. Most people thought Bell cold. Will didn't view him that way, but he'd known Bell before the tragedy. His friend had been a devil-may-care sort of fellow with a sunny disposition. But while their adventures abroad had enlivened Bell to a degree, he wasn't the same. It was as if someone had permanently snuffed out the candlelight within him.

Bell held his glass aloft. "A toast to your new position."

"I'll be bored out of my mind."

"You bore easily." Bell pushed his fist into Will's upper arm. "You know what your problem is?"

"As a matter of fact, I do. I haven't bedded a woman in a week."

Bell shook his head. "Everything has been a little too easy for you—including women."

"And you don't take advantage of easy women?"

"Touché. My point stands. You've never struggled for anything before."

"Neither have you."

"I'm a relatively intelligent man, but unlike you, I can't

just read something and have it branded in my brain. I don't know if it's your confidence or if you're hoodwinking everyone, but you always manage to come out a winner."

Will shrugged. "I decide I want something, and I pursue it."

"This is the first time you've come face-to-face with a real obstacle."

Will laughed. "Give over. We had plenty of obstacles during our travels. You can't have forgotten the time we tumbled the twin sisters in Paris, and their brother showed. Lord, I didn't know if he'd take our coin as recompense or not."

"That incident is a perfect example of how you charm others to get your way," Bell said. "You made him feel as if he were your old friend and an equal to boot. By the end of the night, he was so taken with you that he completely forgot or didn't care that we'd bedded his sisters."

"He was also drunk," Will said. "And the sisters were more than willing if you will recall."

"I believe that was the first and only time a woman tried to rip my clothes off," Bell said. "We had some wild adventures."

"We will again. All I need is money," Will said.

"You know I have the blunt and could finance the journey," Bell said, "but then I'd become your family's enemy."

"There's got to be a way around my situation."

"It's a challenge," Bell said.

A slow smile spread across Will's face. "You're brilliant."

"I assume you intend to explain."

"What could be more challenging than the gaming table?" Will said.

Bell frowned. "It's not a good idea to gamble what you don't have to lose."

"As far as I'm concerned, I have nothing to lose," Will said. "You know my memory. I'll walk away with a bloody fortune."

Bell set his glass aside. "It's risky."

The risk made it all the more exciting. Will clapped Bell on the shoulder. "We'd best leave Fordham to his snoring. Tomorrow, I'll dazzle him with my winnings."

White's, thirty minutes later

A thrill sizzled through Will's veins as he and Bell strolled into the gaming room. "I feel lucky tonight," Will said.

Bell cast a sideways glance at him. "Remember, get out while you're ahead and watch the waiters. It's easy to lose track of how often they top up the glasses."

He'd no intention of playing conservatively. His superior memory had always served him well in card games. Tonight he meant to gain the fortune he needed for his passage to the Continent. He acknowledged that in order to win he had to be prepared to lose. Long ago, he'd determined that nerves could undermine a man's judgment.

Bell joined him at the green baize table. Will ordered a brandy and so did Bell. The game was vingt-et-un. Will outwardly tamped down his excitement, but inwardly, a thrill pulsed through his veins. Luck played a part, but strategy was involved as well. The latter could make or break a man. Will had played the game numerous times and trusted his ability to play well, because of his excellent recall.

The cards were cut, and Palmer, an acquaintance, had the highest card, making him the dealer. The goal was to reach twenty-one or under and beat the dealer. The suite didn't matter.

Palmer dealt the first card to the other seven players. Everyone but the dealer could view his card. Will had a nine. A minimum bet of twenty pounds and a maximum of fifty was set. Will bet fifty. Bell bet the minimum.

After all the players placed their bets, Palmer dealt the second card. Will viewed his card—a jack. His cards now equaled nineteen. The dealer did not have a pontoon, two cards equaling twenty-one. Each player had the opportunity to add cards. When it was Will's turn, he said stick, because the odds of going over were great. This meant he couldn't add to his stake, but he knew staying the course was important.

Bell viewed his cards and said, "I'll buy one." He increased his stake by another twenty pounds, for a total of forty.

The dealer's hand went over twenty-one. "Paying on nineteen," he said. Will showed his cards. No one had a pontoon, two cards equaling twenty-one, or a five-card trick, five cards totaling twenty-one. Either of those situations would have meant the dealer had to pay double the stakes. Will was satisfied with his initial win of fifty pounds. Bell won forty pounds.

Will memorized the previously played cards as the dealer added them to the bottom of the deck without shuffling as the game required. Remembering the cards out of play was a critical part of Will's strategy. His sharp memory made all the difference, as it gave him an enormous advantage.

Palmer dealt the first card in the next game. Will had a four. The minimum increased to fifty and the maximum to seventy. Will absently sipped his brandy and bet sixty. Bell bet the minimum.

Will's next card was an eight. He bought one card equal to his initial stake, the minimum the game required, for sixty pounds again. When he lifted the card, he kept his expression shuttered. It was a ten, meaning he'd gone over and lost. Momentary disappointment needled him, but he could take this single loss in stride.

Bell won fifty.

In the next round, the stakes increased to a minimum of seventy and a maximum of ninety. Will viewed his first card—a nine. He bet ninety. Bell bet seventy. Will glanced at his friend sideways. Bell probably meant to play conservatively all night.

Will downed his brandy. The second card was a three. He bought a card, for ninety. The third card was a seven, putting him at nineteen.

Bell bought another card at seventy. The dealer paid out on nineteen. Will bit back a satisfied smile as he'd won one hundred and eighty.

Bell lost seventy pounds and threw in his cards. "I'm done."

"It's early yet," Will said.

"I'm ahead by twenty. I've had enough."

Will shrugged and signaled a waiter for another glass of brandy.

Bell leaned toward him. "Keep your wits about you."

"Go on, then." Will turned his attention back to the table. After three games, he was up one hundred and ten.

During the next five games, Will found himself up and down. The stakes kept rising, but his winnings now consisted of a mere twenty pounds. For a moment, he thought of Bell's words. Get out while you're ahead. No, he wouldn't quit now. There was never any certainty, but he had plenty of stamina left. When this night ended, he intended to walk away a very rich man.

The dealer changed hands. After several minutes of negotiation, Palmer sold the bank to Lord Hunter. For some odd reason, the hair at Will's nape stiffened. He told himself to ignore the weird sensation and concentrate on the game.

Hunter dealt the cards. Will was aware of the waiter topping up his glass. He sipped and glanced at his card. He had a seven. The stakes were set at a minimum of one thousand and a maximum of three thousand. Will placed an initial bet of one thousand. Two chairs down, Yarborough, a portly man of middle years, bet two thousand and mopped his sweaty forehead with a handkerchief. Will cut his gaze away, unable to watch a nervous player. It made him edgy.

He took another drink. His blood was pumping fast as he viewed the second card. It was a five, putting him at a total of twelve. For a moment, he wrestled with the decision of whether to buy one more card. Ordinarily, he wouldn't question it, and that got under his skin. Deuce take it. He wasn't superstitious like most gamblers. Strategy and a good memory were all he needed. Will glanced at Hunter briefly. "I'll buy another—one thousand again."

Will's heart thumped as he lifted the card. It was a seven, putting him at nineteen. Hunter went over twenty-one and paid out on nineteen. Will's winnings now stood at two thousand and twenty pounds.

His excitement increased as he memorized the cards that were out of play. He could practically feel the win coming. Hunter dealt the cards. Will's first card was an eight. The bet was set at a minimum of two thousand and a maximum of four. Will bet two thousand and forced himself to focus on the play and not the money. His second card was a three. Will downed the remainder of his brandy and bought a card, for two thousand again. His mouth felt a bit dry as he viewed the card. That card was a ten. He'd gone bust. Will slowly inhaled. He was right back at two thousand and twenty pounds.

For a moment, he considered quitting, but he needed a big win if he wished to gain his freedom from his family. Will was confident the tide would turn soon.

The waiter brought Will a new glass of brandy. He sipped it and realized he was a bit foxed, but he still had his wits about him.

In the next round of play, Will viewed his first card—a three. He bet the minimum of two thousand. His second card was a five. Will bought another card. It was a five. He bought a third one for two thousand again—a four. Tension rippled all around him as his fellow players must have sensed Will was on a roll. He forced himself to concentrate, but damn, his mouth was as dry as dust. He bought another card for two thousand, putting him at a total of ten thousand pounds, including his previous win of two thousand. Will could almost hear those around him holding their breath as Hunter dealt the card.

A trickle of sweat beaded down the back of Will's neck. It was a four. He struggled not to show his triumph, but the devil take it, he wanted to shout it to the roof. A five-card trick meant the dealer paid double. He exposed his cards, certain he'd won twenty thousand pounds and his freedom this night.

Hunter turned up an ace and a king, a pontoon that trumped Will's hand.

A collective gasp went up. Voices erupted all around him, but he heard nothing. Will felt as if he were floating above himself and watching the disaster unfold. His ears buzzed like a bee. He had to pay Hunter double his stakes. Twenty thousand pounds.

Hunter told everyone to lower their voices, reminding them of the rules of playing. Will could see the undisguised elation on the man's face. He wanted to hate him, but all he felt was numb.

He forced himself to finish his brandy and smiled. "Gentlemen, I'm out."

When he rose from the table, he nearly stumbled. The copious amount of brandy he'd drunk made it all seem unreal. He walked unsteadily over to Hunter and somehow managed to scrawl out a vowel for the debt. God only knew where he would get the money to pay it.

Bell strode over to him. "What the deuce? I heard the news."

"Not here," he said.

He was in a daze and more than a little foxed as he carefully negotiated the stairs. A servant at the door helped him into his coat. Bell led him outside. When Will dropped his gloves, Bell retrieved them. "Steady, old boy. My carriage will be here shortly."

When it arrived, Bell managed to shove him inside.

Will closed his eyes, and his last thought was that he'd lost.

Someone shook his shoulder. Will's mouth was as dry as a desert. His head felt as if someone were pounding on it like a drum. Disoriented, he opened his eyes to find Bell staring at him. His friend wore a banyan robe over his shirt and trousers.

"How did I get here?" Will croaked.

"You don't remember?" Bell said.

"No." Will sat up, leaned forward, and held his head in his hands. He was in his shirtsleeves.

"My valet managed to get you out of your coat and waistcoat before you passed out on the sofa."

"I was roaring drunk."

Bell walked over to the sideboard and returned to him with a cup of tea. "It's not very hot, but you're bound to be thirsty."

Will drank the tepid tea. "What time is it?"

"Eleven o'clock."

The bell rang. Will felt as if it were clanging inside his head.

A few minutes later, Fordham entered the drawing room and collapsed on a chair. "You look like the devil, but I suppose that's to be expected."

Bell sat in the other armchair. "Do you recall what happened at the gaming table?"

"I lost twenty thousand bloody pounds I don't have," Will said.

"You've got to make a decision quickly," Bell said. "The debt has to be paid."

"I suppose I could escape to the Continent. I wouldn't be the first or the last."

"Be reasonable," Bell said. "You've got no money. A new geographic location isn't the answer. You'll be among strangers. How will you live?"

Will sat back. "What else am I to do?"

"Let me take care of the debt," Bell said.

"No, I can't let you."

"You don't have the blunt," Bell said. "Hunter isn't going to forgive the twenty thousand."

Bell had inherited an enormous fortune. Will didn't know the extent of his friend's wealth, but Bell had described it as obscene. Though he was tempted, Will didn't want to take advantage of their friendship. "I appreciate your offer, but I don't know how I would ever be able to repay you."

"Your brother is bound to hear about it," Bell said.

"Not for a fortnight at least," Will said. "He went to Devonshire to meet with his man of business. When he returns, I'll have to ask him to pay it." He huffed. "What's one more black mark?"

Bell folded his arms over his chest. "I imagine that will come with strings attached."

He would spend years working as his brother's steward to repay him. "I don't have any other option."

"There is one other way out of your predicament," Fordham said. "You won't like the idea, but it is an alternative."

Will looked inquiringly at Fordham. "Well, what is it?"

Bell snorted. "You must be in really bad shape if you can't guess."

"You mean marry an heiress?" Will said.

"There are worse fates," Fordham said.

Will shook his head. "No, absolutely not. I've got enough meddling relatives. The last thing I want is a wife making demands."

"Marry a mouse," Bell said. "Pick someone who is too timid to raise objections. Wait a few months, and by then, she'll be relieved when you take that journey to the Continent."

It was the first time Will had thought of Bell as cold-blooded. "Who would let a devil like me marry their daughter?"

Bell shrugged. "The lady and her family benefit as well. She marries into a prominent family, and you pay back your debt. No one will bat an eye if you make a marriage of convenience, but if you fail to pay the debt, you lose your honor."

"No, there's got to be another way." If only his soaked brains would dry, he might think of a solution.

"If I were you, I'd have a look at the wallflowers. They're desperate, and you're a prize," Bell said.

"Ironically, marriage is your ticket out of England," Fordham said.

Men married for money all the time. It was an accepted practice. "I won't deceive an innocent lady and her family."

"If you choose a lady who is dangerously close to being on the shelf, her family will likely be grateful," Bell said. "They'll know you're marrying her for the money, but in return, she makes a respectable marriage. No lady wants to be a spinster; no one will respect her. Given the lady's lack of prospects, she'll probably be relieved."

Bell had made it sound as if he'd be doing a wallflower a favor. "I'll think about it."

"Don't think too long," Bell said. "Hunter won't wait forever, you know."

"What about Lady Eugenia?" Fordham said. "She's definitely in danger of being on the shelf, according to my sisters."

"She's Beaufort's sister. He'd kill me if I even looked

at her," Will said. "You know friends' sisters are off-limits."

"What about that tall redhead? The one who is bosom friends with Lady Georgette," Fordham said. "Does she have any brothers?"

"How would I know?" Will said.

"She's been out for several years and is accounted a wallflower," Bell said. "I don't recollect any brothers. Isn't she a friend of your sister-in-law?"

"Yes," he said.

"It should be relatively easy to gain an introduction," Bell said.

Fordham grinned. "Congratulations. We found you a bride."

Will scowled. "Trust me. Miss Hardwick is the one woman who wants nothing to do with me."

Fordham and Bell exchanged amused glances.

"What?" Will said irritably.

"You like challenges. She's a challenge," Bell said.

"Even better, her father is rich," Fordham said. "My sister said she has fifty thousand pounds."

Temptation gripped him. But he couldn't imagine how he would ever persuade Red to marry him. First off, he'd better stop calling her Red, since she didn't like it. He had managed to charm her a little in the library. But if he suddenly showed up with a posy, she would be suspicious. "There's a problem," he said. "I don't have enough time to court her properly."

"So make it a whirlwind courtship," Bell said.

Will scrubbed his bristly jaw. "She's too clever. When she figures out I'm only interested in her money, she'll give me the cut direct."

"There's one way to ensure she'll marry you," Fordham said. "Compromise her."

Bell whistled. "Who better than the devil to pull that off?"

"You've both gone mad," Will said.

"Your family is already pressing you to wed," Fordham said. "When they find out about the debt, they'll realize they've got the upper hand. You'll end up married anyway."

"God, I've mucked things up." He'd stupidly let his greed overcome his better judgment, but he'd been so certain he'd win. In truth, he'd never faced a serious setback before. This was much worse than a setback; it was a bloody debacle.

"You've got two choices," Bell said. "Apply to your brother or marry the heiress. Which will it be?"

No matter what he did, he'd end up a blackguard, but then he already was one. He might as well do it on his own terms. Will blew out his breath and met Bell's gaze. "Marriage," he said.

Bell nodded. "I'll let Hunter know you expect to come into the funds soon."

Thirty minutes later, Will got out of a hackney. A fine mist dampened his greatcoat and the chill made him feel worse as he trudged up the walk to Ashdown House. When he reached the bottom horseshoe step, a pitiful cry alerted him. He looked behind one of the giant bushes and saw a kitten. The scrawny thing bleated repeatedly. Will squatted and held out his hand. "Scared?" he murmured.

The kitten backed up a bit and continued to cry.

"There's no one to take care of you." He used to collect stray dogs and cats when he was young. For some odd reason, he thought of all the times his family forgot about him when he was a boy. They were all so busy. He was the youngest, and often shuffled off to the nurse, the usual aristocratic method of dealing with brats. He remembered wishing he had a brother close to his age.

When he was five, they'd left him at church. It was one of the family's favorite stories. They hadn't even missed him, until the rector had returned him home. His father had thought it funny. His mother had wept, and naturally everyone had gone to console her. None of them had known he'd been sad and a little scared, but that was a long time ago.

Will scooped up the cat and strode up the steps. "Hush, Poppet. I'll keep you safe."

He wrapped his coat over the damp kitten, but Poppet continued to cry. He figured it was hungry. "I'll get you some cream in the kitchen," he murmured.

Jones, the fastidious butler, wrinkled his nose when Will handed Poppet to him. The kitten had gray fur and white paws. "He smells a bit from the wet," Will said as he shrugged out of his greatcoat.

Jones examined the kitten. "It's a she," he said in a disapproving tone.

Will retrieved the crying kitten, and Jones wiped his hands with his handkerchief. "I'll call a footman to deal with the animal."

"No, I'll take care of her." He didn't want Poppet to be shooed out of the way of the busy servants. So he strode off toward the back stairs. "Little girl, let's get you some nourishment."

When he walked into the kitchen, he startled Cook and

the maids. They hastily curtsied and stared at him as if he'd grown a pair of horns. "I found her. She's hungry."

Cook smiled. "I'll get her a bowl of cream and mash up a bit of fish."

Will squatted and watched as Poppet lapped up her meal. Afterward, the kitten stretched out on the flagstone. Obviously, she was exhausted.

One of the maids produced a basket lined with old newspapers. She curtsied. "You can leave her here, sir. We'll see to her."

He shook his head. "I'll take her with me and bring her back tomorrow morning." He put Poppet in the basket and carried her to his bedchamber.

After setting her near the fireplace for warmth, he sat on the carpet and petted her. He figured his morose mood stemmed from last night's loss and would pass. In truth, he felt a bit sheepish for even thinking about the time his family left him at church. Good Lord, the massive amount of brandy he'd drunk had clearly made him gloomy—that and the monstrous debt.

The kitten squeaked at him. He rubbed her soft fur and thought it might make both of them feel a bit better.

Chapter Three

One week later

Amy reluctantly handed Emma back into Julianne's arms and took a seat. A crowd of matrons and their daughters were admiring her sketches in the Dowager Countess of Hawkfield's drawing room.

Last week, Madame DuPont had perused her sketches and declared them magnificent. The modiste had set her seamstresses to work creating gowns from two of Amy's designs. They had finished in time for the viewing today. Amy had approved Madame DuPont's fabric recommendations and made several suggestions as well. Excitement had bubbled up inside her, because the gowns turned out even better than she'd expected.

After the maids collected the tea tray, the Dowager Countess of Hawkfield announced it was time to begin. Amy joined Madame DuPont at the round table. The modiste began to unwrap the first gown. Amy drew in a deep breath and faced the ladies. "Madame DuPont and her talented seamstresses made up two of the designs I sketched. You will note the rich color of the fabric— burgundy velvet trimmed at the neckline with frills…"

Amy trailed off as the ladies gasped. A thrill went through her as she turned to find Madame displaying the gown with the help of her assistants. This was what she'd yearned for but had not quite allowed herself to hope for.

"It is absolutely stunning," the dowager countess said.

"We paired it with a white cashmere shawl trimmed with burgundy fringe," Amy said as one of the assistants draped it against the gown.

"I wish to have something similar made up," Georgette said. "I am uncertain about the dark color. Amy, what do you think?"

"With your blond hair, I think coquelicot would work well. The poppy color is still rich, but will not overwhelm your complexion."

Amy turned her thoughts to the next gown as Madame's assistants were already busy displaying it.

The ladies' eyes widened. Amy smiled because their reactions confirmed her private belief that her designs were unique. There was so much in her life that she had little power over, but knowing that others found her designs remarkable filled her with confidence she'd sorely lacked most of her life.

She took a deep breath and began her description. "This gown is far more ornate than the previous one. The underskirt is an ivory silk, heavily embroidered with gold paillettes, cannetille, and gold lamé. The hem is trimmed in a gold fringe. The collar is an airy lace stitched along the neckline from the shoulders reaching all along the back." The lace was doused with liberal amounts of starch to keep it upright.

After everyone admired the gown, Georgette assisted Amy by passing around additional sketches. Several matrons summoned Madame DuPont, who discreetly handed out her cards.

Twenty minutes later, Amy announced she had one other creation. She walked over to the sideboard and opened a small parcel. Then she presented a tiny muslin gown with embroidered roses to Julianne. "I thought Emma Rose should be dressed in the most stylish of infant apparel."

"I adore it, Amy." Julianne's blue eyes were shining. "Thank you."

Several ladies surrounded Amy and complimented her designs. For the first time, she found she enjoyed the attention. More important, she felt more assured of herself than ever before. As she spoke to the other ladies, she had no trouble formulating replies. Perhaps it was because the topic was one in which she had a great interest and knowledge. She knew it would not always be this easy, but today marked an important turn for her.

Patience, Lady Montague, regarded Amy with wonder. "You are incredibly talented. I hope you will consent to design gowns for my sisters and me." Patience looked over her shoulder. "There, you see Hope and Harmony are examining the ivory silk with the gold trim."

Two maids brought in the tea tray again, and the ladies returned to their chairs. Amy did likewise and blew out her breath, relieved that all had gone so well. After she accepted a cup of tea, Hester, Lady Rutledge, eased into the chair next to her. "Miss Hardwick, you acquitted yourself exceptionally well today." Her lined eyes twinkled. "The gown for little Emma was a lovely gesture."

"Thank you. I enjoyed sharing my passion with others."

"I believe you are something of a late bloomer," she said. "This will be your year. Mark my words." Then she lifted her quizzing glass. "Oh, there is Mrs. Jenkins. Excuse me. I must have a word with her."

Sally, Catherine, and Julianne stepped forward. "We could not even get close to you for all the other ladies who wanted your attention," Sally said.

"You have surprised everyone, Amy," Catherine said. "Your singular accomplishment puts all other feminine ones to shame."

"I don't think so," Amy said. "At any rate, I think it's the enjoyment of whatever you choose that counts the most."

Julianne took Amy's arm. "Would you mind meeting my husband's grandmamma?"

"I would enjoy it," Amy said.

As they walked along, Julianne looked at her. "Grandmamma's hearing is poor, but she wishes to compliment you."

"I'm honored," Amy said. "My grandparents died long ago. I think it is important to spend as much time as possible with the elderly."

Julianne smiled as they approached the elderly lady. Her hair was completely white and her skin a little marred by age spots. But Amy could envision her as a beautiful young belle. Amy curtsied and looked directly at the lady. "I am honored to meet you."

She had a beautiful smile. Then she pointed at the

gown that Madame DuPont was wrapping for transport. "Pretty," she said.

"Thank you."

She touched her own hair and then pointed at Amy. "Are you Scottish, dear?"

"No, I am not."

Patience hurried over to them with Emma on her shoulder. "Oh, dear. Grandmamma believes anyone with red hair is Scottish. We've no idea where she got that notion. Aunt Hester implies she knows, but refuses to tell us. I don't even want to think what it might be if Hester won't talk about it."

Amy and Julianne laughed. Then Amy noticed Madame DuPont regarding her. "Please excuse me."

Amy joined Madame DuPont. "Thank you for having the gowns made up on such short notice. I'm gratified that our combined efforts received such acclamation."

Madame inclined her head. "So am I. It was time well spent for me. Several of the ladies took my card and promised to visit my shop." She gave Amy an assessing look. "Your designs are original. I have more than a few competitors in this business. I wish to make you a proposition."

Amy regarded her with a wary expression.

"I will pay you handsomely for the exclusive use of your designs," Madame said. "I believe we both would benefit from the association—if you are amenable, that is."

Amy caught her breath. She'd never dreamed anyone would offer compensation for her designs.

"I would, of course, keep the financial aspect of our arrangement confidential," Madame added.

Amy hesitated. Her grandfather had been a shopkeeper, and she had no prejudice against those who earned an honest living. However, her parents had kept the origins of her mother's great fortune a secret, because they knew the beau monde discriminated against those who engaged in trade. At the same time, she was torn. Her parents approved of her sketches and were proud of her accomplishment. Amy couldn't wait to write to them about today's success. But she had no need of money and did not believe it worth taking the risk.

There was more than just pretty gowns at stake. Ladies were judged so harshly on their appearance—at least in comparison to men. Amy understood that others were drawn to beauty, but it was not as important as one's character. Yet, she knew firsthand how much one's appearance could affect one's life.

If she were to accept Madame's proposition and word somehow leaked, it might hurt her parents—and her chances of making a good marriage. As Amy's thoughts raced, she glanced at the ladies milling about and caught Lady Boswood watching her through narrowed eyes.

She quickly looked away. Georgette's mother was a high stickler for the proprieties. She would rake Amy over the coals if she ever discovered she was engaged in trade.

"I will pay you five shillings per sketch," Madame Dupont said.

Amy caught her breath, for it was a great deal of money. Madame had promised to keep the matter private, and they would both benefit. But the risk of discovery was too high. "Madame DuPont, I appreciate your offer, but I am more than willing to offer my sketches without compensation. I do not need the money, and I'm sure you would not object to my refusal. I assure you my pleasure in knowing that others wish to wear my designs is enough for me."

Madame DuPont regarded her with a shrewd expression. "I view this from a business perspective," she said. "The compensation is my assurance that you will provide the designs on a timely and regular basis. Without it, you will not feel as obligated. The social whirl will take up much of your time, and if pressed, you may well put other things ahead of providing the designs. Frankly, I also believe that an agreement between us will ensure that I have exclusive rights to your designs. My business is very competitive, and if one of the designs is copied elsewhere, it could adversely affect my business."

Amy frowned. "Are you saying you will not feature my designs unless I take compensation?"

"I believe it is my best interest, as I have described to you."

She understood the modiste's concerns, but she found it difficult to make a decision, because she worried about discovery. Yet she wanted her designs featured in the shop. She wanted others to wear her creations. She wanted to design gowns for ladies with imperfect figures—gowns that would transform those who did not fit the image of the perfect English rose.

There was another matter, one she didn't like to contemplate, but she must think of her future. If something happened to her father and mother, Amy knew that her father would have arranged ample funds for her support, for he was a wealthy man. Although Amy knew little of legal matters, she imagined solicitors would be involved, and they might well have a say in her expenditures. The idea rankled, but if she had her own secret funds, she would have some control of her purchases.

She took a deep breath, knowing she was taking a

risk, but it was some reassurance as well. "Madame, your silence on this matter is imperative," Amy murmured.

"You have my word." Madame regarded her with a slight smile. "When may I expect more designs?"

"A fortnight," Amy said, "if that is acceptable."

"Of course. Thank you, Miss Hardwick. I believe our association will prove fruitful for both of us."

Amy nodded. The nervousness ebbed away, and she found comfort in knowing that she would have some control over her future. She need not marry a man she knew was all wrong for her. Best of all, she would be renowned for the gowns she designed and respected for her talent.

Lady Boswood and Georgette were approaching. Georgette's closed expression spoke volumes. Ever since Amy had taken up residence with her friend, she'd noted that Georgette's manner grew stiff whenever her mother was in high dudgeon about something. Amy often felt nervous around Lady Boswood. She often felt as if the woman were examining all of her flaws and comparing her unfavorably to her daughter. Georgette was aware of her mother's competitive nature and abhorred it. Other times, like now, Georgette's naturally vivacious manner disappeared, and she would listen only to her mother. Amy supposed it was her friend's only defense against a mother who insisted upon controlling her daughter.

Lady Boswood's smile was tight when she reached Amy. "Well, have you basked enough in your praise this day? Or should we give you a few more moments?"

Evidently, Georgette's mother resented her for garnering attention. Amy recollected Julianne telling her to have a care round Lady Boswood. An uneasy feeling took hold of Amy. She resolved to be as inconspicuous as possible in that lady's presence. Amy did not doubt her ability to fade into the background. After all, she'd had many years of practice. "I am ready to depart whenever it is convenient for you," she said in a neutral tone.

"Miss Hardwick, we meet again."

She gritted her teeth, having recognized the devil's distinctive voice: velvety deep with a hint of wicked laughter. Slowly, she turned round to find him standing with a gray kitten in his arms. She barely had time to register the kitten's white paws when feminine cries interrupted them. Before she could say a word, all the other young ladies rushed toward him. Amy stepped away as they surrounded him and cooed over his kitten. One would think none of them had ever seen a cat before. Of course, the kitten wasn't the real attraction.

How foolish. They knew his rakehell reputation, and it drew them like moths to a flame. It was the mystique of a bad boy. Well, he was no boy. He was a grown man and had no scruples.

"What a sweet kitty," Sally cried.

Catherine looked at him through her lashes, an affectation Amy despised.

"What is his name?" Catherine asked.

"Poppet is a little lady," he said, petting the kitten.

Catherine and Sally both looked as if they might melt into puddles on the floor.

Amy silently scoffed. Little lady, indeed. The man was a consummate flirt, if ever one existed. She turned to Georgette, certain her friend was similarly disgusted, but Georgette swept past her and pressed through the crowd of ladies. "May I hold her?"

When he handed the kitten over to Georgette, she

nuzzled it. "Sir, I believe she has picked up the scent of your cologne."

"Ah, that would explain why she's been bathing herself," the devil said. "Should I give her a proper bath?"

When the other ladies giggled, Amy rolled her eyes. He probably had some specially made potion designed to turn a woman's brains to mush. No, he needn't even try to impress. He was the sort of rake who relied upon his considerable good looks to get exactly what he wanted. Although it pained her to admit it, even she wasn't entirely unaffected by his handsome face and athletic build. But his looks did not make up for his lack of character.

He was a pleasure seeker who, from all accounts, spent his time wenching and drinking. Amy could not fathom why ladies thought these bad qualities made him alluring. They seemed to like him better because he was a rake. All he had to do was mesmerize the females with his twinkling dark eyes and boyish grin. Why, he probably came here with his cat for the sole purpose of winning the admiration of the ladies.

"Georgette, dearest," Lady Boswood called out in a sweet tone that sounded practiced. "We must leave now."

Thank goodness. Amy could not bear another moment of watching all the ladies flirt with him. No doubt his head would swell to monstrous proportions from all the attention. Of course, she wasn't jealous. She didn't like him—not even a little.

Lady Boswood took her daughter by the arm and marched off, leaving Amy to trail behind. As Amy passed Mr. Darcett, he grinned at her. She gave him a freezing look. The spark in his eyes let her know she'd made a tactical error. Clearly, he saw her disapproval as some sort of challenge.

She would ignore him. The worst punishment she could deal him was to look through him as if he didn't exist. There would be no fun in it for him if she didn't provide him with the miffed reaction he expected.

The next evening

"Everyone is admiring your gown," Georgette murmured as they walked through Lord and Lady Broughton's ballroom. "You're becoming quite famous for your fashions."

Amy smiled. She felt elegant tonight in sheer lavender fabric over a satin slip. The sleeves, neckline, and hem were trimmed in blond lace. She especially liked the pretty lavender satin bows ornamenting the bottom of the skirt.

The dancing had yet to start. Amy was determined not to shrink back if any gentlemen approached. If no one requested her hand, she would hold her head high and converse with others. Because of her tendency to grow anxious in crowds, she had thought of several questions to ask others in the event she grew nervous. Doing so would give her a measure of courage. She most certainly would not run off to hide this night, the way she'd done at the Beresfords' ball.

They had not gotten far when Sally hailed them. "I'm glad to find you in this crush. Oh, my stars, Amy. Your gown is stunning once again. I insist you design one for me, although I cannot possibly carry off your elegance because I do not have your height."

"Thank you, Sally, but your gown is very pretty. I love the lace on the flounces."

"Do you really? I wasn't certain about it, but now I feel reassured, since you approve."

Amy applied her fan. "It is warm in here. Let us get a cup of punch."

As they started off for the refreshment table, Amy looked at Sally. "Have you seen Julianne this evening?"

Sally shook her head. "I asked the Dowager Countess of Hawkfield about her, but she said that Julianne did not wish to attend without her husband. He apparently had to make a journey."

"Ah, there they are," a familiar masculine voice called out.

Amy turned to see Lord Beaufort hailing them. Moments later, he and his friends Charles Osgood and Lord Caruthers joined them. Old habits nearly overwhelmed Amy, but she forced herself to meet the eyes of the gentlemen and smile.

Beaufort took Georgette's gloved hand and bowed over it. As he gazed at Georgette, his blue eyes filled with tenderness, and in that moment, Amy sensed he was madly in love with Georgette.

"Miss Hardwick, you are the very person I have been seeking," Mr. Osgood said.

Amy smiled at him. He had grown a great deal taller since last year. His face had filled out, and he was no longer a lanky boy. "You are looking quite dashing this evening, Mr. Osgood."

"I fear I'm overdue in making my apology," he said.

She blinked. "I beg your pardon?"

"A year ago, I stepped on your toes during a dance." He laughed. "I begged my elder sisters to teach me so that I wouldn't humiliate myself again. Will you allow me to make amends by dancing with me?"

"I would be delighted to partner with you." Osgood was not classically handsome, but he'd acquired a bit of polish in the year past, and she found his self-deprecating sense of humor charming. She was gratified to see Sally and Lord Caruthers following them to the dance floor.

Beaufort and Georgette joined the dancers. With his blond hair and dark brows, Beaufort had the sort of heart-stopping face that made women take a second and third look. He winked at Georgette from across the line. She blew him a kiss. He laughed and clutched his chest. Amy suspected Beaufort would win her friend's heart before the Season ended.

Their sweet flirtation made Amy wonder why Georgette had expressed hesitancy about Beaufort previously. Perhaps Georgette had overcome her doubts. Then an odd thought occurred to Amy. Georgette's father kept telling his daughter that she need not rush into marriage. At the same time, however, Lady Boswood continually pressed her daughter to wed. Georgette never openly argued with her mother, but now Amy wondered if Georgette was silently rebelling against her. If so, Amy doubted Georgette was even aware of her behavior. It was clear to Amy that Lord and Lady Boswood were confusing their daughter with opposite opinions. Amy meant to speak to Georgette about it when they were alone tonight, because she hoped to help her friend sort out her feelings.

The musicians struck up the lively tune of a country dance, and Amy focused all her attention on the steps. She felt exhilarated, because she wasn't sitting on the sidelines watching. She was dancing with Mr. Osgood, who was a wonderful partner. Granted, she'd danced a few times with elderly gentlemen at country assemblies, but only once before had she danced at a London ball, and ironically that had been with Mr. Osgood. She let all of her inhibitions float away and enjoyed herself.

When they met in the middle and turned forward, she smiled at Mr. Osgood. "Your sisters taught you well. You are quite accomplished."

"Thank you. I'll have to tell my sisters that you approved of my dancing," he said.

"Do you still write poetry?" she asked.

He laughed. "My sisters read my poems and told me to give it up. What was the word they used to describe it? Ah, now I remember—horrid."

She laughed. "Did they really?"

"Oh, yes," he said as they turned in a circle. "My real object in writing poetry involved a fantasy. I envisioned myself brooding by a column and all the ladies falling madly in love with me."

Amy laughed. He'd obviously acquired more than a little polish in his manners, which made him rather charming.

When the set finally ended, she was out of breath and laughing at one of Mr. Osgood's jokes. Georgette and Lord Beaufort followed them to the refreshment table for punch. Amy felt exultant. In a mere fortnight, she'd made great strides toward shedding her wallflower reputation.

After Mr. Osgood excused himself, Amy found herself suddenly apart from the others. Beaufort had led Georgette off, and Sally was nowhere in sight. Amy refilled her cup. As she surveyed the ballroom, her gaze landed on the one person she'd despised for years: the cruelest lady in the ton, Elizabeth, now Lady Edgemont.

Amy involuntarily stiffened. A horrible memory gripped her. Two years ago, Elizabeth had walked past the wall-flower row with her flock of friends. Amy had looked at her lap to avoid making eye contact with those mean girls. She would never forget Elizabeth's words. *Oh, look at the poor ugly duckling. Do you suppose she will ever be a swan?*

Their cruel laughter had stung Amy like a dagger to her heart.

Elizabeth's husband walked over to her and leaned down to speak. With a sullen expression, she shrugged one shoulder. Lord Edgemont spoke again, and this time he looked exasperated. Elizabeth shook her head. When he walked off, she regarded his retreating back with a venomous expression.

Shock rained over Amy. All these years, Amy had imagined that Elizabeth had managed to get everything she'd ever wanted in life. When Elizabeth had become engaged to Lord Edgemont last year, Amy's eyes had welled with tears. The injustice had seared her. She'd imagined Elizabeth leading an idyllic life as Lady Edgemont. Now she realized that the woman she'd thought of as her nemesis had not found happiness in her marriage.

Amy wondered why she didn't feel triumphant. She ought to take heart that justice had finally prevailed, but she took no satisfaction in knowing that Elizabeth had not made a fairy-tale marriage. Elizabeth had said and done horrible things to Amy and her friends. Under the circumstances, Amy could not understand her reaction to what she'd witnessed. She ought to gloat. She ought to feel that Elizabeth had gotten exactly what she deserved. She ought to want Elizabeth to be miserable. But she didn't, even though she had every reason to hate Elizabeth.

Then she realized that only shallow and cruel people derived pleasure from the misery of others. She didn't need to avenge herself. Elizabeth was her own worst enemy. She would never know happiness, because she was unfeeling and mean-spirited.

Amy refused to dwell on Elizabeth any longer. She set her empty cup aside and decided to look for friends. Tonight, she would test her fortitude by joining a group. If she got a cold reception, she would simply excuse herself and move on.

Determined to break free of the worst of the crowd, she lifted her skirts and headed away from the refreshment table. She grew a bit frustrated due to the dense crowd. When she halted and craned her head, someone grasped her elbow. With a gasp, Amy looked up into the devil's dark, laughing eyes.

"Did I surprise you?" he said.

He'd spoken in a rumbling tone of voice, one he probably used to seduce his paramours. "Are you in the habit of grabbing women?" she asked.

The devil chuckled. "Only you."

She scoffed. Before she knew what was what, he'd tucked her hand into the crook of his arm and held it fast as he walked away.

She could feel the hard muscle in his upper arm even through his wool sleeve, and for some reason, that made her uneasy. "Let me go."

He looked amused. "You wound me. I long for your company."

"That is your misfortune," she said. "All I long for is your absence."

He guffawed, drawing attention from several scowling matrons.

"Hush," she said. "People are staring."

"Let them." His gaze traveled down the length of her body, making her feel as if he were mentally peeling the layers of clothing away. "I like your gown," he said. "It shimmers in the candlelight."

A giddy feeling bubbled up inside her. Many ladies had expressed enthusiasm for her designs, but his simple statement about the shimmery overskirt touched her in a different way. He'd not flattered her. He'd admired the gown she'd designed, and she was too proud of her talent to resist his admiration.

He regarded her with an amused expression. "I thought you would rebuke me for intercepting you."

She'd foolishly let his compliment go to her head. A devil like him would use flattery to get what he wanted. "Why did you?" she asked. *Why would a sinfully handsome man like you pursue a plain lady like me?*

"Can't you guess?" he said.

"No, and I'm not in the mood for riddles."

He tipped his head as if he meant to confide something, and a faint, spicy scent drifted to her. "You are so suspicious," he said.

"I have good reason." She noticed his lashes were thick and lush. He met her gaze and she fancied she saw intention in his expression. She looked away, uncomfortable with his too warm regard. For her own good, she must withdraw from his escort at once. "It has been interesting, but I must meet my friends," she said. "Now if you will excuse me."

"Not yet," he said.

"Mr. Darcett, I—"

"Ah, we've arrived at last," he said.

He'd sufficiently distracted her so that she'd not realized

he meant to take her to the dance floor. Her lips parted as she stared at him. "You did not even ask."

"I assumed you like to dance."

She glared at him. "You are outrageous."

He turned toward her, and his breath whispered over her cheek. "Admit it. You find me utterly irresistible."

"You are a cad, a bounder, a—"

The musicians struck up the opening bars of a country dance, cutting off her words. He stood across from her and looked as if he were trying to hold back laughter. She ought to walk away, but others would take notice. He'd acted in a high-handed manner, but only a fool would create a scene.

The music started. He bowed. She curtsied. Then he stepped forward and she met him. He grinned when they passed each other as they changed sides. She decided to ignore the flirtatious way he looked at her and focused on the steps, moving one position down the line. All the years she'd sat on the wallflower row, she'd committed the dances to memory. However, it was one thing to observe and quite another to dance. She'd acquitted herself well with Mr. Osgood, but then that gentleman did not disturb her the way the devil did.

They joined hands with another couple, turning and turning until the music changed. She crossed to the other side, facing Mr. Darcett again. Not long after, she met him in the center, and they turned forward. This time, they walked side by side to the top of the line. His hand rested on her upper back, and the firm pressure made her feel as if he'd branded her. He locked his gaze with hers, and Amy's breath hitched in her throat. This time there was no amusement in his eyes, only intensity and something forbidden.

They parted and met again, clasping hands, all the while turning, turning, turning. The entire time, he never took his arresting gaze off her. She felt her resistance melting, and she suddenly wished he would say or do something ridiculous, because his dark eyes were tugging at her like a swift current.

Mercifully, the movements required they change sides and move one place down the line again. She tried to keep a serene countenance, but she could not avoid looking at him. He winked, and somehow she felt more at ease with his teasing. He liked to provoke her, but she was familiar with his antics.

Once more they met in the middle and clasped hands as they turned together. She looked past his cheek, desperate to avoid direct eye contact with him, though she wasn't sure why. Then he spoke near her ear. "Look at me," he said, his voice low and a little rough.

Her heart beat faster when she met his dark gaze. He held her captive with his eyes. She was faintly aware of the cheery melody and of his chest rising and falling. The sensible part of her shouted to break free of this dizzying hold he had over her, but she could not do it.

She told herself it would be madness to fall under his wicked spell. She told herself it was only a dance. She told herself she was in no danger from him. She told herself that even a devil like him must observe the proprieties.

They parted again, but her relief was temporary as she met him in the middle. They turned toward the bottom of the line. Once again, his hand rested on her upper back. She glanced at him from the corners of her eyes only to find him watching her with a sultry expression. When they parted to opposite sides of the line, she breathed a sigh of relief.

The orchestra played the final notes with a flourish. She curtsied and meant to escape, but he offered his escort, and there were too many others watching to refuse him. He looked into her eyes again as he led her away, and she averted her face, realizing he was an expert at ensnaring women with his gaze.

"I would ask if you would like punch, but I fear you might decide to get even and pour it on me," he said.

She turned to find him grinning at her. "I suppose it is past time I forgive you."

"Hallelujah," he said.

She laughed. As he led her through the ballroom, she was aware of others watching their progress. She knew that merely being seen with him might cause a stir, but she would escape him soon enough.

When he handed her a cup of punch, she gave him an assessing look. "I am a little tempted to spill it on you."

He gave her a thousand-candle smile. "I have much to atone for, I see. Well, Miss Hardwick, how may I redeem myself—short of allowing you to douse me?"

"You might regret asking. After all, you would be obligated to do my bidding," she said.

"What would you oblige me to do?"

"Since you are known as the devil, I think the worst punishment would be to require you to mend your wicked ways," she said.

He edged closer to her. "I might require your assistance. All of my lessons were learned at the School of Hades—according to the scandal sheets."

"Then you must do one good deed each day to make up for all the bad ones." She glanced at him from the corners of her eyes. "How many bad ones are there?"

"This week?" he asked.

She nodded.

He leaned forward. "Two."

She narrowed her eyes. "Are you telling the truth?"

"Absolutely ... not."

She laughed and drank her punch. When she finished, he set the cup aside. "Would you care to sit in one of the adjoining drawing rooms?"

She hesitated.

He leaned his head down. "It's noisy and crowded here."

She had misgivings, but since others would be about, she saw no harm. "Perhaps for a short while." He offered his arm again, and she clasped his sleeve. Amy realized that her acquiescence had nothing to do with polite refusals and everything to do with his abundant charm.

He meant to seduce her for her fifty thousand pounds.

Long before he'd arrived at the ball, he'd planned every move, every word. He'd mastered the art of seduction, but he'd known his typical methods would meet with resistance. She wasn't the sort of woman who would fall prey to praise of her beauty. Miss Hardwick was not beautiful. The word that fit her was *unique*.

He'd not even struggled to figure out how he might draw her into his web. The night she'd worn that dramatic gown with the green ribbons and silk roses, he'd instinctively known that she intended to become the most fashionable lady in the ton. Tonight, he'd seen her green eyes light up like the ballroom chandeliers when he'd told her that he liked her shimmery gown. He'd known then that he'd hooked her.

Every moment was calculated to chip away at her

defenses. He'd honed his skills for years and had always gotten exactly what he wanted from women. But he'd never tried to lure an innocent before, and, more than once, he'd felt a twinge of guilt. He'd hardened his stony heart, because his only other alternative meant confessing to his brother, and he'd spend years working off the debt that his brother would have to pay. And Will knew if that happened, he would never leave the shores of England again.

During the dance, he'd drawn her in with his eyes. He let his own desire kindle, so that it would reflect on his face. Will had sensed her capitulation, and then the orchestra had played the last notes.

He'd known he couldn't let her go, so he'd reverted to charming her. Now he had her in the palm of his hand. He led her through one crowded drawing room and into another that was equally full of people.

Others watched them with raised brows, but he kept walking. He escorted her into another smaller room where the fire burned low. Three elderly gentlemen eyed them.

"Come, we're obviously disturbing them," he said, leading her out into a dark corridor.

"I think we had better return to the ballroom," she said.

He sighed. "We'll have to shout over the noise. I just wanted to find a place where we could talk."

"Balls aren't the best place for conversation," she said.

He walked over to a door and opened it. "Ah, a pianoforte. It's a music room. We can talk in there."

"It's dark in there," she said.

"By Jove, you're right."

He heard her sharp intake of breath.

"Mr. Darcett, if you think I am foolish enough to follow you into that room, you are sadly mistaken."

He tugged her hand. "No one will know. It's not as if we haven't been alone before."

"You purposely lured me here," she said in a shocked tone.

"I didn't know this room existed." It was the truth, but he'd figured he could find an abandoned room. Then he would use his considerable skills to melt her resistance. He'd go just far enough that she would feel guilty and ashamed. Then he would offer to marry her, because he'd dishonored her. She might refuse him, but he'd persuade her that it was the right thing to do. He didn't see any other way around it, because he didn't have weeks to court her.

She pulled her hand back. "I may have been foolish enough to fall for your false charm," she said, "but believe me, it won't happen again."

He tried to think of a way to salvage the situation and decided an apology was his only option. "Forgive me. I overstepped the bounds. I will return you to the ballroom now."

"No. Do not ever, ever come near me again," she said, her voice trembling a little. She lifted her skirts, whirled round, and hurried to the landing.

A sour sensation wrenched his chest. He watched her until she disappeared. Then he leaned back against the wall. "Fuck," he muttered.

He'd done a lot of bad things in his life. Over the years, he'd seduced many willing women and left them after his lust cooled. He'd told himself they had agreed and knew it wouldn't last. Each time, he'd walked away with nary a care in the world and forgotten them.

But he'd never sunk lower than he had tonight.

• • •

Once she'd gained the next landing, Amy made her way into the ladies' retiring room. She was grateful to find it mostly empty.

After claiming an empty chair, Amy took a deep breath to calm her nerves. She knew his reputation, and still she'd fallen for his false charm. Oh, but he was quite accomplished at enticing a woman. How many before her had fallen for his deceitful ploys? She scoffed, knowing that countless women had probably willingly allowed him indecent liberties.

Why had he chosen her? Because he thought she was an easy mark. That night in Lord Beresford's library, he'd told her he found her intriguing. She'd known he was lying. Tonight, however, she'd walked right into his trap. He'd taken advantage of her and now she felt stupid for letting him trick her.

Obviously, he was a vile deceiver and didn't care about anyone but himself. She would not blame herself. Granted, she knew his reputation, but she'd thought she was safe at a ton ball. Clearly, the proprieties meant nothing to him.

She sat there for a while, indecisive. The last thing she wanted was to encounter him again, but she had done nothing wrong. She refused to allow him to spoil another ball for her. Part of her wanted to remain in the retiring room longer to calm her nerves, but others had seen her walking with the devil. If she didn't return to the ballroom soon, someone might notice. She didn't want to stir up any suspicion.

Amy rose, shook out her skirts, and headed back to the ballroom. Once inside, she found herself surrounded by the same group of ladies who had flocked round the devil at Ashdown House.

"Oh, my gracious," Sally said. "Everyone saw you dancing and walking with the devil."

"I am so jealous," Priscilla said. "However did you manage to capture his attention?"

"Indeed," Charlotte said. "Everyone is dying to dance with him, and you looked as if you wanted to kick him."

Amy affected a bored expression. She would never admit he'd tricked her. "He insisted on dancing and wouldn't leave my side afterward." She sighed. "I finally managed to escape him."

Sally, Beatrice, Catherine, Charlotte, and Priscilla all gaped at her.

Mr. Osgood, Mr. Benton, and Mr. Portfrey joined them, precluding any further discussion of the devil. Everyone spoke at once, with the exception of Amy. She found it impossible to follow several conversations at the same time and took the opportunity to survey the ballroom. Fortunately, the devil was nowhere in sight, but he could be lurking somewhere in the crowd. If she encountered him again, she would give him the cut direct.

Mr. Osgood turned to her. "Miss Hardwick, would you do me the great honor of taking a stroll out to the landing, where it is cooler?"

"Yes, thank you." He was everything a gentleman should be—kind, respectable, and gracious. Any lady would be lucky to have him as a suitor, but she cared for him only as a friend.

He led her through the crowd and out onto the landing. There were a few couples standing near the stairwell, but he took her over to a wall niche with a statue of Diana.

"Thank you," she said. "My ears were ringing in the ballroom."

"Miss Hardwick, may I speak plainly?" he said in a solemn undertone.

"Of course."

"I saw you dancing with Darcett," he said.

She regarded him warily.

"Frankly, I grew concerned when he led you into the adjoining drawing room," Mr. Osgood said. "Are you aware that his reputation is unsavory?"

She found his concern a little endearing. "I would have to be deaf and blind not to know."

"Yet you allowed him to escort you."

"While I appreciate your concern, we were in full view of others."

"Please forgive me. I should not have said anything."

"I take no offense, Mr. Osgood. I think it is very kind of you to warn me, but I assure you that I'm in no danger of falling for his wiles." Not anymore, she silently amended.

He offered his arm. "Shall we return to the ballroom? You undoubtedly wish to dance."

"Are you asking me?" she said, smiling.

"May I have the honor?" he asked.

"Yes," she said.

They turned, and Amy hissed in a breath as she met the devil's dark eyes. He stood with his back to the railing. His lips curved a little in the slightest of smiles. Then he inclined his head. As Mr. Osgood led her away, she could practically feel the devil staring at her.

"You seem discomposed," Mr. Osgood said.

"Not anymore." She vowed never to let the devil disturb her again.

• • •

Will stood with his back against the railing. No doubt she thought Osgood safe company.

She was no fool. He'd pushed too far and too fast tonight, and she'd rebuked him soundly. Ordinarily, he played the seduction game with more finesse, but desperation had led him to miscalculate, the same way he'd done at the gaming table. Now he'd lost again. After tonight, she would never speak to him. He didn't blame her.

Bell emerged from the ballroom and joined him. "You seemed to have her in the palm of your hand. Then I saw her with Osgood."

Will turned and looked down at the checkered marble floor below. "Leave it alone."

"Something went wrong," Bell said.

"I'm done with this scheme." He felt a little ill just thinking what he'd planned to do to her.

"What will you do?"

"Go to my brother when he returns," he said.

"There are other wallflowers."

"I can't," he said.

Bell glanced at him. "Why?"

"It seems I have a conscience after all."

Chapter Four

Georgette came to Amy's room early the next morning and flopped on the bed.

Amy rubbed her eyes. "It's very early, and we did not get home until very late last evening—or, rather, morning."

"I'm sorry, but I had to talk to you. You know my mother will sit and listen to us in the drawing room after breakfast. So I must speak to you now."

Amy sat up. "What is it?"

"You will not believe what happened at the ball last night," Georgette said.

Amy thought about her horrid encounter with Mr. Darcett, but she said nothing because Georgette was clearly agitated and needed her. "Tell me."

"My mother embarrassed me last night. I overheard her telling Mrs. Jenkins that she expects Beau and me to be engaged shortly." Georgette jerked up to a sitting position. "How could she do that to me?"

"Oh, dear."

"She means to have her way. Yesterday, she told me to be sure to make myself agreeable to Beau. I asked her what she meant, and she chided me for being impertinent."

"You were having a wonderful evening with Beaufort last night," Amy said.

"Something else happened." Georgette's face crumpled. Amy found a handkerchief on the bedside table.

Georgette dried her tears. "Beau asked me to walk with him in the ballroom, so of course I said yes. Then we saw his mother and mine sitting together. They beckoned us. I suspected trouble, and I was right. They made a big to-do about what a handsome couple Beau and I make. Then his mother said there would surely be wedding bells before the end of the Season. I could feel my face burning the entire time."

"I'm sorry. It does sound rather embarrassing." The story made Amy appreciate her mother all the more. She'd often thought Georgette's life was so much easier than her own, but now she knew that her friend had her share of problems.

"It got worse," Georgette said. "Beau actually cupped his ear and said he thought he heard bells."

"I think he is in love with you," Amy said. "I know you care about him."

"Don't you see? There are all pushing me to marry him. It is as if it is a foregone conclusion, and I'm simply supposed to agree, because everyone has expectations." Georgette hugged her knees. "I feel as if they are all taking away my choice."

"Georgette, if you love him, do not let others come between you and Beau."

"Amy, he is pushing me as well. He assumes that we

will marry. Imagine how you would feel if your parents were prodding you to marry Mr. Crawford. And add to that his assumption that you will marry."

"He has not directly mentioned marriage, but he has hinted," Amy said. "And I really didn't appreciate it when he asked my father's permission to correspond with me, when I never gave him leave to make the request."

"So you do understand," Georgette said. "We should have the right to decide for ourselves."

Amy sighed. "There is one big difference. Mr. Crawford does not love me, and I'm fairly certain that Beau loves you."

"What happens after marriage?" Georgette said. "Will Beau continue to make assumptions? Will he make decisions for me, without asking? Will I ever have the right to make my own choices?"

"Perhaps you should talk to Beau about your concerns."

"Yes, you're right." Georgette frowned. "Amy, you were gone from the ballroom for a long time. I saw you walking with Mr. Darcett."

She related the story to her friend. "I knew he was an unprincipled rake, but I thought I was safe with so many others about."

"Why would he do such a thing?" Georgette said. "It is one thing for him to parade around with some of those immodest widows, but he knows such conduct is forbidden with maidens."

"I think he believed me to be easy prey." She fisted her hands. How dare he treat her so disrespectfully? The horrid man ought to be ashamed, but he was probably amused by what he'd done to her.

"It makes no sense," Georgette said. "He's a rake. Why

would he risk getting caught alone with a respectable lady?"

Amy swallowed. "Because it is not the first time he's caught me alone."

"What?" Georgette said loudly.

"Lower your voice," Amy said. "I don't want anyone else to know. It could hurt my reputation." Then she told Georgette the story about how he'd found her in the library.

"We will give him the cut direct," Georgette said. "He comes from a very good family, but he is not respectable."

"I hope I never see him again," Amy said. But Julianne was his sister-in-law, and Amy suspected she might encounter him when she called on her friend at Ashdown House. If so, she would look through him as if he didn't even exist.

Later that morning, Amy and Georgette took their places at the round table in Lady Boswood's drawing room. They both brought their needlework, as Georgette's mother insisted they apply themselves to it daily.

"Miss Hardwick," Lady Boswood said, "I saw you dancing with Mr. Darcett last evening."

Amy exchanged a knowing look with Georgette.

Lady Boswood sniffed. "He is a handsome young man, but his reputation is not the best. I am aware that it is gratifying to receive attention from young men, but I would caution you where he is concerned. Promise me, you will avoid him."

"You can be safely assured I will have nothing to do with him again," Amy said. Her temper flared each time she thought of the way he'd gulled her.

"Georgette, I was gratified to see you dancing and walking with Lord Beaufort," Lady Boswood continued. "Everyone says you make a most becoming couple. And I expect one day you will be a countess."

Georgette bent her head to her needlework. Her fingers were trembling a little. Amy felt bad for her friend. She wondered when her friend would ever have the courage to stand up to her mother, but Amy acknowledged that it would probably do more harm than good.

A footman arrived with a tray of mail. Although Amy was eager to know if her mother had written, she concentrated on her needlework. A lady did not openly show her impatience.

Several minutes later, Lady Boswood handed a letter to her daughter. "It is from your aunt Marianne. And here is a letter for you, Miss Hardwick."

At long last, Amy thought. She was sure it was from her parents, but when she looked at the address, her heart sank like a stone to her stomach. This was not her mother's handwriting.

Lady Boswood's face flushed. She unfurled her fan and applied it. "It is exceedingly warm in here. I don't know why the servants insist upon building up the fire."

Georgette regarded her mother with wide eyes, with good reason, for the room was comfortable.

Lady Boswood rose. "I must attend to the menu in my sitting room. Georgette, I trust that you and Miss Hardwick will occupy yourselves by answering your letters. You know my opinion on idling."

After Lady Boswood left, Georgette shook her head. "This is not the first time that my mother has complained about the heat. It certainly makes her very ill-tempered."

Amy shrugged. Lady Boswood seemed ill-tempered much of the time. However, her face had flushed bright red. "Perhaps she isn't feeling well."

"She has been very irritable," Georgette said. "Well, I'm glad she is gone, because I have no intention of reading Aunt Marianne's letter. I'll write to her later."

Amy broke the seal on her letter. "But how will you respond to her when you have not read her letter?"

"She always complains about her various ailments, and then she asks when I intend to marry. So I write the same letter to her each time." She regarded Amy with an impish grin and started speaking in a sugary voice. "Dear Aunt Marianne, I hope this letter finds you in better health. Mama and Papa are well. My brothers and their wives are well. I am still unmarried, but Mama has high hopes for me. Yours truly." Georgette's twin dimples showed as she grinned.

"You are incorrigible," Amy said, laughing. Then she unfolded her letter.

"Is it from your parents?" Georgette asked.

Amy sighed. "No, it is from Mr. Crawford."

Georgette hurried over to Amy and sat beside her. "What does it say?"

"I just now broke the seal."

Georgette regarded her with a sly expression. "Read it aloud."

"You had better read your aunt's letter and respond kindly. What if she intends to leave you her fortune?"

"Ha. She's more likely to leave me her stinky old hound, Herbert."

Amy laughed. "Is your aunt really that horrid?"

"No, she's worse," Georgette said. "Oh, well, I'll be dutiful and read the old curmudgeon's letter."

Georgette grumbled under her breath while unfolding it. Amy smiled, but it faded when she started reading Mr. Crawford's correspondence.

Dear Miss Hardwick,

I hope this letter finds you in good spirits. For myself, I fail to understand the attraction of London with its reportedly dirty environs and criminal element. To be frank, I am at a loss as to why you would choose London over your own wholesome home in the country.

You know my objective, though I have not yet tendered that which I still hope you wish to hear. I was saddened by our parting. In all honesty, I was shocked that you would tell me not to wait for you. It was my understanding that you went to London at the request of your friend, but now I wonder if there were other reasons. I do not wish to offend you with suspicions. Perhaps you might write and reassure me that nothing has changed in your regard for me.

Yours sincerely,
F. A. Crawford

"Amy?" Georgette said. "You look troubled."

She looked at her friend. "He still has not given up on waiting for me, even though I made it clear that I would not make a commitment. Apparently I wounded him. I did not wish to do so, and now I feel awful."

Georgette set her letter aside. "First of all, if he felt so strongly, he ought to have proposed, but he did not. I wager he had ample opportunity to do so. Second, he went behind your back to ask your father's permission to write. In doing so, he ensured he could plead his case. But it was wrong of him. He is trying to manipulate you. Do not feel sorry for him," Georgette said. "If his spirits are dampened, it is his own fault."

Amy folded his letter. "I believe he means well, but he is not without fault, and neither am I."

Georgette shook her head. "Why do you say that? You have done nothing wrong."

"Yes, I have." She smoothed the folds of the letter. "I said that I came to London to be with you, and that was true. But I neglected to tell the whole truth. I came here for myself, because I wanted one season where I wasn't sitting on the wallflower row, and I wanted to find love. And I did not tell Mr. Crawford that last part. Perhaps I should have, but I think that would be harsh. My decision to tell him not to wait was the kindest thing to do."

"I suppose you will answer his letter."

"Yes, I must. I dread the task, but I think it is important that I tell him that we are not well suited after all. And I will wish him well." She took a deep breath and released it slowly. "And then I must somehow explain my decision to my parents. I believe they are under the misapprehension that I wish to marry Mr. Crawford."

"Will they be disappointed?" Georgette asked.

"I doubt I'll ever know. They would be unlikely to tell me." Amy wondered how she would ever tell them that she had considered marrying Mr. Crawford to please them. Then it occurred to her that they might be better off not knowing. Mama and Papa would blame themselves and feel that they had failed her. But Amy knew that her confusion and reticence in this matter had led her to make mistakes.

Amy rose from the chair. "I will write to Mr. Crawford now. I fear if I do not do so that I will put it off, because it is an unpleasant task." She took the letter with her upstairs to the little desk, drew out a sheet of paper, and opened the inkwell. At first, she froze as she sought the best way to tell him that there was no future for the two of them. Then she realized that simplicity and brevity would be the best course.

Dear Mr. Crawford,

I received your letter today and am sorry to have been the cause of any pain. It was unintentional. In your letter, you expressed shock that I asked you not to wait for me. In all good conscience, I could not. I determined that our interests and temperaments are very different. Yet my admiration for you is such that I have been conflicted for some time. After much reflection, however, I have concluded that we are not well suited.

I hold the highest esteem for you and admire you very much for your devotion to the church. I know you put great store by being an example as well as a spiritual leader to the parishioners.

I hope that we will remain friends, and I sincerely wish you all happiness.

> *Yours truly,*
> *Amy Hardwick*

Amy sanded and sealed the letter. She didn't know if she would ever meet a man who would love her, but she had no doubt that her decision about Mr. Crawford was in both of their best interests.

• • •

Georgette was embroidering a handkerchief for her father in the drawing room while Amy worked on her sketches. The afternoon light was good, and Georgette felt content. She liked to embroider because it made her feel peaceful.

The bell rang. Perhaps it was one of her father's political fellows. They sometimes met with her papa in his library.

Footsteps sounded outside the drawing room. Her mother's voice sounded cheerful, and Georgette knew before she ever heard his voice that Beau had called. She had just seen him last evening. Sometimes he was too persistent, but she did not know his reason for calling and shouldn't make assumptions. When her mother entered, she regarded Georgette with her typical plastered smile. "Georgette, look who could not wait to see you again?"

Georgette and Amy rose and bobbed curtsies.

"How are you today?" Georgette asked.

He handed her a bouquet of wildflowers. "Thank you," she said.

She would have appreciated them more if he'd thought to bring flowers for Amy as well, but she told herself he was a man and wouldn't think of these things.

"Please be seated," Lady Boswood said. "It's always a delight to see you. Is it not, Georgette?"

Her mother's stiff conversation never failed to grate on Georgette's nerves, but she could not show it. "This is a surprise," Georgette said. "I had not expected to see you so soon after last night's ball." *I should be flattered by his persistence, but I'm starting to feel smothered.*

Beau smiled. "I hoped you would take a drive in the park with me."

She looked sideways at Amy and started to suggest they stay indoors, but her mother interrupted as usual.

"But of course Georgette wishes to drive with you," Lady Boswood said. "Run along and put on your spencer for warmth, dear. And do take your parasol."

She had no choice, but her mother always made the decisions. Then it occurred to her that she could decide. After all, her mother would not lecture her in front of Beau. "Perhaps we could stay indoors. We can converse while Amy and I work."

Amy looked up from her drawing. "Oh, please don't miss your outing because of me. I'm thoroughly engrossed in my sketches and would not be good company anyway."

Lady Boswood clasped her hands. "There, all is settled."

Georgette remained silent on the drive to Rotten Row, but the clacking of horse hooves and shouts from street vendors prevented casual conversation. Her temples ached a little as they often did when she had to bite her tongue over some inane or acerbic comment her mother had made.

Beau smiled at her and then returned his attention to the road. Georgette knew she ought to be happy. Any other belle would gladly snatch Beau away, given the opportunity. He had a ready smile and light blue eyes, so different from her darker blue ones. His top hat covered his blond hair of varying straw and sunshine yellow hues. There was no doubt that he was handsome, witty, and nice. But his determined courtship sometimes overwhelmed her, and of course her mother encouraged him to call as often as possible. Perhaps it was time to tell him that courtship shouldn't be a race, but that might wound him. She truly liked and cared for him. It would be better to say nothing. She was just a little out of sorts because her mother had acted so obsequiously earlier.

When they reached Rotten Row, the promenade was in full swing. Georgette knew that Beau was proud of his smart curricle and loved to rattle on about it. She would listen with a little smile until he realized he'd forgotten himself and bored her silly. Of course, she loved the sound of his voice, and he'd answered in a gruff tone that her liked her voice, too.

Her spirits lifted, because the sun was shining, and now that she was away from her mother, she didn't feel as if others were pushing and pulling her. Georgette twirled her parasol and waved at Sally and her brother. As Beau drove along, they both waved at many acquaintances.

Beau leaned toward her. "Look, there are my friends," he said, raising his voice. "I'll pull off the road for just a moment."

"Very well."

After he pulled over and saw to the horses, Beau helped her climb down. She'd been a bit afraid of climbing down the big yellow wheels when he'd first taken her for a ride, but now she felt comfortable as long as he assisted her.

A breeze stirred the leaves overhead. The tall oaks provided shade. The scent of the scythed grass tickled Georgette's nose.

Beau escorted her to greet Charles Osgood and Lord Caruthers. "Well met," Beau said.

Georgette bobbed a curtsy. "I hope you gentlemen are enjoying the lovely day and the promenade."

"Well, we were hoping to attract the attention of some pretty ladies," Osgood said.

"I have the prettiest lady in England," Beau said. "And she's all mine."

She thought it a little funny that he'd spoken of her as if she were a possession like his curricle, but it didn't signify.

Someone farther down the path called out and waved. It was Beau's mother, Lady Wallingham, and her daughter Eugenia.

Georgette pasted on her society smile, but Lady Wallingham was every bit as ridiculous as Georgette's own mother. Lady Wallingham had one advantage over Lady Boswood in that she didn't appear to be ill-tempered.

Lady Wallingham prodded poor Eugenia to walk faster. Georgette certainly understood how Eugenia felt. Why did some mothers not understand the fine art of subtlety?

A somewhat large woman, Lady Wallingham clutched her chest and huffed upon catching up to them. "Oh, my, I didn't want to miss you." She prodded Eugenia again. "Do make your curtsy."

Georgette decided to rescue Eugenia. "Have you met Lord Caruthers and Mr. Osgood?"

Before Eugenia could answer, Lady Wallingham interrupted. "Oh my, yes, all of my son's friends call frequently. But of course, I'm looking forward to having you come along with us to visit Beau's grandmother this Saturday."

"Goodness, it must have slipped my mind," Georgette said, not quite hiding her sharp tone. "Or perhaps I missed the invitation?" She imagined Lady Wallingham and Beau clasping her arms in a game of tug of war.

"Mother, I have not asked Georgette yet," Beau said.

Caruthers and Osgood exchanged amused looks.

"Oh, well, hurry and do so," Lady Wallingham continued. "You don't want her to make other plans." She patted Georgette's hand. "I'm sure you would consult my dear son first," Lady Wallingham said. "I know you would not wish to disappoint him."

Georgette wanted to say that Beau ought to consult her, but of course, she must keep silent to avoid causing a scene.

"You are such a lovely couple," Lady Wallingham said. "By summer, our family will no doubt have a new member."

Lady Wallingham's statement was the last straw. Georgette could no longer force herself to smile. Everyone made assumptions about her and assumed she would acquiesce. She simply could not bear it.

Caruthers bowed. "Ladies, Beaufort. Osgood and I are off now. Have a pleasant evening." The two climbed into Caruthers's curricle. With a deft tug on the reins, Caruthers drove onto the main path again and disappeared among multiple other conveyances.

Georgette turned to Beau, meaning to ask him to return her home, but his eyes widened a bit. He must know she was vexed, because she was not trying to hide it.

"Georgette, perhaps you would allow me to escort you for a walk," Beau said.

"Oh, what an excellent idea," Lady Wallingham said. "Eugenia and I will visit some of our acquaintances. Do be mindful of the horse droppings, Lady Georgette. You don't wish to ruin your slippers."

Georgette took Beau's arm. He led her away from the promenade and farther into some of the more rustic areas. When they were well away from the crowd, he stood with his back against a tree. "I'm sorry my mother blurted out the invitation like that. I told her that I would ask you, but sometimes she doesn't think before she speaks."

"Well, we both have ridiculous mothers," she said.

"They are our mothers, and regardless of their faults, they deserve our respect." He smiled. "And really all you have to do is placate them."

"No, Beau. You do not understand. If I placate them it means that I bow down and do whatever they want or expect of me. I have almost no say in my life, because everyone decides what is best for me. No one ever thinks to consult me first."

He cupped her face with his hands. "Do not worry. Our mothers are just excited that we are courting. So am I."

She turned her face away, hating that she must say the words, but if she did not stand up for herself now, everyone would continue to manipulate her into doing what they wanted.

"Georgette, what is it?"

She regarded him. "I need everyone to stop pushing me so hard."

He frowned. "What do you mean?"

She inhaled on a shaky breath. This would not be easy to say. "Everyone, including you, is trying to rush me. No one says it directly, but they are not subtle about it either. Both of our families assume we will marry. And that troubles me, Beau."

His expression grew alarmed. Then he took her by the shoulders. "Georgette, I thought we had an understanding."

"Nothing was ever spoken. No one ever asked me."

"It was understood," he said. "I called on you. We kissed last winter. And yes, you have led me to believe you wished to marry me."

"I'm not saying that I don't want to marry you," she said. "I'm saying that I need more time."

"Don't you know how I feel about you?"

"All I ask is that we slow down a bit. I feel as if we're racing ahead in this courtship."

His mouth thinned. "Every night when I go to bed, I imagine having you there with me."

Oh, dear heavens. "Beau, you should not mention that in my presence."

"Why? I know you're a respectable young lady, but I do think about being intimate with you. Those feelings aren't wrong."

"I know, but we aren't married."

He drew her into his arms. "We could be."

She averted her face and blinked back her stupid tears. "You're not listening."

He pulled her flush against his body. "It's just hard to wait."

She gasped at the hard ridge of his sex against her stomach.

"Please don't be afraid," he said.

She narrowed her eyes. "This is why you're in such a rush to marry. You want to bed me."

He laughed. "Where did you hear that expression?"

"I have three elder brothers." She pushed on his chest. "You didn't answer me."

He kissed her softly on the lips. "I will do my best to honor your request to slow down, but I don't want to wait too long."

She stepped out of his arms. Beau still did not understand. He'd just assumed that she would marry him. And that made her wonder what else he would assume without asking what she wanted. "You had better escort me home."

"You're overset again," he said. "What is wrong?"

"If you had listened, really listened, to what I said a few moments ago, you would not have to ask me that question. But you are like our mothers. You make assumptions about the decisions you believe I will make." She shook her head. "Beau, don't take me for granted. And I think it would be better if I did not go with your family to call on your grandmother. It will set expectations of our future, and I am far from being decided."

He clenched his jaw and strode away, leaving her to follow in his wake. She struggled to keep up. Eventually, he halted, turned around, and walked back to her. He halted a foot away, and the distance seemed like a mile. "Forgive me for losing my temper. I have made assumptions, but your every word and deed encouraged me."

"Beau, I think you had better take me home now." He didn't understand, and she suspected he never would. Her heart felt heavy as she realized he didn't see that he was still making assumptions.

"You're making me suffer because my mother blurted out the invitation to the call on my grandmother," he said. "I saw your smile fade away. It's not fair to blame me. I can't control my mother."

"Beau, it's not fair for you to assume that I will leap to do your bidding. That includes visits to your family, carriage rides, dances, and, most of all, weddings," she said. "If I don't stand up for myself, everyone else will continue to assume that I will acquiesce to whatever they believe is best for me."

"It's called courtship," he said.

"You are pressing me, and you don't want to admit it. Take me home, Beau."

"You just want to make things more difficult than they are," he said.

"No, I just want to have a say in my life."

Chapter Five

One week later

Amy took advantage of the morning sunshine to work on her designs. She envisioned a gown with a Vandyke collar. Along the bottom of the gown, she drew silk tulle flounces. At the end of the paper, she made a note recommending aqua silk satin for the fabric and silver lamé embroidering the flounces.

A knock sounded. Frowning, Amy rose. "Come in."

Georgette let out a disgusted sigh. "I will be so glad when this card party is over tonight. Mama is fretting over every little detail. She actually chided me for sneezing."

Amy laughed. "Oh, dear."

"The servants are scurrying about, and my father recommended I steer clear," Georgette said. "Then he shut himself up in his library. I wish I could hide in there, too."

"Your mother is just anxious for everything to turn out well," Amy said.

Georgette sighed. "It cannot have escaped your notice that she insists on perfection. I have to bite my lip to keep from telling her to stop haranguing everyone."

Amy pitied Georgette for having to endure such a temperamental mother. "You understand her and manage well in spite of her flaws."

Georgette's eyes widened. "Oh, are those new sketches?"

"Do you like this one?" Amy asked.

"Oh, yes. High collars are all the rage now."

"Here is a walking gown I drew with long sleeves," Amy said. "There are three rows of lace at the shoulder and two rows at the bottom of the skirt."

"I like that one as well. Are you planning to show them to Madame DuPont?" Georgette asked.

"Yes, when I draw a few more." Amy felt a bit uncomfortable about hiding the matter of compensation, though she had taken none yet. She felt Georgette did not need to know. In truth, the less she knew the better.

"It is so exciting to think of others wearing your creations," Georgette said.

A knock sounded at the door. Georgette went to answer, and Lizzy bobbed a curtsy. "Miss, her ladyship requests you attend her in the drawing room."

Georgette sighed.

"Should I come as well, Georgette? Perhaps I can help," Amy said.

"You have two letters, Miss Hardwick," the maid said, pulling them out of her apron pocket.

"Read your letters," Georgette said. "I'll attend my mother."

After Georgette left, Amy sat at the desk. She wrinkled her nose upon recognizing Mr. Crawford's handwriting. The other one was from her mother. She decided to read the vicar's letter first and be done with the unpleasant business.

Dear Miss Hardwick,

Six times, I have read your short missive and fail to understand why you have lost all affection for me. My spirits have been so lowered, that I finally sought your parents' counsel. I admitted to them that I fear you have transferred your tender feelings to another.

My dear, please tell me that all my worries are the product of my imagination. Until I receive such reassurance, I will be pining for your presence. At this moment, I am tempted to journey to London to see for myself that you are unaltered since last I saw you, and that you are the same sweet country girl. But let me say no more on this subject. I believe it obvious where my tender feelings reside. All that is required for my happiness is a comforting word or two from you.

Yours truly,
F. A. Crawford

She could not fathom why Mr. Crawford had trouble interpreting her letter. Amy felt that she'd been clear and concise in her explanation. She was more than a little surprised about his claim of tender feelings. Before she'd left home, he'd never said anything that indicated he felt affection for her. But apparently the moment he realized she no longer welcomed his suit, he suddenly fancied himself in love, though he'd not gone so far as to use the word.

Since she had told him she no longer believed they would suit, she decided that any further correspondence was unnecessary. If she were to write to him, he might interpret her letter as encouragement, and that would not be good for either of them. She tossed his letter on the fire and broke the seal on her mother's letter.

After unfolding the letter, Amy smiled. Papa left the correspondence to Mama as he said she had more delicacy and always managed to strike the right tone. Amy's chest tightened just a little, for she missed her parents.

Her mother's letter started out with assurances that she and Amy's father were in good health. They were surprised that she had rebuffed Mr. Crawford, but Papa had said the vicar could sometimes be a dry old stick. Her mother stated that she trusted Amy's judgment, though she was somewhat surprised that Amy had told him not to wait for her just prior to leaving for London.

The sudden timing leads me to believe there might have been a disagreement. In your letter, you were very firm that you no longer welcome him as a suitor. Are you certain, daughter? I feel compelled to ask because Mr. Crawford appears to be truly distraught and was under the impression that the two of you had an understanding.

We hope you are enjoying the London Season and look forward to your return this summer.

She was uncertain what to make of her mother's letter. In the end, she decided Mama meant to caution her to be certain for Mr. Crawford's sake. Amy had no doubts about her decision.

The letter made her long for her parents. She had never been away from them for such a protracted length of time, and she missed them very much. She wished they had come to London after all. But she would make the most of the time she spent with Georgette. Amy suspected that her friend would marry Beaufort this summer, unless something drastic occurred. This season would likely be the last time that Amy and Georgette would spend so much time together. It made Amy a little sad, because she'd had so much fun with Georgette and Julianne the last two years in London.

Her gaze strayed to the letter. Tomorrow, she would write to her mother and father. She would confirm her decision about Mr. Crawford and reassure her parents. Then she would focus on her activities since arriving in London. Amy looked longingly at her sketchbook, but she knew it would be rude not to volunteer to help with the preparations for the card party.

Amy placed the sketchbook in her trunk for safekeeping and left her guest chamber. She didn't look forward to Lady Boswood's mercurial moods, but she was accustomed to keeping her thoughts from showing on her face. The remainder of the day might be trying, but she looked forward to playing whist and conversing with friends tonight.

Will took a deep breath before entering the library. He did not look forward to informing his brother about the debt, but procrastination would only make him feel worse. Will swallowed hard, knowing that his brother would rip him to shreds for gambling what he didn't have to lose.

He would make no excuses. All he could do was

promise to pay the debt with the salary he earned as land steward. He would spend years working just to pay the debt. But he'd done this to himself and must face the consequences.

Will stepped inside. Hawk set a leather case on his desk and looked up. "Will, I just returned."

"Yes, I know, but there is something I wish to discuss with you."

"Not now," he said, sorting through the stack of letters on his desk. "I wish to bathe and see my wife."

"Right," he said. "I won't disturb you then."

"Meet me here tomorrow morning at ten sharp. We'll go over your duties then."

Will hesitated, because he didn't want his brother to find out about his debt from someone else.

"These will have to wait until tomorrow," Hawk mumbled as he sifted through letters.

"Lady Boswood is holding a card party tonight," Will said. "All the family is attending."

"I'll check with my wife, but I'd rather not attend. I'm done up. Why don't you escort our mother? She'll like that."

"Certainly," he said. "Tomorrow, then."

Hawk regarded him with a weary frown. "Is all well with you?"

He was anxious to get this over with as soon as possible, but Hawk was exhausted. "It can wait." What would another day matter?

Amy smiled as she left the card table with Lord Caruthers. They had won, but now she wished only to converse with others. Several ladies had complimented her jade gown with the standing lace along the shoulders and back. She was enjoying herself far more this season than any other and was glad that she'd come to London.

Some of the gentlemen had expressed disappointment that Lady Boswood had insisted the stakes in the games must remain low. Amy wasn't the least bit surprised. Georgette's mother adhered to a strict moral code.

Lord Caruthers took her to the refreshment table, where they saw Sally with Mr. Portfrey. After a few minutes of small talk, the gentlemen left, and Sally went upstairs to the retiring room.

Amy finished her punch and walked about the room. Her confidence had risen in the short time since coming to London. She might not be a diamond of the first water, but others admired her for her elegant gowns and even wanted to wear her designs. She'd spent too many years feeling inferior. While she was a bit troubled that she'd not tried harder before, Amy knew she could not change the past. She would focus on tonight and her future. For now, she was happier than she could ever recall being.

She'd made a circuit of half the room when she spied Cecile, Lady Eugenia, and Bernice sitting in a row of chairs with the matrons. They were her oldest friends and had sat with her year after year on the wallflower row at balls, watching the dancing but never participating. Last year, she'd not spent as much time sitting with them, because Georgette and Julianne had taken her under their wings. This year, she'd avoided the wallflower row and thus had spent no time at all with them.

Cecile caught her eye and waved. Then she spoke to Lady Eugenia, who in turn nudged Bernice. Their smiles decided Amy. She could not ignore her friends simply because they were sitting with the dowagers. When she approached, they moved to make a place for her. Amy knew a moment of hesitation, but a chair was only a chair. And she'd not spent time with her dear friends since coming to London.

"You look beautiful," Eugenia said.

Amy's face heated. "I will never be beautiful, but thank you for your kind words."

"We heard that you have become the fashion darling of the ton," Bernice said. "We're very proud of you."

"I've done nothing special, really. I just started drawing designs for my own amusement," she said. *You should despise me because I ignored you at the previous two balls.*

"You are too modest." Cecile pushed a drooping curl off her cheek. "Amy, you are the picture of elegance. Your hair and your gown are perfect. When I look at you, I think it is possible to learn to dress in the first stare of fashion."

"Thank you for the compliment." Amy noted that Cecile's bodice and puffed sleeves were too tight, making her appear plumper.

Eugenia leaned forward. "Would you give us fashion advice?"

"Surely your dressmaker is better suited to assist you," Amy said.

"I dare not trust mine again." Bernice touched the high ruff collar at her neck. "This is a perfect example. The modiste said it was very fashionable, but I have to hold my chin up. It makes my neck ache."

The collar, in the latest Gothic fashion, did not flatter Bernice's round face and short neck at all. "It is difficult to look your best when you are uncomfortable," Amy said. "I learned that lesson the hard way."

"Would you call on me next week?" Eugenia said. "Cecile and Bernice will attend. We would very much appreciate your advice."

"I'm not an expert," she said.

"Please say you'll come," Eugenia said. "We've missed you and hope you can advise us."

She'd missed them, too. "Very well. I'll share with you what I learned from friends and fashion plates."

Bernice clasped her hands. "I knew you had not forgotten us."

Amy maintained her smile, but Bernice's words struck her heart. She promised to call soon and then excused herself. As she walked away, she fanned her heated face. Bernice's words echoed in her mind again and again.

I knew you had not forgotten us.

Her chest burned with shame. She had ignored her friends, because she didn't want anyone to associate her with the wallflowers. Tonight, when they had offered her a chair, she had not wanted to take it. How could she be so selfish and inconsiderate? How would she feel if Julianne and Georgette treated her in such a shabby manner? She knew what it was to be ignored and shunned.

Something hot rushed up her throat and through her cheekbones. She mustn't humiliate herself and create a scene. As she walked through the crowd, Amy kept drawing in air in an effort to maintain her composure. She was perilously close to tears, but she didn't want to go to the retiring room where others would notice her discomposure. Once free of the doors, she brushed past the crowd on the landing and hurried down the stairs.

She'd thought of going to the library, but she saw gentlemen emerging from there. In a panic, she turned right and fled down the servants' stairwell. She stood outside the door leading to the kitchen and used her gloved hands to wipe the tears from her face, because she didn't have a handkerchief.

Amy pressed her hand to her aching chest. When she had slighted her friends, they had been nice to her. They ought to have called her a two-faced friend or ignored her, but they had welcomed and complimented her. While she'd never meant to hurt them, she'd done so all the same. She'd only thought about herself and her determination to break free of her wallflower label. Outwardly, she'd transformed into the fashion darling of the ton, but inwardly, she'd allowed something ugly to sprout, and she was ashamed.

Pots banged and laughter rang out from the kitchen. Then a voice sounded close to the kitchen door. Her heartbeat drummed in her ears. Realizing that someone might come out and find her, Amy turned left and tried the door to the wine cellar. It was open. She stepped inside, closed the door, and released a relieved breath. It was rather cool inside, but at least she was safe from prying eyes.

Footsteps clipped on the floor.

She held her breath and flattened her back against the cold wall. Her legs trembled. Oh, God, who was it? She squinted in the darkness. Should she make a mad dash for the door? Or should she wait to see if the other person would leave? She inched along the wall, and then a candle flame wavered.

The footsteps clipped closer and closer. Her heart pounded. *Please, please, please go away.*

"Who goes there?"

The voice startled her. No, it couldn't be. She must be

having a nightmare. But she knew that voice all too well. Drat it all. What was the devil doing here?

He drew closer. In the dark cellar, the single candle cast flickering shadows over his face. "Miss Hardwick, did you follow me?"

"I did not," she said, sniffing. "What are you doing here?"

"Admiring Boswood's excellent wine collection," he said. "I saw the butler accidentally leave the door open and came to investigate. But you still haven't answered my question."

"Leave me be." She sniffed again.

"Are you weeping?"

"N-no." Her face burned. Of all the people to witness her cry, it would have to be him. The devil. The man who had tried to trick her into going in a dark room alone.

She heard the whisper of cloth, and then he handed her a handkerchief. "Dry your eyes."

Amy blotted her face and handed it back to him.

"I'll find another candle; those stairs are dark. Don't move," he said.

The minute he stepped away, she turned round to escape, but she bumped her hip into a stack of crates and hissed in her breath. He came to her side in a few long strides. "You're injured."

"It's only a bruise," she said. In truth, it hurt. She knew her hip would be purple and tender for some time. Lizzy would see it when she helped her undress tonight.

"There's a candle branch, but you'll arouse suspicion if you carry that. Stay still until I can locate a second candle," he said. "You don't want to fall and hurt yourself. You'll have difficulty trying to explain how it happened."

Of course it was the sensible thing to do. She worried

her hands, wishing he would hurry with that candle. His features were indistinct in the darkness, but she could make out his movements as he walked about. She had no idea how much time passed, but she grew increasingly anxious.

"Found it," he said.

Thank goodness. She meant to leave as soon as he lit the candle.

He used the flame from the first candle to light the second one.

As he moved around, she saw bottles nestled in diamond-shaped cabinets. There was a long table just beneath. There were more bottles than she'd ever glimpsed in all her life. Lord Boswood's collection must add up to a tidy fortune.

Mr. Darcett walked toward her. "I'll escort you to the door. You go upstairs first. I'll wait for a few minutes before coming upstairs."

She nodded.

When he offered his escort, she took it. The faint scent of sandalwood soap clung to him. Her mouth dried as they neared the door. All she wanted was to escape unobserved. Hopefully, the redness had left her nose and cheeks by now. All that mattered was leaving quickly and undetected. As they neared the door, footsteps clipped on the other side.

Her heart stampeded. She held her breath, terrified they would be discovered.

Mr. Darcett beckoned her and turned round. He led her farther back into the cellar, where they hid behind a stack of crates and blew out the candles. Her nerves jangled. Mr. Darcett was so close, she could hear his breathing. *Please, please, please don't let anyone discover us.*

A key scraped inside the lock and turned over.

Amy covered her mouth.

The footsteps retreated.

"Bloody hell," the devil muttered. "We're locked in."

"I wish we could find a private place," Beau said.

Georgette sat on the window seat with him and adopted a demure expression. "My mother would notice if we left."

"You know my intentions," he said. "If you would let me, I would propose tomorrow."

"Not yet. I don't want Amy to be uncomfortable," Georgette said. "She might feel that she must leave."

"I'm frustrated," he said.

She knew what he meant. At the park, she'd felt the long, hard ridge of his sex against her stomach, but she needed more than his desire.

"Do you know how much I want you?" he whispered.

Georgette lowered her eyes. "I know, but there has to be more. I have to make this decision. If I don't insist upon it, you and our mothers will continue to assume you know what is best for me and make plans, without even consulting me."

"You know what I feel for you," he whispered. "Once we're married, our families won't interfere."

She gave him a dubious look.

"If you do not mean to let me propose this season, then be honest," he said. "I cannot go on without some reassurance. We can be engaged while Miss Hardwick resides with you. At least then, we'll be allowed some privacy."

"Please, just give me a few more weeks. Amy needs me, too."

"I think she's doing very well this season," Beau said. "I'll agree to wait for three weeks."

"No, Beau, that's too—"

"Three weeks," he said. "No more."

"You're making demands," she said.

"There must be a time frame. I know you'll put it off if I don't insist upon it."

"That is quite enough." When she rose, he stood and caught her arm.

"No, Georgette. I'm tired of the diversions and excuses."

"Then you are free to court someone else," she said.

His jaw tightened. "Very well. I wish you all the best."

Panic beat in her chest. "No, I didn't mean it. I just feel rushed."

"Make up your mind. I can't live with your indecision forever." He looked out at the card tables. "Smile. Your mother is coming this way."

She lifted the corners of her lips to hide her turmoil. He was pushing her to make a decision, when marriage lasted a lifetime. She was supposed to be ready to take this step, but she didn't feel ready at all. She didn't want everyone telling her when to be ready; she wanted to feel ready.

Her mother arrived. "Lord Beaufort, do you mind if I have a private word with my daughter?"

"Not at all." He bowed and strode away.

Georgette feared her mother had noticed them quarreling and held her breath.

"Have you seen Miss Hardwick?" her mother asked. "Lady Wallingham reported seeing her leave the card room in a distressed manner a half hour ago."

"Perhaps she is in the retiring room now," Georgette said. "I'll have a look."

A few minutes later, Georgette walked into the retiring room, where she found Eugenia. "Have you seen Amy?"

"The last time I saw her she was leaving the card room, but that was some time ago," Eugenia said.

"Thank you. Perhaps she's not feeling well and decided to rest," Georgette said. Afterward, she checked Amy's room, but it was empty, and Lizzy had not seen her. Georgette thought it odd that Amy had disappeared, but perhaps she had already returned to the card party.

After entering the drawing room, Georgette walked about but did not see Amy. She stopped to speak to the Dowager Countess of Hawkfield and her daughters. "I missed seeing Julianne. I hope she is well."

"Oh, yes," Patience said. "Hawk just returned home today, and they wanted to spend a quiet evening together."

"Provided little Emma cooperates," the dowager countess said. "By the way, have you by any chance seen my son William?"

"No, I have not," Georgette said. She thought it a coincidence that Mr. Darcett and Amy were both missing, but she couldn't forget what Amy had told her about her last encounter with him.

"More than half an hour has passed since he left the room," Hope said.

"Perhaps he had another engagement."

The dowager countess fanned her face. "He escorted us this evening and would not leave us."

"I'm sure he'll return soon." She curtsied and walked round the ballroom until she reached Beau, who was speaking to Mr. Osgood and Mr. Portfrey. "Beau, may I have a word with you?"

He regarded her warily as he took her aside. "What is it?"

She bit her lip and blamed herself for making him unhappy. "Have you seen Mr. Darcett?"

"Briefly when I arrived. Why do you ask?"

"The Dowager Countess of Hawkfield asked me if I'd seen him, so I thought perhaps you knew if he had left."

Beau shrugged.

"Have you by any chance seen Amy?" she asked.

"No, not for some time," he said. "We have two missing guests?"

"I'm sure it is a coincidence," Georgette said.

"Probably," he said in a gruff tone.

She felt awful, because she really did have tender feelings for him. "Beau, I'm sorry. Please be patient with me."

Beau looked grim as he met her gaze. "You complain that everyone makes decisions for you, but you have made a decision."

She knit her brows. "I don't understand."

"You decided that I could not propose and that we must wait to marry," he said. "And I have no say at all."

"I think we had better bang on the door," Amy said.

He'd lit the candle branch, set it on the floor, and removed his gloves. Then he bent and looked at the keyhole. "Give me one of your hair pins."

"Do you actually know how to pick a lock?" She would not put anything past him.

"No, but considering the circumstances, I thought I'd try. Please lend me a hair pin."

She removed her long gloves and held them in one hand. When she pulled out a pin, a lock fell over her breast.

He eyed her hair. "It's long."

She held out the pin. When he took it, his fingers

brushed her skin. She drew in a sharp breath at the tingling sensation.

The candlelight cast shadows over his face. He stood still as a statue, but his breathing sounded a bit faster.

His silence disturbed her. "The lock," she said.

"Right." There was a rough timbre to his voice. The moment stretched out. Then he turned away and bent to examine the keyhole again.

Relieved, she inhaled and exhaled slowly. She tried to convince herself that it was only a momentary, accidental touch, but she'd never felt anything like it before. Then again, there was no one quite like the devil.

He pushed the pin inside the keyhole and worked on the lock. As he poked and prodded, she grew increasingly anxious. "Try not to bend the pin."

A huff escaped him. "I'll help you put your hair to rights after I unlock the door."

She scoffed. "You? A lady's maid?"

"It's not as if you have another choice."

She tapped her toe. "Let me know when you tire of your labors. Then I'll bang on the door."

"Only the butler has the key," he said. "He is probably at his station in the foyer."

"Yes, but surely a servant will come round if we pound on the door repeatedly. We can ask him to alert the butler."

"*If* they hear us," he said. "The lock is our best hope."

"Really, that pin will not release the lock."

"Your faith in me is overwhelming." After a few minutes, he made a frustrated sound, stood, and took off his coat. Then he laid it on the floor, kneeled, and poked the pin inside the lock again.

She leaned against the wall and watched him. At one

point he rolled up his sleeves and looked back at her. "Would you mind holding the candle branch for me?"

"Not at all." After she approached, he handed it to her. "Hold the light close, so I can see."

The candlelight illuminated a dusting of black hair on his forearms and the bulge of muscle in his upper arms. "You are very fit for a rake." The moment the words popped out, she wished she'd kept silent.

"I fence, box, and ride," he said. "I grew accustomed to daily physical activity while traveling." He pulled the pin out. "It's mangled. Give me another."

"My hair will be in ruins, and you'll never get that door open with a pin." Did he not understand that others would take one look at her disheveled hair and conclude the worst?

"Let me try," he said. "We'll fix your hair afterward."

"If I knock on the door, it may alert someone."

"You can try," he said. He wasn't sure they should be found alone. Someone, probably one of his female relatives, might get the idea to make them marry.

Miss Hardwick set the candle branch on the floor and banged on the door.

Will retrieved his coat. "Let's look on the bright side," he said. "Chances are they'll run out of wine or sherry and send for the butler to open the door."

She knocked again.

"You'll bruise your knuckles," he said, reclaiming the candle branch. "We might as well enjoy a bottle of one of Boswood's finest wines while we wait."

"Getting foxed will certainly help."

"There's a world of difference between a glass or two of wine and getting foxed." He handed her the hair pin.

"You can fume and fuss all you want," he said. "I'm planning to take advantage of the situation." He set the candle branch on the table and searched until he found a corkscrew. "Excellent. Now what should I have? Madeira or port?"

She followed him. "Madeira."

He lifted his brows in a comical manner. "You plan to unbend?"

"One glass won't hurt."

"Suit yourself. I'll drink the rest."

"Notice I expressed no surprise whatsoever," she said.

He selected a bottle, inserted the corkscrew, and pulled it out with a pop. He looked round. "No glasses. We'll just have to drink out of the bottle."

"That's disgusting," she said.

He lifted it to his lips. "Ah," he said. "Excellent vintage. My compliments to Boswood."

She took the bottle and sipped out of it. "I can't believe I did that."

He laughed. "I'll keep your disgusting secret."

"Ha-ha." She drank again. "Is that a chair by those barrels?"

He walked past the barrels and lifted the chair. When he returned with it, he sat and patted his thigh. "We'll share."

Her jaw dropped. "You actually think I will sit on your lap?"

"We've only the one chair," he said.

"If you were a gentleman, you would offer me the chair, not your lap."

"But I'm the devil. Be a sweetheart and bring the bottle."

She marched over to him and held the bottle over his head. "I swear I'll drench you if you don't get up."

He stood and made a leg. "Your chair, Mademoiselle."

When she sat, he walked past the barrels again and returned with another chair.

"You lied."

A wicked chuckle escaped him. "You dashed my fondest hopes."

She snorted and sipped from the bottle.

He rummaged in his waistcoat pocket for his watch and walked over to the table to consult the time by the candlelight. "It's midnight. I'll leave the watch here. Remind me to retrieve it when we're rescued."

"I don't know how long the party will last," she said.

He knew it might last another two or three hours, but he said nothing.

When he returned to the chair, she took another sip of wine and handed him the bottle.

He took a drink. "Why were you crying earlier?"

She said nothing.

"Did someone wound you?"

"Quite the opposite."

"You were crying because someone was nice to you?" He sounded incredulous.

"No. I wounded my friends."

"I find that difficult to believe. Julianne said you're very kind."

She released a long sigh. "I mistreated them."

"What happened?" he said, his voice rumbling. "Truly, it can't be that bad."

Oh, yes it is," she said, her voice quavering.

He took a drink. "Since I'm the expert on badness, maybe I should be the judge."

She huffed, unable to believe she was actually speaking

to him about it. No doubt the wine had loosened her tongue.

"If you tell me, I might be able to help. It's hard for you to be impartial."

She looked at her lap, ashamed of what she'd done. "I ignored friends that I've known since my come-out. I didn't want anyone to associate me with the wallflowers again." Her eyes welled with tears. "I'm ashamed."

He handed her a handkerchief. "It's understandable," he said. "We are judged by the company we keep, especially in the ton."

"I should have risen above it," she said. "The worst part is that they welcomed me despite the horrible way I treated them."

"It's not irreparable. Since they still consider you a friend, you have the opportunity to right the wrong. Introduce them to your other friends."

"They're acquainted with them, but I need to make the effort to bring them together and ease the way." She looked at him. His face was in shadows, and she couldn't see his expression. "You are the last person I would expect to give good advice. Thank you."

He cleared his throat. "I'm sorry for what happened the last time we met." Of course, she didn't know he'd meant to compromise her to gain her fortune. He still felt like a rat for his dishonorable plans. Tonight, it seemed worse, because she'd let down her guard and exposed her vulnerability.

"I thought about forgiving you for my own sake," she said. "Holding grudges is poisonous. Now I think I will forgive you because there is kindness in you."

He took another drink. "Make no mistake. I have very little to recommend me."

"You have a wonderful, large family," she said. "I envy you. I always wanted brothers and sisters."

"You must have cousins, aunts, and uncles."

"My cousins are much older than me." She sighed. "I was something of a surprise to my parents. I came along late in their marriage. They called me their little miracle."

He sipped the wine and handed her the bottle. "Why didn't your parents come to London?"

"They don't care for the city, the way I do. So I told them not to bother. Then Georgette asked me to join her for the Season, and I accepted." She took a sip.

"Where is your home?" he asked.

"Malmesbury, in the county of Wiltshire."

"Ah, the Cotswolds." He envisioned an aging couple sleeping soundly in their nightcaps, unaware that their *little miracle* was presently trapped alone with a notorious rakehell. Bloody hell.

He finished the bottle and took it to the table. "Would you like more wine? I could open another bottle."

"Why not? I'm feeling a little giddy."

"Miss Hardwick, are you foxed?"

She laughed. "I should not laugh. We're stuck here."

"Oh, we'll be discovered sooner or later." He thought she'd had more than enough wine tonight. The subject of wine reminded him that he needed to bring up a sensitive subject. "This is rather indelicate, but we drank a lot of wine. I saw a dry chamber pot in the adjoining workroom."

"Oh, I'll wait," she said, her voice squeaking.

He sighed. "It might be a while before we're discovered. Please, go first."

She took the candle branch and hurried past him with her head bowed. He would explore the workroom after she returned. He hoped to find something for them to sleep on, though he couldn't imagine locating anything that would cushion the hard floor.

When she returned, he noticed she was shivering and draped his coat over her shoulders. "Better?" he asked.

"Yes."

He went to relieve himself. Then he investigated the straw in the open wine crates, but there wasn't enough for a makeshift bed. The straw would have proved dashed uncomfortable, but now he wondered how they would manage to sleep at all.

Will returned with the candle branch and consulted his watch. He winced. It was three o'clock in the morning. He would try one last effort to keep them from having to spend the night in this cold cellar. He turned to her. "I think we should try to call out for help."

"Yes, I agree." She followed him to the door. "You would think Lady Boswood would have missed us."

They all had probably noticed them missing, and he wasn't sure what the consequences would be. Lady Boswood had undoubtedly checked with the butler and upstairs maids about their disappearance, but no one would think to inquire with the cook or scullery maids.

When they reached the door, he squatted down. "Help, we're locked in!"

He tried again. "Help!"

Will called out several more times. There was no response. They'd missed their opportunity for escape when the butler had come to the door earlier. Of course, they had wanted to avoid discovery and had not counted on the butler locking them inside. With a weary sigh, he rose and dusted off his knees.

"You're giving up?" she said.

He looked at her. "I'm sorry, but no one is about."

She lifted her skirts, ran to the door, and banged her fists on it again. When he tried to pull her away, she fought him. "Release me!"

"If anyone is around, your caterwauling will bring them running."

"I hope so, you brute."

He took her hand and dragged her along with him. "Now, now, you'll make me blush with all your compliments to my person."

"I despise you even more."

"That's unfortunate. I was rather hoping I could turn you up sweet."

"You—you—"

He halted. "Hush. Like it or not, we're stuck here. There is insufficient straw to make a rudimentary bed, we have no fire, and the temperature is dropping. We're both exhausted, and the chill will only get worse as the night progresses. I propose we share our body heat."

"What?" She looked incensed.

He cupped her cheek. "Your nose is red and your cheek is cold, and to be perfectly honest, I'm more than a little chilled in my shirtsleeves." He sighed. "If you will allow it, I'll sit up, and you can lie on me for warmth. Then I'll cover us both with my coat."

She nodded and bowed her head.

"Let us find the spot with the least amount of draft." He took her hand. "Do you need to relieve yourself again?"

Her face crumpled.

"I don't mean to be impertinent. I'm trying to make

us both as comfortable as possible under unsatisfactory conditions."

She handed him the coat, took the candle branch, and scurried to the workroom. He paced to keep warm. When she returned, he led her to one of the chairs and placed his coat over her. "I'll be right back."

He strode off to take care of his own bodily needs. Afterward, he untied his cravat and removed the neck cloth. He chafed his arms as he strode back to her. She wiped her face with her glove and turned away. He crouched beside her. "Amy, I'll keep you warm and safe tonight."

She sniffed. "I didn't give you leave to call me by my Christian name."

"You may call me Will—it's short for William."

"They will try to m-make us m-marry, w-won't they?"

Reality was sinking in for her, but he saw no reason to belabor the point. "It's cold, and your teeth are chattering. Come," he said, helping her out of the chair.

He left his neck cloth on the chair and led her to a corner. When he sat against the wall, he held his arms out to her. She gingerly crawled onto his lap. He draped his coat over them and pressed her head to his shoulder. When she wiped her eyes again, he kissed her forehead. "Try to sleep."

"I don't think I can," she whispered.

"Are you cold?"

"Not so much anymore, but you are hard all over," she said.

He chuckled, and his breath frosted in the air. "And you are soft all over."

She looked at him. He kissed her cold cheek and caught a faint whiff of rose-scented soap lingering on her skin. Their mouths were only inches apart. The tension between them drew out and tightened like an invisible rope. He tried to convince himself that kissing her would count as a survival measure, but of course, he just wanted to taste her.

"Stop me if you mean to do so," he whispered.

Her breathing grew faster, but she said nothing.

"On the count of three," he said.

Oh, dear God, I don't think I can deny him.

"One," he said, his voice rumbling.

He is a devil and cannot be trusted.

"Two."

You're ruined already.

"Three," he said in a rough tone.

Kiss me before I lose my courage.

He trailed his lips lightly over her mouth. The kiss was butterfly gentle and fleeting. No man had ever kissed her before. She wanted to savor the sensation as he lifted his lips, but it was only a momentary pause before he kissed her again. The sound of his lips meeting hers mesmerized her. He applied a little more pressure and reached round her, pulling her closer until her breasts were nestled against his rock-hard chest. There was something very exhilarating about being in a man's arms.

Of course, she must stop him, and she meant to do so, but he drew his tongue over the seam of her mouth. Her lips parted involuntarily, and then he swept his tongue inside. Shock kept her still, but as he slid his tongue inside and withdrew repeatedly, she lost the ability to think of anything beyond his intimate invasion.

Only the devil would kiss like this.

When he lifted his lips, she inhaled. The masculine

scent of him curled inside her, curbing her ability to listen to the voice of reason. Once again, he covered her lips, only this time, he sucked her tongue into his mouth. She felt strangely possessed by him. Or was it merely the wine muddling her brain? Whatever it was, she couldn't find the strength to tell him he mustn't kiss her in this wicked manner. Unfortunately, the wanton inside her kept saying, *Yes, yes, yes.*

"I can taste the wine on your tongue," he said in a low rumble that made her breath hitch. Then his tongue filled her mouth. He slowly withdrew part of the way, and then he repeated the pattern again. And again. And again. She felt boneless, slightly lethargic, and curiously excited at the same time. Truly, he must be a devil to know tricks to make her forget everything but his wet, intimate kisses.

He nuzzled her neck. "I love the scent of your skin." Then he trailed damp kisses down her neck and sucked on her throat where her pulse beat. He licked her there, startling her. She had no time to think, for he traced his tongue along the low neckline of her gown. She bit her lip to keep from crying out as he outlined the tops of her breasts. When he dipped his tongue in the hollow between her breasts and cupped them, she drew in a shattered breath.

Will touched his forehead to hers and rubbed her back. Of course, he was aroused, but their breath frosted in the air, and she was a virgin. He pressed her head against his shoulder again and nuzzled her hair.

She placed her slender hand over his chest. "Your heart is beating so fast."

He tightened his hold on her, a little undone by her innocence. She'd not known how to kiss him back, but she'd caught on quickly. The women in his life had always been independent, worldly, and temporary. He'd bedded them and shared a few laughs, but he'd never let them get close. He sought pleasure, not intimacy.

Will tried to convince himself that they could somehow manage to extricate themselves from an enforced marriage. But it was the wee hours of the morning, and he knew that others must have noticed them both missing. There was no escaping until the servants stirred in the morning. He considered bribery, but he didn't have any money with him. At any rate, if one servant was alerted, he would report to the butler who had the keys, and the butler, who undoubtedly was loyal and trustworthy, would report the incident to Boswood.

Amy's deep, even breathing drew his attention. She was asleep. Dormant protective feelings filled his chest. He supposed their enforced captivity had created a situational bond between them, but he knew it wouldn't last. If they were forced to marry, they would likely live separate lives like most couples of the ton: he with his traveling and she with her gown designs.

He sighed. There was nothing more he could do tonight. He would deal with tomorrow when it came.

Chapter Six

The next morning

What shall I tell Miss Hardwick's poor parents?" Lady Boswood cried.

"Mama," Georgette said, "I'm sure there's a perfectly reasonable explanation."

"No, there isn't," her mother screeched. "She's disappeared off the face of the earth."

The Marquess of Boswood entered the drawing room and cleared his throat. "Madame, the physician is here with a tonic for your nerves."

As a maid led Lady Boswood away, Georgette looked at her father gratefully. When it came to emergencies, her mother was hopelessly inept.

Last night, word had leaked out during the card party that the devil and Miss Hardwick were missing. A great hue and cry had commenced, but none of the guests or the servants had seen them for quite some time. More than a few guests had mentioned an elopement because everyone had seen the pair flirting at the Broughtons' ball. Georgette prayed it wasn't so, because of the scandal.

The Dowager Countess of Hawkfield mopped her tears. "Gypsies must have stolen them."

Hawk paced the drawing room. "I cannot imagine Will kidnapping Miss Hardwick. He resisted my sisters' efforts to make him a match. Why would he steal a bride?"

"I cannot fathom Amy leaving with him," Georgette said. Amy had made her poor opinion of Mr. Darcett clear, and Georgette could not understand how the devil had managed to persuade her friend to elope. Amy always used caution and was mindful of the proprieties. She knew an elopement would cause a terrible scandal. Amy would not want to hurt her parents. Considering all these factors, Georgette could not believe Amy had willingly run away with the devil. But if she wasn't with him, where was she?

The bell rang. A few minutes later, Hester, Lady Rutledge, ambled into the drawing room. "Is it true my nephew ran off to Scotland with an heiress?"

Hawk managed to settle his aunt and explained that no one knew for sure what had happened to the unlikely couple.

Lord Boswood stroked his chin. "There's something very odd about this business. Both went missing at approximately the same time. I hate to mention it, but we must consider that there may have been foul play—and in my own home, no less."

"But Papa, we know everyone who attended the party," Georgette said.

"Perhaps the butler saw something suspicious," he said and walked over to the bell to summon him.

Five minutes later, Mr. Hoffman arrived, looking stoic as usual. "My lord," he said, bowing.

Lord Boswood explained the circumstances. "Did you or any of the other servants observe anything unusual last night? Even the smallest incident might be of use in our search for the young people."

"Nothing out of the ordinary, my lord."

Boswood stroked his chin. "Were there any unusual sights, sounds, or smells?"

Hoffman shook his head. "I can check with the cook, but we were serving a cold collation last night, so I doubt there are any clues there."

"How could they just disappear?" Hawk asked. "The butler didn't see them leave via the front door."

"Amy was wearing a ball gown. She would not have gone out in the cold night without a wrap, and outerwear is Mr. Hoffman's responsibility," Georgette said.

"We assume they are together," Boswood said. "It seems likely."

Hawk cleared his throat. "Have *all* of the rooms been checked?"

Mr. Hoffman's composure slipped for the first time that Georgette could ever remember.

"My lord, I inadvertently left the wine cellar unlocked for a short while last night. When I realized my mistake, I returned and locked the door," the butler said.

The marquess stared at him. "Did you enter the wine cellar before locking the door?"

"No, my lord."

"Did you hear voices or a noise of any kind?"

"No, my lord."

"Dear God, they must be locked in the wine cellar," Georgette cried.

The marquess held up his hand. "Everyone please be calm. We do not know yet if that is in fact what became of Miss Hardwick and Mr. Darcett. Now, Hoffman, if you will lead the way, Lord Hawkfield and I will accompany you to the wine cellar."

After her father left, Georgette looked at Beau. "I cannot sit and wait."

He took her arm. "Come, I will escort you there."

Someone shook his shoulder. "Will, wake up."

He blinked and found his brother staring at him. "What the deuce?"

When Amy gasped, Will realized he was cupping her breasts and dropped his hands. After he stood and assisted Amy to her feet, he rubbed his eyes only to find Hawk examining the empty wine bottle from last night. His brother looked at him with an odd expression.

Will held up his palms. "There was nothing else to drink."

Amy brushed ineffectually at her skirts. Will realized she was nervous and took her arm. "Be calm. We're rescued. Everything will be fine now."

Boswood cleared his throat. "Beaufort, Georgette, let us inform the others that we found Miss Hardwick and Mr. Darcett safe and sound."

"Papa, I wish to speak to her," Georgette said.

Beau took her arm. "We should give them privacy."

The marquess regarded Hawk. "We will await you in the drawing room."

Hawk cleared his throat. "Will, there is an issue that we must address. We had better go upstairs."

"What issue?" Amy asked.

Will wanted to put his arms round her to comfort her, but he didn't dare in front of his brother. He exchanged a meaningful look with Hawk. "I wish to speak to Miss Hardwick privately. We will be along momentarily."

Hawk took him aside. "Be quick about it. The scandal sheets are likely to be full of tales."

"What?" he said under his breath.

"Talk to her briefly, and then come upstairs."

After Hawk left, Will took Amy's cold hands and squeezed them in an effort to reassure her. "I want to prepare you. They may try to make us marry." He knew they would, but he wanted to soften the blow as much as possible.

She flinched.

"I'll fight it," he said. "We did nothing wrong. We just got locked in the wine cellar."

"I can't believe this. It was an accident." She worried her hands. "We didn't do anything really bad."

"We spent the night together."

She leaned toward him. "Surely they wouldn't make us marry because we kissed."

"Hush. Don't mention that—never give away ammunition," he said.

She grasped his hands. "You will persuade them, won't you?"

"I'll do my best," he said. But he didn't hold out much hope.

Thirty minutes later, in the drawing room

"You will dishonor her?" the Dowager Countess of Hawkfield cried.

"Mama," Will said, "I'm not dishonoring her, because I never dishonored her in the first place." He was breathing hard as everyone stared at him with disbelief. "I swear she's as pure as the driven snow." He'd tried for her sake, but he was getting nowhere with any of them. Even Hawk felt marriage was necessary.

Aunt Hester arched her gray brows. "And how would you know that if you hadn't gone fishing?"

"Oh, oh, oh," the dowager countess cried.

Will noticed Amy clasping and unclasping her hands. "It's ridiculous to make us marry because we got locked in a wine cellar accidentally."

"The bald truth, Darcett, is that your reputation is, ahem, not the best," Boswood said. "To be honest, most of the guests last night thought you had abducted her."

The dowager countess wept again.

Hester rolled her eyes. "Louisa, stop that sniveling. This isn't the end of the world. Well, it's probably the end of Will's bachelor days, but he'll survive."

"Aunt Hester, I counted on your support," Will said. "I didn't hurt her."

"I beg to differ," Boswood said. "Whether by design or accident, the two of you went missing together and were locked in by yourselves all night. The gossip has already spread."

"That brings a question to mind," Beau said. "How did the two of you end up in the wine cellar in the first place?"

"It was an accident," Will and Amy said simultaneously.

Hester snorted. "You're a poor excuse for a rake if you can't lie any better than that."

Boswood folded his hands over his belly. "It's never

about the truth; it's always about the perception. And in this case, the gossip has leaked and the damage is done. It affects both of your families as well."

"The sooner you accept the inevitable, the sooner you'll adjust your mind to the changes," Hawk said. "Everyone in the family will support you."

Amy's face crumpled. Will sat beside her and gave her his handkerchief.

"Let us give Miss Hardwick and Mr. Darcett a few minutes of privacy," Boswood said. He walked over to Amy. "If you are ever in need of anything, you must come to me. You've always been a special friend to my Georgette, and I'll do my best to see that most people know that it was an accident."

She dabbed at her eyes while everyone filed out of the drawing room.

Will took Amy's cold hands and squeezed them in an effort to reassure her. "I tried, but it seems gossip has spread far and wide."

"I cannot believe this. I feel as if this is all a bad dream, and I will awaken to find my life has not changed."

"I wish to speak to you, because we will likely spend very little time together in the next few days. Matters will likely progress quickly. No doubt my female relatives will begin planning the wedding within hours."

"How can we marry when we barely know each other?" she said, her voice trembling.

"We spent the night alone. Unfortunately, it is common knowledge. We don't have a choice."

"But it was an accident," she said.

No one would believe a rake like him hadn't taken advantage of her. "It is the only way to salvage our reputations." Actually it was to save her reputation, since his was ruined long ago.

"I am still in disbelief," she said.

"This is not what either of us planned, but we'll make the best of the situation."

"What will I tell my parents? Oh, God, I cannot even imagine their shock upon learning the news."

"If you wish, I will write to them," he said.

She looked at their joined hands. "That is very kind of you, but I think it would be better if they received the news from me."

"Try not to worry. Years from now, we will probably laugh over our wine cellar adventure."

"I'm sure you're right," she said without conviction.

Will's head felt light from weariness as he walked along the gravel walk behind his brother and mother. All he wanted was a bath and his bed. After they entered the foyer, the butler collected their wraps, and the dowager countess headed for the stairs.

Hawk turned to Will. "I need to speak to you."

"Can't it wait? I'm done up."

"No, it cannot," Hawk said.

Bloody hell. His brother knew about the debt. "Right," he said and followed his brother into his study.

Will slumped in a cross-framed armchair. "You know about the debt."

Hawk surprised him by taking the adjacent chair, rather than sitting behind his desk. "I presume that was the reason you wished to speak to me yesterday."

He nodded.

"You're hardly the first man to fall prey to the gaming

tables." Hawk sighed. "I'll pay it on the condition that you never gamble again."

"It's my responsibility, and I will pay it."

"You have no money," Hawk said.

Will arched his brows. "I expect to come into funds soon."

Hawk stared at him.

"I didn't plan last night, if that's what you're thinking." Of course he wouldn't admit he'd had designs on her fortune prior to last night's debacle.

"I deduced as much," Hawk said. "If you'd intended to seduce her, you would have chosen more comfortable accommodations." He sighed. "Let me pay the debt for now, so that word doesn't get back to Hardwick."

Will nodded. "I will repay you, and I will stand by our agreement to work as your land steward."

"I'm glad. It's difficult to find a man who has all the right qualifications. You know the property well and have a lot of experience with people from all walks of life. And you're smart as a whip—when you're not gambling."

Will pinched the bridge of his nose. "I expected you to rip me to shreds for the debt."

"I've made bad mistakes, as you know, but what counts is how you deal with it afterward," Hawk said. "You came to me and took responsibility."

He said nothing, because he was weary and could no longer think.

"Will?"

"Hmm?"

"The circumstances of your marriage aren't important. It's what comes after the wedding that matters. I wish you both happy. Now get some rest before you collapse."

He swallowed hard. "Thank you."

Aunt Hester's town house, two hours later

Hester had insisted that Amy stay at her town house upon hearing that Lady Boswood had taken to her bed in a nervous state after last night's incident.

"I know it's difficult, gel, but the letter must post by express. You don't want your parents to get this news from someone else who has heard an exaggerated account."

"I understand the reason," Amy said. A fog enveloped her brain. None of this seemed real. In the space of a few hours, her entire life had turned upside down. God only knew what was in store for her in the future.

Hester set out the paper, pen, and inkwell. "Do you prefer privacy or would you like some assistance?"

Amy's hand trembled as she picked up the pen. She set it aside. "I just need a moment t-to calm myself."

"You can dictate the letter to me," Hester said. "I'll add a postscript to the letter letting your parents know that you were a little nervous."

She shook her head. "They will worry more if I do not write the letter myself."

"Very well. I will sit on my sofa, and if you need assistance writing the letter, just let me know."

Dear Mama and Papa,

I love you both very much. I have news that will no doubt shock you. I regret to inform you that I will marry soon due to unusual circumstances. A gentleman named Mr. William Darcett and I were accidentally locked into a wine cellar overnight. I am unharmed, but you must know that there is a great

*deal of gossip circulating, and I wished you to learn
the news from me, rather than strangers. I have been
compromised.*

   *I am presently staying with Lady Rutledge, Mr.
Darcett's aunt, until the wedding. I do not yet know
when or where it is to take place, but I beg you to
come to London at your earliest convenience. Please
believe that I am unharmed, safe, and sound. There
will be a big adjustment, I'm sure, but I will persevere.
I miss you both so much and look forward to seeing
you at the wedding.*

Yours truly,
Amy

Amy closed her eyes momentarily after writing the
word *wedding*. She still felt as if she were caught in
a dense fog and could see no farther than the cold mist
swirling round her.

"Are you finished, Miss Hardwick?" Hester asked.

She swallowed hard. "Yes, I am."

"Do you wish me to review it for you?"

"No, I feel confident of the wording. Thank you for
your support and the offer of your home during this difficult time."

Hester patted her hand. "We are to be family now."

Amy sanded the letter. When she applied the seal, she
faltered. Then she bit her lip as Hester arranged for its
delivery. It was one of those indelible moments she knew
would be stamped on her memory forever. There would
be many more in the days ahead, and she would have to
maintain her composure.

Oh, dear God, she must marry the worst rake in England.

The next morning

"Have one more cup of tea with me," Hester said.

"Thank you," Amy said as the servant carried away the plates. She'd managed to eat a little breakfast, but her vexation had not abated.

Will's prediction that others would take over their lives had begun immediately after their rescue from the wine cellar.

"I've always said a cup of tea will smooth over even the most difficult of times," Hester said as she poured for them.

"My mother says the same thing." Amy bit her lip. Right now, she wanted her mother and father very much, but she also dreaded the moment when she must face them. They would not lecture her, though she believed it would be far easier than watching them try to be cheerful and brave for her sake.

Yesterday, she'd managed to write the letter to her parents without shedding tears, thanks to Hester's pragmatism. Amy had faltered only once, but Hester had reassured her that all would work out well. That moment would be forever burned in her memory. There would be many more in the coming days, and she would have to put on a brave face during all of it.

Amy wondered if the letter had arrived yet. She kept picturing her mother breaking the seal in the parlor and reading it aloud to her father. She envisioned her mama stumbling over the word *compromised*. Papa would push up from his favorite chair and rummage for his spectacles. Then he would sit beside Mama, take the letter, and read the astonishing news, because he would not believe it until he saw the words.

He would take Mama's hand and try to reassure her. Her parents would speculate about the man she must marry. They had never met William Darcett and probably did not even know of his existence, because until recently, he had been gone from England for many years.

At some point, her father would amble over to the window. Amy knew him well. He would blame himself for not escorting her to London this year. Papa would believe he could have prevented his only daughter from being harmed. Her chest hurt thinking of her poor parents receiving such shocking news.

"So, you are to marry William."

Hester's voice recalled Amy to the present. She could think of nothing positive to say, so she remained silent.

"I remember when he was born," Hester mused. "Louisa and her husband were elated to have another boy. They waited several years for the arrival of their spare, though I think that an awful way to refer to younger sons." She sipped her tea. "Like all young men, he's spent several years sowing his wild oats, a few too many on the Continent in my opinion. His mother feared he would never return home. Louisa will be glad to see him married and settled."

"They cannot be happy about the circumstances," Amy said. *Neither could he,* she silently amended.

"Oh, my dear, these things happen. You must not be fearful. William has a good heart," Hester said.

He'd been kind to her last night, but no matter what his aunt said, he was known for his dissolute lifestyle. She had no illusions about how difficult this marriage would be.

"You will learn to make the best of your situation," Hester said. "You are marrying into a wonderful family. I think it is lovely that you and Julianne will be sisters by marriage."

"Yes, that will make me very happy," Amy said. She had always wanted a large family, and to be part of one with Julianne would be wonderful. "I am very much looking forward to knowing all the family better."

"I knew that would cheer you," Hester said.

"There is still so much that must be decided. I do not even know when we will marry or where we will live. It is so unsettling," Amy said.

"All will be worked out in good time, and probably far more quickly than you may be prepared for. You will make the adjustment. It will be easier if you establish a routine. There is comfort in that for both husband and wife."

She swallowed. "I know so little about him."

"But soon you will," Hester said. "He will call after luncheon to propose. You must wear your prettiest frock."

Oh, dear God. It is real and irrevocable.

Her stomach tightened. Everyone said they must marry, but she knew very little about him, and none of it was positive. She tried to imagine living with a man she didn't know, and everything inside her wanted to flee. Amy tried to tell herself that he had been kind last night and concerned about her, but that did not reassure her in the least. She could only imagine what was in store for her. His reputation was terrible, and she suspected very little of it was exaggerated. How could she marry a hedonistic man? How could she live with a man who would undoubtedly be unfaithful and profligate? But if she did not marry him, her reputation would be in shreds, and she would bring even more shame upon her parents than she had already done.

The bell rang. A few minutes later, a footman entered. "Express mail for Miss Hardwick."

Amy ripped the seal with shaking fingers. The letter from her parents was short and to the point. *Do not despair. We love you and will make haste for London.* Chill bumps erupted on her arms. "My mother and father will arrive tomorrow," Amy said, blinking back tears.

"Of course," Hester said, reaching over to pat Amy's hand. "By the time they arrive, you will already be engaged to William."

She wished with all her heart that she could turn back the clock and start yesterday over again. How could she marry the worst rake in England?

"Ah, my dear, I wish I could do more, but you are stronger than you know," Hester said. "You will prevail, no matter what comes."

Early that afternoon

The butler walked in. "Mr. William Darcett."

Amy rose. *Please God, help me get through this day.*

He strode in, wearing a green coat, fawn trousers, and polished black boots. When he bowed, Amy curtsied.

"Aunt Hester, thank you for receiving me," he said.

She lifted her quizzing glass. "Shocking."

He grinned. "What?"

"Your eyes aren't glowing red, and I see no traces of horns or a forked tail." Hester dropped her quizzing glass.

He laughed. "It's a sad day for the scandal sheets."

Hester snorted. "You gave them enough fodder to last for a month. No doubt the papers will embellish every detail."

Will winked at Amy. "I hope they include the Gypsies," he said. "That was my favorite part."

"Your mother is a sweet woman, but she was always fanciful," Hester said. "Well, that's the kind explanation."

Their interaction intrigued Amy. Clearly, they were close-knit and accustomed to teasing. She'd imagined that everyone would react somberly to last night's scandal. Instead, they were jesting as if nothing of great import had taken place. But it had, and her life and his would never be the same.

"I will leave the two of you alone on the condition that you do not run off to Gretna Green or take up with Gypsies," Hester said.

Amy managed a little smile. Will bowed as his aunt ambled out of the drawing room.

When the door closed, Amy's anxiety climbed. How could she accept him when only yesterday she'd had little respect for him?

He clasped her hands and gazed into her eyes. In the sunlit room, amber hues reflected in his dark eyes. He had lush black lashes, but his thick dark brows and prominent cheekbones were the portrait of masculinity.

He was the sort of man who turned feminine heads as he strolled through a room. He was the sort of man who could charm a woman out of her petticoats in a flash. He was the sort of man who could have his choice of beautiful women.

At that moment, she felt certain that this striking man regretted having to marry her. He did not want her. How could he? Then again, she didn't want to marry him, either. Oh, God, this would be the greatest test of her for-titude. Every other obstacle and heartache paled in comparison to this marriage of convenience. She wanted desperately to find one good thing to cling to, but she couldn't fool herself.

She bowed her head, knowing this would be a disaster. How could she go through with this sham of a marriage? She was taller than many men, and far too thin. Everyone would look at the two of them and pity him. But he would not want for beautiful, willing women. She knew how most ton marriages worked. Gentlemen took mistresses. Many were quite blatant about their liaisons. How would she bear the humiliation when he rejected her and turned to others?

"You're trembling," he said.

She sought words, but as always, her brain froze when anxiety pulsed through her veins.

"Please look me in the eyes."

She lifted her gaze to him. He was so handsome he took her breath away.

"There is something I need to ask you," he said. "Lord Boswood called this morning to inquire about us. After I reassured him that all was well, he told me something that we must discuss."

"What is it?" she whispered. God, what else could go wrong?

"I learned this morning that there is another man in your life."

She blinked. "You mean Mr. Crawford?"

"Do you have an understanding with him?"

"No," she said.

"Boswood said he writes to you."

"Mr. Crawford asked my father for permission to write to me without my knowledge."

"I see."

She sighed. "Mr. Crawford courted me for a short time, but I ended it before leaving for London. I also wrote a letter telling him that we do not suit. I do not believe he will write again."

"I'm relieved," he said.

He'd stunned her. She would have thought that he would grasp at an opportunity to avoid marrying her, but then it occurred to her that he was probably relieved because marriage to her would allay the scandal.

"My parents will arrive in London late tomorrow," she said.

"I know," he said. "I wrote to your father. He will call on me at Ashdown House tomorrow. I will formally request your hand in marriage then."

Her gaze flew to his. "Why did you write to him?"

"I don't have the best reputation," he said. "I hoped to reassure your father. It probably did little good, but I felt it worth making the gesture."

"Thank you," she said, more than a little stunned. The letter he'd written indicated he wasn't completely without feelings or scruples. Of course, people weren't simple. They all had good and bad qualities. Amy knew her father would not be pleased that she was marrying a rake, but William's gesture showed that he cared, at least to some degree, about others and that gave her hope.

"I obtained a special license," he said. "We will marry the day after tomorrow."

She couldn't breathe for a moment. "So soon," she whispered.

He cleared his throat. "My family insists we must hush up the gossip quickly."

Two days. There would be no time to have a special gown made up for the occasion. But she had many others. She must think of the blessings, but for a moment, absolutely nothing came to mind.

Then she remembered how much she'd worried that she would never marry. Now she would have a husband. It was frightening to know so little about him, but he must feel very much the same way. Perhaps they could help each other though the difficult times.

"I wish there were a map that we could consult to help us navigate our lives," he said. "We'll have to create our own and do our best when we must travel over rough terrain."

She suspected they would face a great many bumpy roads over the years. "Will we live at Ashdown House?"

"Only temporarily. After the wedding, I will consult my brother's man of business and ask him to suggest suitable properties near Richmond. I will work as my brother's steward for the next year. Perhaps you would accompany me and help select a suitable property."

The prospect cheered her. "Oh, yes, I would enjoy choosing furnishings and decorations."

"Right. You draw gown designs," he said.

She kept her expression as serene as possible. At least he'd not objected to it. She couldn't bear to give up her dress designs; it wasn't who she was, but it was an important part of her life. The thought that a man could take something away from her that she cherished made her uneasy. But he had not objected, and she would not borrow trouble.

She was more troubled that he did not know she had

agreed to accept compensation for her designs. There was no doubt in her mind that he would disapprove of her involvement in shop matters. While certain professions were considered respectable for gentlemen of the ton, a lady who accepted coin for her work would be considered inferior. Society would shun her if they knew.

Amy thought the attitudes outmoded and pompous. More important, she did not know if Will was responsible with money or not. The day might come when she would be thankful that she'd saved the money she earned. Part of her thought the deception a poor way to start a marriage, but this was no love match. Neither of them was under any illusions that this was anything other than an attempt to salvage their reputations.

Was she making excuses or was she making a smart decision? Considering his reputation, she concluded that it was in her best interest to set aside a nest egg.

"I have something that belongs to you," he said. "I've been meaning to return it." He rummaged inside his coat and withdrew the silk red rose that had gone missing since the Beresfords' ball.

"Where did you find it?"

"On the carpet in the Beresfords' library," he said. "I don't know why I kept it."

A stray thread was still attached to it.

"I thought you might need the rose so that you could wear the gown again," he said.

"Thank you." She didn't tell him that the gown was so renowned that she could never wear it again unless she changed the ribbons, lace, and roses.

He lowered his gaze and scuffed the toe of his boot on the carpet.

"Is something wrong?" she asked.

"I don't have a pretty speech prepared."

He'd just won a tiny corner of her heart. "You do not need one."

He clasped her hands and kneeled. She gazed into his dark eyes and her heart squeezed. Why did she feel perilously close to tears? Because this man would be her husband until the end of their days. She found herself blinking back tears. In the past twenty-four hours, she had become a veritable watering pot.

His eyes were shining as he met her gaze. "Amy, will you make me the happiest of men and marry me?"

"Yes, I will marry you." *Lord, please walk beside us.*

Will stood. When he cupped her cheeks, he wiped the stray tear streaking down her face with his thumb. "May I kiss you?"

"Yes," she whispered.

He kissed her gently on the lips.

She wanted so badly to believe that it would work, that they could forge a life together and be happy.

They would be married for the rest of their lives. Until now, she'd thought all of her choices were gone, but she realized she did have a choice. She could decide to make a mockery of the vows she would take or she could do everything possible to make this marriage work.

She must be brave and exert herself. He would be her husband soon, and if she focused on his needs, she might be able to make him happy. In turn, he might reciprocate. God willing, this marriage of necessity might stand a chance. She met his gaze and her skin prickled a little. "I will do everything in my power to see to your comfort and happiness."

He lit up with that thousand-candle smile. "I like the sound of that." He draped his arms round her and pulled her flush against him. She gasped, making him chuckle. The hard contours of his muscular body were pressed all along her thighs, stomach, and breasts.

"Put your arms round my neck," he said in that rumbling voice she'd come to recognize.

She did his bidding, and when he angled his head, she was glad to have his shoulders as an anchor. He kissed her openmouthed and her knees felt a little weak. She parted her lips for him, and as their tongues tangled, his hands slid down to her bottom. His mouth was wet, and his body emanated heat through the layers of his shirt and waistcoat. Against her belly, she could feel something hard. She'd heard unseemly talk in the ladies' retiring room and knew he was aroused.

Her breasts suddenly felt heavier and heat traveled to her most intimate place. She wanted something, needed him to possess her. And she wanted to run her hands over his body, but she wasn't quite that brave.

He broke the kiss. His breathing was labored and fast. "I think we'll do very well together," he said. "Very well, indeed."

She prayed he was right.

Chapter Seven

Harry Fordham's rooms, that evening

A toast to your engagement," Fordham said.

"Here, here," Bell said.

"Cheers." Will sipped the champagne and sprawled in one of Fordham's cast-off leather chairs. He didn't much feel like celebrating—not when he knew he'd changed the course of Amy's life and taken away her choices.

"You're a lucky dog," Fordham said. "Down twenty thousand, and then you bag a bloody heiress."

Will gritted his teeth and set the glass on the side table. He was breathing harder than usual.

"Old boy, is something wrong?" Fordham said.

"She's going to be my wife," he gritted out.

Fordham grew still and eyed Will warily. "My apologies for the bit about bagging an heiress."

"Accepted," Will said.

Bell regarded him with a keen expression. "You surprise me."

"I didn't bag her." He leaned forward with his elbows on his thighs. "We got locked in a bloody wine cellar all night. Friends and family insisted we had to marry to tamp down the scandal."

"No offense to the future Mrs. Darcett, but you are coming into a fortune," Fordham said.

Will thought about the scared look on Amy's face the day after. She'd had every right to be wary of him after he'd actually tried to compromise her.

"Let us go to White's," Bell said. "We'll get Will foxed."

He didn't want to celebrate the fortune she would bring. Not long ago, he would have reveled in getting exactly what he wanted. But she'd looked frightened when she'd accepted his proposal. He'd felt awful, because she was a respectable, innocent young lady and deserved better. She didn't want him, and he couldn't blame her.

"Will, you want to go, don't you?" Fordham said, watching him with an uneasy expression.

He really didn't, but he'd be damned if he showed it. "Cheers to that," Will said. He'd go to White's and drink himself stone-cold drunk. Maybe then he wouldn't feel so damn guilty about getting exactly what he wanted—her fifty thousand pounds.

The next day

Amy busied herself with her sketches in Hester's Egyptian drawing room, but her nerves threatened to rattle her. She just had to do something to help control the anxiety. She felt more in control of her life while drawing designs for gowns. For short snatches of time, she could focus on something other than her impending marriage to a man who was almost a stranger to her.

Soon Will would arrive to escort her to Ashdown House. Hester had left earlier to call on a friend and would meet them there. Now that they were engaged, they no longer required a chaperone.

Today he would present her as his fiancée to his family. Even though she had met his mother and sisters, she was anxious to make a good impression. She hoped they would approve of her, but part of her wished she could suddenly transform into a petite blond-haired beauty. As soon as the thought entered her head, she let out an exasperated sigh. She mustn't let those old feelings of inferiority take over again. Her new life was beginning, and if she were to find any happiness, she must start by believing she deserved it.

The butler entered the drawing room and announced Mr. Darcett. Amy pinched her cheeks and rose. When Will entered, she curtsied. He crossed the room with his hands behind his back. In shock, she noted his eyes were bloodshot. Oh, dear God, she'd known he was a rakehell, but seeing the proof shook her. But what was there to be done now? She'd accepted his proposal. If she cried off, the gossip would hurt her family and his as well.

He handed her a posy. "Roses from my mother's conservatory."

"Thank you," she said.

She walked to the bell. "I'll ring for a maid to bring a vase."

He strode over to the glass case with the faux mummy. "My aunt has a fondness for anything strange. She and my grandmamma are my favorites. I especially like that Hester doesn't mince words."

"She is plainspoken, but she is also very wise," Amy said. "She has been a great deal of help to me."

"It is all a little unsettling, isn't it?"

So he was feeling at sea as well.

The maid arrived and promised to put the flowers in a vase. Will offered his arm, and Amy clasped his sleeve. He looked at her as he led her out of the drawing room and down the stairs. "My friends wanted to celebrate my engagement last night. I fear you're seeing me after a night of revelry."

He was no stranger to it. She wondered if this was what she could expect from him every night. She doubted he would give up his wicked ways simply because they were forced to marry.

"If I were half as dissipated as the scandal sheets intimate, I doubt I could crawl out of bed each morning," he said.

She wondered how many beds he'd crawled out of over the years, but she would not voice the words.

"I like your green jacket," he said.

She smiled at the term he used. "It is called a spencer."

"You look very well in it," he said, leading her through the great hall.

"Thank you," she said.

"It's perfectly molded to your figure." His eyes danced.

"You are unseemly," she said under her breath. He was flirtatious.

He leaned his head down. "Guilty as charged."

"You're pouring on the charm today."

"Well, I was hoping to be rewarded for it."

She lifted her brows. "I beg your pardon?"

They reached the foyer. He retrieved his hat and gloves while she put on her bonnet and gloves. Then he led her out.

He looked at her with a mischievous grin the entire time they walked toward the carriage. She couldn't help but return his smile. His innate ability to charm made him seem entirely frivolous, but she'd discovered another side to him in the wine cellar. He'd understood her guilt about the way she'd treated her friends. She'd been surprised by his advice and hadn't thought he would care enough to offer it, but then she didn't know him well enough to make those assumptions. If this marriage were to stand a chance of succeeding, she would have to look past her perceptions of him and discover the man behind the rake-hell façade. She could only hope there was more to him than what she'd seen on the surface.

When they reached the carriage, he helped her negotiate the steps. Then he climbed in and sat next to her. She caught the faint scent of sandalwood, and something else, something male and primitive.

When the horses started, he set his hat aside and turned to her. "Now, about that reward."

"You're impatient." She let the bonnet partially hide her from him.

He plucked the bow loose and took the bonnet off. There was something arresting and exciting about a man untying a bow and removing a bonnet. She felt a little vulnerable without the bonnet, but when he nuzzled her cheek, she found herself mesmerized by the scent of his skin and the soft way he feathered his finger along her jaw and the shell of her ear.

Her pulse sped up. She moistened her lips. He angled

his head and kissed her. When he deepened the kiss, she kissed him back, because she liked kissing him, and he was her fiancé.

Her fingers threaded through the crisp strands of hair at the nape of his neck. His dark hair was thick, wavy, and silky to the touch. He parted his lips and touched his tongue to her mouth. Without hesitation, she opened for him, and this time, he tasted her in a leisurely manner. She surrendered to his slow siege and gave herself up to sensation: the ragged sound of his breath, the scent of sandalwood on his skin, and the warmth of his big hands cupping her face.

When he broke the kiss, he leaned his forehead against hers. His breath was coming faster. "I've started something we cannot finish."

Her face flushed. He meant... oh, heavens.

A smile spread across his face. Then he tickled her waist. She shrieked.

"Hush, the driver will think I'm tupping you in the carriage."

"You're what?" she cried. She wouldn't tolerate foul language.

"Sorry. Poor choice of words."

"Does that mean what I think it means?" she said, her voice rising.

"I cannot read your mind. What do you think it means?"

"You're bad," she said.

"Wrong answer. Try again."

She laughed. "I should scold you." Oh, he knew how to use charm to get what he wanted. She imagined he also knew how to escape what he didn't want, with the notable exception of having to marry her.

"But you won't," he said. "Because I think you secretly like it."

"I will not tolerate crude language."

"You must admit I diverted you."

"That was not your aim," she said. "You wanted to shock me."

"No, I wanted to kiss you," he said, his deep voice rumbling.

She caught her breath at the heated look in his eyes.

The carriage rumbled along for some time, and then it turned. He looked out the window. "Ah, there is Ashdown House in the distance."

Her mouth dried, a bad omen, for she would be tongue-tied and judged harshly for her inability to converse. This first meeting was critical, because she was meeting them as his fiancée. She didn't want to disappoint him, but if she allowed her anxiety to overwhelm her, she would embarrass him.

He reached over and clasped her hand. "Don't be nervous. You know almost everyone. They will adore you."

"How can they, under the circumstances?"

"You worry for nothing. My female relatives are delighted I'm getting leg-shackled."

She looked at her lap, hating that he'd used that derogatory expression. He probably hadn't even thought twice about it.

"If it's any consolation, I'm not looking forward to facing your father," he said. "I fear he'll plant me a facer."

Her jaw dropped. "My papa would never hit you."

"You're his only daughter, and I've got the devil of a reputation, if you'll pardon the bad pun. He's likely to cut up nasty over what I've done to his little girl."

"In my letter, I told my parents it was an accident," she said.

Will shook his head. "He's not going to care."

"My father is a very gentle and amiable man," Amy said.

"Does he own a pistol?"

"He has guns for shooting birds."

Will released an exaggerated sigh. "I'm not long for this world. Kiss me before I die."

When he reached for her, she laughed and put her hand on his chest. "No. The carriage is slowing, and you will observe the proprieties."

He winked. "For now."

Will escorted Amy through the foyer and into the great hall. He squeezed her hand, because she was as skittish as a doe.

He stopped at the stairwell and decided a bit of humor would help ease her anxiety. "Behold Apollo, my mother's naked statue. Aunt Hester threatened to clothe the ugly thing in a toga if my mother didn't get rid of it. Mama accused Hester of having revolting taste, because of the faux mummy. Everyone was in an uproar over who had the worst décor."

"You're jesting," she said.

He shook his head. "No, I'm not. My family is rather eccentric."

"William, why are you dawdling?" Patience called out.

He looked up at the landing. "Hello, sister."

"Everyone is waiting," she said, beckoning him with her hand. "Hurry along."

"We'll be there momentarily," he said. "Amy wishes to admire Apollo."

Patience rolled her eyes and walked back to the drawing room.

"Patience has four boys, including Peter, who helpfully waters my mother's hothouse flowers."

Amy smiled. "He uses a watering pot?"

"No. Peter is like a dog—only he prefers his grandmother's flowers rather than trees."

Amy laughed. "Will I meet the infamous Peter?"

"He's in the nursery with the other children, all of whom are probably terrorizing the nurse."

Running footsteps sounded above. "Uncle Will!"

"Speak of the devil," Will said. "Peter, go back to the nursery before your mother sees you've escaped."

When Peter climbed on the banister, Amy gasped. "Oh, dear God, he will hurt himself."

"He does it all the time."

Peter slid down backward on his stomach. "Wheeee!"

"You must catch him," Amy cried.

Will laughed. "Watch."

When Peter reached the bottom, he flipped off like a monkey and ran back upstairs. "Again," he cried.

Will ran after him. "Peter, stop!"

The drawing room doors opened. Amy recognized Montague, Patience's husband. He hurried out and tried to grab his son, but Peter ducked, spun around, and ran in the opposite direction.

"Peter, come back here!" Montague roared.

The boy's laughter rang out.

Patience and Hawk came out of the drawing room.

"He's headed for the back stairs," Will yelled as he took off after Peter.

"I'll catch him coming up from the kitchen if he

escapes you," Hawk shouted as he ran down the main stairs. He paused at the base and bowed. "Welcome to the madness, Miss Hardwick. Do watch out. We have a wild boy loose."

Soon everyone spilled out onto the landing. Julianne walked to the rail with Emma on her hip. The babe was grinning, as if entertained by all the commotion. "Amy, please come upstairs," Julianne said. "Will and Marc will catch Peter eventually."

"That boy will be the death of me," Montague said. "Where is that nurse?"

"Probably writing her resignation letter as we speak," Hester said. "Who can blame her?"

"Oh, dear," the dowager countess said. "What must you think of us, Miss Hardwick?"

Hester ambled to the rail and looked down. "No doubt she thinks we're all dicked in the nob."

"Hester, please mind your language," the dowager countess said.

"Bah," Hester said. "Come along, gel. We don't bite. Well, one of his Patience's brats does, but I forget which one. They're all horrid."

"Hester, they are my children and your great-nephews," Patience cried.

"Not by choice," Hester said.

Amy lifted her skirts and started up the stairs. Hope met her halfway. "Do excuse us. I wish I could tell you that this is not the normal state of affairs, but I don't wish to mislead you."

Amy laughed. They perfectly fit her vision of the large family she'd always dreamed about. "I'm sure it is not always quite this chaotic."

"Yes, it is, but you'll grow accustomed to it," Hope said. "We might as well have tea. Who knows how long it will be before they corral Peter?"

When they reached the landing, Harmony offered to check on the nurse. "She is no doubt quivering in fear for her position."

"It's a miracle the woman has lasted this long," Hester said. She regarded Amy. "Patience's youngest brat, Thomas, tried to scalp her last week."

"He did not," Patience said. "He only cut a small lock."

"We should have named him Mischief," Montague grumbled.

"Let us all return to the drawing room," the dowager countess said. "We left Grandmamma sleeping on the sofa."

Everyone turned when a voice rang out.

"Success! One naughty boy caught," Will called out.

Amy looked over the rail. He was marching the glum Peter across the great hall. Will met her gaze and a dazzling smile spread across his face. In that moment, she envisioned him with their son one day. Something flickered in her chest like a feeble candle flame.

"Are you Scottish, dear?" Grandmamma shouted.

Will smiled as Amy shook her head. Grandmamma thought anyone with red hair must be Scottish.

"I always liked those kilts the Scotsmen wear," Grandmamma hollered.

"What she really wants to know is what they wear or don't wear underneath those kilts," Hester said.

"Oh, Hester, we do not speak of such things," the dowager countess cried.

Hester snorted and adjusted the tall feather in her turban.

Amy's shoulders shook with laughter. She seemed completely at ease as she petted Poppet, who sat on her lap purring.

"Miss Hardwick, I understand your parents will arrive soon," Patience said.

Amy lowered her eyes. "Yes, I have not seen them yet."

Will reached for her hand and squeezed it. He suspected that Amy would remain anxious until they arrived.

The butler, Jones, entered. "Mr. and Mrs. Hardwick and Mr. Crawford."

Amy gasped and looked at Will. "I had no idea Mr. Crawford was coming."

"Have no fear," he said. "I can dispense with him."

Amy leaned toward him. "What do you mean by dispense?"

Will arched his brows as he helped Amy rise. If her former suitor intended to make a claim on her, he was in for a startling surprise.

"What could he possibly want?" she said.

"William, who is Mr. Crawford?" the dowager countess asked.

"My rival, I suspect," he said.

"Oh, dear. Oh, my goodness," his mother said.

All the color had drained from Amy's face.

"Steady," Will whispered. "I'm sure there's a logical explanation."

A portly gentleman with a bald spot and unfashionable gray whiskers escorted a tall lady inside. Like Amy, the lady had red hair, though hers was not as bright. Then a short man dressed in clerical garb entered, regarding the surroundings with a slightly patronizing smile. Will presumed this man was the famous vicar and wondered what he wanted.

Amy's eyes were a bit misty. He offered his arm. "Will you introduce me to your parents?" Will murmured.

She nodded.

As he led her to them, he could feel her hand trembling on his sleeve.

"Mama, Papa, I wish to present my fiancé, Mr. William Darcett."

Mrs. Hardwick curtsied. Her husband bowed.

Amy went into her mother's arms. "I missed you."

Will met her father's eyes and offered his hand. Mr. Hardwick's grip was strong, but he looked more than a little careworn.

"On behalf of my family, I wish to welcome you and Mrs. Hardwick to our home," Will said. "Please make yourself comfortable."

Mr. Crawford cleared his throat.

Will put his hands on his hips. "We weren't expecting you, Mr. Crawford. To what do we owe your visit?"

"I am here in a spiritual capacity."

"Really? I find that interesting, given that no one in my family requested your spiritual guidance."

Crawford's face mottled. "I am here to advise Miss Hardwick."

"Mr. Crawford, I understand that at one time you courted my fiancée," Will said. "I'll be honest, since you are a man of the cloth; I rather suspect spirituality is not your reason for journeying to my family's home—uninvited I might add."

"You presume to know my reasons," Crawford said, "but I wonder at yours."

"Let's get to the point, shall we? Why are you here?"

"I wish to speak to Miss Hardwick privately," he said.

Will narrowed his eyes. "If you wish to speak to her, do so. But there will be no private meetings."

"I only want to ensure that she knows she has a choice. Miss Hardwick, you do not have to marry this infamous rake. I will overlook your lapse in judgment."

"What lapse of judgment are you talking about?" Will asked, frowning.

"The one that landed her in a compromising position," Crawford said. "I want Miss Hardwick to know that I am still willing to marry her under these less than satisfactory circumstances."

Amy frowned at him. "Mr. Crawford, I am engaged, and even before that, I made my position clear. I do not wish to wound you, but I do not wish to marry you, either."

"You don't know your own mind," Crawford said.

Will arched his brows. "Sir, I beg to differ and must insist that you do not make derogatory comments about my fiancée."

"Do not twist my words," Crawford said. "You have clearly turned her head. Miss Hardwick, end this engagement now. Even though he has tainted your reputation, I will gladly marry you."

"Maybe they should fight for her," Aunt Hester said. "You know, like those stags that lock horns."

"Hester, please," the dowager countess said. "They are not animals."

"They're men; not much difference," Hester said.

"Why must you say such things?" the dowager countess said.

"Because it's true," Hester said. "I've had five husbands, you know."

"Crawford, you might want to make your apology

now," Mr. Hardwick said. "Darcett is a big fellow and likely to squash you."

"Mr. Crawford, will you accompany me to the balcony?" Amy said.

Will gritted his teeth. "Amy, may I speak to you?"

"Sir, how dare you address her in such a familiar manner?" Crawford said.

"I dare, because she is my fiancée." Will narrowed his eyes. He didn't like anyone interfering with his life, especially not some puffed-up vicar. He wished Crawford would insult him so that he'd have an excuse to bloody his holier-than-thou nose.

Amy regarded Will with an alarmed expression. "I need to speak to Mr. Crawford."

Will patted her hand. "I would prefer you did not go off alone with other men."

"Sir, I am a vicar," Crawford said.

"I don't care," Will said. "You're not taking her off alone."

"William," Amy said with a tight smile. "May I speak to you for a few moments?"

He grinned. "I thought you would never ask."

She took him aside. "What is the matter with you? You are acting as if you're jealous of Mr. Crawford."

He scoffed. "I'm not jealous, but I'm not letting any man go off alone with my fiancée—especially that sanctimonious pri— Never mind. I don't like him."

She released a sigh. "I only want to speak to him privately to prevent wounding him in front of the others. He will listen to me, and I must insist that you allow me to take care of this matter."

He hesitated. "I don't like it."

"This conversation will end in probably less than ten minutes. Now, please excuse me."

With more than a little effort, Will squelched the urge to follow Amy and throw "his holiness" over the balcony.

Fifteen minutes later, she returned to the drawing room with a serene expression. Mr. Crawford was not so tranquil. His face could easily be described as almost purple, and his expression was decidedly mulish. Hawk took the vicar aside and spoke to him. Crawford made a curt bow, muttered something, and followed a footman out of the drawing room.

Will crossed the room to speak to Amy. "What happened?"

"Nothing happened. I simply reminded him of all the reasons that we did not suit, and I wished him well in his search for a bride," she said.

Will narrowed his eyes. "You did not tell me everything," he said. "He tried to persuade you to throw me over."

"I told him that I would not have married him, even if I were not already affianced to you," she said.

"Mr. Hardwick, please be seated," Will said as he led Amy's father inside Hawk's study. "My brother is making arrangements for Crawford's departure."

"He insisted upon accompanying us." Hardwick shrugged. "Crawford seemed a sensible fellow until my daughter rebuffed him. If you want the truth, I think his pride took a hit, and from that moment on, he was determined beyond all common sense to win her. Went about it in a stupid manner, but there you have it."

"Can I interest you in a brandy?" Will asked.

"I suppose so," Hardwick said.

Will poured two fingers in each glass and brought one to his future father-in-law. "The solicitors will arrive shortly, and we can deal with the settlements then. But I wish to formally request your daughter's hand in marriage."

Hardwick swirled his brandy. "I have questions for you first."

"Fire away, sir."

"My daughter insisted in her letter that the two of you accidentally got stuck in that wine cellar. Frankly, I find that rather suspicious."

He explained the circumstances. "We had planned to leave separately and ended up locked inside."

Mr. Hardwick took a deep breath. "Look me in the eyes. Did you violate my daughter?"

The question shook him, even though he hadn't. "No, sir."

"You spent the night with her."

"It wasn't a choice. The temperature dropped. It was cold enough that our breath frosted in the air. There was nothing but the hard floor and two wooden chairs. I knew she was exhausted and overset. So I held her on my lap, and covered us with my coat. She was able to sleep."

Hardwick narrowed his eyes. "What are you leaving out?"

"I kissed her." Hardwick didn't need to know the details.

"After many years of marriage, my wife and I had given up on children. And then one day, Mrs. Hardwick told me the stunning news. We were both in our early forties. We call Amy our little miracle."

"I know. She told me." Her parents obviously adored her.

"I daresay there is a great deal about her you *don't* know," he said. "And frankly, I am worried. You've got a bad reputation."

"I've definitely sowed wild oats," he said. "I traveled

on the Continent for four years, three more than most men on their grand tours." He looked out the window, remembering. "I met Amy not long after I returned to England. It was at my brother's wedding."

"You conceived a partiality for her a year ago?" Hardwick said.

"No. She didn't much care for me, I'm afraid."

"And why was that?" Hardwick asked.

"I teased her and followed her about for my amusement." He turned to Hardwick, feeling a bit abashed. "It was sort of a game, I suppose. I would say something to annoy her, and she would retort."

"Amy?" he said. "She's always shied away from that sort of thing."

"Well, I was very annoying."

"Do you have a profession, Mr. Darcett? Or are you a gentleman of leisure?"

"I will take over as land steward for my brother shortly after the wedding."

Hardwick finished his brandy and stared into the empty glass. "Amy is a grown woman, but she will always be my little girl."

"I understand, sir."

"I doubt you do." Hardwick regulated his tone, but his expression was fierce. "I'll be honest with you. The very thought of allowing my daughter to marry an infamous rakehell makes my stomach curdle."

Will set his brandy aside. "It is beyond my comprehension to really understand how you feel. I cannot change my past, but I will not abandon her."

"To be clear, I'm only granting you permission to marry her because the scandal would destroy her reputation,"

Hardwick said. "If you ever hurt her, you'll have to answer to me."

"I will treat her with the respect she deserves."

When Hardwick regarded him with obvious skepticism, Will realized his words probably sounded hollow to the man. He leaned forward with his elbows on his thighs. "We barely know each other. She's scared."

"Those are the first words you've said that don't sound glib and cocksure," Hardwick said.

Will's face actually heated. His aunt Hester had always said he was a born charmer. God knew he'd used it to his advantage all his life. He hadn't fooled Hardwick, and Will found himself respecting the man. "I'll admit something to you."

"Oh?" Hardwick said.

Will gave him a wry smile. "She's the one woman who saw through me." She'd probably learned more than a little wisdom from her astute father.

Hardwick laughed. "Good for my daughter." He paused and added, "I meant what I said, Darcett."

"I know, sir."

"Well, I've held your feet to the fire, and you passed the test—barely."

Will huffed. They both knew Amy deserved better than a rake like him.

"You have my blessing." Hardwick fumbled in his coat pocket, withdrew a handkerchief, and polished his spectacles.

Will walked over to the window to give the man a moment to compose himself. As he stared out at the familiar, rustic landscape, he recalled Amy's stunned expression yesterday when he'd told her he was relieved. Thank

God neither she nor her father would ever know the reason for it.

Amy followed her future sisters-in-law upstairs to a bedchamber. "This was my room before I married," Patience said. "There is something I wish to show you." She opened a wardrobe and held up a white embroidered gown with a train.

"The lace is beautiful," Amy said.

Patience smiled. "It was my wedding gown. Harmony and Hope wore it as well. Julianne wore a different gown that she had made up."

"Patience's gown was much too long for me," Julianne said. "Taking up the hem would have ruined the embroidery."

"You are tall enough for it," Patience said. "My sisters and I hope you will consider following the tradition by wearing it at your wedding."

Her heart turned over. "Thank you. I would be honored." Oh, this would be so much better than having a gown made up.

"Let us see if it fits," Patience said.

At first, Amy was a bit shy about undressing before them, but they kept telling her funny stories about Will when he was a boy while Patience helped her don the gown.

"When he was all of five years old, he ran away from home," Hope said. "Mama was frantic."

Harmony laughed. "There is a reason she suspected Gypsies had stolen you and William."

"Why is that?" Amy said.

"You need a bit of background," Patience said. "Will was in a snit about something and said we would all be sorry when he left home forever. No one took him seriously. Several hours later, we realized he was missing. Our father sent riders out in all directions. Unbeknownst to us, Will had found some Gypsies on the road. Eventually, Papa found him filthy and happy as a lark mending utensils."

"Mama has never stopped worrying that Gypsies will steal him," Harmony said, laughing.

"He was always running away," Hope said. "One time, he insisted he was walking to China."

"His interest in traveling started at an early age," Amy said. Privately, she wondered why a young boy would run away so often.

His sisters exchanged knowing looks but said nothing. Amy wondered if she'd said something wrong, but for the life of her, she couldn't figure it out.

"The gown fits Amy almost perfectly," Patience said. "We'll pin the bodice a little tighter in the back, and then she will be set, except for a bonnet."

Amy looked at her reflection in the cheval mirror. "I have a length of long lace that I think would make a perfect veil."

"What a stunning idea," Julianne said. "You can hold it in place with my gold bandeau. That way, you will wear something that all of us wore at our weddings."

"Thank you all for making this special for me," Amy said.

"Of course we want it to be special. You are to be our sister," Patience said.

Amy knew that having sisters was far more special than any gown.

The dowager countess insisted that Amy and her parents join them for dinner that night. Amy found herself a bit fatigued. She had always needed time alone with her thoughts, but there had been no chance for that today.

Will leaned toward her. "You look a bit done up."

"I am a little tired," she said.

"We'll be husband and wife tomorrow. I still cannot quite credit it."

"I know. Everything has happened so fast that I haven't had a chance to really let it sink in," she said.

"We'll take a postponed wedding trip to Brighton this summer if you wish."

"I'd like that. I've never been there." She wondered if he meant it or if he was one of those men who made promises on the spur of the moment and forgot all about them when something more interesting caught his attention. She told herself to give him the benefit of the doubt, but doing so was far easier said than done. When the desserts arrived, Amy begged off.

"Ah, but you must try just a bite of my favorite— almond cheesecake," Will said.

When he drew close with the fork, he looked at her mouth. "Open for me," he murmured.

She did his bidding. The combination of almonds and lemon was so divine, she closed her eyes momentarily. After she swallowed, she met his gaze. His dark eyes were intent on her. Then he leaned closer and whispered, "You make dessert a sensual experience."

"Will," she whispered. "You mustn't look at me in that manner." He regarded her from the corners of his eyes. "I find myself anxious for tomorrow night."

His words made her even more nervous. She had a rudimentary idea of what happened in the marriage bed, but making herself vulnerable to a man whom she knew so little about frightened her. How could she engage in intimacies with him when there were no tender feelings involved? The clink of a spoon on a glass brought the conversation to a halt. Everyone looked to the head of the table, where Hawk stood with his wineglass. "I wish to propose a toast to Will and Miss Hardwick. May you have a wonderful wedding and a happy life together." Then he grinned. "And now for something a bit more substantial than good wishes. It occurred to me that a newly wedded couple might appreciate a bit more privacy than they're likely to find at Ashdown House. As it happens, there is an empty dower house on the property. Since Will and his bride have not had time to purchase their own home, I thought they might make use of the cottage. I took the liberty of hiring servants, and there are some existing furnishings there. A bed, for example."

"Marc!" Julianne said to her husband. "You are unseemly."

He chuckled. "And you're surprised?"

Will winked at Amy and faced his brother. "We'll take the cottage and the bed."

Amy clasped her trembling fingers and lowered her gaze to the table. Everyone was trying so hard to make this seem as if it was a celebration. She kept her eyes downcast, because she didn't want anyone to see how much she dreaded this marriage.

"Oh, dear. We do not speak of such indelicate matters," the dowager countess said.

Hester snorted. "Never mind your mother, Will. She's only worried about acquiring more grandbrats."

Chapter Eight

$\mathcal{H}$e was getting married.

Will's heart thudded in his ears. He stood before the altar, feeling more than a little solemn about the vows he would make this day. His friends would never believe that he felt a responsibility to Amy. He supposed his father had drummed some principles into him, and part of him was a bit sad that his father wasn't here to witness his wedding. But then, his father had died before even Will's sisters had married.

"Dearly beloved, we are gathered together here in the sight of God, and in the face of this congregation, to join together this man and this woman in holy matrimony."

Will looked at his bride from the corner of his eye and caught his breath at the lace veil caught up with a gold band gleaming in her red-gold curls. His shy bride had a flair for the dramatic.

Lady Georgette looked a bit teary-eyed as she stood

beside Amy. Will glanced at his brother, and Hawk gave him an encouraging smile.

Then the rector was addressing him. "Wilt thou have this woman to thy wedded wife, to live together after God's ordinance in the holy estate of matrimony? Wilt thou love her, comfort her, honor, and keep her in sickness and in health; and, forsaking all others, keep thee only unto her, so long as ye both shall live?"

"I will," he said.

The rector turned to Amy. The solemn vows washed over him until she answered in a clear voice. "I will," she said.

"Who giveth this woman to be married to this man?"

Mr. Hardwick answered, "I do."

Will took her slightly trembling right hand and repeated after the rector. "I, William Joseph Darcett, take thee, Amy Marie Hardwick, to have and to hold from this day forward, for better, for worse, for richer, for poorer, in sickness and in health, to love and to cherish, till death us do part, according to God's holy ordinance; and thereto I plight thee my troth."

Her green eyes were wide as she repeated her vows. The entire ceremony seemed a little unreal to him, and he suspected she felt the same way.

Will took the gold band and slid it onto her long, slender finger. "With this ring I thee wed, with my body I thee worship, and with all my worldly goods I thee endow." Unexpectedly, he felt the weight of his responsibility to her. *She was his wife*.

The rector lifted his chin. "For as much as Amy and William have consented together in holy wedlock, and have witnessed the same before God and this company, and thereto have given and pledged their troth either to the other, and have declared the same by giving and receiving of a ring, and by joining of hands; I pronounce that they be man and wife together, in the name of the Father, and of the Son, and of the Holy Ghost. Amen."

When the ceremony ended, Will turned to her. Something tender unfurled in his chest as he gazed upon his wife. "Mrs. Darcett, I believe you are the most breathtaking bride in all of England."

"You look beautiful," Georgette said after the wedding breakfast at Ashdown House.

"Thank you. Please call upon me soon," Amy said. "I will miss you."

"I will call after a decent interval." Georgette kissed the air by her cheek. "I wish you happy."

Afterward, Amy fingered the gold band on her finger. It felt a bit heavy, but she knew she would grow accustomed to it. After all of her worrying and a largely sleepless night, she'd felt calm upon the conclusion of the ceremony. She'd worried for years that she would end up a spinster; now she was married. Her skin tingled a little as she recalled the tender look in Will's eyes and the words he'd said. *Mrs. Darcett, I believe you are the most breathtaking bride in all of England.* Her husband had made her feel pretty for the first time in her life.

Georgette disappeared into the crowd when William approached. He took Amy's hand and fingered the wedding ring. "You didn't eat much."

"I suppose I'm too distracted." In truth, she was nervous, but she didn't want him to know.

"Ah, here are my friends," Will said. "Amy, may I introduce Bellingham, better known as Bell, and Fordham."

"Better known as useless but loyal," Fordham said with a bow.

Amy laughed. "It is a pleasure to meet you, Lord Bellingham and Mr. Useless."

"I like her already," Fordham said, laughing.

She noticed Bell was far more reserved than Fordham. Amy found the way he studied her a bit disconcerting, but she thought it must just be his way. "After Will and I are settled, you must both come to dinner. I wish to know his friends better."

Fordham winked at her. "Will you serve roast beef and Yorkshire pudding?"

"Is that a badly disguised request?" She wondered how anyone could resist Fordham.

"Please?" Fordham said with a grin.

Amy smiled at Will. "Should I say yes?"

"You had better or he'll not stop begging," Will said.

After his friends left, she took Will's arm. "Let us make a circuit of the room and greet everyone."

There were a great many guests, including the Duke and Duchess of Shelbourne as well as the Marquess and Marchioness of Boswood. Amy made a point of introducing Bernice, Eugenia, and Cecile to Will.

"Congratulations," Eugenia said. "We are all very happy for you."

Will caught Amy's eye. "I'll give you a moment with your friends."

Her heart softened. He'd understood she needed to speak to them. When Amy turned to her friends, they each hugged her. "You surprised us," Cecile said.

"I imagine you're aware of the circumstances. I'm very sorry I wasn't able to call on you," she said, fighting back her sorrow over the way she'd treated them. "I have missed you."

"Do not tear up," Bernice said. "This is your wedding day, and we want you to be happy, Amy."

Amy inhaled. "You are right, and someday I will attend your weddings."

When Will returned, Amy hugged each of her friends once more, and then she took her husband's arm. After they had spoken to almost everyone, Will took her hands. "Are you ready to leave?" he asked.

She nodded, though she wasn't ready at all. "I wish to say good-bye to my parents."

"Let me escort you to them," he said.

"Mama, I will miss you," Amy said.

Her mother hugged her. "Be happy, Amy."

She would try, with all her heart, to find happiness in this marriage.

Amy's father took her arm. "I can't believe my little girl is all grown up and married now."

She hugged him hard. "I love you, Papa."

"We will miss you," Mama said.

Her papa removed his spectacles and polished them. She saw a suspicious sheen in his eyes.

"I will come to see you as soon as I am able, Papa."

"You are married now, but we hope you will be able to come home on occasion." He shook Will's hand. "Take good care of my little girl."

"I will, sir," he said.

She hugged her mother and father once more. Then she took Will's arm and soon they were emerging from the grand doors. Excitement tugged at her heart. She was married. Really and truly married.

An open carriage awaited them. Will threw coins for the children. And then he sat beside her and kissed her as the carriage rolled away.

Will led her to the cottage. "In Wales, the bride is always carried over the threshold for luck."

"I'm no dainty miss." The enormity of marrying him rushed over her. Once again, she felt as if this weren't really happening, that somehow she would awake to find it all just a strange dream.

When the butler opened the door, Will lifted her in his arms.

She gasped, making him chuckle.

"You may be tall, but you're light."

She wrapped her arms round his neck. Her face heated as Will stepped over the threshold. While she felt she mustn't take his charming ways to heart, she was a little undone by his romantic gesture.

He set her down in the foyer. They walked into the great hall, where the servants had lined up for inspection. There was Saunders, the butler, and Jenkins, the valet. Mrs. Beasley, the housekeeper, was a robust woman. Anna, the lady's maid, curtsied. A footman, three maids, the cook, two scullery maids, and two sturdy laundry women made up the rest of the servant staff.

The housekeeper offered to show them about the place.

"Perhaps tomorrow," Amy said. "I think I will be better able to concentrate then."

"Yes, of course, Madame."

Her world tipped sideways again at being addressed as Madame. She was no longer Amy Hardwick. She was Mrs. Darcett. Why did it feel as if she were losing her own identity?

Will led her upstairs and opened a door. "This is your bedchamber."

Anxiety knotted in her chest at the sight of the bed. She looked out the window. Her stomach felt jittery when she thought of what would happen in that bed tonight. He was her husband, but he was little more than an acquaintance.

"If you prefer something different than the blue bedding, you may change it," he said.

"I like the blue counterpane and blue bed hangings very well." She walked over to the desk and looked out the window. "The view of the trees is soothing, and the light is good for my sketches." Her words sounded flat and superficial to her own ears.

He joined her by the window. She caught her breath as he removed the gold bandeau and set the lace veil on her shoulders. He ran his fingers lightly all along her jaw. Then he took her hands in his and fingered the gold band on her finger.

He tipped her chin up and kissed her briefly on the lips. Afterward, she looked out the window again, and he suspected she was more than a little nervous about their wedding night.

"The weather is fine. Would you like to walk?" he asked.

"Yes, I would like that very much. I must change first."

He pointed at the connecting door. "Knock when you're ready."

She hoped the walk would lessen her anxiety.

He held her hand as he led her along the path. His palm was warm, and his hand engulfed hers. She ought to feel reassured, but all she felt was a horrible panic building up inside her once again.

The path turned, and massive oaks formed a canopy of branches and leaves. She could not fully appreciate the rustic scenery when she was riddled with apprehension about her future.

Over the years, she'd envisioned how it would feel to marry. She'd imagined feelings of euphoria upon hearing a man declare his love for her. More than anything else, she'd wanted a happy union like her parents'. Marriage was supposed to be a holy bond, but the only bond she shared with Will was the resignation that they must marry to save their reputations.

She must stop dwelling on the negative aspects. There was no going back now. They were bound by holy matrimony for the rest of their lives, and she was determined to try to make the best of things. Perhaps if they conversed, she wouldn't feel so nervous. "The shade must be nice in the summer." The words sounded inane to her, but she'd needed to say something.

He adjusted his stride to accommodate her. "I like that you walk rather than mince like so many women."

She smiled tentatively at him. The spring breeze was a little cool, and she was glad that she'd donned her blue spencer. At any rate, it looked very well paired with her sprigged muslin gown. Of course, he wouldn't notice.

They walked for a while, and then he turned to her. "Are you always this quiet?"

His question felt like a criticism, but she remembered what Georgette had said. "Do I strike you as aloof?"

"No, you strike me as thoughtful. What are you thinking?"

I'm terrified because we are strangers to each other. She would not voice the words, for it would not help matters. Instead she would focus on him. "Tell me a little about yourself."

"I traveled for many years and only returned to England last summer for my brother's wedding."

"Will you tell me about your journeys?"

"My friend Bellingham and I traveled through Paris and Italy with no idea if we would find lodgings or not. I grew accustomed to making do in all sorts of circumstances," he said. "But the adventures made up for any small hardships."

"Give me a specific example of how you made do," she said.

"Once, the servant girl in our lodgings got ill, and there was none other to be had, because the rain was pouring. I figured it couldn't be too difficult to make a pot of tea. Four tries later, I managed to produce tea that wasn't full of leaves." He grinned. "I even taught myself to cook eggs." He grinned. "If we're ever in need, I am capable of feeding us tea and eggs."

She smiled. "That is a relief."

"The best part of traveling is meeting people from all walks of life. You learn to appreciate their talents and their trades. Our clothing and coin marked us as men of wealth, but we didn't advertize our aristocratic origins so that others wouldn't fawn over us. It's not something I can experience in England, where I'm known."

Aristocrats rarely mingled with those they considered to be inferior, though there were exceptions, such as Brummel. Her family was considered part of the landed gentry. For her sake, her parents had kept the source of their fortune a secret. They had wanted her to reach as high as possible in society. Given what he'd said, he probably wouldn't care that her grandfather had been a shopkeeper, but she suspected other members of his family would disapprove.

"You loved traveling," she said.

"Those days are over."

She paused as the realization set in. "Because of me."

"No. My family objected."

"You weren't ready to give it up," she said.

"A grand tour usually lasts one year. I spent four abroad."

She didn't miss the implication. He had not wanted to stay in England. But what had held him back? Had he succumbed to family pressure? Or was there another reason he'd agreed to stop traveling?

"I accepted a position as my brother's land steward."

"How do you like it?"

"I haven't begun yet. Look, there's the oak with the tree house ahead," he said. "Let's make a run for it."

She never had a moment to protest, because he took off. When he stopped, she clapped her hand to her chest, because she was a little out of breath.

He wasn't at all. "Look," he said, pointing up to the branches.

She saw the ladder and the little wooden house in the tree. "I've never seen one before."

He shed his coat and handed it along with his hat to her. "Be ready. I'll hand down something to you. All right?"

"Yes," she said, wondering what in the world he meant to retrieve.

Then he climbed the ladder nailed into the tree as if he'd done it hundreds of times before. She supposed he probably had.

Amy drew closer to the tree. "I'm here if you wish to drop something to me."

He poked his head out. "Very well."

She caught a blanket.

He looked down. "I confess I put it up here earlier. We need something to sit on so you don't ruin your pretty skirts," he said. "Step back. I'm climbing down with a basket."

She gasped as he swung out with a basket on his arm. "Be careful. You don't want to fall."

He chuckled.

She held her breath, but she needn't have worried. He was sure of foot and athletic. Her husband was strong and far more muscular than most of the gentlemen of her acquaintance.

He set the basket down and beckoned her with his hand. She went to him and held the basket while he shook out the blanket over the grass. After he removed his coat, he helped her to kneel. He took out two wineglasses and a bottle. Grinning, he uncorked it. "Hold the glasses for me so I don't spill."

"What is this?" she said, smiling.

"Wine for our private celebration." He poured. "A toast to our marriage."

She clinked her glass to his. While she sipped the wine, she thought it rather sweet of him to plan this little outing.

"Bell and I used to sit along the Seine and dine on a simple meal of bread, ham, cheese, and wine." He drank. "Like peasants."

"Did you keep a journal or make drawings?" she asked.

"No." He tapped his head. "It's all here."

"Were you not afraid that you would forget?"

"I have an excellent memory, but you probably would

have drawn pictures of all the ladies in their French finery," he said.

"Perhaps I'll draw you," she said.

He set his wineglass aside, rolled on his side, and propped his head in his hand. "How do you like this pose?"

She smiled a little. "Is this indolent pose representative of you?"

"At the moment, yes."

She sipped her wine and set it on the grass.

He reached for her hand. "I have a confession."

She looked at him warily and wondered if he were about to tell her something he ought to have admitted before he'd proposed.

"I want to kiss you."

She wet her lips and realized only afterward that it had been an unconscious act. "Oh."

He sat up and took her bonnet off. Then he cupped her face. His scent enveloped her as he gazed into her eyes. He angled his head and kissed her. When he touched his tongue to her lips, she opened for him. She knew what to expect and liked the way he tasted her slowly and then with more intention.

Then he was urging her to lie down with him.

"Will?"

"Mmm," he said, slipping one button free on her spencer.

She caught his hand. "We shouldn't."

He threaded his fingers through hers. "Amy, no one ever comes this way. We're safe from prying eyes."

She sat up, put her feet on the blanket, and wrapped her arms round her shins. They were married, but she didn't feel comfortable at all. Acting on desire without any emotional attachment felt wrong.

He sat beside her and crossed his legs. "What is it?"

"Until today, I did not know your middle name," she said.

"I'm not following the logic."

"Don't you see? I barely know anything about you," she said. "Everything has rushed by too fast for me. I do not know your favorite color or if you prefer tea to coffee. I don't know if you're an early riser like me or not. I know about one incident in your childhood, thanks to your sisters. I met your friends only at our wedding today. A week ago, neither of us could have foreseen any of this." She paused and added, "It is as if we've gone about this backward."

"What happened can't be changed," he said. "I thought you had accepted that fact when you agreed to marry me."

"You don't understand."

He let out a long sigh. "No, I don't."

"In the normal course of things, you would have called upon me. We might have taken walks or drives in the park. We would have talked about things that mattered." She looked at him. "We are little more than acquaintances."

"Let me see if I have this correct. You're overset because I did not court you."

Misery flooded her heart. She'd been forced to give up her dream of romance, and he didn't understand the importance to her. "I should have said nothing."

"Amy, tell me what is really troubling you?"

She turned away. "You were right about one thing. This is not what I'd planned."

"What did you plan?" he asked.

"The same thing all little girls dream about: a handsome, dashing prince who declares his undying love." She looked up at the leaves overhead and huffed. "I feel utterly foolish for admitting that to you."

"Is it the physical intimacy that scares you?"

"I need to know you first. I need to feel something for you, other than sheer terror that we may find ourselves utterly incompatible," she said.

He pulled up a blade of grass. "I'm a rake, not a prince, and our marriage will not be the fairy tale you dreamed about."

She whipped her face away, because she didn't want him to see how much his words hurt.

He remained silent for several minutes, and then he spoke in a gruff voice. "If it is important to you, I will grant your wish and court you."

Stunned, she turned her gaze to him. "Thank you."

"I don't want this to go on indefinitely," he said. "There are so many strikes against us. A marriage in name only would be the death knell."

"I agree," she said. "I just need a little time."

After a few moments, his mouth curved in a lopsided grin. "We need to establish the ground rules."

"Rules?" she said, frowning. "That is unnecessary. You need only bring me flowers, and we will talk, so that we can learn more about each other."

"No, that's too easy," he said. "If we're to enjoy this courtship, then it must be challenging. I propose a wedding wager."

"A wager?"

"You have only pin money, so it wouldn't be sporting to make the prize monetary. I have something else in mind."

She smoothed over her expression. *He does not need to know the truth about my designs.* She'd taken no money yet, but the compensation would be a safeguard, in the event he turned out to be a wastrel. Amy had misgivings starting out her marriage with this deception, but this was a marriage of convenience, something she must never forget.

"The duration is a fortnight, starting today," he said.

"Four weeks," she countered.

"Three," he said. "That's my final offer."

"Very well," she said. "What are the terms?"

"If I win you over with my courtship, you agree to stay abed with me and do my every bidding for an entire week." He ran his finger over her bottom lip. "Every bidding."

Her face heated. "What do you mean by winning me over?"

"You'll succumb to my touch and beg me to make love to you."

"Ha! You might as well cede defeat now, because that will never happen."

"I can show you pleasures you've never dreamed existed," he said.

She'd managed to resist the devil's temptation for the most part and figured she had the advantage. "In order to win in this courtship, you must prove that you've mended your wicked ways."

"What?" he said in an outraged voice.

"Those are my terms. It will not be a real courtship if you're spending the bulk of your time engaged in vice and depravity." She regarded him with a smug expression. "You should know I will have spies to ensure that you do not cheat." She had no idea how she would procure spies, but she'd figure it out.

"Me, cheat? Oh, that's a low accusation."

"I'm only giving you fair warning," she said. "And if you fail to meet the terms, I win three more weeks of courtship."

"You assume I'll fail, but I won't."

"You'll have to prove it to me," she said.

"You drive a hard bargain, wife, but I will agree to the terms on one condition."

She regarded him suspiciously. "What condition?"

"Kisses are allowed," he said.

She liked kissing him. "Agreed."

"All sorts of kisses," he said.

She narrowed her eyes. "Define all sorts of kisses."

His low, wicked laughter called to the wanton inside her, but she must resist.

He kissed her cheek and whispered, "I can kiss you anywhere."

"We must remain clothed."

He took her hands and kissed her wrists. "Clothing includes nightgowns and shifts as well," he said, "and we can touch."

"Agreed, but we must keep our clothing on." He would be limited by her clothing. Wouldn't he?

He smiled. "Very well. But there is one other condition."

"You're making it too complicated."

"There is nothing complicated about admiring my own bride. I may not touch you when you're *completely* naked, but I can look."

She gasped. "No."

"Yes," he said. "The advantage will be yours, because I'll be frustrated." He paused and added, "You're allowed to look at me naked, so long as you don't touch."

Her face flamed. "You mean to trick me. I know it."

"Tricks are allowed," he said. "My strategy will be to seduce you."

She lifted her chin. "I might ravish you."

"My wicked wife, do you know how to ravish a rake?" he said, his voice rumbling.

"I may lack experience, but I'm clever enough to figure it out."

He flopped back on the blanket. "Take me, I'm yours."

She burst out laughing.

He beckoned her with his fingers. "Come lie next to me. I want to kiss you."

"You're already failing at courtship," she said. "The idea is to woo me, not demand kisses."

He turned on his side, picked a dandelion from the grass and started plucking the lance-shaped petals. "She loves me. She loves me not. She loves me. She loves me not." He grinned at her. "How am I doing so far?"

"So far, you have managed to charm me."

"That's a good start." He discarded the dandelion and crawled over to her. "Now can I have a kiss?"

"You will have to wait until tonight."

"Please," he said. "Just once more."

She almost said yes, but he apparently liked challenges. And she liked having the upper hand. Amy glanced at him from the corner of her eye and said, "Tonight."

They dined on lobster, among other courses, that evening. He'd seated her next to his place at the head of the table and told her stories of his mischievous exploits at Eton. Apparently, he'd befriended Fordham and Bellingham there.

"I met Bellingham only briefly," Amy said, "but he seems a very intense gentleman."

"He was a devil-may-care fellow until he lost all his family to consumption four years ago."

Amy gasped. "Oh, how awful."

"I worried about him. The traveling helped." Will looked at her. "It was a different world altogether, and what you leave behind sort of fades. I don't know if that makes sense or not."

She nodded. "I think I can understand on a lesser scale. The spring season is such a fanciful whirl, and every year when it ends, I feel a little disappointed upon returning home where the pace is so much slower. Eventually one adjusts again." She looked at him. "It must be far more pronounced with different languages and new sights to see all the time."

"You do comprehend," he said. "Bell needed to focus his attention away from England and the tragedy. Otherwise, I fear he might have gone mad."

"You are a good friend to him," Amy said.

"Well, I had my own reasons for leaving England," he said.

She meant to ask him what he meant, but the desserts arrived.

Will grinned. "Pistachio ices."

After the footman left, Will spooned up the confection. "Open for me."

"I'm not an infant who needs to be fed," Amy said.

"No, you're all woman," he said. "Now open for me."

She let him spoon the ice into her mouth. Then he captured her lips in a decadent tongue kiss. Her head was spinning from the combination of the cold confection and the warmth of his mouth.

When he lifted his mouth, his eyes held a sultry expression. He handed her the spoon, and she understood what he wanted. She spooned the dessert into his mouth as he caught the back of her head. She met his mouth and tentatively touched her tongue to his. He quickly became the aggressor. Excitement raced through her veins, and every instinct within her wanted more of his kisses, more of him.

He stood and pulled her chair back. When she rose, he gazed into her eyes, mesmerizing her. He slid one finger featherlike all along her jaw, leaving a tingling sensation. Then he offered his arm. When she clasped his sleeve, her thoughts scattered. She was all too aware of the scent of his wool coat and the strength of his arm.

"I want to change into something comfortable. May I come to your room in half an hour?" he asked. "I wish to begin courting you tonight."

She regarded him warily. "The rules apply."

"I will abide by them," he said in a low voice that made her more than a little breathless. He knew exactly what he was doing, but she refused to let him win her over until he'd proven he was reformed.

"What is this sly expression?" he asked as he led her up the stairs.

"You have nothing to be suspicious about. I, too, intend to abide by the rules."

When he opened her door, she stepped through. He blew her a kiss and said, "May the best mate win."

Half an hour later, her maid, Anna, finished braiding Amy's hair. After the maid left, Amy slipped on a white linen robe over her shift and reclined on the chaise longue with her sketchbook. The fire made the room just toasty enough for comfort. The mantel clock struck the hour. Her gaze flew up to it, and then the connecting door sighed open.

She looked over her shoulder, and for a moment she couldn't breathe.

He wore only a brown banyan robe over trousers and no shirt. Black hair liberally dusted his chest. He held a book. "May I join you?" he asked.

"Yes, of course." She felt a little embarrassed clothed only in her thin nightgown and robe. When she started to sit up, he shook his head and pressed her back. "There's enough room for both of us."

"It will be a tight fit," she said.

He took her sketchbook and set it aside. "You can work tomorrow. It's our wedding night."

She'd only wanted to keep occupied, so she wouldn't be nervous, though there was no reason for it, given their wager.

When he put his knee on the cushion, she had no choice but to move over.

He lay beside her and grinned. "We're perfectly snug."

Those were not words she'd expected from a rake. She looked at the book. "You intend to read to me?"

He nodded. "It is a poem that I thought you might like."

She suspected some ridiculous trick, such as a naughty limerick, but she said nothing.

He turned the pages. "Ah, here it is. 'The Passionate Shepherd to His Love.'"

"Christopher Marlowe," she said.

He kissed her lips quickly and then began to read.

"'Come live with me, and be my love; and we will all the pleasures prove...'"

Amy listened to him read the familiar lines in his deep, distinctive voice, and she couldn't help admiring her handsome husband. He had full lips and sharply defined cheekbones and jaw. But his eyes were the most arresting feature, because of his thick lashes and dark brows. She noticed a tiny scar by his right brow and wondered how he'd gotten the injury.

His voice mesmerized her. She thought it rather sweet of him to choose the pastoral poem. Then again, she'd better not take any of his efforts to woo her seriously. He was determined to win this wager and admitted he intended to use trickery if necessary. No doubt he thought to lull her and then make his move. He probably planned to seduce her, but she would not let him.

" 'Then live with me, and be my love,' " he said, closing the book.

"You read very well," she said.

He set the book on the floor and clasped her hand. "Tell me about your childhood."

"You're only asking because I insisted it must be part of the courtship for us to get to know each other."

"You're my wife. I am curious about you."

"There isn't much to tell," she said.

"You must have played with other children. What were your favorite games?"

"I had a friend in the neighborhood named Susan. We played with my dolls."

When he smiled, his eyes crinkled a little at the corners. "You pretended to be mothers."

"Yes. I had an imaginary husband named Laurence Lancelot."

When he laughed, she pushed on his shoulder to no

avail. "I thought it an elegant name. Of course, he looked like a prince with golden hair. He also rode a white steed and carried a lance."

"Laurence Lancelot and his lance." Will laughed. "Was it a long lance?"

"Oh, very."

He guffawed.

"What is so funny?" she said.

"Nothing," he said. "So did your imaginary Prince Laurence Lancelot kiss you?"

"Oh, yes. I substituted a pillow for Laurence."

He smiled. "What else?"

"He kneeled at my feet and regularly declared his undying love for me. Unfortunately, he was often called away to fight battles for the king. I wrote him love letters and asked my papa to post them."

"Let me guess. Your papa answered them."

"How did you know?"

"I met your father. He clearly adores his little girl."

She bit her lip. "I didn't realize how much I missed my parents until they came to London."

"I'll take you to see them before autumn," he said. "Who taught you to draw?"

"I had a wonderful governess. She encouraged me to draw and paint with watercolors."

"She recognized your talent," he said. "Even I, who know nothing about women's fashions, can see that your creations are stunning. The night of Lady Beresford's ball, I noticed the striking green ribbons on your gown when you walked inside. Everyone was watching you."

At first, she took pleasure in his compliment, but guilt quickly followed. She was deceiving him about the money she would earn from providing designs to Madame DuPont.

He touched her nose. "Are you afraid I will object to you designing gowns?"

"I didn't know how you would feel about it, but I won't let it interfere with my household duties," she said.

"I wouldn't care if it did," he said. "I like having a fashionable wife."

Drat. Why did he have to be so nice about it? Now she felt even guiltier, but she mustn't show it.

He leaned over her, and her heart beat a bit faster. When he kissed her, she parted her lips slightly. He gently touched his tongue to hers, and when he retreated, he angled his head in the other direction, repeating the pattern. She dared to kiss him back. It was exhilarating to taste him and run her fingers through his silky hair.

When he came up for air, his eyes were darker and a bit glazed. He took her hand and placed it on his hard chest. His heart was pounding. She gazed into his eyes. "Is this a trick?"

"No. I'm still clothed, for the most part. Besides, you have to succumb to my touch in order for me to win."

"In that case..." She ran her hands over his muscular chest and abdomen. As she feathered her fingers over him, she noticed an arrow of dark hair just below his navel. Her gaze traveled to his trousers, and her eyes popped wide open. Good heavens, she could see a bulge in his trousers—a very large bulge.

His eyes were closed, and his breathing grew faster.

"Will? What are you doing?"

"Trying very hard, pardon the pun, not to lose the wager."

"Oh."

He opened his eyes. "We could forget about the wager and the first two courses and move on to dessert."

"No, we will not forget the wager, and I know you're not actually referring to food. The terms stand as agreed," she said.

He stood and helped her to rise. Then he pulled her braid over her shoulder and untied the ribbon.

"My hair will tangle when I sleep if I don't keep it braided," she said.

He met her gaze. "I want to see it down."

How could she deny his request when he had agreed to court her? She reached to loosen the braid, but he caught her hand.

"Let me." He unraveled the strands slowly. When he finished, he combed his fingers through her hair. He arranged the heavy locks over her shoulders and brushed her breasts with his fingers.

She caught her breath at the pleasurable sensation, drawing his attention.

"I like that it's red," he said.

She looked at him dubiously, but he continued to comb his fingers through her locks.

"Promise me something," he said.

"What is it?"

"Never cut it."

She recalled Lizzy telling her that gentlemen preferred long hair and decided she would grant his wish. "Very well."

"And one last request," he said. "On the day we finally make love, I want you to brush your hair over my skin."

His seductive tone left her yearning for his touch, but she needed more from him than physical pleasure.

He pulled her into his arms. When his hands slid to her bottom, he pressed her against him. She could feel the hard ridge of his sex against her stomach. Then he kissed her quickly. "I'd better leave," he said. "I want you too much."

For a moment, her heart leaped, but the feeble hope died as she realized that for him, it was only about pleasure.

He led her to the bed, where Anna had turned down the covers. When Amy climbed beneath them, he picked up the spare pillow. "You are not allowed to kiss Laurence."

She laughed.

He kissed her cheek, snuffed the candles, and opened the door.

Temptation to call him back gripped her for a second, and then her good sense prevailed.

"Good night," he said.

The door clicked shut.

He'd made her smile over his silly jest about Laurence.

She stared up at the unfamiliar canopy. Tonight, she'd sworn to be on her guard, and yet she'd fallen for his charms once again. He'd read her the pretty poem and beguiled her when he'd asked her never to cut her hair. At times, he'd seemed sincere, but she lacked the objectivity to discern between the charming rake and the man beneath the façade. The latter troubled her the most. Earlier today, he'd mentioned his family disapproved of his traveling, and then he'd distracted her. Perhaps she was making too much of it, but her instincts told her there was more to the story.

She realized she'd ceded something to him already. He'd won another little corner of her heart, and it scared her. She mustn't forget that he saw the courtship only as a game that he meant to win. He was a rake, through and through. If he won, he would lose interest quickly, and then he would likely betray her.

Amy bit her lip. He was her husband, and she'd told him that she would do everything in her power to see to his comfort and happiness. But she mustn't let herself fall in love with him, because he would surely break her heart.

Twenty minutes later, Will washed and climbed into bed. He'd been hard as a rock and had done what all men did to relieve the lust when there was no willing partner available.

He climbed into bed and clasped his hands beneath his head. This afternoon, she'd turned her face away when he'd told her that their marriage would not be the fairy tale she'd dreamed about. His damned conscience had pricked him. He'd agreed to court her, because it was their wedding day, and she'd looked so forlorn.

I need to feel something for you, other than sheer terror that we may find ourselves utterly incompatible.

Immediately afterward, he'd regretted his decision, because he'd known she wanted something from him that he wasn't capable of giving. He'd proposed the wager, with the expectation she would refuse. She'd risen to the challenge and surprised him.

He had the gnawing feeling that she'd played him like a pianoforte.

Will had known what she wanted—a relationship based on tender feelings. There had been women in his past who had stated they wanted only a liaison, but at some point, they would start to cling. He'd always made a graceful exit and never looked back.

Will shoved the memories of his former paramours back into the farthest corners of his brain. He meant to win the wager and had gotten off to an excellent start. She'd been skittish, but he'd managed to put her at ease and make her laugh. As for reforming, he figured he could avoid the usual rakehell lures for three weeks. He rather looked forward to seducing his wife. Granted, he would likely be frustrated, but the anticipation would undoubtedly increase her desire and his as well. He grinned as he thought about the wicked plans he had in store for her.

When that third week ended, he would gradually distance himself. He grew bored quickly and knew that his desire for Amy would eventually burn to embers. For her sake, he would be discreet about his liaisons. Given the circumstances of their marriage and his reputation, she probably expected him to be unfaithful.

He was fooling himself. Amy was no mouse. She would not overlook a liaison the way so many other wives of the ton did. The thought arrested him. What would happen if he ultimately failed, as he no doubt would, to give her what she wanted?

He tried to dismiss the implications, but they hung over his head like a thundercloud.

Chapter Nine

The bathwater was luxuriously warm, and the scent of the rose soap was divine. Anna added more warm water to the bath, and Amy leaned back in the hip tub. For the first time since she'd found herself locked in the wine cellar, she felt relaxed. "Anna, you might as well go on about your duties. I wish to enjoy the water until it cools."

After Anna left the bathing room, Amy let her thoughts drift. She was lethargic, likely a result of the anxiety that had plagued her for days. She closed her eyes and must have dozed, because the click of the door closing startled her. When she turned her head, she found Will watching her.

Her face grew hot, and she covered her breasts with her hands.

His boots clipped on the marble floor until he stood over her. "You're naked."

"You might knock," she said.

"I'm allowed to see you naked." His gaze swept over her body. "Stand up."

"Please return to my room. I'll meet you there after I dry off and put on a robe."

He shook his head. "I intend to watch."

"You're embarrassing me," she said.

"I'm your husband. You'd best accustom yourself to being naked in my presence. At the end of three weeks, you'll be spending a great deal more time naked in bed with me."

"If you win," she said.

"Oh, I will."

"You're failing at courtship," she said, desperate to be rid of him. Oh, she wished he would leave and give her privacy. The water had cooled, but she couldn't make herself get out of the bath with him watching.

"I'm abiding by the rules," he said. "You ought to thank me. No other husband would let his bride stay chaste on their wedding night."

She didn't doubt it, but she refused to let him win that argument. "Our situation is irregular. We would never have married if not for the scandal."

"You have chill bumps on your arms. Get out of the bath before you freeze."

"Not until you leave."

"Very well, but you will lose the wager," he said.

"No, I will not."

"Yes, you will, because you're not abiding by the established rules. But that's perfectly fine with me. I'm more than eager to take you to bed this morning."

"You do not care about my tender sensibilities," she said.

He took out his watch. "You have two minutes to get out of that bath or you lose the wager."

"That was not part of the agreement," she said.

"One minute," he said.

She stood and climbed awkwardly out of the tub. Then she grabbed a towel, intending to cover herself with it, but she dropped it.

He bent to retrieve it, and his gaze traveled up her legs. Then he smiled when he looked at her sex. "Red," he said.

"The towel, if you p-please," she said.

He rose and gave it to her. "You're shivering."

She applied the towel as quickly as she could. Her face burned the entire time. Then he handed her the robe. She slid her arms into the sleeves and tied the sash.

When he reached for her, she marched past him. Oh, she was furious with him.

He followed her into the bedchamber. "I did not break the rules."

"You are a cad," she said. "You did not care that I was embarrassed."

"Do you care that I'm frustrated? Do you care that I wanted desperately to make love to you last night?"

"You agreed to the rules," she said.

"So did you."

"I wish I'd never..." She closed her mouth before she said something she would regret.

"Never what, Amy?"

"Forget I said anything." She'd almost told him she wished she'd never married him. It was a petulant thing to even think, and she was ashamed of herself.

"No. Finish what you started," he said.

She looked at him. His expression was severe. "Will, I suspect you came here looking to start a row."

He shook his head. "I picked wildflowers for you this

morning and hoped to find you still in bed. I'd planned to order a tray sent up for us."

She saw the bouquet of dandelions in a vase sitting on the night table and winced.

"When I heard the sound of water, I came to you. I can't have what I want until I prove I'm worthy of you—"

"Will—"

"No, let me finish. All I wanted was to look at my bride."

"Will, I'm modest." She couldn't tell him that she'd feared he would look upon her and find her wanting. Her breasts were small, and she was too thin. Worst of all, she'd feared he would compare her to all the beautiful women he'd taken to bed. No doubt he was disappointed after his first glimpse of her body.

He took her hands. "I suppose I've got a black mark today."

She lowered her eyes. "Thank you for the flowers."

He lifted her face. "At the risk of earning another black mark, I'll admit something to you."

Her pulse quickened, wondering what he meant to say.

"Do you recall when I told you that I watched you walking in the Beresfords' ballroom?"

She frowned. "Yes."

"You were so tall and regal in that gown. I imagined then that you must have long, shapely legs." He grinned. "I was right."

She looked into his eyes, stunned that he was pleased with her.

"I suppose I shouldn't mention what else I wondered."

"Now you must tell me," she said.

"Well, I believe I mentioned it when you got out of the bath."

She blushed, remembering the one indecorous word he'd uttered: *red*. "Do you ever stop thinking about—that?"

He grinned. "That what?"

"Making love," she said.

"Sweetheart, I'm a man. You would be appalled if you knew how much we think about—that."

"You're trying to pull the wool over my eyes."

He pulled her into his embrace. Good heavens, he was aroused.

"We're clothed," he said. "In case you want to touch me."

He smelled so good—like sandalwood, starch, and him. "I don't know." He was a little too eager, and she was far from unaffected by his embrace. If she didn't watch out, he'd win the wager, and all her hopes of kindling tenderness between them would die out.

"If you'll be sweet to me, I'll be sweet to you," he said.

She found it difficult to resist his charm, and he was trying. "Tonight," she said. "First course, only, with clothing."

He gave her a dazzling smile. "I'll count the hours."

"Speaking of hours, the servants have probably set out breakfast. We should go downstairs. I'll ring for Anna. After I dress, I'll knock on your door."

"Amy?" he said.

"Yes?"

"I am very determined to win this wager."

She laughed and pushed him away. "Go now, so I can dress."

Georgette clasped Beau's arm as they walked out into the garden. "There's a bench along the row of hedges," she said. The shrubbery was tall enough that it would conceal them from her mother's watchful eye.

The wind riffled his blond hair. "I'm surprised your mother relented and let me walk with you alone," he said.

"Papa told her that she was being too fussy after he caught me moping."

Beau found the bench and sat beside her. "Why were you moping?"

She looked at her lap. "I miss Amy."

"It has been only two days since you saw her at her wedding," he said.

"Everything will change now that she's married. It's the same with Julianne. Now she has an infant and a husband."

He said nothing.

She knew what he was thinking. If she married him, she would join the ranks of her friends. "We were as close as sisters, but it will never be the same again."

"Georgette, I've wondered about something, and I haven't said anything, because it is indelicate."

"Then perhaps you shouldn't say anything."

"I have to know, because I can't stop thinking about it."

She turned her head slightly and let the bonnet hide her anxious expression.

He tugged on the ribbon. She reached to stop him, but he batted her hand away. Then he took off the bonnet. "Look at me while I speak to you."

She met his gaze. He had the most amazingly beautiful blue eyes, but they were clouded today.

"Are you afraid of making love?" he asked.

She averted her gaze. "You are too immodest."

"Georgette, look at me and tell me the truth."

She looked at him, inhaled and exhaled without speaking.

He cupped her cheek. "I knew it."

Her temper flared. "I'd have to be an idiot not to be apprehensive."

He chuckled. "You like it when I kiss you, don't you?"

"Yes," she whispered.

"And I think you liked it when I touched you, although we were both nervous. It's a bit difficult when you're afraid of being caught."

"Beau, that's not the entire reason."

He stiffened as if he expected her to say something that would wound him, and that made her feel awful.

"It isn't you," she said. "I don't like change very much."

"It's a part of life," he said, "and it can be wonderful, if you embrace it."

"I'm two and twenty and afraid of growing up. There, I've admitted that I'm a silly, childish goose."

His lips parted. "Why didn't you just tell me?"

"Because I was embarrassed."

He looked at her thoughtfully. "Your brothers have all married and left home. Your two closest friends have married. And I have been pushing you to let me propose. My guess is you're feeling overwhelmed by all the changes."

"Yes, but now I feel even worse about it, because in comparison to Amy I'm lucky. I cannot even imagine how she's bearing up in such a marriage—to a man she despises."

"One thing at a time," Beau said. "First of all, your fears of change are not all that unusual. It's natural to feel apprehensive about how a change will affect you. Second, you must not feel badly about yourself, because of your friend's difficult situation. I think it's awful that they had to marry, when they were accidentally trapped."

"I fear he will mistreat her," she said.

Beau shook his head. "I won't lie to you. He earned his bad reputation, but I saw the two of them dancing. There were enough sparks between them to catch fire. And she encouraged him afterward, by allowing him to escort her round the ballroom. A number of people remarked about the two of them flirting."

"But he is reputed to be a horrible rake," she said. "I fear he will betray and humiliate her."

"I'm not defending his rakish past, but he comes from a good family," Beau said. "He did not abandon her, and believe me, there are plenty of men who would have done so. The material point is that only they can make their marriage work. There is nothing that you or anyone else can do. For what it is worth, I heard he is to take over as his brother's land steward. Let us hope that this is a sign that he's changing for the better."

"Thank you," she said. "I've been so worried."

He regarded her with a solemn expression. "I never meant to distress you, but I did. My attempts to rush you were selfish and only resulted in you wanting to push back. I hope you will forgive me. From this moment forward, I promise to listen, and will respect your wish to make your own decisions." His jaw clenched. "I hope that you will give me another chance, because I don't want to think about a life without you."

"Beau, thank you. There is no other man I want. I just needed to be sure of my feelings without everyone pushing and prodding me."

He squeezed her gloved hand. "I know. I will give you the time."

All she'd needed was to know that he would respect

her enough to let her make her own choices. She smiled at him. "You know my mother approves of you."

He regarded her as if he were trying to hold back some strong emotion.

"My father told me he likes you."

"I'm honored," he said.

"Beau, I love you with all my heart," she said.

"Oh, God," he said.

"And I didn't say that because my friends are married now. You know I have a mind of my own."

"Yes, I know," he said.

"I love you because you understand my foibles and fears, and also because you're so handsome you dazzle my eyes."

He laughed.

"But mostly, I love you because you understand how I feel and respect that I am capable of making good decisions. I love you because you're patient and kind and you kiss very well."

"I didn't think it possible to love you more, but I do," he said.

"You can kneel," she said. "Oh, never mind. You'll get your trousers dirty."

"I don't give a damn about the dirt," he said, kneeling.

Her eyes welled with tears as he took her hands.

"I love you so much. Please make me the happiest of men and marry me," he said.

"I will marry you," she said.

He rose, drew her to her feet, and gave her a lush kiss that left her breathless. "Your father is home. I want to ask his permission."

"You may," she said. "Mama will be beside herself with

happiness." She gave Beau a sassy grin. "And then I shall shock her by telling her that you proposed in the dirt."

Will came to her room, wearing trousers and the banyan the way he'd done the previous night. "No poetry tonight," he said. "We'll talk instead."

She sat on the chaise with her hands clasped.

"You let your hair down," he said, smiling. His hair was a bit rumpled and there was a bit of stubble along his jaw.

"I wanted to please you."

"I like that you want to," he said, threading his fingers through her long locks.

"I want you to believe that I'm a good wife, and I want you to look forward to seeing me."

"I have an idea. Let us lie on the bed and talk," he said.

She cut her gaze over to the bed. "That might not be the best place."

"Are you reneging on your promise this morning?"

"No, but—"

"Then the bed is the most comfortable place for talking and touching," he said.

She suspected this might prove to be a fatal mistake, but she vowed to keep her virtue mostly intact until she won the wager. "Very well, but you must behave."

He took her hand and led her to the bed. Then he took off his banyan. "You might as well dispense with the robe. We'll be plenty warm beneath the covers."

She rather thought she'd be safer with the extra layer of the robe, but that was ridiculous. He wasn't about to pounce on her and lose the wager.

After she climbed beneath the covers, he followed and

turned on his side. "Amy, why don't you face me? I doubt there's anything interesting on the canopy."

She did feel a frisson of unease, but she turned toward him. "What do you want to talk about?"

"It's your turn to ask questions," he said.

"Well, there is something I realized today. You lost your father several years ago. I tried to imagine how I would feel, and it occurred to me that it must have been a very difficult time for you and your family."

He sighed. "He died of a heart seizure unexpectedly. It was hard on my mother and sisters." They had wanted to draw the whole family closer and talk about his father. His mother had idolized his father as if he'd been a saint.

"How old were you?"

"Seventeen." His mother and sisters had looked to Will for comfort, but he hadn't known how to deal with his own grief, much less theirs. His brother had been equally inept at trying to console them. With more than a little shame, Will recalled being relieved when he'd gone back to school after the mourning period.

"I'm sure your mother and sisters were glad to have your brother there to take over the reins."

Will hesitated. "Hawk had left home years before. He and my father didn't get on very well."

"Did they have a falling out of some sort?"

"My brother got into serious trouble when I was twelve. No one talked about it, but everyone knew something was wrong."

"It must have been painful," she said.

His father had covered up a scandal in the making. Will had only learned the truth in the past year.

"You must have missed your brother," she said.

No one had ever said a damn thing when Marc left home. "I resented my father for driving Marc away, but I was only twelve, and no one would tell me anything."

"Marc?" Amy said.

"My brother didn't acquire the nickname Hawk until after our father's death."

She was silent a moment. "You must have felt torn between your brother and father."

He shrugged. "It happened a long time ago. There's nothing to be done about it now."

Amy suspected the events had affected him far more than he wanted to let on.

"Do you remember seeing Brandon at my brother's wedding?" he asked.

"Oh, yes, your cousin," she said.

"He's not my cousin; he's Marc's son."

Amy inhaled on a sharp breath.

"I didn't know until last summer," he said.

Amy was more than a little stunned. Apparently, his family had hushed up the scandal. Now she and Will had brought more problems into their lives. "At least you and your brother are closer now."

"He's six years older, and I haven't spent much time at home."

Amy wondered if he had traveled for so long to avoid his family and all that they left unsaid. "Your new position will bring you closer to your brother."

"Marc is the head of the family. He tries to be fair to everyone, but that never works."

"I think you have a wonderful family, imperfect as all

families are," she said. "Your sisters were very sweet to me. I look forward to knowing them better."

He sat up. "Be careful of my sisters, Patience in particular."

"What do you mean?" She sat up as well.

"Patience tries to rule over everyone. She seems to think that it's her duty to tell others how to live their lives, and she's not subtle at all about it."

"She's the eldest sister, so it's probably just a habit," Amy said.

He shook his head. "I'm serious, Amy. My family could come between us if you're not careful."

"Will, surely you exaggerate."

"You don't understand. If they get wind of something they don't approve of, they hold family meetings. Hawk as the head of the family brings up the subject, and everyone confronts the problem family member. It's like the Inquisition."

"Will, are you not mistaking genuine concern for meddling?"

"The point is they will nose into our affairs if you give them an inch, and I really want a bit of distance from them. I don't want them interfering, so we won't be spending a great deal of time with them."

Her smile faded as the disappointment set in. "I really want to know your family better."

"Amy, they will intrude if we allow it, and no matter how well-meaning they are, they can cause problems. I want to keep what happens in our marriage as private as possible."

"Of course I will keep our private life private." Did he think she would reveal their intimate conversations?

He released a loud sigh. "I did not mean to insinuate

that you would tell them things that should be private. I mean to warn you to be cautious when speaking about us. I think my sisters expect me to mistreat you. They're looking to pounce, so don't inadvertently give them any ammunition."

She thought about what he'd said for several minutes, and then something occurred to her. Amy hesitated to bring up the matter, but after hearing about the way his family ignored problems, she decided to be honest. "You probably will be angry when I say this, but haven't you given your family cause to expect trouble?"

He shot out of bed. "I can see where your loyalties lie."

She threw back the covers, hopped off the bed, and marched around it until she stood before him. "This has nothing to do with loyalty. You are angry because I spoke the truth."

"I'm angry because you're not taking me seriously. I told you about my family because I don't want them to come between us. God knows, we've got enough problems without adding their fuel to the fire."

"Lower your voice," she said. "I won't let you shout at me."

"Never mind. This isn't going to work tonight." He turned round and stalked over to the door.

"You can't resolve problems by sweeping them under the carpet."

He turned toward her, breathing audibly. For a moment, she was a little intimidated, but if she didn't stand up to him now, he would conclude he could run roughshod over her to get his way. On the other hand, she must not forget his pride. "Will, I understand what you are saying about your family. You are right. I don't know them well."

"Obviously," he said.

She'd been honest with him when she'd said he'd given his family reason to be suspicious. He'd accused her of being disloyal, and now she realized that she'd wounded him.

Amy approached him. "I always wanted brothers and sisters, so to me your family seems wonderful. But you are my husband, and you will always come first. Always. And if anyone ever criticizes you in my presence, I will defend you."

He threw his arms round her and held her tightly. She wondered if anyone had ever defended him before. Amy sensed there was more beneath the surface. His sisters had laughed while telling her about Will running away when he was young. At the time, Amy had seen it as a childish prank, but now she wondered if there had been a reason for it. She would not probe again tonight. He needed the comfort she'd sworn to give him.

She kissed his cheek. "Come back to bed with me. I promised you a first course."

He kissed her neck and inhaled. "I think you should design prettier nightclothes for ladies—something sheer."

"I'm sure others would view it as scandalous." She wondered if his paramours had donned sheer night rails, but she decided never to discuss the women of his past, especially in the bedchamber. No good would come of that subject, and she was better off not knowing the particulars.

"I have a request," he said. "Will you be offended if I remove my trousers? I'm wearing drawers."

"I suppose the drawers count as an article of clothing," she said.

He chuckled and walked with her to the bed. Then he grasped her waist, picked her up, and set her on the mattress. She scrambled beneath the covers, turned on her side, and watched him unbutton the falls of his trousers. He shucked the trousers, kicked them up with his foot, and threw them on the chaise. A ribbon tied his loose-fitting drawers, and he was clearly already aroused.

"Are you always this...amorous?" she said.

"I'm a good soldier and ready to salute you."

She fell back on the mattress, laughing.

He eased inside the covers and lay on his side. "What are you serving for the first course, wife?"

"Kisses?" she said.

He pulled her against his body. She could feel his aroused sex against her stomach.

"Let me have a taste," he said.

He gave her a lush tongue kiss, one that made her breathless and tingly all over. When she reciprocated, he made a rough male sound. "You taste so sweet." He kissed her again. His muscular body emanated heat, and she felt him harden against her stomach.

She placed her palms on his chest and swirled her fingers through the hair there. Then she kissed him where his heart was pounding. She decided to experiment and licked one of his flat nipples.

He inhaled quickly.

She licked the other one.

"Lie back," he said, pressing her into the mattress. Then he untied the drawstring of her night rail and pushed it down her shoulders. He helped her free her arms. Then he cupped her breasts and circled his thumbs over her nipples.

She inhaled on a trembling breath.

"You have sensitive nipples," he said. "I'll be gentle."

She'd no idea what he meant until he bent his head and took her in his mouth. When he suckled her, the most indescribable pleasure flooded her veins. Her back bowed. She reached for his head and threaded her fingers through his thick hair.

He switched to her other breast, and she gave herself up to the heated sensations. She realized she was panting, but she didn't care about anything except the wondrous feelings coursing through her. Gradually, she became aware of dampness between her thighs. She didn't understand what was happening to her body, but she felt hollow inside her most private place. A strange need to be filled engulfed her.

He drew on her nipple, and then he licked it. She opened her eyes to find him looking at her breasts, and once again, she wondered if he found her inadequate.

"Your breasts are beautiful," he said. "They're perfectly shaped."

He could not know how happy he'd made her.

"I want to make love to you so badly," he said. "By the time we do make love, we'll probably burn down the bed."

She laughed. "You say the funniest things."

"Oh, I have plans for that eventful night—actually the entire week."

She turned on her side. "If you win."

"I will."

"Tell me your plans," she said.

He touched her nose. "No, it will be a surprise."

"You already surprised me tonight. I didn't know men suckled women."

"Did you like it?"

"You know I did."

He chuckled. "Ah, well, I'd love to stay, but I don't trust myself."

"I wish you would," she said.

"Are you caving in?" he said in a hopeful tone.

"Absolutely not, but I would love to cuddle with you."

"I won't be able to sleep for wanting you," he said. "And don't think to trick me into losing this wager."

"You still have to prove you're reformed."

He kissed her cheek and got out of bed. "Eighteen more days," he said. "You'd better rest up now, before the weeklong bedding."

She threw a pillow at him, and he dodged.

"Oops, I think you killed Laurence," he said.

She laughed.

"Good night, sweetheart."

She didn't take his endearment to heart, but she did feel they had turned a corner tonight. He'd talked about his family and their issues. There was still much she needed to know about Will in order to fully understand him. But for the first time, she held real hope for their marriage.

All along, she'd been pessimistic, even when she'd vowed to see to his happiness and comfort. Tonight, however, she believed that she'd answered a need within him when she'd told him that he would always come first and that she would defend him.

He'd given her a gift as well, though he didn't know it. She'd been so afraid that he would find her wanting, but he was pleased with her. While she believed that establishing an emotional bond with him was more important, she'd learned tonight that lovemaking was a part of that bond. She'd felt closer to him tonight. He'd given her pleasure and made her laugh.

She dared to hope that in time they might share tender feelings.

Chapter Ten

Amy approved the housekeeper's accounts and met with Cook over the menu. Afterward, she retrieved her sketchbook and went to the parlor to draw additional designs. Yesterday morning, she'd received a letter from Madame DuPont. The dressmaker had congratulated her on her advantageous marriage and wished to know if Amy still intended to provide designs. Amy responded with an affirmative and promised to call with new designs next week.

Will strolled into the parlor. "I hoped you might like to go for a walk with me."

"I will gladly take that walk with you. Let me get my spencer, and I'll join you here in a few minutes."

He squeezed her hand. "Take your time."

She felt a bit guilty about agreeing to take her designs to Madame DuPont next week. She'd not even thought to check with Will first, but it felt silly to ask permission. She acknowledged that much of her guilt resulted from the secret she kept from him. The chances of Will discovering her secret were very small. Only Amy and Madame DuPont knew, and the modiste valued Amy's designs too much to do anything that would put her in jeopardy.

As she walked upstairs, her conscience troubled her. Perhaps she ought to tell him about the compensation, but she ought to have confessed that earlier. Now he would wonder why she'd kept silent. How could she tell him that she didn't trust him? For her, it was simply a matter of protecting herself in the event she found out that he was a wastrel. If he discovered that she'd deceived him, he would view her actions as a betrayal. The chance of that happening was minuscule. Madame DuPont would never say a word, and Amy knew the modiste had already benefitted from featuring her designs.

Her reasons were sound, but she was taking a risk, albeit a small one. The only way he would ever find out was if he incurred a large debt, and in that event, he would have no right to object. Why then did she feel so bad about it?

Because she'd developed a bit of a tendre for him.

He was doing more than making an effort to court her. She remembered how he'd shared a painful part of his life last night, and the way he'd hugged her when she'd told him he would always come first. Now she realized that it wasn't entirely true, because she was putting the money she earned ahead of him.

As Anna helped her into the spencer, Amy told herself not to allow her developing feelings to interfere with her good sense. She must be practical until she knew him better. Even though she believed her decision was sound, she still felt a twinge of unease as she left her bedchamber.

She was halfway down the stairs when the bell rang. Will strode out of the parlor and frowned. "The mail came earlier. It seems we have callers. Deuce take it. You would think people would have the decency to leave us in peace."

Voices sounded in the foyer. Amy stepped onto the marble floor and took Will's arm. Then a familiar squeak drew their attention. Poppet ran across the marble floor and rubbed against Will's legs.

"Poppet, where did you come from?" he said, lifting the kitten in his arms.

Hawk and Julianne walked inside.

"Sorry to disturb you," Hawk said, looking a bit abashed. "Your cat cried for three nights in a row, so I thought we'd better bring her to you."

Julianne hugged Amy. "Are you happy?" she said.

Amy couldn't help blushing. "Yes, I am." She'd uttered the words without thinking, but now she realized that it was true. In spite of her grave misgivings, he had been attentive and fair. Of course, she found him charming. He was at his most irresistible when he was jesting or teasing.

"We won't disturb you any longer," Hawk said.

"Nonsense," Amy said. "At least have a cup of tea with us."

"Are you certain?" Julianne said. "I feel as if we're intruding."

"I insist," Amy said.

They sat in the parlor and Amy served tea.

Julianne grinned. "I know you haven't heard the news, because Georgette's mother thinks it's indelicate to write letters to newlyweds."

"What news?" Amy asked.

"Georgette and Beau are engaged."

"I thought I'd never see the day." Amy smiled. "Oh, I am so happy for her. I wish she and Beau would call."

"Beau is traveling with Georgette and her parents to her aunt Marianne's home in Bath," Julianne said.

"Oh, no," Amy said, laughing. She looked at Will. "Georgette's aunt Marianne drinks vinegar thrice daily, complains constantly about her gout, and has a stinky old hound named Herbert."

"Let us hope Lady Georgette warned Beaufort," Will said.

"Julianne, how is little Emma?" Amy asked.

Julianne beamed. "She laughs now, especially at Marc."

Hawk sighed. "Everyone laughs at me. I can't imagine why."

Poppet jumped on Will's lap. "Ugh, your claws are digging into my trousers," he said, sitting the cat beside him.

"Will, there is no rush," Hawk said, "but when you're ready, I'd like to discuss your duties."

"Do take your time," Julianne said. "You have a honeymoon only once."

Amy exchanged a quick glance with Will. They had not consummated their marriage, and for some reason that fact suddenly loomed large in the room. But what they did or did not do in privacy was no one else's concern.

"Take at least another fortnight," Hawk said.

Amy saw an opportunity and leaped at it. "Actually, I have to take some sketches to the modiste next week. Will, perhaps that would be a good time for the two of you to meet."

Will regarded her with raised brows. "Can't you just have them delivered?"

"I need to consult with her about the fabrics," Amy

said. Oh, dear, she was getting deeper and deeper into her deception. The real reason she needed to visit the shop was to pick up the purse, but she could always do that later. "I'm sorry, Will. There's no rush."

He grinned. "You want to shop."

Julianne laughed. "Oh, I think he already knows you too well, Amy."

"I'm found out." She found it difficult to meet Will's eyes.

"Then it is decided," Will said. "I will call on you next week, Hawk."

"And I will go shopping with Amy," Julianne said.

"That would be lovely," Amy said. She would have to take Madame DuPont aside for the money exchange, and that made her uneasy.

"We had better leave the newlyweds to enjoy their honeymoon," Hawk said.

Amy and Will followed them to the door and waved good-bye.

After the carriage rolled away, Amy turned to Will. "I'm sorry. It was thoughtless of me to arrange to call on the modiste."

"Don't worry. I don't think the meeting with Hawk will take long. I may meet my friends at the club while you're shopping. That way, you won't feel as if you must hurry."

Why did it feel as if they were cutting their honeymoon short? She had no one else to blame but herself. If she'd not opened that invisible door, he wouldn't be meeting his friends. That worried her more than a little, because they were undoubtedly rakes and might influence him.

Rain pattered the walkway. "I suppose we weren't destined to walk today," he said.

She wasn't ordinarily given to superstition, but for some reason, the rain seemed like a bad omen.

Over the next week, Amy discovered new facets to Will. He loved chocolate, despised porridge, and liked baked eggs. One morning, he'd brought the newspaper to the table and then, with an abashed look, apologized for reading at the table, but she didn't mind. That had pleased him. Then, while drinking her tea, she'd noticed him perusing the paper very fast. She'd laughed and said he must be looking for something in particular. He'd shrugged and gone back to his paper. His gaze had sped down one column and then the next equally fast. When she'd questioned him, he'd admitted that he read quickly.

She'd not given it a great deal of thought until one day he walked in while she was frowning over the household accounts. No matter how many times she'd added the long column of figures, she got a different sum every time. Frustrated, she'd asked him to check her arithmetic. He'd not even put pencil to paper. Once again, his gaze flew down the column and then he'd given her the answer. At first, she'd not believed him. Then he told her to turn to a new page and cover the final sum. When she did, he surveyed the long column quickly and gave her the answer. She'd uncovered the sum. He was right.

She'd been amazed, but he'd shrugged it off and told her he'd always learned faster than most people. When she'd insisted that he acknowledge his brilliance, he'd sighed and told her that it had caused problems in school. He grew bored easily, and as a result, he'd resorted to all sorts of mischief.

On Saturday morning, it rained again. She found Will

sitting on the floor in the parlor with the mantel clock. "It stopped," he said.

She frowned at the parts on the carpet. "We could purchase another."

"I'll have it fixed quickly," he said.

She sat on the sofa, watching him. "Your sisters told me that you took up with Gypsies when you were five."

He smiled. "I mended utensils for them and then got caned for running away." He started putting the parts of the clock back together. "When I was a lad, I was curious about the mechanisms of clocks. I went to my father's study, moved the ladder for the bookshelves to the mantel, and carried the clock down. Then I took it apart. It was fascinating to me. My father rapped my knuckles for breaking it. I asked him to let me prove I could put it back together. My father didn't believe I could do it. His face turned purple when I successfully finished the job."

"You got into trouble for being smart." She paused. "Will, why did you run away so often when you were little?"

"I don't remember," he said. "I probably just did it to see if anyone would notice I was gone."

She blinked. "Why wouldn't they notice? Surely your nurse kept a lookout for you."

He shrugged. "I would wait until she fell asleep, and then make my escape."

"I cannot believe your mother did not sack that nurse for incompetence," Amy said. "You might have been hurt."

"The nurse was old and had been with our family since Hawk's birth. At any rate, I was quite naughty. I was the youngest and got under foot."

Amy figured he'd wanted attention and had gotten it by misbehaving.

"I learned to use my brains to avoid trouble, and I also figured out how to charm others into giving me what I wanted. Cook adored me. It's a wonder I didn't get fat from all the biscuits and cakes I wheedled out of her."

"I'm not surprised," she said.

"Oh, you weren't easy to charm. In fact, you were quite the challenge." He grinned at her. "That's the reason I couldn't resist you."

"You liked to tease me only for your own amusement."

"I liked it, because you always had a quick retort. You're clever and very talented as well."

"Are you trying to charm me?" she said, laughing.

"Yes, but I meant it." He stood and put the clock back on the mantel. "Voilà. It's ticking."

She clapped.

The rain drummed the roof. She walked over to the window. The wavy glass distorted the view, but the downpour made it even more difficult to see out. His footsteps thudded on the carpet until he stood behind her.

He wrapped his arms around her waist and nuzzled her neck. "I like thunderstorms."

"They frightened me when I was a child."

The room was dim, and his scent filled her head.

"Come upstairs with me," he said.

"It's daytime," she whispered.

"It's darker now with the rain. And I want to kiss and touch you."

Her heart beat faster. "Very well."

He took her hand and led her upstairs. Then he opened his door.

"What if the servants come in?" she said.

He walked over to the table, picked up a key, and

locked the door. Then he set the key aside and came to her. He stood behind her, unhooked her gown, and untied the tapes. Then he unlaced her stays. She didn't want to think how he'd learned to undress a woman so well, but she knew there had been many others before her. Soon, he'd divested her of everything but her shift, stockings, and slippers.

"Leave the stockings on and kick off the slippers," he said.

She stepped out of her slippers. "Your turn."

He gave her that thousand-candle smile, the one that never failed to make her melt.

She managed to get him out of the tight-fitting coat. He untied his cravat and tossed it on the floor. Then he removed the braces. She unbuttoned his shirt, and he drew it over his head. He took her hands and put them on his trousers. Clearly he wanted her to unbutton the falls.

She smiled and let her fingers brush over the bulge in his trousers. When he let out a ragged breath, she enjoyed knowing she had a certain feminine power over him. She wanted to give him pleasure. And though she knew little of lovemaking, she would experiment and pay attention to his reactions to guide her.

When she finished, he sat on the edge of the bed and pulled his boots off. He stood and pulled off his trousers, leaving only his drawers. "We're going to start with the first course and then proceed to the second one."

Amy felt a bit nervous. "What will be served in the second course?"

"I'll show you. It may shock you a bit, but you'll like it."

"Tell me first," she said.

He shook his head, stripped back the covers, and lifted

her onto the mattress. Afterward, he stepped between her thighs and pushed down the layers of her shift and soft stays. Then he urged her to lie back. He joined her on the bed, turned on his side, and cupped her breasts. She closed her eyes as he suckled her. Rivers of pleasure coursed through her body. She felt the dampness between her thighs and arched her back as he switched to her other breast.

He kissed her, and she opened for his tongue. She loved the way he rhythmically tasted her. Then she kissed him back, imitating him. Her breasts felt fuller, and she was breathing harder. Her skin seemed to be on fire. She held his face and tangled her tongue with his again. He trailed kisses down her neck and sucked where her pulse beat. Afterward, he blew on the spot as if he meant to cool her.

She caressed his chest, loving his muscular body. He was her husband—her man. "I like to touch you," she whispered.

He smiled. "I like it, too." Then he put his knee between her thighs and hovered over her. When he tried to touch her, she caught his hand, but he whispered, "I promise you will like this."

Will knew that he would shock her. She might object, but he was determined to make her come. He moved slowly down her body and lifted her shift to her waist. The red hair at the apex of her thighs excited him. When he spread the folds and looked at her, his blood ran hot. She released her breath and nodded. He smiled, slid his hands beneath her bottom, and tilted her upward. He bent her knees one at a time until her feet were planted on the bed. Then he pressed her legs wider. When he touched the folds of her sex, she jerked.

"Easy, love," he said.

He wanted her badly, but she was a bit nervous. Will was determined to take his time and slowly stoke the fire within her. The sight of her half-bared to him made his groin tighten. He ran his hands over her calves clad in silk stockings. God, she had the most fantastically long legs.

"Will, what are you doing?"

"Looking at you." He licked his lips. "It makes me hard."

He kissed the inside of her knee and ran his tongue underneath her garter. The whole time, he looked up at her from beneath his lashes. Her lips were parted, and her eyes held a sultry expression. Then he switched to the other garter. Her tits were rising and falling fast with each breath.

Will winked at her. Then he trailed his tongue all the way up her inner thigh and stopped just short of the red curls that made him hard as stone. He painted a wet trail up her other thigh, only this time he ran his tongue along her soft folds.

She gasped.

He did it again.

"Oh, my God."

Will smiled at his virginal bride's blushing face. "Relax, Amy. I won't hurt you." He caressed her soft folds. Then he spread them a little and found her sweet spot. He gently rubbed her there, and she inhaled on a shattered breath.

He ran his finger down the length of her folds, and his cock got harder as he encountered moisture. One day soon he would watch as he penetrated her, but today, he would focus on her pleasure only. He spread the folds again and touched his tongue to her. She bucked beneath him, and he chuckled.

"What are you doing?" She sounded shocked.

He touched his tongue to her sweet spot again.

"You are wicked."

"I am the devil." Then he touched his tongue to her again and again and again, slowly building up the rhythm and eventually quickening it. He looked up at her. God, her eyes were glazed over. "I'm going to make you come."

"What?"

He laughed, and then he flicked his tongue rapidly. The whole time he watched her writhing on the bed. He could feel the tension building in her body. She was soaking wet, and he had to restrain himself, because he craved to be inside her.

A little high-pitched sound came out of her throat.

He rubbed her again. "Come for me, Amy."

When he flicked his tongue again, her back bowed.

"Will," she cried out.

He leaned over her on his elbows and watched her face as the little death overtook her.

When she collapsed, he kissed her lips gently.

She opened her green eyes and stared at him with an expression of wonder.

He grinned. "Did you like it?"

"You devil. You should have warned me."

He grinned. "You would have protested."

"Probably," she said in a faint voice.

Will rolled to his back. He was still breathing fast. His cock was fully erect and pushing up his drawers.

She turned on her side and looked at him. "You're aroused."

"Yes."

"Will, is there some way for me to reciprocate?"

"Without penetration? Yes, but it might disgust you."

"Were you disgusted when you pleasured me?" she asked.

"No. It excited me."

"Then I won't be disgusted with you."

He turned and opened the drawer to the night table and grabbed two handkerchiefs. "It's a bit messy. I'll ejaculate when I come."

She knit her brows.

"My seed will spill."

"Ah, the reason for the handkerchief." She paused. "I don't know what to do."

Something tender unfurled in his chest at her innocence. "I'll show you."

She kneeled beside him and untied the ribbon on his drawers. He sprang out, and she gasped. "Good heavens, you're huge."

He chuckled. "My sweet wife, you just uttered words every man wants to hear."

She tentatively touched the tip of his cock and swirled her finger round the bit of moisture. He made himself lie still and watched as she lightly ran her finger down the length of his cock and over the sacs. He inhaled, took her hand, and wrapped it round him. Then he showed her the rhythm. She caught on quickly. "Oh, my. It's getting bigger."

The sight of her tits and her tumble-down red hair made him wild with lust. Her soft hand felt so good wrapped round his cock. God, he wanted to be inside her, but she was squeezing him now, and he looked down at her through his lashes. He wanted it to last a long, long time, but his lust for her had been climbing higher and higher every day.

She looked at him and her lips curved in a sly smile. Then she bent down and swirled her tongue round the head.

"Jesus." He'd never in a million years expected her to do that. Most women refused if a man asked.

"Do you like it?" she asked in a sultry voice.

He looked down at her through his lashes again. "God, yes."

She smiled and licked him again as if were some delicacy. He touched her cheek, and then he guided her hand back to his cock. She squeezed him again, and he gritted his teeth as the pressure built and built and built. He'd been hot and hard for too long, and he was burning from the feel of her tongue on him.

Tension gripped every muscle in his body. He grabbed the bedpost with one hand and leaned his head back. The throbbing was intense as it overtook him. His seed started to spurt, and she wrapped the handkerchief round him. Then she grabbed the second one, because he'd soaked the first. It seemed to go on and on and on. When he collapsed, she kissed him lightly on the lips. Then he let the little death take him.

An indeterminate amount of time later, he awoke to find his wife on her knees, admiring his body. Her breasts were half hidden by her hair, and her lips were kiss-swollen.

"You look like an erotic wood nymph," he said.

She met his gaze. "You swooned."

He laughed. "Men fall asleep after they make love." He stretched his arms. "It's still raining. I wonder what we'll do today."

"I think we should stay abed," she said in a chirpy voice.

"What have I unleashed?" he said.

"I liked it," she said, bouncing on her knees.

Her tits jiggled. He figured he'd be hot and hard again soon.

"Can we make love again?" she asked.

"I need a few minutes to recover," he said.

"Oh." She looked disappointed.

"Don't worry. I'll rise to the challenge again."

"Are there other things we can do and still abide by the wager?"

"Yes."

She knit her brows. "I've lost track of the days. I think it's only been eleven days. We still have ten more to go to the third course."

"Your arithmetic is unreliable," he said. "There are only five more days to the third course."

"You lied," she said. "That's a black mark on your courtship."

"I can erase the black mark," he said, pressing her to her back.

"No, you can't."

He tickled her waist.

She shrieked. Then a horrified expression came over her. "Oh, my God. The servants probably heard us."

He laughed. "A minute ago, you were raring to have a go at me again. Now you're prim and proper."

"We had better dress and make ourselves decent."

He wasn't about to let her out of the bed now. "The rain is loud. No one can hear us over it."

"Are you sure?" she asked.

"Positive," he lied as he came over her.

"What is next?" she asked.

He cupped her tits, pressed them together, and flicked his tongue rapidly back and forth between her nipples.

"Will," she cried out.

He'd never suspected that a wanton lay beneath her prim façade, but he counted himself a very lucky man.

On Sunday night, they sat down to dinner. She looked at him. "Are you hungry?"

"I'm starved—for you." He held her gaze. In the candlelight his dark eyes held a sensual promise, one that mesmerized her. This afternoon, he'd shut the door to the parlor and kissed her with unrestrained passion. He was a man with strong appetites. His masculinity excited her, and while she did not yet know much about pleasing him, she vowed to learn.

She intended to make him so happy he would never stray.

After the soup course, the footman brought in the second course. Will gave her a heated smile. She blushed a little, wondering what he had in mind for bed tonight. He ate with gusto, but each time he looked at her, she found herself able only to nibble at the food, because his seductive smiles excited her too much.

When the dessert arrived, he grinned at the cheesecake.

"I know it's your favorite," she said.

He shook his head. "You are."

She found it a little difficult to breathe. Tenderness unfolded in her chest. Her feelings for him were growing little by little. She sometimes wondered if he felt the same way, but she didn't want to press him. She wanted him to be the first to declare his love. Amy admitted it was probably too soon for him. He desired her and often used endearments in bed, but she mustn't allow herself to misinterpret his charm for love.

When the footman retreated, Will placed his hand over hers. "I've been thinking about tonight."

Her face grew warm.

"You're blushing," he said.

"What have you been thinking?" she asked.

He leaned toward her. "We've done almost everything, except consummate the marriage."

She thought of the way he'd slipped his cock, a word he'd taught her, between her legs. The friction had overwhelmed her. She squeezed her thighs together, remembering the pleasure.

"I know we have this wager, but I hoped you would agree to move forward," he said.

She stared at him. "You mean forget the wager?"

"I want to make love to you, unrestrained."

She wanted more than physical pleasure from him, and if she capitulated now, she sensed he would never open his heart to her. "Let us go on as we agreed," she said.

He sighed.

She'd disappointed him and part of her wanted to give him what he wanted, but she was afraid.

"Why?" he said.

Because I think I'm falling in love with you, and I want you to love me. She would not admit it. If she revealed her feelings and he said nothing, she knew it would crush her. "It's not that I don't want to consummate our marriage," she said. "I just have this feeling that all the romance will disappear if we cut short the courtship."

He leaned back in the chair, but he said nothing.

"Will, I know it probably doesn't make sense to you, but it is important to me." Surely he would understand.

He toyed with his fork, but he didn't pick it up. "We need to talk."

His voice had sounded flat and resigned.

Her heart beat a little faster.

He pushed his plate of cheesecake away, uneaten. "Eat your dessert."

Her stomach clenched. "I'm not hungry."

He gave her an enigmatic look. "Neither am I."

The back of her neck prickled.

He stood and pulled her chair back. "Let us go upstairs."

She took his arm and winced when her hand trembled. He was bored with her already. His expression was grim as he led her up the stairs. She disliked this feeling that he held all the cards in their relationship. He'd agreed to the wager, but he'd already tired of courting her. Their marriage had begun on shaky ground, and she'd wanted with all her heart to find happiness with him. Now she feared their marriage was already on the brink of collapse.

He was frustrated with her. Was it too much to ask that she let him make love to her without all these barriers?

He'd agreed to the wager, because the challenge amused him. For her, it wasn't merely fun and games. Tonight, she'd admitted she feared the romance would disappear if they consummated the marriage.

She knew going into this marriage that it was not a love match. Of course, he'd comprehended that she really wanted love when she'd said that she needed to feel something for him. He understood needy women all too well. More than a few had pretended they only wanted to bed him, and then a point would come when they started to cling. He didn't like it when women tried to smother him. Inevitably, they would push him to form an attachment.

When he reached her door, she looked at him. "Knock when you're ready."

He shook his head. "We'll talk now."

Something flickered in her eyes. Then she lifted her chin. "Very well. Please come in."

He led her to the bed. "Let us sit on the edge."

"I'll sit where I please."

When she started to walk away, he caught her arm. "No games tonight, Amy. We need to talk."

He hoisted her up on the mattress and sat next to her.

"You're angry with me," she said.

"I was frustrated and didn't like it when you said you felt the romance would disappear if we consummated the marriage. It felt as if you were holding back in the misguided belief that it would engender tender feelings between us."

"God forbid," she said.

"Sarcasm won't help matters," he said.

She looked at him. "But consummating the marriage will?"

"Why do you wish to continue dangling it like a carrot?"

Amy's mouth thinned, and then she spoke. "What happened when you pursued a woman and she finally let you catch her?"

"What does this have to do with our marriage?"

"Just answer the question," she said.

"I bedded her."

"For how long, Will? How long before you grew bored and went looking for the next challenge?"

He hesitated and told her the truth. "A fortnight at most."

Her smile held no warmth.

"You turned the tables on me," he said. "You challenged me to that wager to keep me interested."

"No, Will. I asked you to court me, because I wanted to do everything possible to make this marriage a happy one. The sacred vows I took meant something to me, and that is why I resolved to do everything in my power to see to your comfort and happiness. But I also realized that we needed to get to know each other, and that is the true reason I wanted you to court me."

He sighed. "I admit the courtship aspect has brought us closer together. We have talked a great deal because of it, and I'm not altogether sure I would have realized the importance of communicating with you without it. I do see that now."

"Will, I need to know you better. I love your kisses and touches, but unless there are some feelings between us, the intimacy will wither quickly."

"I don't know what I'm capable of feeling," he said. "All of my past relationships were fleeting and shallow. But it is different with you, and it all started that night we were locked in the wine cellar. For the first time in my life, I had protective feelings—for you. I worried you would catch a chill, and I hated that you were so scared. I've never felt that way about a woman before."

He saw the tears welling in her eyes and drew out his handkerchief.

She dabbed the handkerchief in the corners of her eyes. "Thank you for telling me. It helps."

He took her hand. "We are only beginning to know each other. Everything else about our marriage has been rushed, but the feelings can't be. You told me what you'd always wanted, and you deserved to marry for love. But we can't change what happened, and I don't want to mislead you."

"No, that would be wrong."

"I can honestly tell you that I like you. I can honestly tell you that I'm proud to have such a talented and well-dressed wife. I can tell you that I enjoy spending time with you, because you're clever, and you make me laugh. And I can honestly tell you that I desire you. It's important to me, and I think it is to you as well."

"If you want to end the wager, we can," she said.

"You have trouble trusting me," he said, "and given my reputation, it's understandable. That's the reason you insisted I mend my wicked ways."

She nodded.

"I think you need some kind of proof," Will said. "More important, I think the courting business is helping us to understand each other."

"I want us to find happiness in this marriage," she said. "I don't want us to live separate lives, and it scares me that you may not feel the same way."

"I'll be honest. I went into this marriage believing that we would end up living separate lives, because of the circumstances and because it's so common in the ton," he said. "My brother said something that I think is true. The circumstances of our marriage don't matter. It's what comes after the wedding."

"I think your brother is very wise," she said.

"It occurs to me that no one expects us to succeed,

and you know how I love a challenge." He smiled a little. "Let's prove everyone wrong."

"I want you to promise me something," she said.

"What is it?"

"Promise me you will be faithful to me."

He swallowed. "I promise to be faithful to you."

She threw her arms around him. He could feel her shaking, and he knew there would be times when he would be tempted. But if he failed he would dishonor her and himself. They were for better or worse bound for life in this marriage.

Chapter Eleven

Will awoke the next morning to find Poppet perched on his chest. "Deuce take you."

Poppet squeaked at him repeatedly. Hell. She was probably hungry. The cat got right up in his face and squeaked as if demanding something. Then it occurred to his wooly brain that he could ring for a servant to bring Poppet's breakfast to his room.

He set Poppet on the bed and got up to put on his trousers from last night. Egad, it was only eight o'clock. "You need to go back to bed," he told the cat.

Poppet swished her tail and squeaked.

"Yes, I know you're in bed, but it's mine." He slipped on his banyan and rang the bell. After the footman arrived, Will gave him instructions and slumped in the leather chair. Then everything that had transpired last night flooded his brain.

"The devil," he grumbled.

Poppet squeaked at him.

Will worried about the implications of their conversation. He'd been honest about his feelings for her, but now he wondered if she expected him to fall in love with her. He'd been smitten a time or two, but generally his interest in women had been based solely on lust. He wasn't the sort of man who needed or wanted close relationships of any kind. God knew, he'd dodged his family members most of his life.

The only person he'd ever stood by was Bell. He wasn't even sure why, other than that he'd seen his friend dying alive right in front of him. As he watched the cat's tail twitch, it occurred to him that he'd rescued stray animals all his life. He'd also rescued Bell.

It was an arresting thought. He told himself it didn't signify and put it out of his mind. After he'd finished dressing, a knock sounded at the connecting door. "Come in, Amy."

His valet left the room, and Will felt a little uncomfortable with her for some strange reason, but he figured it would pass. "Are you ready for breakfast?"

"Yes, today is my shopping expedition with Julianne."

"Right. You're taking sketches to the dressmaker."

She sort of froze for a second, and then she smiled. "Yes, I hope Madame DuPont likes them."

He thought her initial reaction was a bit odd, but he dismissed it. "I'm sure the dressmaker will approve." As they walked downstairs together, he looked at her. "I'll take you in my curricle to Ashdown House, since I'm meeting my brother. Then you and Julianne can spend the day shopping."

"I'm looking forward to it. We haven't spent much time together this season, but now we're sisters," Amy said.

After breakfast, Will drove them to Ashdown House

and escorted her inside. Julianne met them in the foyer. "Amy, if you're ready, we can leave now."

Will kissed Amy's cheek. "Have a lovely time."

"Marc would tell me not to spend too much money," Julianne said.

Will said nothing. It troubled him that he'd needed Amy's fortune to cover his debt, because today he carried a check for twenty thousand pounds signed to his brother. He tried to shrug it off, but the deception bothered him more than a little.

Amy caught his hand. "Invite your friends for dinner. Tell Fordham I'll serve roast beef and Yorkshire pudding."

He grinned. "He'll come when he hears that news." He waved and strode off to his brother's study. Two hours later, Will concluded his meeting with Hawk. There wouldn't be any challenges with the account books, but he looked forward to meeting the tenants and riding about the property.

After leaving Ashdown House, Will drove his curricle to White's, where he found Bell in the coffee room and took a chair across from his friend. "Good to see you," he said.

"Well, how is married life?" Bell asked.

"Better than I expected."

Bell arched his brows but said nothing.

A waiter brought Will a cup of coffee. He took a sip and eyed Bell. "Where is Fordham?"

"Probably passed out from one too many bottles," Bell said. "He likely forgot he was supposed to meet us."

Will grinned and sipped his coffee. "So, what is new in your life?"

"Not much. I pensioned off my mistress."

"No scene, I hope," Will said.

"Of course there was," Bell said. "I got tired of the same old accusations about how I ignored her and took her for granted. It was deadly boring."

Will set his cup on the table. "You found someone else?"

"You know me too well." Bell drank his coffee and set the empty cup aside. When the waiter returned, Bell waved him off. "So you're satisfied with your bride."

Will smiled. "She invited you and Fordham to dine with us this week. If you see Fordham, tell him she's planning to serve roast beef and Yorkshire pudding."

"Very well." He paused. "Speaking of invitations, Elise, my new mistress, is hosting a private card party tomorrow night. Join us," he said.

Will shook his head. Ladies did not attend parties given by courtesans. "No thanks."

Bell let out an amused huff. "Unbelievable."

"What?" Will said.

"You're refusing because you're married."

"The deuce take you. We're newlyweds."

"You'll get bored soon enough," Bell said.

Will glared at his friend. "Careful, Bell. She's my wife."

Bell inhaled. "Right. My apologies."

"Accepted," Will said.

"You surprise me," Bell said. "No offense, but you're not exactly known for long liaisons."

Will traced his finger round the rim of his cup. "It's different when the woman is your wife."

"Having no experience, I can't say as I understand."

"I feel a responsibility to her." He frowned, thinking again of the check he'd given his brother this morning. After their discussion last night, the deception weighed heavily on his mind.

"I know you," Bell said. "Something is bothering you."

"Her father cut up nasty when I formally asked his permission to marry her. I promised the man I wouldn't hurt her." Will looked at his friend. "Hardwick gave his permission only because she would have been ruined if we hadn't married."

"You didn't intend to compromise her at that card party."

"You know I previously tried and botched it," he said. Desperation had led him to that clumsy attempt. Now he was glad he'd failed. If he'd purposely compromised her, she would have known and her father would likely have wanted to kill him. Their marriage would have proved miserable indeed.

"Does she know you lost a fortune gambling?"

He shook his head. "I didn't want Amy or her father to know. Hawk paid the debt to keep it quiet." Will frowned at his coffee cup. He'd gotten her fortune and repaid his brother. All had gone in his favor. Why then did he feel as if he'd eaten something rotten?

"Why the glum expression?" Bell asked.

"This morning, I repaid Hawk the twenty thousand pounds—from her marriage portion."

"You would have gotten the money from the marriage settlement even if you'd married her under ordinary circumstances," Bell said.

"I'd be lying if I said I wasn't relieved that she had fifty thousand. She doesn't know that a substantial portion of her fortune went to pay my gambling debt."

"You're hardly the first man to marry an heiress."

"The incident in the wine cellar was an accident," he said a bit too gruffly. "If she ever found out about the debt, she'd conclude I meant to compromise her."

"You hushed up the gambling debt," Bell said. "How would she ever find out?"

"Of course you're right."

"She's your wife, and you feel a bit of guilt," Bell said.

"There's a part of me that thinks I should tell her."

Bell cleared his throat. "I have a story that may help you with that decision. Five years ago, we went to a gaming hall. Do you remember? We were both green as grass and full of ourselves."

"I remember," Will said. "I puked half the night after drinking too much brandy."

"You were flirting with a tavern wench. I was watching a high-stakes card game. The play went on for hours, and then I saw a gentleman cheat. He netted a tidy sum."

"What happened?" Will said.

"The gentleman, who shall remain unnamed, was my late father's friend." Bell shook his head. "No one else caught it. I felt it was wrong to keep silent, but I knew the man. I couldn't get up the courage to make the accusation. That night, I couldn't sleep. I had a dilemma, and I didn't know what to do. The next morning, I went to my father and told him what I'd seen, but I didn't identify the man. My father told me that in such circumstances, there are three key questions to ask before revealing something. Is it true? Is it kind? Is it necessary?"

"What did you do?" Will asked.

"I knew it was true. As for the kindness part, I felt the man didn't deserve it. I did, however, feel it necessary to reveal the man's identity to my father. He told me I'd done the right thing, and he cut the man's acquaintance."

Will pondered the three questions. "Well, it is true that I gambled, but it wouldn't be kind to tell Amy. I think a confession is not only unnecessary, but it would do more harm than good."

"You've made your decision," Bell said. "Now let the matter go."

Amy felt a bit nervous as she and Julianne entered Madame DuPont's shop.

Madame DuPont greeted them with an elegant curtsy. "Welcome to my establishment."

"I know you wish to confer with Madame DuPont," Julianne said. "I want to have a look at the bonnets and trims."

Madame DuPont inclined her head and faced Amy. "You have brought your latest sketches?"

"I have, thank you."

Amy followed the modiste to a worktable and laid out the new designs. "For this one, I recommend a red satin and the trim would be red velvet just above the lace flounces."

"One moment," Madame DuPont said. "I believe I have a silk that will work well for this design."

When the modiste returned, she brought both a blue and a red satin. Amy reviewed the fabrics. "I prefer the red with the matching velvet."

"Excellent," Madame said. "I agree."

Amy showed her the next one. "I envision a blond silk gauze, silk ribbons, and tulle." Amy laid out another sketch. "This one is an ivory silk ball gown with gold lamé borders. Notice the flounces are a bit more understated." She showed Madame several more designs. "And finally, this one is somewhat different. It is a silk taffeta with long sleeves and lace at the wrists. I paired it with a sheer silk shawl with black embroidery and a black netted veil."

"The last is stunning," Madame said. "May I recommend a black silk ribbon to trim the high waistline?"

"It is an excellent suggestion," Amy said. "I know you like this last one. Are you interested in any of the others?"

"I will take them all," Madame said. She glanced behind her at Julianne and returned her shrewd gaze to Amy. "You have your reticule. I will use a shawl to cover the purse when I return."

After the modiste disappeared behind a curtain, Amy's anxiety kept her on edge. She pretended to be engrossed in the designs, as if matters had not already been concluded. Not long afterward, Madame walked out with a shawl draped over her arm. Amy glanced over her shoulder, but Julianne was examining a bonnet.

Amy closed her sketchbook and retrieved her reticule. She opened the drawstring. Madame dropped the purse inside. The clink of the coins sounded unnaturally loud to Amy's ears, but it was undoubtedly just her nerves. She closed the drawstring. Then she looked up and saw Julianne standing before the mirror and looking at Amy's reflection there.

Amy felt as if her heart had dropped to her stomach. She made herself walk over to her friend—and now sister. "The bonnet looks well on you."

Julianne looked at her reflection again and sighed. "No, I don't think I will take it today." She turned round. "Have you concluded your business?"

"Yes, I have."

Madame curtsied as they departed. The jingle of the shop bell made Amy feel a little ill.

"There is the carriage now," Julianne said, lifting her gloved hand.

When it arrived, they stepped inside.

"Do you wish to visit any other shops?" Julianne said.

"No, not today."

"Amy, be careful. The coins jingle," Julianne said.

Of course they jingled. Amy looked out the window. She'd not even thought about the reflection in the mirror, but then she'd been anxious, because she'd known what she was doing could cause problems.

"I know your parents are wealthy," Julianne said, "and I know your marriage portion was staggeringly large. So I am at a loss to understand why you would accept money for your sketches when you do not have a need."

"My grandfather was in trade. I don't think there is anything wrong with taking money for honest work."

Julianne turned to her. "Then why were you attempting to hide it?"

"Because I know how the beau monde views trade."

"Does Will know?"

Amy winced. "No," she whispered.

Julianne patted her arm. "Tell me the reason you're taking the money."

She tightened the strings of her reticule. "I initially made the agreement with Madame DuPont that day my designs were displayed at your home. Greed was part of it, but I thought I should be paid for the work. You're right. I knew I must keep it a secret. My parents do not reveal the source of their fortune, because it came from my grandfather's trade."

"Amy, you know I will keep our conversation confidential, but I am concerned. You're deceiving Will."

She looked at Julianne. "I know so little about my husband. His reputation is such that I am far from comfortable. He is a rake, and I started to worry that he might also be a wastrel. How could I say that to him? It would be an accusation. But, if I discover he has put us in ruinous debt, we would be in terrible trouble. So I thought to set aside a nest egg, in the event it was ever needed."

Julianne frowned. "Amy, if the worst happened, you could go to your father or my husband for assistance."

She shook her head. "My parents have had to bear the scandal of my marriage. I don't ever want them to worry again." She knew that others in the neighborhood probably gossiped about her marriage to a rake. "If I ever applied to your husband for assistance, it would cause hard feelings between the brothers."

"Amy, if someone else had seen you today, you can be sure the gossip would fly. Then you would humiliate your husband, your parents, and all of Will's family. Is the money worth the risk?"

"I wish to take preventative measures for a while longer. Just until I am assured that he has mended his ways and that I can trust him."

Julianne looked at her. "Amy, if he ever found out you deceived him, he would never trust you."

"I swear as soon as I feel our marriage is on solid ground I will give up the compensation." She wondered if she would ever be able to trust him.

The carriage stopped off at the cottage.

"I'm not encouraging you in this deception," Julianne said. "But those coins jingle, and others will notice. How will you explain when we make all of our purchases on credit?"

"I'm sorry to involve you in this matter. I prefer to stay home now," Amy said.

"Will is expecting you at Ashdown House. Do you want me to give him a message?" Julianne said.

"No. Let me take the purse inside, and then I will go with you." She flew inside the cottage and up the stairs, hating the sound of the clinking coins. Once inside her room, she hid the purse deep in her trunk. In the future, she would ask Madame DuPont to pay in pound notes only. As she closed the trunk, Amy wondered if she was making the right decision. She would simply take it day by day and be far more cautious in the future.

Will sat in the drawing room with Grandmamma. "Amy is not Scottish," he said, pitching his voice louder. "She just has red hair."

Grandmamma patted his hand. "You could wear a kilt."

He laughed. "No. I'll never be caught in a skirt," he said in a loud voice.

"Oh, dear," the dowager countess said. "Grandmamma is quite fixated on Scotsmen."

Marc walked inside. "Oh, Lord, does she still think Amy is Scottish?"

Will laughed. "Yes."

"I hear voices in the hall," Hawk said. "Julianne and Amy must have returned."

When Amy walked into the room, Will and Hawk rose. Amy's subdued expression puzzled him. He'd thought she would be happy after a day of shopping.

"Julianne went to feed Emma and said I should come to the drawing room," Amy said.

Will went to her and kissed her cheek. Then he held her hand and led her to the sofa.

Patience, Hope, and Harmony glided into the drawing room. They spent so much time at Ashdown House that Will wondered why they didn't just move in.

"William, you are very familiar with your wife," Patience said as she sat across from them.

"It's called affection," Hawk said.

Will winked at Amy. "Shocking, isn't it? Married couples being familiar with each other."

She blushed and looked at their joined hands.

"They are newlyweds," Hope said. "Will, it is too bad that you were unable to have a wedding trip."

"We're postponing it until this summer." Will looked at Amy. "Shall we go home?"

"Oh, but you must stay for dinner," the dowager countess said.

He didn't want to spend the evening with his family, and he suspected something was troubling Amy. Will knew his relatives would poke their noses into his marriage. Already Patience had criticized him for openly showing affection for Amy.

Amy leaned closer to him. "Let me speak to your mother," she murmured. Then she sat beside the dowager countess. "Thank you so much for inviting us to dine. I hope you will forgive a newly wedded couple for wanting to spend time alone."

"Of course, dear. I just like having the family here. That's why my girls come so often. It was lonely after my husband died. That was many years ago, but when you're old and gray, time seems to go faster for some reason."

Amy patted her hand. "I will call on you soon. Will

and I started out our marriage backward, so we're trying to get to know each other."

"I'm so glad, dear." She sighed. "William, it seems you married a very sweet girl. Now go have your honeymoon."

The next day, Amy paid a call on the dowager countess as promised. Patience, Hope, and Harmony had called as well. Grandmamma was snoring softly beside Amy. As was custom, all the ladies applied themselves to needlework as they spoke. Julianne joined them for only a few minutes and then left to feed Emma.

Amy found the dowager countess to be a somewhat timid woman who was easily influenced by her daughters, Patience in particular. Amy noticed that Patience criticized Harmony's stitches, which looked perfectly fine to her, but she kept her opinions to herself.

"I'm sure Amy's needlework is perfect," Hope said. "She does design fashions."

"There is no such thing as perfection," Amy said, "and I cannot be impartial about my own needlework."

"Your gown designs are renowned," Patience said. "You must be proud of your accomplishments."

She kept her gaze on her needlework. "Actually, William is proud of my designs."

"Isn't that sweet?" Patience said in a sardonic tone. "Do you not agree, Hope?"

Amy lifted her eyes, stunned by Patience's sarcasm.

Hope's lips twitched. "Indeed, I'm sure he's not hoping to gain anything from complimenting his wife."

All three sisters laughed.

A hot blush crept into Amy's face. She kept her gaze on her needlework and said nothing, but she didn't like what they had insinuated. Obviously, they were teasing, but underlying their words was their belief that his compliments were not genuine.

"Amy, I'm sorry. We did not mean to wound you," Patience said. "It's just that we know our brother. He is a charmer and not above scheming to get whatever he wants."

She couldn't disagree completely. Charm did seem to flow in his veins, and there was something irresistible about his fun-loving nature. Their wager was a prime example. But she didn't know him well at all.

"It would behoove you to take his compliments with a grain of salt," Hope said.

"He is restless and unlikely to settle in one place for any length of time, but perhaps you're just the one to tame him, Amy," Harmony said.

Amy threaded the needle into the cloth. She almost made an excuse to leave, but she'd made a promise to Will, and she would not break it. "I have found that sometimes we believe we know someone when we do not. It is true I have not known Will very long. But he is my husband, and I told him that he would always come first. I also swore that I would defend him if anyone ever criticized him."

The three sisters exchanged surprised looks. Patience cleared her throat. "Amy, we love our brother, but we know that he earned his devilish reputation. We're hopeful that you're the one who will reform him. We couldn't help but notice that you're a little smitten with Will. We just wanted to make sure you understand him."

"If you believe that he is incapable of being sincere, then I conclude you do not know your brother at all," Amy said. "And I will not allow you to criticize him in my presence. Please excuse me." She rose, only to find Hawk closing the door. "Amy, please be seated."

"Perhaps we should give you privacy," Patience said.

"Sit down, Patience, because this mostly concerns you."

"I really must go," Patience said, gathering up her needlework.

"Patience, I'm calling an impromptu family meeting right now," Hawk said.

Amy noted the arrested expression on Patience's face. "I did nothing wrong, Hawk."

"I was standing outside the door and heard every word," Hawk said. "At this moment, I'm ashamed of all three of my sisters."

Amy covered her mouth, remembering Will's warning. Part of her wished she'd said nothing, and yet she couldn't live with herself if she didn't defend him.

"They were only teasing," the dowager countess said.

Hawk regarded his mother. "It was unkind, Mama."

"We're family, and being a part of a family is supporting each other," Hawk said. "I could not stand back and listen to my sisters tell Amy that her marriage to our brother didn't stand a chance. Patience, you influence Hope and Harmony. I'm not excusing them, but you're the one who sets the tone, and they have always followed your lead. Will is our brother. He and Amy have recently married and are just now getting started on their life together. What I'm asking from all of you is to leave off the criticism and focus on lending your support to Amy and Will.

"We're a big brood," Hawk said. "We all have different personalities and interests. But we should stand united as a family and remember to count our blessings and keep our focus off the negative."

Patience sighed. "You're right, Marc. Amy, please accept my apology. We do love Will very much, but sometimes you see other people only through the perspective in which you know them. Please do not take an insult, but I had heard that you were a wallflower. I expected a shy, mousy woman with no conversation or backbone. You are the exact opposite."

Until that moment, Amy had not realized how much she had changed in such a short time, but she'd taken control of her life, even when uncontrollable events had occurred. She looked at Patience. "I always wanted a large family. I was so touched when you loaned me your wedding gown. I had no brothers or sisters and hope that we can all grow closer over time."

"I think Will is very lucky to have married you," Hope said. "He has changed for the better. Now that he has married you, he will give up his dreams of traveling. Before you entered his life, he was determined to journey to Switzerland, but everyone in the family agreed that it must stop. We feared he would stay away for years as he did before."

Patience sighed. "He meant to leave, and we urged Hawk to cut off his quarterly allowance. Will was furious, but he needed to settle into a career."

Amy did her best to shutter her expression, but inside she was alarmed. Little wonder that he objected to his family's interference. But why had he not told her the truth about the measures his family had taken to keep him home?

Chapter Twelve

Amy spent the day overlooking all the preparations for tonight's dinner party. Bellingham and Fordham would dine with them tonight, and Amy wanted everything to be perfect. The maids had polished every surface to a shine. The food was under preparation, and now all that remained was for Amy to dress. At one point in the afternoon, Will had laughed and told her that his bachelor friends wouldn't notice, but she had been adamant.

Amy had meant to speak to Will about the information his family had divulged, but she'd decided to wait another day because his friends were joining them for dinner. She was troubled that he'd not told her about it, but perhaps he just felt that it was water under the bridge. When speaking of the past, he often said it was over and nothing could be changed. He wasn't one to look back. But clearly, the traveling had meant very much to him.

That evening, Anna persuaded Amy to wear her jade silk gown with a low neckline. As Anna finished dressing her hair, a knock sounded. "Thank you, Anna. That will be all," Amy said. Then she called Will inside.

He opened the door and walked toward her with his hands behind his back. "Stay at your dressing table."

"Why?"

He looked at her in the dressing mirror. "Close your eyes."

"Why?"

"Just do it. And no peeking."

She closed her eyes. He reached round her. She felt him drape a necklace round her neck. His fingers worked on a clasp.

"Now you can open," he said.

She gasped at the sight of the glittering emerald necklace. "Oh, it's beautiful, but where—when?"

"It was the day you went shopping with Julianne, and I'd gone to White's to see Bell. I realized I'd never given you a wedding gift. Since you haven't complained, I thought your gift should be extravagant. Oh, yes, there are matching earbobs as well. But I'll let you put those on."

"Anna must have been in on the surprise," Amy said.

He grinned. "And I see she persuaded you to wear that gown."

Amy donned the earbobs. "Will, they're beautiful." She turned to him. "Thank you."

He took her hands and helped her rise. "I'm glad you like them. Do you know you actually surprised me that day? You went shopping and came home empty-handed."

She kept the smile on her face, but her stomach tightened. Neither she nor Julianne had made a purchase because Amy had inadvertently exposed her secret. Her guilt gnawed at her, and for a moment, she was tempted to confess, but not tonight, when his friends were coming to dinner. She didn't want anything to mar this night.

"I do wish you had allowed me to invite two other ladies to make the numbers even at the table," Amy said. "I have friends who would be delighted to meet Bellingham and Fordham."

"I've no doubt your lady friends would be delighted, but my bachelor friends can smell a matchmaking scheme a mile away." He kissed her lingeringly on the lips. "Do you realize there are only seven more days until one of us wins the wager?"

"I never did find any spies, but then we've not been apart except that one day," she said. "Well, except for the day I called on your mother." She told Will what had transpired, with the exception of the information about his travels. He thanked her for defending him and admitted Hawk was right about his sisters. Will was also impressed with the way she'd dealt with Patience that day.

A thoughtful expression flitted through his dark eyes. "By Jove, you're right. We've spent every evening together, *not* eating dessert."

She laughed and touched the necklace again.

He smiled. "I wonder who will win."

"It may be a draw. I was certain at the time you proposed the wager that you would fail, but you've proven yourself quite romantic," she said. "Flowers, poems, and jewelry. Our conversations were the best part of all."

He cupped her face with his warm hands and gazed into her eyes. An intense giddy feeling flooded her heart. The tender feelings had grown gradually over the last two weeks. She told herself that it was too soon. Yet the heart has no time line.

If they had engaged in a traditional courtship before marriage, they would not have spent as much time together. They would not have conversed for hours in the candlelight or touched each other intimately. In an ordinary courtship, they would have had to monitor their conversation, because they would have been chaperoned in a drawing room. They would not have been able to talk freely about things that mattered. But as a married couple they had been able to do that. Even though it was a marriage of necessity, they had agreed to honor their vows. As Will had said, no one expected them to succeed. She would never forget his words. *Let's prove them wrong.*

She listened to her heart and acknowledged the truth. She had fallen in love with him.

"What are you thinking?" he asked.

She wanted to tell him, wanted to confess her love for him, but she must wait for the right time. Tonight he had given her a gift. Perhaps it was her turn. She placed her hand over his chest and felt the steady beating of his heart. "I wish to give you a gift tonight."

"Oh, what is it?"

"I wish to cede the wager to you," she said.

"What?" He looked stunned.

"I want you to win. Tonight, I want to make love to you, without any barriers or rules," she said.

"Thank you." He kissed her, softly at first, and then with hunger. His mouth was hot and the kiss was lush and very, very erotic. He slid his hands down her back and then covered her bottom. When he pressed her against his body, his aroused cock pressed into her abdomen. When he ended the kiss, his eyes were dark with passion. "I just realized that you're delaying gratification once again."

"I am?"

"You gave me a gift, but I have to wait until after my friends leave to, er, open the package."

She playfully swatted him. "You are so bad."

"I think we've established that," he said.

She smoothed his lapels. "Not so much anymore."

He lifted her hands, palms up, and kissed her wrists. "You continue to surprise and amaze me."

"So do you," she whispered.

"We had better go downstairs, because that bed is tempting me, and I want a leisurely loving," he said.

She took his arm and inhaled his unique, masculine scent. Her chest fluttered, and she realized it was joy filling her heart.

"Ah, that was an excellent dinner, Mrs. Darcett," Fordham said, pushing a curly blond lock off his forehead. "I say, that still sounds very strange. I never thought to see this devil become a married man, but you're smiling. I assume you're making him mind."

Amy laughed. "Actually, sometimes it's the other way around."

"Oh, ho," Fordham said. "So she's a bit of vixen, eh?"

Will winked at her. "My wife has managed to surprise me almost on a daily basis."

"Leave it to Will to find the best wife—in a wine cellar no less," Fordham said.

Bellingham shook his head. "Fordham, do try to have a bit of decorum."

He winced. "Sorry, Mrs. Darcett."

"Don't worry. I took no offense."

"It's certainly a different path to the altar," Will said.

"Mind you, I don't think I ever want to step foot in another wine cellar. It was deuced cold in there. The wine, however, was excellent."

Bell's chest shook. "I should have guessed you would take advantage of Boswood's fine collection. How many dead soldiers were there?"

"One." Will looked at Amy. "Our term for empty bottles. I've buried more than a few over the years."

"Speaking of wine, let me top up the glasses," Bell said, lifting a bottle of claret. Afterward, he raised his glass. "To Mr. and Mrs. Darcett. I wish you both happy."

Amy was intrigued by Bell. He was as tall and muscular as her husband. Like Will, he had dark hair, but his was shorter. "My lord, you traveled with my husband for many years."

He turned his intense bright blue gaze upon her. "Yes, we wandered the Continent for four years. It was quite an adventure."

"I went as well," Fordham said, "but my family called me home after only six months. I got in a spot of trouble."

"You are trouble," Will said, laughing.

"True, but maybe one day I'll meet a woman willing to take me on as a husband." He grinned at Amy. "Do you happen to have any single friends who don't mind a fellow with scuffed boots and a sad lack of funds?"

"Why do I suspect that you would flee if I were to offer to introduce you to my eligible friends?" She liked Fordham. He was charming in a self-effacing manner.

"I say, Darcett must have told you the truth about me. Now I'm doomed. You'll never let me near your friends."

Fordham leaned across the table. "You probably shouldn't, if you wish to keep them as friends."

Laughing, she looked at Will. "Is that true?"

"I'm afraid so," Will said.

She returned her attention to Bellingham. "My lord, you must know my husband very well."

"Yes, he is like a brother to me," Bell said. "He asked me to accompany him on a grand tour following a difficult period in my life. No doubt he told you that I lost all my family to illness?"

"Yes, he told me." Amy admired him for addressing the issue directly. People often buried painful experiences rather than confronting them.

Bell sipped his wine. "Our journeys proved fascinating and helped me to overcome the worst of my grief."

The shock and pain must have been horrific. Thank God Will had been there to help his friend. "Do you plan to travel again?" Amy asked.

"I thought of journeying to Switzerland, but finding the right traveling companion is somewhat difficult," Bell said. "The conditions are often a bit too rustic, and not everyone can laugh and make do the way your husband did. He's quite versatile. Did you know he can make a pot of tea and cook an egg?"

Amy smiled. "Yes, he told me that he learned to do that out of necessity." Privately, she realized Will had wanted to journey with Bellingham. He'd meant to escape his family in much the same way he'd done when he'd run away as a child. But why? What was he running away from?

"Since you're back in England, do you ever consider marrying, my lord?" Amy asked.

"Why? Do you have eligible friends?" Bell asked.

"As a matter of fact, I do," she said.

"Shocking," Bell said. "Generally, the hostess invites her friends and makes sure I meet them, whether I wish to or not."

Amy grinned. "To be honest, I wanted to even the numbers at the table, but Will insisted that neither of you would appreciate my matchmaking efforts."

"If your friends happen to have papas who are plump in the pocket, I might find myself miraculously in love," Fordham said.

Amy laughed. When she turned her attention to her husband, she saw him exchanging a cryptic look with Bell. Perhaps they thought Fordham's jest in poor taste.

After the footmen removed the dishes, Will gave Amy a heated look. "Time for the third course."

Her face grew warm at his reference to their private jest. She wondered if she would always associate love-making with food.

"Mrs. Darcett, I understand you have a career," Fordham said.

"It's not a career," Will said. "Amy enjoys designing fashionable gowns."

"A dressmaker in London makes up the gowns from my sketches," Amy said. "I consult with her about the fabrics and trim."

Fordham frowned. "It sounds like a career to me."

"It is her pastime," Will said. "Amy is talented and enjoys drawing."

Bell regarded Amy. "Never mind our thickheaded friend. He doesn't know the difference between trade and amusement."

She kept her expression as serene as possible and

told herself to put it out of her mind for the time being. She mustn't dwell on her deception in front of Will, because she might inadvertently give away her discomposure.

"Amy, would you like more wine?" Will asked.

"No, thank you," she said.

Will poured more wine for himself and his friends. He handed a glass to Fordham. "I assure you my wife is not engaged in trade."

"Sorry, Mrs. Darcett," Fordham said. "I didn't think. Of course you wouldn't engage in trade."

"I take no offense." She thought of that moment when Julianne had told her to use care, because the coins jingled. The memory shamed her, but she must not dwell on it now. The best thing would be to change the topic, but she froze, as she always did when she grew anxious.

Luckily, Bell asked Will questions about his position as land steward. The three men discussed the topic for a short time. Then Will turned his attention to her. "Sorry, sweetheart. We forgot ourselves. Will you forgive us?"

"There is nothing to forgive. I know nothing about your position, but I'm more than happy to listen," she said. She had just made herself sound like one of those silly ladies who had feathers for brains.

"You indulge us, Mrs. Darcett," Bell said. He eyed Will. "You're a lucky fellow. She's one in a thousand."

"I think so," Will said.

"You both put me to the blush," Amy said. She could not take pleasure in their approval of her when she was deceiving her husband.

Will grinned. "You blush frequently, wife."

"I'm sure you have plenty to do with that, Darcett," Fordham said.

Will winked at her. She lowered her gaze, knowing he would think her abashed.

The footmen brought in the desserts: nuts, sweetmeats, fruit, and cheesecake.

"Ah, I had a feeling my wife would serve cheesecake tonight," Will said.

Apparently Bell and Fordham liked cheesecake as well. Amy ate only a few bites. Her heart was heavy, when she ought to rejoice that Will had proven himself to be a wonderful husband. No matter how hard she tried, she still couldn't shake off Will's statement. *I assure you my wife is not engaged in trade.*

She must refuse to take compensation for her sketches in the future. Tonight, she'd ceded the wager to Will, thereby effectively putting her trust in him. She couldn't live with this deception, for it would ruin their blossoming relationship. The next time she took sketches to Madame DuPont, she would inform her that she no longer required compensation. She need not explain her reasons. Madame DuPont was only interested in profit. But what if she refused the sketches?

When the gentlemen finished their desserts, Will retrieved the bottle of port from the sideboard. "Amy, we could bring our port to the drawing room, if you wish."

"No, stay and take your time. I have some embroidering to finish." When she rose, Will and his friends stood.

"Enjoy your port," she said.

Will escorted her to the door. He was proud to have such a clever and generous wife. She'd impressed his friends and had a facility for drawing out others in conversation. He liked that there was no vanity in her. Far too many women in his past had practically demanded compliments. Unlike them, Amy focused her attention on others.

She fingered the gems at her throat, making him smile. He'd intended to wait until after the wager concluded to give Amy the emeralds, but he'd wanted her to wear them at dinner. "You were magnificent tonight," he whispered. He lifted her hand and kissed it. "I won't be too long."

After she departed, he returned to the table and poured drinks for his friends. She'd stunned him earlier when she'd ceded the wager. Now the anticipation of making love to her made his groin tighten. He bit back a grin as he thought of a way to tease her. She would express outrage when he insisted she must stay abed with him for the remaining seven days.

"You're a lucky devil," Fordham said as Will passed round the drinks.

"I am," he said.

Bell sipped his port. "She's accomplished, clever, and unique. But then, you've always somehow managed to come out a winner. In this case, you married one."

"Too bad she doesn't have any sisters," Fordham said.

"She has friends," Will said.

"What? I must have suffered momentary madness. I'm sure the urge to wed will pass as soon as I leave the honeymoon nest," Fordham said.

Will snorted.

Fordham took out his watch. "Gentlemen, I promised to visit my mistress. I'll see you at the club, I'm sure."

After he left, Bell arched his brows. "Join me outside for a cheroot?"

"I'll walk out with you."

Once they were out of doors, Bell took out a case and offered a cheroot to Will.

"No, thanks." He didn't want to go to Amy's bed stinking of smoke.

Bell lit his cheroot and inhaled. "You're different with her."

"True. I try to avoid vulgar habits in her presence."

Bell blew out a smoke ring. "That's not what I meant."

He'd known. "Events transpired. We adjusted."

"There's an example of the difference. You used the word *we*, not *I*."

"She's my wife."

Bell flicked ashes. "You're besotted."

"Tell me to go to hell in advance," Will said.

"Let me guess. You're recommending I marry."

"You're the lone survivor," Will said. "Perhaps you are meant to carry on your family's legacy."

Bell stubbed out the cheroot. "I don't believe in meant to be. There's only sight, smell, sound, and touch. If there is anything else, it's long dead to me."

Will gazed up at the full moon. "There is something else." He looked at Bell. "You're alive for a reason."

Amy tried to focus on embroidering the little gown for Emma, but her conscience troubled her. She'd told Julianne that the money she took for her sketches was a precautionary measure. At the time, she'd thought it wise to wait until Will had proven he would not beggar them, but she was the one who was putting their marriage in jeopardy.

When Amy had married Will, she'd had ample reason

to distrust him. But after the conversation at dinner, she could no longer fool herself. He wasn't the one who had betrayed the trust in their marriage. She'd kept her dalliance in trade a secret, and then she'd taken a risk that had alerted Julianne. Even after Julianne had confronted her, Amy had insisted she needed more time.

Just because he didn't know did not make it right.

The day she'd accepted Madame DuPont's offer of compensation, she'd known it was wrong. She'd nearly refused, until the modiste offered her five shillings per sketch. Amy had always felt the ton's attitude about trade was hypocritical, and so she'd persuaded herself that she had every right to accept compensation. But secretly flouting the proprieties counted as hypocrisy.

Julianne was right. If anyone caught her accepting coin, the gossip would spread and humiliate members of both her family and Will's.

Now she had a dilemma. The time to have admitted to him that she had accepted money for her sketches had long since passed. If she told him now, he would want to know why. She'd already deceived him and could not make matters worse by lying. But if she told him the truth, he would not care about her excuses. Her only defense—that she'd hidden money in the event he gambled away a fortune—would insult him and quite possibly destroy the bond they had worked so hard to establish.

Shame made her feel a little ill. She'd betrayed her husband and put Julianne in the middle of her scheme. Amy didn't want the money any longer, but she had no choice but to leave it secreted in the bottom of her trunk until Will was gone, and she could safely take the purse back to Madame DuPont.

• • •

"Amy?" Will said.

She gasped and turned to find Will and Bell entering the parlor.

Will laughed. "You were so deep in thought."

"Please join me," she said, rising.

Bell shook his head. "I came to thank you for the excellent dinner, but I'll not intrude any longer. Until we meet again." He bowed and retreated.

Will crossed the room and sat beside her. "You seem a bit anxious."

"Oh, it is nothing," she said.

His eyes held a tender expression. "Sweetheart, are you having second thoughts? If you're not ready, I won't press you."

He was so considerate that it made her chest ache. She did not deserve him, but she must push her guilt to the farthest corners of her brain and focus all of her attention on him. "Will, I haven't changed my mind."

He helped her rise. Then he escorted her upstairs. She told herself that it was in both their best interests to keep her secret. Their relationship was still in the fragile stage. She would live forever silent about her deception, because she would rather have it hanging over her head than wound him with the suspicions that had led her to deceive him.

When he reached her door, he looked at her. "I want to take your hair down tonight."

She nodded. When he closed the door, guilt made her stomach clench. All this time, she'd held herself up as the righteous person in this marriage, but he'd never failed her. Since the night they were locked in that wine cel-

lar, he had acted honorably. Not once had he shirked his
responsibilities. He'd agreed to court her, and he'd held up
his end of the bargain. He'd gone to his club only on the
day she'd suggested a shopping trip. Ironically, she was
the one who had failed him. And God willing, he would
never know.

Chapter Thirteen

At the sound of the knock, Amy rose from the bed. "Come in."

Will entered, wearing the banyan and trousers. He held a bottle and two glasses. "You left the necklace on. I'm glad."

"What is this?" she asked.

"A liqueur I discovered in Italy." He set it on the bed table. Then he pulled the turned-down covers all the way to the end of the bed. Afterward, he hoisted her onto the mattress, making her laugh. He poured about two inches of the amber-colored liqueur in the glasses and handed her one. "To dessert," he said, touching his glass to hers.

She laughed. Then she sniffed the drink. "Is it strong?"

"A little, but it's very sweet. And tastes of almonds," he said.

She sipped it. "Oh, it is a bit strong, but it's very good."

He shrugged off the banyan and sat beside her on the mattress. "I thought you would like it. There's a story."

She sipped again. "Tell me."

He swallowed. "An Italian artist intended to paint a Madonna and chose a model. Supposedly, she was a widow of little means, but she wished to give a gift to the painter for the great honor he had bestowed upon her. According to the tale, the widow made a secret concoction that included brandy."

When he kissed her, she could taste the liqueur on his mouth and tongue. She sipped from her glass again. "It's so sweet it's sinful."

He sipped again and smiled. "I want to paint you."

"You paint?"

Laughter lurked in his eyes. "In a manner of speaking. I'll show you in a bit." He lifted his chin. "Drink some more."

She sipped. "I see your plan. You think if I get a bit inebriated, I won't be nervous."

"I agree that might prove beneficial, but I had something else in mind."

"If you're intending to paint me, you've no paint, canvas, or easel."

He swirled his finger in the liqueur and painted her lower lip.

"Oh," she said, laughing.

His eyes danced mischievously. "Are you done with your glass?"

"No." She laughed. "I'm jesting."

"I'll be patient." He leaned toward her and licked her lip. "Mmmm. You taste so sweet."

"What a surprise," she said. Oh, she was a little giddy.

He reached over and pulled on the drawstring of her nightgown.

She took another sip of the liqueur and handed him the

glass. He set the glasses aside. "Guess what I'm thinking about?"

"Painting?"

"Actually, I was thinking about getting you naked."

"But I thought you wished to paint me," she said.

"I wish to paint you nude." He winked. "Will you be my model?"

"Certainly. I will be your Madonna."

"Madonna's been done before. I was thinking Amy."

"What will you call your painting?" she asked.

He pulled the pins from her hair. "The bride undone." He set the pins on the table. Then he combed his fingers through the curls and arranged them so that they flowed over her breasts.

She drew in her breath and let it out slowly. He stood and removed his trousers and drawers. He was aroused, and the sight sent desire eddying through her veins. His sculpted body was all hard angles and planes. She reached out to touch his hot chest. When she trailed her hand down to his cock, his nostrils flared. She closed her hand round him and squeezed gently. He shut his eyes momentarily, and when he lifted his lashes again, his expression was glazed.

He grasped her night rail and pulled it over her head. Then he urged her to lie back on the pillow. He sat beside her and retrieved one of the glasses with liqueur. He dipped his fingers inside and painted her lips, her earlobes, and dabbed at her neck. Then he licked her lips. Her breathing grew faster. He tasted her earlobes and nipped one with his teeth.

"Oh," she said.

"Don't like that?"

"You surprised me."

"It's all right. If I do something you don't like, then you must tell me. If I do something you like, you should tell me as well," he said.

She inhaled and exhaled slowly. He bent his head and suckled her neck. Then he set his hand on her stomach. "Don't be alarmed. I'm going to pour a bit on you."

Oh, heavens. She'd never thought he would do something like that.

He dribbled the liqueur between her breasts and down the length of her stomach. Once again, he set the glass aside. Then he knelt between her legs and licked his way down her body. Her stomach trembled a bit the entire time.

"Sit up for me." His voice rumbled.

She did as he asked. He retrieved the glass and painted her nipples liberally. Then he took a sip and set the glass aside. He kissed her openmouthed, and she tasted the sweetness on his tongue. His hands cupped her breasts. She clung to his shoulders, and when he bent his head to suckle her breast, she arched her neck, sending her hair spilling down her back as desire engulfed her. A high-pitched sound came out of her throat. Oh, God. Oh, God. Oh, God. She was on fire.

When he lifted his head, she gazed down his torso and saw that his cock was fully erect. He lay on his back and brought her on top of him. His fingers combed through her hair again, and she let her curls brush along his chest. His expression grew increasingly ardent as she moved down his torso. Now and then, she planted kisses on his hot skin. When she let her hair sweep over his cock, he hissed in his breath.

He rolled her to her back and kissed her deeply. "Draw your feet on the bed," he said. Then he slid his big hands underneath her bottom and tilted her up. He looked up at her from beneath his thick lashes. Then, watching her, he stuck two fingers in his mouth. The look in his eyes should have incinerated her.

He caressed her folds and slowly inched one finger inside her. "You're wet."

She inhaled on a ragged breath.

He slipped another finger inside her and moved ever so slowly. "I'm stretching you. If you feel any discomfort, you must tell me."

She was breathing fast. "I like it."

He stilled the movements. "Squeeze my fingers."

She looked at him in confusion.

"Tighten your inner muscles," he whispered.

She did and caught her lip with her teeth at the exquisite sensation.

"Again," he said.

She whimpered.

"Feel good?"

"Yes," she whispered and squeezed his fingers again.

"Don't stop," he said. Then he slid his body down the bed. When his tongue flicked high among the folds of her sex, she cried out. A wicked laugh escaped him, but he didn't stop. His fingers moved in and out, stretching her, and then the waves of pleasure gripped her.

Will positioned his cock, and entered her as the rhythmic contractions of her orgasm continued. A wounded sound came from her throat. He slowly slid all the way home and framed her face. "Sweet Amy." He kissed the tears on her cheeks. "I tried not to hurt you."

Her nails bit into his back.

He stayed very still. She was so tight inside, and God

help him, it felt so good. But he would not move, because he could feel the tension in her. He kissed her lips. "Sweet, sweet girl."

She opened her eyes.

"Sorry it hurts," he said.

After a few moments, she sighed. "Oh, it's better when I'm not so tense."

He moved a little inside her. "Did it hurt?"

"No," she said, smiling.

He eased in and out as slowly as he could and gazed into her eyes the whole time. There was an expression of wonder on her face.

"Wrap your legs around me."

When she did, he hissed in his breath at the feeling of her soft, slim thighs cradling him. "I love your legs," he said.

He bent to kiss her again, but his control started slipping. Will bared his teeth, focusing on a slow and steady rhythm, but the pressure built and built and built. The sounds of wetness drove him to the edge. The instinct to pump faster gripped him. He was breathing hard and losing himself to the erotic sensations. She clutched him with her arms. He stilled and pressed higher. Then she squeezed him with her thighs. The erotic spasms started, and he gave himself up to the pleasure as his seed spilled inside her. The throbbing went on and on and on, the sensations stronger than any he could ever remember. When he was spent, he collapsed atop her, completely and utterly sated.

Sleep had claimed him

He was heavy, but she didn't want to let him go. He was

still inside her, and she loved the feeling, even if she was a little sore. She gazed at the fan of his black lashes. Her strong, muscular man looked a little vulnerable while sleeping.

He'd made her feel beautiful and wanted.

A rush of tender feelings flooded her heart. While he continued to sleep, she dared to whisper the words. "I love you."

He'd tried so hard to be gentle with her, but his need had overcome him. She'd watched him the whole time, focusing on his pleasure. Toward the end, he seemed to have been in something of a frenzy, pumping faster and faster. Then he'd strained inside her, and she'd felt him throbbing.

Smiling, she gently brushed a lock of his black hair aside. His eyes opened. He looked disoriented for a moment. She kissed his smooth cheek, realizing he must have shaved this evening. Her husband was considerate.

He pushed up on his elbows and cleared his throat. "I must be crushing you." His voice sounded sleep-scratchy.

"I like holding you," she said.

He rolled over onto his back and looked at her. "Are you all right?"

"Yes, more than all right."

"Sorry I wasn't more considerate."

"You were," she said.

"I need to take care of you."

"Will?"

He got out of bed, looked at the sheets, and winced.

She saw the bloodstains and sought to reassure him. "I'm fine, Will."

He drew the covers over her. "I'll be right back."

She watched him walk to the bowl and pitcher. He wasn't the least bit modest.

Will poured water from the pitcher into the bowl.

When he started to wash himself, she looked away. A few minutes later, he walked to the bed with a damp cloth and towel. He stripped the covers back. Realizing his intent, she tried to protest, but he put his finger over her lips. "Shhhh. Let me take care of you."

Her face heated as he applied the cloth.

"I should probably sleep in my own bed tonight until you're recovered," he said.

"I wish you would stay with me."

"It's too tempting to say no." He snuffed the candles, climbed into bed, and faced her. "If I should get amorous during the night, you must stop me. Your body needs rest."

The idea that he might awaken during the night and want to make love stunned her. She supposed there was much she still had to learn about her husband. "Are all men as eager as you?"

"Probably," he said, yawning. "Let's spoon."

"What?"

"Turn your back to me," he said.

"Where is my night rail?"

"We're sleeping naked," he said, pulling her to his chest and cupping her breast.

"Oh, I like this," she said.

"Me, too. Sleep," he muttered.

His deep, even breathing was the only sound in the room. "I love you," she whispered again.

Upon awakening, he'd shocked her and had to explain about morning erections.

"You're jesting." She was lying on her side with the sheet pulled over her breasts, and her lovely red hair was spilled all over the pillow.

"It's the truth," he said. "Men get erections throughout the day, me included."

"I don't believe you."

"It's quite obvious with the current fashion for tight trousers," he said.

"I'm not in the habit of staring at men's crotches," she said in a shocked voice.

He burst out laughing.

She wrinkled her nose. "Aunt Hester was right. Men are animals."

He ripped the sheet off her. "Grrrr," he said, crawling over her.

"Wiiiiiiillll!"

"Got you in my trap, and now you're my breakfast."

She laughed and tried to push him away.

"You don't believe me, do you?" he said.

"No."

"Well, since you declared defeat in our wager, you have to stay abed with me for six more days."

"What? No! I ceded the wager to you as a gift. That's not the same as defeat."

He grinned at her outraged expression and shook his head slowly. "That wasn't part of the rules."

"You just lost the wager," she said. "I win three more weeks of courtship. The fun is over for you."

Deuce take it. She looked serious. "Let's compromise," he said.

She narrowed her green eyes.

"Seriously, I'd planned to still court you. By the way, have I mentioned how enticing you look in nothing but that emerald necklace?"

"That's not courtship. That's lust," she said.

He almost said the latter was the goal of the former, but that would probably get him kicked out of bed. "There is still a great deal for us to learn about each other," he said. "You have to admit we have fun together, too."

"I'm not staying in this bed for six days," she said.

He sighed. "I had my heart set on it."

"Will, be practical. We can't eat in bed."

"Yes, we can." He caught himself before saying he'd done it any number of times. Even the slightest hint about his former paramours would likely earn him a permanent black mark. Besides, none of them had been truly special. As Bell had said, Amy was one in a thousand.

"If we stay in this bed, I know you won't be talking," she said.

He bent his head and kissed her nipple. "I can talk while I make love."

"Will, there are practical matters—a bath, clean sheets, and your heavy beard makes you look like a pirate."

"Oh," he said. "I'm being a selfish brute. You probably need to recover anyway."

"From what?" she said.

Hope leaped in his chest. "I thought you might be a bit sore, last night being your first time and all."

She knit her brows. "No, sore isn't the right word. It's actually sort of a pleasant feeling."

"Amy?" he said.

"I'll compromise," she said. "Three more weeks of courtship."

He groaned.

"There is one other condition," she said.

"You're torturing me," he said.

"I'm very sorry, but I demand that you make love to me every night."

He laughed and rolled onto his back, taking her with him. "It's time for your riding lesson."

"We have no steed," she said.

"Yes, we do," he said. "Lean forward, love. You'll like this."

He stroked her folds and dipped two fingers inside her. "You're soaked."

"Oh, my."

"Put me inside you," he said.

She did as he asked and slowly pressed down until she was fully seated. "Oh, I like that."

"Come closer to me," he said, "and ride."

She moved slowly. "Oh."

"Feel good?" His voice rumbled.

"Yes." She felt self-conscious at first, but she soon gave herself over to the sensations. He cupped her breasts and suckled first one nipple and then the other. She reached for the pleasure he'd shown her. He closed his hands over her hips. The emerald necklace lapped at her neck as she moved.

"I like watching your tits while you ride," he said.

His earthy words should have shocked her, but the way he'd spoken called to the wanton inside her. Then she sensed the moment was upon her. Amy cried out as the pleasure rushed through her like a waterfall. She tumbled over and over. The powerful sensations racked her body. She stilled as her inner muscles contracted over and over again. Then she collapsed on his chest.

He rolled her over, and she realized their bodies were still joined. This time, he thrust inside her without reservation. She clasped her hands round his neck, and he never took his dark gaze off of her. "You are mine," he said.

"Yes." He possessed her, and she wanted it. Wanted all of him. He was *her husband. Her man. Her heart.*

The ropelike muscles in his strong arms tensed as he increased the tempo of his thrusts. He was breathing fast, and she loved watching his expression. He was a lusty man, in his prime, young and strong. She wondered if she would ever stop marveling that this beautiful man wanted and desired her.

He bared his teeth, thrusting faster and faster inside her. She wrapped her legs round him and squeezed.

"God, yes," he said, hissing in his breath. Then he pushed until he could go no farther, and she felt him throbbing inside her. When he collapsed atop her, she caressed the damp strands at his nape, and though he was heavy, she welcomed the weight of his body.

"Sorry," he mumbled and rolled onto his back. Then he caressed her cheek and closed his eyes.

Two hours later, he took her for a long walk through the woods. There was something he needed to discuss with her. He didn't know why it hadn't occurred to him before. He supposed it was because they had postponed consummating the marriage. But he figured they'd better talk about it before it was too late, if it wasn't already.

He took her to the old swing not far from the tree house. "I'll push you," he said. She smiled as he sent her higher and higher. Eventually, he let it slow. "Amy, there's something that occurred to me a little belatedly."

She looked at him inquiringly. "What is it, Will?"

"Well, you know lovemaking can have consequences," he said.

"Yes, I know," she said.

"We never talked about children," he said.

She shrugged. "I just assumed they would come along. Are you worried that it will be like my parents?"

"No, not really," he said. "It's just that we didn't take any precautions."

"What do you mean?" she said, frowning.

She didn't know there were preventive measures. He squatted beside the swing. "You understand what happens when I spill my seed, right?"

"Yes," she said.

He blew out his breath. "Well, I could have withdrawn from your body to prevent getting you with child."

Her smile faded. She looked in the other direction and let her bonnet partially hide her face. "I always wondered how courtesans managed."

He figured she was thinking of the women in his past. "It's damned foolish to keep ladies ignorant of basic facts of life, especially when it concerns your own bodies."

"You sound almost angry about it," she said.

He wouldn't tell her about some of the uglier things he'd witnessed at school and abroad. Young, pregnant women who lost their livelihoods, while the scoundrels who impregnated them walked away free as birds. He was fortunate that Hawk had instructed him about the use of French letters to prevent disease and pregnancy.

Will helped her to rise and held her hands. "I just want you to know that you have a choice—or I should say, we have a choice to make. It was stupid of me not to even think of it. Last night, I was more worried about making sure I didn't...hurt you."

She looked at him. "I knew you wouldn't hurt me, Will."

"You know there were others in my life, and you know there were never any serious relationships. The thing is, I worried because I'd never made love to a virgin before. I didn't know what to expect."

"You acquitted yourself very well."

He smiled a little. "The choice is yours. Do you want to let things happen naturally or do you want to delay a family?"

"Do you have a preference?" she asked.

"Since we're still getting to know each other, we might want it to be just us for a little while longer."

"Yes, I agree," she said. "Even with a nurse, a babe still requires a lot of attention, especially with feedings."

He held her hand as they walked back to the cottage. "My friends are very impressed with you."

"I liked them," she said. "They are very different in their characters. Fordham is something of a charmer, though not nearly as handsome or clever as you are."

"He can be a slow top at times, but he's a loyal friend."

She sighed. "Bell, on the other hand, is something of a mystery. His manners are polished and his conversation all that it should be. But I sense that he holds back a part of himself, as if he doesn't want others to get too close."

"You've pegged him," Will said. "But enough about my bachelor friends. We have three more weeks of courtship."

"So what should we talk about today?" she asked.

"I think we should go for a drive during the fashionable hour," he said. "I want to show off my fashionable wife."

• • •

She hadn't wanted to go out into the social whirl so soon. In truth, she'd wanted to stay in their idyllic little cottage. Of course, there had been issues, but they had managed to resolve them. And she was feeling easier now that she'd made the decision not to take any more coin for her designs. In truth, the guilt over her deception had spoiled her pleasure in creating gown designs. As the days went on, she hoped that her bad feelings would dissipate, but for now, she meant to concentrate all of her attention on Will.

He was proud of her and wanted to show her off to the ton. Of course, she was delighted that he was pleased. No, she was stunned, after all the years she had sat on the wallflower row, believing herself too plain, too tall, and too shy to attract the attention of any man, much less one as handsome as her husband.

Will had made her feel desired and attractive. When she was alone with him, she had learned to shed her inhibitions and felt herself worthy of being loved. But while he was an attentive lover, he'd never directly expressed tender feelings for her. She counseled herself to be patient. He'd told her he wasn't certain what he was capable of feeling, but she must trust that, in time, he would come to love her. Yet she found it difficult to hold back her own declaration. Only when she was certain that he was asleep did she find the courage to whisper what was in her heart. But now, he was expertly steering his curricle along the crowded, noisy streets of London, and she felt as if she were crossing from her private honeymoon world into the public social world. Anxiety flooded her chest. Supposedly their marriage had alleviated the worst of the scandal, but she knew that others would stare and gossip. There were a number of cynical and cruel people in the ton who thrived on controversy.

"Amy, there is nothing to be nervous about. I want to see that sweet smile, and I promise to make you laugh today. We're going to drive along Rotten Row. I doubt people will point their fingers and stare, all because we accidentally got locked in a wine cellar—or stolen by Gypsies if you prefer."

She laughed. Then she sighed. "You're right. If I cower, they will assume the worst."

"Actually, the park is the easiest place to make our first appearance as husband and wife. I need only tip my hat and you can wave your pretty gloved hand. Ah, here we are." He drove along the path and winked at her. "Oh, my, everyone is looking at us." He looked sideways at her. "Are my devil horns showing?"

"No, I'm so very sorry. You must have forgotten them," she said.

He grinned at her. "Surely my forked tail is swishing behind me."

She looked behind the seat. "Oops, I think you lost it along the way."

"Drat, my bad reputation will be in tatters," he said.

She laughed and waved as they passed Lady Wallingham, who was openly staring at them.

"I suppose she thinks we should hide our indecent selves in the country," Will said.

She grinned at him. "I rather like being indecent with you in the country."

"This may prove to be a very short drive," he said.

"I have a very virile husband," she said.

"I'm so tempted to kiss you in front of everyone, but we'd probably have to face the inquisition at Ashdown House if I did."

She leaned forward. "Oh, look. It's Georgette and Beau." She waved enthusiastically.

Will pulled his curricle alongside Beau's and pointed ahead. "Follow me."

Georgette waved at Amy. "Oh, she looks radiant, and I'm sure Beau is thrilled," Amy said.

Will drove off the path and jumped down. Then he reached up for Amy. He pretended that he was about to drop her, making her laugh. A group of passing matrons walking along held up their quizzing glasses to get a better look.

When Beau halted his vehicle, Amy bounced on her toes as Beau helped Georgette descend.

Amy hurried to her friend and clasped her hands. "Congratulations to you and Beau. I've missed you."

"Oh, heavens, I wanted to write, but you know my mother and her ridiculous ideas about the proprieties," Georgette said. "Why she thinks newlyweds shouldn't be disturbed with mail is beyond me."

"Julianne told me your mother forbade you to write to me. When did you return from your aunt's house?" Amy asked.

"Yesterday, and not a moment too soon. Aunt Marianne's old hound, Herbert, gobbled up a tray of biscuits and cast them up on Mama's slippers."

Beau laughed. "I've never heard such screeching in all my life."

"Mama's nerves have still not settled. She's taken to her bed, and Papa is hiding in his library. All is back to normal," Georgette said, laughing. "But look at you, Amy. Your cheeks are rosy, and you look very happy."

"I am," she said as Will clasped her hand. "But when is your wedding taking place?"

"In a fortnight," Beau said. "The banns were read last Sunday, so just twice more, and then we will marry. Afterward, we will retire to the country and live with my family."

"Eugenia will be my bridesmaid," Georgette said. "I do hope you will come to the wedding."

"Of course we will," Amy said. "I'm very happy for you both."

Beau asked Will a question about his curricle. The two men went over to examine the wheels.

"Oh, heavens," Georgette said. "Beau will go on for hours about axles and such. I pretend to be fascinated for his sake. But never mind that. Walk with me a little way and tell me how you really are."

"I will likely astonish you," Amy said. "You know I was apprehensive about this marriage, with good reason. It was so strange at first, because we knew very little about each other. But we are getting to know each other, and I am truly happy."

"I'm glad," Georgette said. "And really, how could he not love you?"

Amy's smile faded. "Our marital relationship is still developing."

"Are you in love with him?" Georgette asked.

Amy shaded her hand above her bonnet brim and looked out at the path. "I haven't told him."

"He seems smitten with you," Georgette said.

"He said he is proud of me," she said. It was so much

more than she'd hoped for, but still it fell short of her ultimate dream of marriage.

"That is very reassuring," Georgette said.

"Well, there can be no doubt about you and Beau," Amy said, turning the conversation back to her friend. "Now tell me all about your plans for the wedding and the honeymoon." Georgette told her about the dress that Madame DuPont was creating, and she explained that she and Beau would journey to the Lake District in Scotland for their honeymoon.

All of Amy's happiness ebbed slowly away. She found herself wishing she'd not expressed such jubilance over her marriage, because she felt foolish. In truth, she'd been ecstatic over the progress of her marriage, but when she compared her situation to Georgette's, Amy realized she'd been thrilled over a marriage of necessity. She'd been happy with second-best, until hearing Georgette's news.

"I'm very glad I saw you today," Amy said.

"Lady Wallingham is planning a ball in celebration of the engagement," Georgette said. "You must attend."

"Yes, of course." Amy's stomach tightened a little at the prospect of appearing at a public ball. She told herself that all would be well, and of course she couldn't disappoint Georgette, but it seemed that the idyllic time she and Will had spent alone was quickly coming to a close.

They turned round and walked back to the curricles. Amy waved as Beau drove Georgette away.

"Do you want to walk?" Will asked.

"No, I have a slight headache." She'd manufactured the headache, because all of her happiness had burst like a soap bubble.

"I hope you're not unwell," Will said.

"It's only a headache," she said.

"I'll take you home to rest."

During the drive home, she told herself to be happy with the progress of her own marriage and not to compare her situation with that of her friend. In truth, she'd been quite happy until Georgette had said words that had made reality sink in. *And really, how could he not love you?*

Her husband didn't love her. He liked her. He was proud of her. He enjoyed spending time with her. And he desired her.

She told herself it was enough, that it was far more than she'd expected from this marriage. It could have been so much worse. In truth, she'd never held out real hope for her dreams, even before she'd journeyed with Georgette to London. The only two men who had ever expressed interest were exact opposites: a vicar and a devil. Ironically, they shared one similarity—neither loved her.

With a deep breath, she vowed to expunge this foolish envy and return her focus to her shared goal with Will. They would prove everyone wrong about them. Everyone would see that they were delighted with each other. No one would forget that he was the worst rakehell in London, and no one would forget that she was a wallflower. But they would not see what they undoubtedly expected: a couple living separate lives.

That afternoon, she had gone to her room to rest and shortly thereafter discovered the reason for her dampened spirits. Her monthly cycle had begun. She ought to have known, but she'd told herself the slight ache in her back was a result of the lovemaking. Ordinarily, she kept track, but with all the upheaval in her life, she'd completely forgotten. She drank some tea dosed with willow bark that made her a bit sleepy and eased some of the cramping.

Poppet followed Will to her room. "Amy, do you still have a headache?" he asked.

The kitten jumped on the bed and sat on the pillow beside Amy. "My monthly cycle started," she said.

"Oh." He sat on the edge of the mattress. "I hope it's not too uncomfortable."

Here was more evidence of his vast experience with other women. His gentle manner made her even more cross. "I don't feel well," she snapped, "and yes, it is uncomfortable."

He winced. "Can I bring you anything? Or perhaps rub your back?"

"No, thank you," she muttered. Oh, she was in a horrid mood.

He rose. "Try to rest."

She did manage to doze. The sigh of the door opening awoke her, and she realized the room had gotten considerably darker. Will walked in with a candle. "Ah, you're awake. Are you feeling any better?"

"The tea Anna made helped me sleep," she said.

"I don't want to disturb you," he said. "I'll just go round to the club and let you rest." He kissed her cheek. "Go back to sleep now. I'll check in with you tomorrow."

After he left, she felt very sorry for herself, because her back hurt and she was irritable. She'd given her trust to him, but it was much easier to trust him when he was at home with her. Now he was gone, and she missed him. She wished the outside world would go away, and that it could just be the two of them, plus the servants and Poppet of course.

Most of all, she wished Will would come home and talk to her.

Will could not help noticing that Amy had not been herself all week. She withdrew inside herself and said little. She was never sharp-tongued, but she was also not forthcoming. Will grew tired of this strange behavior quickly, because it seemed too much like moping to him.

On Friday morning, she'd joined him for breakfast and seemed to be her old self again. He set his newspaper aside. "Monday, I start my position. I'll be working at Ashdown House most of the time, when I'm not out inspecting the property."

She set her toast aside. "I wish we had more time alone."

He patted her hand. "We'll still talk at night. By the way, we received an invitation from Lady Wallingham to a ball in one week. Sorry, I'd misplaced it, but I sent an acceptance late yesterday."

"Georgette told me at the park. It is to honor her engagement to Beau," Amy said.

He frowned. "I assumed you wished to attend a ball given in your friend's honor."

"Of course I do," she said with no enthusiasm.

Will's temper snapped, but a footman came in to clear the dishes.

He rose. "Amy, please come with me to the parlor."

She sighed and walked with him. Once there, he sat with her on the sofa. "Amy, what is wrong? I understand you did not feel well earlier in the week, but since you came down to breakfast, I assume you've recovered. What I don't understand is why you're ill-tempered about the ball in your friend's honor."

She looked at her tightly clasped hands. "I prefer not to reveal it, because it is unworthy of me, and I should have let it go before now. I will do so immediately and will not perturb you again."

"I insist," he said, "because you have been in a bad temper since the day we saw your friend and Beau at the park. Did you have a falling out with Georgette?"

"No, I did not."

"Then tell me what is wrong, because I'm weary of your petulance."

"I have been resentful, without cause, and envied a dear friend. I am well aware I should not begrudge her."

He frowned. "Then why did you? She is a good friend to you."

"Sometimes it can seem that others' lives are so much easier. Sometimes your friend gets what you want more than anything else in the world. You don't resent them for getting it, you only resent that you cannot have it. That is why I have been in a foul mood, and I'm ashamed to admit it."

He shook his head. "I don't understand; you're speaking in generalities."

"Have you ever wanted something very badly, but circumstances conspired against you?"

He thought of that day when his brother had told him that he would withhold his quarterly allowance to prevent him from traveling. "Yes."

"Georgette made an offhand remark. It was meant kindly. She has no idea that it stung me, and I wish to leave it at that."

"You will not resolve this resentment until you release it."

"There is no resolution, Will. I was simply reminded

that I will never have what she has. I was perfectly content until she made the remark, and I will find contentment again. I just have to accept things as they are, rather than as I wish them to be."

"You are unhappy because of this lack in your life. Tell me what it is you need, and I will give it to you," he said.

"You cannot give what you do not have to give," she said. "Please excuse me. I wish to write a letter to my parents."

Will went for a ride because he was frustrated with Amy. He hoped a jaunt through the property would clear his head so that he could figure out what his wife wanted so badly that he supposedly couldn't give her.

When he returned home two hours later, he muttered "women" under his breath as he trudged up the path to the cottage. Damnation, he would make her tell him. She was the one who insisted they talk all the time, and now she suddenly wanted to retreat to silence. That was just too damned bad.

He stomped into the foyer, no doubt leaving dust on the floor. Will decided to confront her and tell her that enough was enough. He strode across the marble floor and strode to the parlor where he heard voices. He found Amy entertaining three of her friends: Eugenia, Cecile, and Bernice. They were looking at Amy's sketches.

"Sorry," Will said. "I didn't mean to interrupt."

The ladies rose and curtsied. "We were on the verge of leaving, sir," Lady Eugenia said. Cecile and Bernice regarded him with obvious apprehension. They apparently believed he was the devil.

"Amy, we look forward to shopping with you next week," Lady Eugenia said.

After the three ladies departed, Will joined Amy on the sofa. "I hope I didn't scare your friends away."

"No, they only wished to call and set a date for shopping," she said. "They want my fashion advice."

He nodded. "I went for a ride, because I was frustrated and wanted to see if I could work out what you felt was lacking in your life that made you envy your friend. You said I couldn't give you what I didn't have to give. It took me some time to figure it out, because I was thinking it had to do with something visible. Then I recollected the night we quarreled, and I realized that you had told me the day we married. You wanted the fairy-tale romance."

"It doesn't signify," she said. "I allowed momentary envy to cloud my judgment. No good ever comes from comparing yourself to others. I know that, but I'm human, and I responded with petty resentment."

"That night we quarreled, I told you honestly how I felt about you, but it seems that you are unhappy because of the circumstances of our marriage after all. You agreed to show the world that we are happy. And we both promised to remain faithful to each other."

"Will, I meant all of those things, and I think you know that I was happy and delighted—and then I had that conversation with Georgette and let envy overrule me."

"Did she say something that overset you?"

Amy was silent a moment. "She did not know that her words would wound me."

"What did she say?"

Amy's hands were clutched tightly in her lap. "It was one of those comments that people often toss off that are not insincere, but are mostly meant to buoy the other person. I did not expect my feelings to rise up the way they did. It was a shock to me."

"What did she say?" he asked once more.

Amy said nothing. He remained silent. While it was his nature to immediately respond to another's comment, he made himself wait for her to formulate her reply.

She wet her lips. "She said, 'And really, how could he not love you?'" A mirthless little laugh escaped her. "You see, it was nothing at all, and I am so sensitive that I made more out of it than I ought to have done so. I sulked and failed in my vow to bring you comfort and happiness."

His chest tightened. He didn't like the feeling. "We both knew this marriage would be a challenge," he said. "We took vows, and we made our private commitments to our union. I thought we were in accord."

"When we drove to the park, you noticed my anxiety. I didn't want our time alone in the cottage to end so quickly. I felt and still feel that our relationship is new and vulnerable. I didn't want to expose our marriage to society, but it wasn't so difficult while driving along Rotten Row. Of course, I was thrilled to see Georgette again. I told her that I was truly happy, because you and I were getting to know each other. Then I realized that it did not sound nearly as special when I shared it with Georgette. I wanted her to be more enthusiastic. I didn't want to hear that she thought the developments in our marriage were *encouraging*. I wanted to hear that she was thrilled for me. I viewed my happiness from her perspective and realized the reality had fallen short of my girlhood dream.

"She is my dear friend, and I envied her because she had time to have a wedding dress specially made. I envied her because she will have an extended wedding trip. I envied her because I know that Beau is in love with her. I envied her because everything has come easily to her and almost everything, save my fashion designs, has come hard for me.

"Because of that, I have had low expectations for myself all my life. I actually considered marrying Mr. Crawford, even though I thought him too critical, because my parents seemed to like him. I came very close to marrying a man because it was sensible, and I thought it would please my parents. If not for Georgette's counsel, I might have made that mistake."

"Instead you made a worse mistake with me," he said.

"Will, I may have thought that when we were compromised, but my opinion of you has changed a great deal since that time. I expected the worst, and you have abided by our every agreement.

"I am the one who has let doubt creep in. I am the one who insisted you prove yourself, but I have not lived up to my commitment to make this marriage work. You were right that I have trouble trusting you. I know that is a problem, and I will try to overcome my fears. I am likely to fail more than once, but I hope you will be patient with me."

"I will try, but I cannot promise that I won't grow exasperated and angry with your mistrust. Turn that around, Amy, and ask yourself how you would feel if I did not trust you."

She winced. Of course he had no idea that she had deceived him, and once again, she had demonstrated her hypocrisy. She took his large hands in her own. "It occurs to me that if I expect trust from you, I must give it as well."

"Amy, we cannot stay in the cottage forever. Sooner or

later the butterfly must leave the cocoon. I understand your concerns, given the circumstances of our marriage, but hiding will only make it worse. However, if you ever find yourself in company with those who make you uncomfortable for any reason, you must find me, and I will take you away. There is no reason to subject ourselves to cruel and malicious people, and we both know plenty of them exist in the ton."

Chapter Fourteen

Amy was a bit nervous as Will escorted her into the foyer at Lord and Lady Wallingham's home. This was the first social function that they would attend as a married couple. She tried to avoid looking directly at anyone, because she feared others were likely staring at them. Scandal of any kind drew the ton like bees to nectar.

Tonight she wore a gauze gown with blue sprigs over a white satin silk slip. The bodice and flounces were trimmed with blond satin leaves. In her hair, she wore a wreath of silk roses. She had worried that the roses would look awful with her red hair, but Will had told her it was the next best thing to seeing her hair flowing and loose. She wanted him to be proud of her tonight. She had always felt lacking because of her plain looks. In the privacy of her bedchamber, Will had made her feel desired. But tonight, she wished very much that she could be beautiful for him.

Unlike her, Will seemed perfectly at ease as he led her

up the stairs. He waved at someone and continued on to the receiving line. He looked handsome, of course, in his black coat and trousers. Amy was aware of others whispering. She did not look at them. As they moved down the line, they greeted Lady Wallingham.

"Well, isn't this sweet? How lucky you are, Miss Hardwick, to have married Mr. Darcett, for he is a handsome young man."

Amy heard the unspoken words. *What a pity he was forced to marry a plain woman.*

Will gazed at Amy. "Lady Wallingham, you are mistaken. I am the lucky one, since Miss Hardwick consented to become Mrs. Darcett."

"Oh, yes. How silly of me to forget. Of course she is Mrs. Darcett now," Lady Wallingham said. "But now, dear, you must come and say hello to Eugenia."

When Amy came to Eugenia, her friend squeezed her hand. "I'm so glad you came."

Just before they stepped into the drawing room, Will slowed his steps. "Amy?"

She looked at him.

He captured her gaze and held it. Her skin prickled. He said nothing, but there was something new in his eyes. She sought the word and realized it was tenderness.

Amy caught her breath, wondering if it could be possible that he was developing more than just a fondness for her. She told herself not to get her hopes up, because she didn't want to risk heartache.

Not long afterward, Lady Wallingham approached them. "Now, now, Mrs. Darcett, you must not live in your husband's pockets. It is not the thing at all." She followed those inane words with inane laughter.

"Ah, but I'm wicked and have never met a rule I didn't itch to break," Will said. "So I will keep my wife in my pocket for now."

When Amy looked at Will, he regarded her with that heated look she knew so well. He set his hand in the curve of her lower back, and she welcomed the possessive gesture. Indeed, he made her feel cherished. He leaned down and said, "You look magnificent tonight."

Amy's heart squeezed. His approval meant the world to her.

He leaned down a bit as he spoke. "Dance with me?"

She smiled. "Thank you."

As they neared the dance floor, the musicians played the opening bars of a waltz. She leaned closer to his ear. "I've never danced it."

"I will lead, and all you need do is follow." The music started, and he twirled her round and round and round. He never took his gaze off her, and she wondered if he could see the love shining in her eyes. In her head, she heard one-two-three, one-two-three, one-two-three.

Amy glanced over her shoulder. "Oh, Will, look. Grandmamma is moving her hand in time to the music."

"I suppose it's loud enough that she can hear it," he said.

"I wish she were a bit steadier so that you could waltz with her," Amy said.

"I think that can be arranged, Mrs. Darcett." He took her hand and led her off the dance floor. Amy smiled a little at Will when she noticed others remarking on their early exit. But in a moment, those cynical people would witness something very special, something that would give them pause when referring to him as the devil.

He walked over to his grandmamma and bowed. Then

he held out his hand. A sweet smile spread across her face as he helped her to stand. Then he hoisted her small slippered feet on top of his shoes. The voices in the drawing room gradually receded as others gathered round to watch Will dance with his grandmamma. Patience came to stand by Amy and handed her a handkerchief. She blotted the corners of her eyes.

When the music ended, Will escorted Grandmamma slowly back to her chair. In the pause before the musicians struck up the next tune, Grandmamma hollered at Amy, "Are you Scottish, dear?"

Amy and everyone else laughed. She made a point of greeting Will's sisters and the dowager countess. A few minutes later, Will approached. "I'm walking out in the garden with Bell. Says he wants to discuss something with me. I'll be back soon."

"Take your time. You've not seen much of your friends lately."

"The same could be said for you," he said. Then he leaned closer to her. "We won't stay long. The dancing has made me hungry for you."

She felt a little breathless at his words. "Do not delay the gratification too long," she whispered.

He gave her a wolfish grin, and then he strode out of the ballroom.

The wind was a bit cool out in the back garden. There were lanterns in the trees, but the guests apparently did not want to brave the cool air, with the notable exception of Bell.

Bell took out a cheroot. "Care for one?"

Will shook his head. "No, thanks."

Bell lit the cheroot from one of the hanging lanterns. "Marriage is making you soft."

"Actually, it's making me hard."

Bell snorted.

Will stared up at the sky full of chimney smoke. Still, he could make out a half-moon and stars.

"Hunter is here tonight," Bell said.

"Oh?" The hair on Will's nape stiffened.

Bell inhaled and blew out a smoke ring. "He is spending lavishly all over town. I've heard others at the club talking about his winnings that night and your losses. More than a few believe you intentionally compromised your wife in that wine cellar and married her for her fortune."

"They can bloody well think what they want. I know the truth and so does my wife."

"She doesn't know about your gaming debt," Bell said. "You've got two choices. Either you keep silent in hopes that she never discovers the truth or you confess."

Amy would despise him for the deception. He ought to have confessed everything to her, but he'd thought it kinder to keep the information from her. At the time, he'd believed the chances of Amy finding out were negligible. Now the risk loomed over him like an approaching storm. Will knew the gossips were watching and waiting for him to make a misstep. He'd given them plenty of fodder, but he no longer felt like the man who had reveled in his devilish reputation.

If he told Amy, he would hurt her. She'd struggled with her doubts about him, but she'd promised to give him her trust. They had worked hard to make this marriage work, but his deception could ruin everything. He wanted to wait it out, but he knew it would be cruel to let someone else inform her. "I have to tell her."

"Explain the circumstances," Bell said. "The gambling had nothing to do with her. You only wanted money to travel."

"Yes, and then I tried to compromise her at Lord and Lady Broughton's ball. She'll know that I was fortune hunting." Now he stood to lose far more than a fortune, because she would never trust him again after learning of his deception.

Amy stood talking to Georgette and Beau about their plans. "I will consult with Will, but perhaps the two of you would visit us over the summer."

"That sounds like an excellent idea," Beau said.

"I agree," Georgette said. "Amy, will you and Mr. Darcett continue to live in the cottage?"

"We haven't discussed it, to be honest. It is convenient to Will's position and is cozy. I guess I've grown rather attached to it since it is our first home."

"We will live with Beau's parents," Georgette said.

"It's an enormous house, and we'll have our own apartments," Beau said.

Amy wondered if Georgette would prefer to live in her own house, but of course she would not broach the subject in front of Beau. She figured Georgette would grow weary of Lady Wallingham's interference and insist upon a home of their own.

Georgette frowned at the hem of Amy's gown. "One of the satin leaves is loose. You had better have that repaired before it falls off."

"Oh, you're right," Amy said. She excused herself to

visit the retiring room. A familiar-looking woman with brown hair and a longish, foxlike face fell into step beside Amy as she climbed the stairs.

"You don't remember me," she said. "You're Mrs. Darcett."

"I apologize for not recollecting your name, but you do look familiar," Amy said.

"Lady Hunter, formerly Caroline Fielding," she said.

"Oh, yes," Amy said. She remembered the story that Caroline had chased Hunter for years. Hunter had kept his distance until it appeared he had a rival.

"There is something I wish to discuss with you privately if you are amenable."

Amy frowned. A warning clanged in her head. Why would this woman she was barely acquainted with wish to speak to her privately? Then it occurred to her that the woman might be seeking a dress design. "Lady Hunter, if this concerns fashion, there is a shop where I can direct you."

Lady Hunter wet her lips and leaned closer. "This concerns a gambling debt. I'm worried. I know what it is to be a gaming widow."

Amy thought that Lady Hunter was more than a little strange. "You are mistaken, Lady Hunter. Now, if you will excuse me, I am in a rush." She hurried ahead on the steps, glad to escape the strange woman.

As Amy entered the retiring room, she admitted that if Will had not spent every night at home with her, she might have grown alarmed. A maid hastily procured thread and a needle and quickly secured the leaf.

Afterward, Amy walked over to the pitcher and bowl to wash her hands. As she dried them, Amy realized she was being unfair and hypocritical. He wasn't the deceptive partner in this marriage. In truth, her deception never quite left her. Every time she walked past her trunk she thought of the full purse inside, and the secret that she was keeping from her husband. She knew it was wrong to keep this matter from him. Soon, she must sit down and admit her dishonesty. He wouldn't like it, but she would take full responsibility and tell him that she was done with it. She just needed to find the right time.

A few minutes later, Amy descended the stairs to find Will in the great hall looking up at her. He smiled, and her heart contracted. She slowed her steps as the giddy emotions flooded her chest.

He met her at the base of the steps and took her hands.

"How is Bell this evening?" she asked.

"The same as always. Smoking his cheroots and saying a great deal in as few words as possible," Will said.

Amy laughed. "He does seem to be a thoughtful person."

Will leaned closer. "Do you mind if we depart early?"

"Not at all," she said. "We will say good-bye to Georgette and Beau. Then we will thank Lady Wallingham and leave."

They walked through the crowd and found Georgette and Beau. Amy hugged Georgette. "I look forward to your wedding and know that you will be happy."

Georgette hugged her. "I am so happy for you, Amy, and fear that I didn't express it well the last time we met. I look forward to visiting you and Mr. Darcett this summer." Georgette's eyes welled with tears. "I doubt either of us expected to be married by the end of the Season. I have missed you, but I know we will always be friends."

"I imagine we will exchange many letters," Amy said. "You will always be the sister of my heart." Then she and Will bid Georgette and Beau good-bye for the evening.

They had taken only a few steps when Lady Wallingham minced over to them. "You cannot be leaving already. Why, it's barely midnight."

"I have an early day planned tomorrow," Will said. "Thank you, my lady, we enjoyed the ball."

As Will led Amy out of the ballroom and down the stairs, she was glad to escape the crowd. She recollected that odd woman, Lady Hunter, but decided not to mention it until they were in the carriage. There were a number of guests on the stairs, and Amy felt it wise to watch what she said in a place where others might eavesdrop.

After collecting his greatcoat and her wrap, they walked to the waiting carriage. Even though the night air was cool, her face grew a bit warm as she anticipated Will's lovemaking tonight. She always felt closest to him afterward, when they were sated and spooning, to use Will's term for their cuddling during sleep. Of course, she also loved his playful side in bed. He knew how to make her laugh and how to enslave her with his touch.

He handed her up the carriage steps, followed her inside, and rapped on the roof. Then he put his arm around her shoulders and kissed her cheek. For a short while, the carriage lulled her, and her thoughts drifted. She'd vowed to trust him and never to compare their lives to others'. From this point on, she must focus on the positive aspects of her marriage to Will, and there were many. She would not wish a marriage on any couple who were effectively strangers, because of the vexation. But obstacles did help one to grow in character.

"Warm enough?" he asked.

"Yes, thanks to your body heat."

He kissed her lingeringly.

"Oh, I forgot to tell you something," Amy said. "I spoke to Georgette and Beau this evening about the possibility of visiting us this summer. I did tell them that I must speak to you first, but they were all for the plan."

"I have no objection. They are welcome," Will said.

"I was sure you would agree or I would never have suggested it," Amy said. "So you see, I know quite a bit about you now."

He chuckled. "I'm sure we'll learn far more in the weeks and months ahead," he said.

"Something else occurred to me tonight," Amy said. "The cottage was supposed to be a temporary residence, if my memory serves me correctly. To be honest, I find it cozy, especially since we are newlyweds. And I am rather attached to it, since it is our first home. It's also convenient for your work."

He kissed her on the lips. "I agree with all of your points."

After arriving at their cottage and divesting themselves of their outerwear, Will led Amy upstairs. When they reached her door, she frowned. "I almost forgot a strange incident tonight. Do you know Lord Hunter?"

He did his best not to show his shock. He noted that Amy wasn't angry. She looked a bit curious, but nothing more. A bead of cold sweat trickled down the back of his neck. "Yes, I know him. Why do you ask?"

"His wife tried to detain me on the steps tonight. I believe the woman may be suffering from some sort of nervous condition, for she seemed very intent. She also used a term that I've never heard—*gaming widow.* I assume her husband is a high-stakes player and that has undoubtedly affected her. But to stop a person who is all but a stranger to her is very odd, I think."

He opened her door.

"Is Lord Hunter a high-stakes gambler?" she asked.

"Yes," he said. Amy had provided the opening, and he knew he should tell her, but he wasn't prepared. He felt like a devil for keeping silent now, but he feared losing her. He needed time to think how to explain the events to her.

"I feel sorry for her, but I intend to keep my distance," Amy said. "She seems more than a little strange to me."

Will released his breath slowly. "That would undoubtedly be for the best," he said. A knot formed in his chest. "Let me undress you," he said, stepping behind her.

She looked at him over her shoulder and smiled.

After he'd stripped her down to her shift, he took the pins from her hair. He loved watching it fall down. Then he unlaced her stays and slid her shift off her.

She untied his cravat. "I like undressing you," she said.

"I like it when you undress me," he said, as she helped him out of the tight sleeves of his coat.

She regarded him with a sultry expression as she unbuttoned the falls on his trousers. When her fingers brushed over his aroused cock, she smiled up at him from beneath her lashes. He drew his long shirt over his head. When he finally stripped off his drawers, he was hot all over.

Right now, he needed her. He lifted her on the bed and came between her thighs. Then he pulled her to a sitting position and gave her a lush tongue kiss. He felt an intense need to be as close to her as he possibly could. Tonight he could not hold back, because somewhere in the recesses of his brain was the niggling fear that he might lose her over this deception. He pressed her back onto the pillow and started his kisses on her forehead and worked his way down her cheek and her long, graceful neck to the tops of her breasts.

He wanted to worship her with his tongue and his mouth. As he suckled her, he caressed her soft, silky waist and hips. Then he lifted her long, long legs over his shoulders and touched her intimately, slowly at first and then with gathering speed. The sound of her labored breathing and her wet folds drove his desire higher. He wanted her. He wanted to possess her in every way possible, and not just this one night, but for the rest of their days together, God willing.

Will slid two fingers inside, where she was hot and tight. His lust for her climbed higher as he gazed upon the slick folds and rubbed her sweet spot. She was writhing on the bed now, her red hair tangling all around her. He had to join with her, had to find release from the damning secret he'd kept from her. God knew he would never tell her that he'd needed her fortune. Amy was strong, but she had a fragile side as well, and it would kill him to wound her—to destroy her trust and make a mockery of their relationship.

He could no longer delay. "I need you now," he said.

She wrapped her arms round him. He pushed inside her until he could go no farther. Then he bent his head and plunged his tongue inside her mouth over and over and over. Then he was moving inside her, a slow dance as her body answered his. He couldn't take his eyes off her. So often he was energetic, but tonight he wanted it to be slow, leisurely, and about them together, not just one partner at a time. He reached between them to caress her sweet spot and watched her come undone with that amazing red hair spilling all over her pillow. He wasn't far behind her. When the pressure built to a fever pitch, he gave in to the instinct to pump faster. He forgot everything but sharing their bodies and the incredible pleasure she gave him. As the erotic sensations took over him, he pushed in until he go no farther while his cock throbbed over and over and over again. When he collapsed, he realized he'd forgotten to withdraw. But what was done was done. As he drifted off, he heard Amy's voice.

"I love you, Will."

He was in a state between dreaming and wakefulness. It was still night. The raw scent of their earlier lovemaking was all around him. His cock was hard as stone, and her sweet little bottom cushioned him. Her breast filled his hand. He rolled her nipple between his fingers, and she made that little feminine sound again.

"Will?" she whispered.

He rolled on top of her. "I want you again."

She wrapped her arms and legs round him. He positioned his cock and slid inside her, where she was still wet and hot. He pressed in and out slowly, frequently pausing to kiss her lips and her breasts. Judging from her little feminine sounds, she liked it very well. He understood enough about a woman's anatomy to know she wouldn't come like this. So he reached between them to rub her sweet spot. She writhed beneath him, arching her back, and it felt so damned good to be inside her, because she fit him like a tight glove. As the pleasurable sensations increased in intensity, he started to lose his focus. Then she came apart with a little cry. As she contracted all around him, he came and looked into her eyes in wonder as the erotic sensations took them both simultaneously. As he gazed at her, something blinding happened to him. His chest seemed to expand inside and a rush of feelings completely overwhelmed him. When they were both spent, he gently rolled her to her side, with their bodies still joined, and cupped her cheek. "Amy, I love you."

Her eyes welled. "I love you, too, Will."

The next day, Will carried a picnic basket that he'd asked Cook to put together. Amy carried a blanket and held his hand as they walked along the tree-lined path. Sun rays speared through the lush green leaves, and joy filled her heart.

Early this morning when Will had left her bed, she'd privately thanked God for this wonderful gift of love. The day Will had proposed she'd been filled with fear and disillusionment. She'd believed that all her dreams of a loving husband were dashed forever. Now it seemed like a miracle had taken place. She would never forget the look of wonder on his face when he'd told her that he loved her.

Amy knew that in the years to come they would have disagreements. She remembered times when her mother and father had argued. They'd never done so in her presence, but she'd known by the redness in her mother's cheeks and the stubborn expression on her father's face. But they had always made up within a day. Their love for each other had overcome any conflict. Now Amy believed that the love she and Will shared would see them through any troubling times.

The only shadow over their lives was her deception

about her sketches, but she knew what she must do, even if it meant giving up the chance to have her designs made up into stunning gowns. Tomorrow, she would take care of the matter. Part of her wanted to keep it a secret. He would never know, unless she told him. But how could she live with a lie of omission? She could tell him part of the truth. Madame DuPont had refused to do business with her unless she took compensation. It was the dressmaker's insurance that she would have exclusive access to Amy's designs. Amy knew she ought to confess everything, but if she told him she'd feared he would gamble and beggar them, it would wound him. She didn't want to spoil this happy new beginning for them. In years to come, she would remember her deception whenever she felt miffed about some minor transgression of his.

"Ah, there is the tree house," Will said. "I thought we should celebrate where we first started our marriage."

She smiled. "I approve."

When they arrived at the spot, Will helped her spread the blanket. Then he set the picnic basket there, and they sat on the blanket. He captured her face with his big, warm hands. "I love you, Mrs. Darcett." Then he kissed her gently. "I didn't know it would be like this. When we made love last night, I kept thinking how much I needed you, and then a rush of feelings came over me. I've never experienced anything like it before."

"I didn't think it possible for us to fall in love, and I am overjoyed," she said.

He lowered his gaze. "I love you, but I don't deserve you."

"Will, please don't say that."

He swallowed. "I've done bad things. I've been selfish and treated others cavalierly."

"We've all made mistakes," she said. "You can't change the past, but you have already learned from it. I've made mistakes, too," she said. "I've hurt others."

"Not by design," he said. "But I will speak no more of my dissolute past. Today is for celebrating." He opened up the picnic basket and retrieved two glasses. "Hold them, please, while I open the wine."

He poured wine into the glasses, and she handed him one.

Will touched his glass to hers. "To love."

"To love," she said.

She sipped her wine and then set out the plates. They dined on thin slices of ham, chicken, cheese, and crusty bread. He ate heartily, while she nibbled on the food. Amy found that love had a way of overruling her stomach.

When they finished, she packed away the plates, and he topped up the wineglasses. "Tomorrow, I start my position as land steward. I find myself reluctant to leave you," he said.

"I will have a good dinner waiting for you and cheese-cake for dessert."

He grinned. "I prefer you to cheesecake."

She laughed. "Well, perhaps I mean to turn you up sweet first."

"I may not be able to wait until after dinner," he said. Then his smile faded. "I just realized I was inconsiderate last night. We'd agreed to wait for children, and I might have gotten you with child."

"Will, if that happens, I know we will both love the babe. That day when you caught Peter, I looked down from the stairs and imagined you with our own son one day," she said.

"Did you really?" he asked.

"I did. I know you will be a good father," she said.

He took a deep breath. "I want to be sure that all of our children get equal attention."

As the youngest of his family, he'd probably felt slighted at times. She'd wondered if he'd run away and gotten into mischief for that reason. Amy felt certain that his family had meant well; it was just part of being the youngest. "Will, you told me that you resented your father for driving your brother away. Did you have problems with your father?"

"It was Hawk's choice to leave. Afterward, my father lavished attention on me. He'd never done so before. At first, I liked it, but I grew to resent him. He'd noticed me only because my brother had left. I felt guilty after he died. After that, I spent most of my boyhood summers with Bell."

"After you left school, you went on your grand tour with Bell," she said, "and you didn't come home until four years later."

Will stared at her. "What are you insinuating?"

"The day I called on your mother, your sisters told me that your brother took measures to prevent you from traveling again. They feared you would never come home again."

"They succeeded," he said. "And they also managed to interfere in our lives. I knew this would happen."

"I told you that you would always come first, and that I would defend you," she said. "And I did. I told them that they didn't know you very well if they believed you lacked character. Your brother defended you as well," she said. "And your sisters admitted they were wrong."

"If you think they will change, you will be disappointed," he said.

"That is what they thought of you," she said, "and I told them they were mistaken. You have proven to me that you are a good man."

He pulled up a fistful of grass, but said nothing.

"Will, in a sense, you've been running from your family since you were a child," she said.

"What? That's ridiculous," he said.

"I understand why you were angry when your family took strong actions to keep you at home," she said. "But I keep thinking if you had left, you might not have returned."

He clenched his jaw. "Let me guess. You think I should embrace my family, warts and all."

"Actually, I think they need to embrace you," Amy said.

He looked startled.

"I think people form opinions of others and label them. It's very easy to let those labels become part of your identity. When others called me a wallflower, I just accepted it. Then when I thought this would be my last season, I was determined to break free of that identity. So I took on another one, and I was proud to be identified as the fashion darling of the ton. But that's not who I am deep down. We all take on these identities and let them define us. Patience sees herself as the elder sister. She feels it is her duty to criticize, but that's not who she really is at all. The real Patience cares that her mother is lonely and spends time with her mother, as do Hope and Harmony.

"As a child, you misbehaved to get attention and took on the identity of a bad boy. You let it define who you are for years, but that is not the Will I know. The Will I know dances with his grandmother and makes me laugh. The Will I know didn't abandon me when we were compromised. The Will I know reads me poetry and plans celebrations like this one. I love you, Will, for who you really are."

He pressed her down onto the blanket and kissed her deeply. "There are things I need to tell you, but not today. Today, I simply want to love you."

She brushed aside the dark lock that fell over his brow. "The past doesn't matter. I love you for the man you are today."

She waved as Will rode off to Ashdown House the next day. Afterward, he would be inspecting bridges on the property. When he'd left, she hurried upstairs. A leather case held her new designs and the purse with the coins. She had stuffed handkerchiefs on top of them to cushion them and meant to return the money to Madame DuPont. Amy could not keep that money hidden in their cottage anymore. She couldn't bear its presence. When she'd returned it all, she would confess everything to Will. She would explain how her doubts and fears had led her to do something she'd known was wrong, but she could no longer live with it.

Fear lifted the hair at her nape, and a little voice warned her not to ruin their happiness. She should tell him soon, but he had only just declared his love. What would a few more weeks matter?

She hugged herself, thinking of the moment he'd looked wonderingly into her eyes and told her he loved her. Amy wanted to hold on to that happiness for now. She would find the right time to tell Will. But not now when they had just declared their love.

Thirty minutes later, Amy entered Madame DuPont's shop.

The modiste came to greet her. "Mrs. Darcett, I hope you have brought me sketches."

"I have, but first, I must speak to you. Is there a private place?"

The modiste nodded. "This way," she said, gesturing with her hand.

Amy followed the modiste into a small, private sitting room.

"May I offer you tea?" Madame said.

"No, thank you." She took out the sketches. "Before you review them, I have something else for you." She took out the purse and handed it to the modiste. "I cannot keep it," Amy said.

Madame DuPont regarded her shrewdly. "Your new husband does not approve, and you do not wish to keep secrets."

"He approves of the sketches, but he doesn't know about the money. I know you wished to compensate me to ensure I would keep to my end of the business bargain, but I cannot do it."

"I understand," Madame DuPont said.

"Do you still want the sketches? I know it is your policy to have an exchange of money to ensure consistent delivery."

"If I refuse, you will take them to one of my competitors. I would be a fool to refuse."

Amy knit her brows. "Was that the real reason you insisted on payment?"

The modiste smiled. "Absolutely. It was my assurance that you would never take them to one of my competitors."

"Here are the sketches." Amy followed the modiste back into the shop in order to review fabrics and trims for the designs. As they emerged from the corridor, Amy looked up in surprise to find Patience and Julianne in the shop. "I didn't know you would be here."

Julianne looked at her with a guarded expression. "You could have ridden with us."

"I brought my sketches for Madame DuPont." Amy laid them on a counter. "Here is one you may like with a rolled velvet trim."

Madame DuPont followed Patience to a dressing room for a fitting of a new gown. Once they were gone, Julianne turned to Amy. "I thought you were done with this scheme."

"I returned the money today." She hugged her. "I felt so terrible putting you in the middle of my deception, and I could hardly bear to walk past my trunk, knowing the money was in there. I've learned my lesson about deceiving those you love."

Julianne smiled. "Do you love Will?"

"I do, and he loves me." Her arms tingled. "Against all odds, our marriage of convenience is a love match after all."

Julianne hugged her hard. "I am so glad for you. No one deserves happiness more."

"It is very freeing to be rid of those coins. Now all that remains is to tell him the truth."

"The only really terrible thing you did was to hide it. Focus on that," Julianne said.

"The only thing that troubles me is that he may find it hard to trust me again."

"Perhaps, but be forthcoming and over time his trust in you will be restored," Julianne said.

"Thank you," Amy said.

"I'm so glad you're here," Julianne said. "I need your advice on the ribbon for this silk blond lace." She laid the lace against a green satin. "What do you think?"

Amy shook her head. "The lace is too frilly for satin." As they walked about the shop, Amy advised Julianne about a different fabric that would work with the lace. "Red is a very good color for your dark hair. See how the white lace enhances the red silk."

"Oh, yes. I'm so fortunate to have a sister who gives me fashion advice," Julianne said.

Amy thought she was very fortunate to have sisters and brothers to add to her own small family. But most of all, she was fortunate to have a husband who loved her.

The next afternoon, Amy was perusing fashion plates when the butler announced Lady Hunter. Amy frowned and almost told the butler to turn her away with the usual polite excuse of not being at home, but the woman's persistence indicated that Lady Hunter would not be satisfied until she had Amy's full attention. "Very well, please show her up."

Amy stood when Lady Hunter entered. "Please be seated."

After taking a chair, Amy came to the point. "Lady Hunter, this is the second time you have sought me out, even though we are not well acquainted. I sense you have a specific purpose."

To Amy's shock, the woman tried to offer her a purse.

"No, I will not take your money," Amy said. "Why would you do this?"

"You needn't pretend with me. I know my husband benefited," Lady Hunter said.

Amy thought the woman deranged. "Lady Hunter, I believe you should go now."

"I know Darcett married you soon after my husband won twenty thousand pounds at his club," Lady Hunter said. "I thought you would have need of money."

"I have no idea what you are talking about." Amy stood. "Please leave."

"I knew it," Lady Hunter said. "You have no idea. He married you after he lost twenty thousand to my husband."

Amy clutched the chair arms as she sat. "You must be joking."

Lady Hunter shook her head and pulled out a slip of paper. "I found Mr. Darcett's vowel on my husband's desk."

Oh, God. Amy's hand shook. It was Will's handwriting.

"I am so sorry," Lady Hunter said.

Amy forced herself to meet the woman's eyes. "I beg you to say nothing of this to anyone."

"I understand. Believe me, I understand," Lady Hunter said.

Amy kept her composure just long enough for Lady Hunter to leave and then she fled upstairs to her bedchamber. She refused to let herself cry. Instead, she called Anna in and said, "Have all of my belongings packed as quickly as possible."

The maid gasped. "Madame, surely—"

"Just do it," she cried. She was shaking all over as she sat at her desk to compose a letter to her parents. She wrote quickly and gave no explanations. But as she wrote the words, she suddenly slowed and set the pen aside.

They had betrayed each other. Did one type of betrayal

trump another? Was one sin worse than the next? She had kept secrets from her husband. He had apparently married her for her money so that he could pay the gambling debt.

She knew it was true, and it hurt so much. He'd told he loved her. She bent over and wept. Why would he deceive her about his feelings? Or had he? She no longer could determine the truth about him. Her face crumpled, and her heart felt as if he'd thrust a dagger in it.

Where did they go from here?

Her first instinct had been to flee, but of course she could do no such a thing. She must confront him with her own betrayal and his.

Will strolled inside the cottage with a posy of wild-flowers behind his back. "Is Mrs. Darcett in the parlor?" he asked the butler.

"No, sir. She's kept upstairs most of the day."

He frowned and went upstairs, wondering if she was feeling poorly. When he knocked on her door, he heard rustling within. When she answered, he caught his breath. Her face was white and her eyes swollen. "Come in, Will."

"Oh, my God, what has happened?" When he tried to take Amy's hands, she stepped back.

"I had a visit from Lady Hunter today."

His neck prickled. "You know?"

She went to her desk and retrieved a small piece of paper. Bile rose to his throat. It was his vowel.

"I didn't tell you because I knew you would think I had married you for the money."

"Didn't you?"

"You know that I tried to get us out of marrying after we were caught in the wine cellar."

"Nonetheless, you did not tell me that you paid a fortune—from the money I brought to the marriage—to cover a gambling debt."

"No, because we had to marry, and I didn't want to be the cause of additional wounds."

"I have something to tell you, Will."

"Don't leave me," he said.

"Do you remember the night your friends dined with us? And the discussion about trade? I lied by omission. I took compensation for my sketches, and do you want to know why? At first, I wanted to have the money as assurance in case I didn't marry, and then when I learned we must marry, I kept it from you. And the reason is because I feared you would gamble and beggar us."

"I feel sick," he said.

"So do I, Will."

"I meant to tell you, because I didn't want you to hear it from someone else," he said. "I just wanted to wait for the right time."

"The right time would have been the day you proposed to me," she said.

His temper snapped. "And when were you planning to tell me that you were taking money for those sketches?" he said, his voice rising in anger.

She gave him a bitter smile. "I just wanted to wait for the right time. I wasn't even sure I should tell you, because you would ask why I did it. I knew it would cause a deep rift if I told you that I didn't trust you. Given your reputation, I had every reason to doubt you."

"You sat calmly at dinner when Fordham mentioned trade," he said. "You didn't bat an eye. Worse, you trusted that dressmaker to keep your secret, but you didn't trust me enough to tell me the truth. If that had gotten out, you would have humiliated me and both of our families."

"I gave the money back to the dressmaker, because I felt guilty," she said. "But what about that gaming debt, Will? How many people know? Do others think you purposely compromised me in that wine cellar to cover the debt?"

He flinched.

She turned and walked over to the desk chair to sit. "I can't bear the mortification. How am I to hold my head up, when everyone is gossiping about me? I will be pitied. I'm not strong enough to face scandal again."

He knelt before her and took her hand. "Amy, we can weather this storm. We've faced difficulties before and overcome them."

She looked at him and then she inhaled sharply. "Oh, my God. I just realized that night you tried to lead me into that dark music room, you meant to compromise me."

His heart stampeded. "Amy, I told you I was a selfish man. I felt awful afterward, and you forgave me."

"I didn't know you did it because you wanted my fortune," she cried. "You must have been elated when we were trapped in that wine cellar."

"You know I tried to get us out of that situation," he said.

Tears streaked down her face. "Was it an act? Did you simply make the effort, so that I wouldn't put two and two together?"

"No, I didn't. I swear it." God, this was going very badly. "Amy, I love you. We will work through this as we have previously."

She blotted her face with a handkerchief. "The problem is that I cannot trust you, and I daresay you cannot trust me. We both made a commitment, but the entire time, we were deceiving each other. How can we reconcile without trust? It is impossible."

"You know I'm a changed man because of you."

"Are you, Will?"

"You know I am, and I know you are stronger because of our relationship as well. We're married for as long as we shall live. I know it won't be easy, but we've come this far. I don't want to give you up."

"I'm sorry, Will. I think you had better go."

"I can't leave you like this," he said.

"Will, I'm planning to write to my parents and make arrangements to go home."

"No!" He fisted his hands to hide the fact that they were shaking. "I won't let you leave me."

She shook her head. "I just think that a marriage based on mistrust cannot thrive. We were never meant to be. Our marriage was based on an accident. I'm sorry, Will, but I don't think we can get past this much deception and mistrust."

No. He refused to let her leave. "You're my wife. We took vows. If you will give me the chance, I will make this up to you," he said.

"There's been too much damage."

"What are you saying?" he said.

"I will write to my parents tomorrow and make arrangements to return home. We will live separate lives just as you envisioned. You can travel with your friends, and I will live quietly in the country."

Will paced his room, trying to figure out how to save his marriage. He didn't want to lose Amy. After everything they had been through, he refused to give up now, but he didn't know what to do. All he knew was that he loved her too much to let her leave him. God, he'd spend the rest of his days worshiping the ground she walked on if she would only give him another chance.

He was breathing hard and having trouble thinking, but he had to think.

Will slumped on the edge of the bed. A familiar squeak sounded. He looked back at his pillow to find Poppet swishing her tail. She padded over to him and rubbed against his arm. "I don't feel well right now, Poppet," he said.

The cat squeaked at him. Will held her on his lap and petted her. He thought about the day he'd taken Amy out for a picnic. He'd been like a green boy with his first girl. Then she'd told him that he'd taken on the identity of a bad boy at a young age and let it define him. He knew it was true. All those years, he'd taken on the role of the devil-may-care spare heir and tucked away his resentments toward his father. He'd wanted to avoid seeing the pain of his family after his father's death and had done everything he could to keep his distance. Amy had been right. He'd been running from his family for years. If Hawk had not withheld his quarterly funds, Will knew he probably would never have come home.

He'd never appreciated his family, because he didn't want anyone to get close to him. For years, he'd wandered the Continent and had countless, temporary liaisons with women. Each time one of them started to express tender feelings, he'd walked away without an ounce of remorse for the way he'd treated them. He'd done it because he didn't want to risk his own heart.

Damn his sorry soul to hell. After he'd proposed to

Amy, he'd planned to live separate lives. She didn't know he'd meant to abandon her so that he could travel. But after they had married, she had insisted that they get to know each other, because she wanted more from him than a toss in bed. He'd fallen hard for her, and now his chest hurt like the devil.

"I can't do this alone, Poppet," he said.

He needed advice. He would have to swallow his pride, but he'd do whatever it took to win back his wife. Will set Poppet on the bed. She squeaked at him, but he ignored her and walked over to the pitcher. He poured cold water into the bowl and splashed his face. Then he walked out of his room, down the stairs, and had a groom bring round the curricle.

He drove to Ashdown House and realized he'd forgotten his hat only when Jones, the fastidious butler, eyed him with distaste. "Is my brother at home?" he asked.

"Yes, sir. He's in the drawing room with everyone else."

Oh, Lord, he'd have to face the whole family. Will trudged through the great hall and saw Peter looking down at him from the landing. "Don't even think about sliding down the banister," he growled.

Peter laughed and ran off.

Will climbed the steps and opened the door to his mother's drawing room. Sure enough, everyone was there, including Aunt Hester. They all stared at him.

Hawk stood before the hearth and frowned. "Will, we're holding a family meeting, but we didn't want to disturb you and Amy. It's only about Peter."

Aunt Hester adjusted the tall white feather in her ugly purple turban. "Peter pissed on the roses again."

"Oh, Hester," the dowager countess said. "We do not use such language."

Hester snorted.

Grandmamma regarded him with concern and beckoned him to the sofa. He sat beside her, and she reached over to pat his hand. "What is wrong?" she shouted.

He tried to control his breathing. "I need help."

Hawk's jaw dropped. "Will, you know we will do whatever we can, but you must tell us what is wrong."

At first, pride made him hold his tongue, but pride would gain him nothing. He inhaled. "I really was a devil." He told them everything, including his plan to compromise her. He thought they would rebuke him, but they all just gaped at him.

"She is the one who told me that I've been running from my family all my life. I didn't realize it. I just kept old resentments bottled up inside me and went about my selfish life. God, I'd even planned to abandon her so that I could travel. I thought we would live separate lives, but she insisted I court her. She wouldn't let me run roughshod over her. I liked her, but little by little, I started to care. And then I fell in love with her.

"She believes the trust is broken beyond repair, but I don't want to give her up," Will said. "And you might as well know she's humiliated and believes she cannot face society again. Everyone thinks I married her for her fortune." He leaned forward with his elbows on his knees. "I don't know what to do."

"Will, we are not without influence," Patience said. "Everyone in this room will dispel those rumors. We all know you were trapped accidentally, and you married her to avoid the scandal."

Will lifted his chin. "Is it possible?"

"It's more than possible," Hawk said. "I know Boswood

would vouch for you. Your misguided friends can dispute the gossip as well. I can't believe the three of you cooked up such an idiotic fortune-hunting scheme."

"She saw through me," Will said. "I ought to have known. From the first moment I met her, she let me know exactly what she thought of me, and it wasn't positive."

Julianne stood with the babe on her hip. "Patience, will you please take Emma Rose to the nurse, and please ask her not to let the boys scalp what little hair Emma has. Marc, will you call for the carriage while I get my shawl?"

Then Julianne smiled at Will. "I'm going to get our girl."

He sighed. "She will probably refuse."

Julianne shook her head. "She won't."

After Julianne left, Will paced the drawing room and kept looking at the clock. The low sound of conversation buzzed, but he paid no attention. He was edgy and restless. So he kept pacing. After thirty minutes, his hopes dwindled. Julianne had sounded confident, but Will feared Amy was adamant. He slumped in a chair, but he couldn't sit still, so he got up and paced again.

Another half hour passed, and the door opened. He spun around only to see his bewildered friends.

Hawk glared at both of them and told them to be seated. "When Amy arrives, you will both claim responsibility for that scheme to compromise her," Hawk said. "And then the pair of you are going to dispute all the gossip that Will married Amy for her money."

"Hawk, don't blame them. I agreed to it," Will said.

"I don't give a rat's arse," Hawk said. "Sorry for the vulgarity, Mama. Hope, pass the smelling salts to our mother."

"Oh, dear," the dowager countess said as Hope held the vial for her.

Bell frowned at Will. "Your wife knows about the gambling debt?"

"Of course she does," Hester said. "Why do you think we called you here?"

Bell's mouth curved just the slightest bit. "You must be the infamous Aunt Hester."

"I am indeed," she said, looking him over. "If I were forty years younger, I'd have you leg-shackled in a week. In my day, I was quite talented at catching husbands."

"Oh, Hester, must you say such things?" the dowager countess said.

Will looked at the clock. Another forty-five minutes had elapsed. He walked over to the window and clenched his jaw. Then he shut his eyes. *I know you're not interested in bargaining, Lord, but I swear I'll get on my knees and beg if you'll send her to me.*

After a while, soft footsteps padded over to him. "Will, come sit and have a cup of tea," Harmony said.

He shook his head, because he didn't want anyone to see the anguish on his face.

Will didn't know how much time passed, but it seemed an age to him. The voices in the room were subdued, but he couldn't focus on them. It was all he could do just to keep from falling apart.

His brother walked over to his side and put his hand on Will's shoulder. "If this doesn't work, we'll figure out a new plan," he said. "Just hold steady."

Will knew all was lost. "Thank you, but she means to return home. It's now or never, and I fear it is the latter."

"Last spring, I thought I'd lost Julianne forever. Don't give up, Will."

The clock struck the hour. His face contorted with the

effort to keep the misery inside. Then voices sounded from beyond the closed door. He couldn't look, because he couldn't bear to get his hopes crushed.

The door sighed open and everyone exclaimed at once.

"I told you I would bring her," Julianne said.

Will inhaled and turned to face her. Amy's face was a little pale and her eyes were red. Everyone kept talking, but he comprehended nothing. He wanted to go to her and comfort her. Bu if he did, she might well rebuff him.

Then he recollected the bargain he'd made and knew that he was going to have to make a sacrifice. All the voices in the room dwindled as he strode over to Amy. "I made a bargain with the Lord. I didn't think he'd listen to a devil like me, but he sent you as I asked. Now I have to honor it, even though I'm about to surrender my pride and dignity." He dropped to his knees and took her hands.

A collective gasp resounded.

Will took a deep breath. "I love you, and I don't want to live without you. If you'll give me one more chance, I swear I'll read you poetry, take you on picnics, and tell you I love you six times a day. I'll even let Laurence sleep with us."

Her eyes filled with tears as gasps rang out.

Will looked over his shoulder. "Laurence is a pillow."

Hester snorted. "Get on with it, Will."

He turned his pleading gaze to Amy. "I'm sorry I broke your trust. It's true I tried to compromise you, but you were too smart to fall for my botched plan. And then, after we married, I didn't tell you, because I cared about you, and I knew it would wound you."

Tears rained down her face. "I didn't tell you about the money I earned for the designs, because you had a bad reputation, and I feared you might beggar us by gambling. But it was wrong of me. I should have been honest from the beginning."

He swallowed hard, because he was having trouble controlling his emotions. "Please don't leave me," he whispered. "I love you, and I don't want to live without you."

"You are my husband, and I took a holy vow. I made mistakes, too," she said. "But I suppose we were both more than a little scared when we married and made bad choices. I do love you, and I promise from this moment forward that I will always be honest with you."

Oh, God, she was taking him back. "Amy, I pledge my honesty to you as well. More important, I pledge my life and my love to you, if you will have me."

"I will have you, because I do not want to live without you," she said.

A rousing cheer went up. Will rose and leaned down to kiss her. Then he whispered, "Come live with me and be my love."

Tessa Mansfield has broken a
matchmaker's number one rule:
Never fall in love with the groom.

Please turn this page for
an excerpt from

How to Marry a Duke.

Chapter One

London, 1816

The belles of the beau monde had resorted to clumsiness in an effort to snag a ducal husband.

Tristan James Gatewick, the Duke of Shelbourne, entered Lord and Lady Broughton's ballroom and grimaced. A quartet of giggling chits stood near the open doors, dangling their handkerchiefs as if poised to drop them. Determined to avoid playing fetch again, he strode off along the perimeter of the room.

With a long-suffering sigh, he conceded he'd contributed to this national disgrace. Ever since the scandal sheets had declared him the most eligible bachelor in England, he'd rescued twenty-nine lace handkerchiefs, five kid gloves, and twelve ivory fans.

If only he could have convinced himself to choose a bride based upon the inelegance of her fumbling, he might have wedded and bedded the most inept candidate by now. Alas, he could not abide the thought of spending a lifetime with Her Gracelessness.

He surveyed the crowd looking for the hostess of this grand squeeze, a useless endeavor. The crème de la crème swarmed the place like bees. The din of voices competed with the lively tune of a country dance, making his ears ring. He'd rather eat dirt than subject himself to the dubious delights of the marriage mart, but with his thirty-first birthday approaching, he could no longer pretend he was invincible. The dukedom had been at risk far too long.

Someone tapped a fan on his shoulder. He paused to find Genevieve and Veronica, two of his former mistresses. Seeing them together, he realized how alike the striking widows looked. Both were tall, dark-haired, and curvaceous. He canvassed the cobwebs in his brain and realized all of his past lovers had similar attributes. Well, those he could recollect.

Tristan bowed and lifted each of their hands for the requisite air kiss. "Ladies, it is a great pleasure to see you again."

"Were your ears burning?" Veronica said in an exaggerated boudoir voice. "You are the subject du jour."

"I am delighted," he lied. He'd grown increasingly frustrated with the notoriety the papers had whipped up. How the devil he'd ever find a bride in this circuslike atmosphere evaded him. But find one he must.

Genevieve tittered. "We were comparing you to all of our other gentlemen admirers."

He'd bedded more than his fare share of mistresses, but this situation was certainly unique among his experiences. "What did you conclude?"

Genevieve leaned closer and squeezed his arm. "We agreed you were the naughtiest of all our lovers."

He regarded her with a wicked grin. "Praise indeed."

Veronica glanced at him from beneath her lashes. "How does it feel to be England's most sought-after bachelor?"

High-pitched giggling rang out from behind him. He rolled his eyes. Not again.

Genevieve's shoulders shook with laughter. "Watch out, Shelbourne. A bevy of little misses are stalking you."

He grimaced. "Rescue me?"

The two women laughed, blew him a kiss, and drifted away, leaving him to the predators. When he turned round, the four silly chits he'd seen earlier halted and stared at him, agog. Given their youthful faces and puritanical white gowns, he surmised not one of them was a day over seventeen. He needed a wife, but he'd no intention of robbing the proverbial cradle.

When they continued to gape at him as if he were a Greek statue come to life, he took a step closer. "Boo."

Their shrieks rang in his ears as he walked off into the crowd. Ignoring the avid stares directed at him, Tristan squeezed past numerous hot, perspiring bodies, and not the kind one hoped to find naked and willing in bed. With more than a little regret, he banished thoughts of Naked and Willing in order to concentrate on Virtuous and Virginal. First he must locate Lord and Lady Broughton. Perhaps his hostess would introduce him to a sensible young lady of good breeding. Perhaps pigs would fly, too.

He might have avoided all this nonsense if his dear mama had cooperated. When he'd informed her of his bridal requirements a month ago, she'd swatted him with her fan and told him he had rocks in his head.

A loud bang nearly sent him ducking for cover. Feminine gasps erupted all around him. Alarmed, he sought the source of the disturbance and realized it was only the slamming of the card room door. The gentleman responsible for this discourteous act was none other than his oldest friend, Marc Darcett, Earl of Hawkfield.

Tristan hailed Hawk with a wave and walked in that direction. Intent upon reaching his friend, Tristan failed to notice the impending danger until something crunched beneath his shoe. A quick glance to the floor confirmed his worst fear—the thirteenth incident of a dropped fan. Damn and blast, he'd crushed it.

He lifted his gaze, expecting a devious mama and her blushing daughter. Instead, a petite young woman with honey-blond hair stood staring at his shoe. She said something that sounded suspiciously like *ashes to ashes, dust to dust.* With all the voices ringing in his ears, he assumed he'd misheard.

Though he was tempted to walk past her, he couldn't ignore the fan he'd broken. "I beg your pardon," he said, bending to retrieve the mangled ivory sticks.

"You are not to blame. Someone jostled my arm."

Her excuse was the worst he'd heard yet. He didn't even bother to hide his cynicism as his gaze traveled up her white gown. Blue ribbons trimmed her bodice, drawing his attention to her generous décolletage. He continued his perusal to her heart-shaped face. She watched him with twitching lips. Pillow-plump lips. He inhaled on a constricted breath. Lord, with that mouth she could make a fortune as a courtesan.

Her long-lashed eyes twinkled. "Sir, if you will return the remains, I will see to its burial."

Her witty remark stunned him. Belatedly, he realized he was grinning up at her. She probably thought he'd fallen for her ruse. Exasperated with himself, he grasped the broken sticks, rose, and placed the ruined fan in her small gloved hands.

He met her amused gaze again, noting she did not simper or blush. She was no miss fresh out of the schoolroom. "I apologize for the damage. Allow me to make reparations," he said.

"It is quite beyond repair," she said.

"I insist upon compensating you for—"

"My pain and suffering?" She laughed. "I assure you the fan's death is a relief to me. Look, you can see it is exceedingly ugly."

They'd not had a proper introduction, and yet, she'd invited him to come closer. He decided to oblige her and find out if her intentions extended beyond droll quips. While she chattered about a dim shop light and putrid green paint, he stole another glance at her mouth, picturing those lips damp and kiss-swollen. Slow heat eddied in his veins.

She continued speaking in an unreserved manner as if they were old friends rather than strangers. "Even my maids refused to take the fan," she said. "So I decided to carry the pitiful thing at least once."

A footman carrying a tray of champagne paused before them. She lifted up on her toes like a ballerina to place the ruined fan upon it. Pint-sized she might be, but her flimsy skirts outlined a deliciously rounded bottom. He liked voluptuous women, and his practiced eye told him this one had the body of a goddess.

His blood stirred. He wanted her.

A warning clanged in his head. She was probably

married, and he never dallied with other men's wives. Then again, maybe she wasn't. He found himself hoping she was a willing and lonely widow, but he meant to do more than hope.

"Poor little fan. May you rest in peace." She pirouetted and gave him a dazzling smile. "There now, I'm done mourning."

She was exceptionally clever, but without the brittle artifice common among the ton. He caught her gaze, willing her with his eyes. "Now that the funeral is over, perhaps you would allow me to escort you to the refreshment table." And thence to a more private location.

"You are too kind, but I must return to my friends."

Triumph surged inside him. She'd said friends, but made no mention of a husband. "Will you allow me the *pleasure* of your company a little longer? I mean to persuade you to accept my offer."

"I have dozens of other fans," she said. "Your apology is more than sufficient."

She intended to play hard to get. Since he'd come of age, women had always pursued him. At the prospect of a chase, excitement raced through his blood. But he must proceed with caution. If he'd misjudged her, she would take offense. A smile tugged at his mouth. He knew exactly which card to play.

He reached inside his coat and produced his engraved card. "Take it. In the event you change your mind, send round a note." If she refused, he'd have his answer. But if she accepted, he'd have her name. And soon her.

When she started to reach for the card, he held his breath. *Take it, little charmer. I'll ride you to the stars all night.*

She hesitated and then peered at his card. Her doll-like

eyes grew round as carriage wheels. She curtsied, mumbled something he couldn't hear, and disappeared into the crowd.

Her sudden departure caught him off guard. He took two steps, searching for her, but the crowd had swallowed her. Obviously she'd not known his identity beforehand. But why had she fled?

"There you are."

At the sound of Hawk's voice, Tristan turned.

"I tried to save you," Hawk said, "but that dragon Lady Durmont waylaid me. So who was the latest clumsy belle to accost you?"

"I've no idea," Tristan said. "I take it you do not know her."

"I never saw her face." Hawk frowned. "What the devil were you doing engaging a strange lady in conversation?"

"I stepped on her fan."

Hawk made a sound of disgust. "Follow me."

As he walked with his friend, Tristan frowned, wondering how he could have misread her signals. Then again, the women who pursued him made no secret of their illicit intentions with their risqué innuendos. The mysterious lady had surprised and intrigued him, but she'd not taken the bait, so he dismissed her from his mind.

Hawk led him over to a wall niche displaying a winged statue of Fortuna, goddess of fortune and fate. "Old boy, you've got to be more careful," Hawk said. "These chits are desperate. One of them might trick you into a compromising situation."

Tristan huffed. "A cautionary tale in reverse. Lady Rake seduces unsuspecting bachelor."

"There are plenty of schemers on the marriage mart who would throw away their virtue to marry a duke."

"Ridiculous." He'd never fall for such tricks.

"Forget this bridal business for now," Hawk said. "You needn't rush to the altar."

"I've left the dukedom unsecured for thirteen years." With good reason, he silently amended.

Hawk released a loud sigh. "You're determined to wed."

"Determined, yes. Whether I'll succeed is debatable."

"As usual, you're making matters much too complicated. You're in luck. I have a brilliant plan."

"This ought to prove entertaining," he said.

"It's simple," Hawk said. "Choose the most beautiful belle in the ballroom, get an introduction, and ask her to dance. Then call on her tomorrow and propose. In less than twenty-four hours, you'll be an engaged man."

"You call that a brilliant plan?"

Hawk folded his arms over his chest. "What's wrong with it?"

He huffed. "Most of the beauties I've met are vain, silly, and clumsy."

"You want an ugly wife?"

Tristan scowled. "That's not what I meant."

"What the devil do you want?"

"A sensible, respectable, and graceful woman." He wanted more, but he wasn't about to confess his fantasies.

"If it's a boring and plain bride you're wanting, you need look no farther than the wall," Hawk said, indicating a group of pitiful-looking gels sitting with the dowagers.

Tristan had started to turn away when he saw the amusing lady he'd spoken to earlier. His heartbeat drummed in his ears. She led two gangly young cubs over to the for-lorn girls. The chandelier's soft candlelight illuminated her curly golden hair.

Within minutes, both cubs were escorting wallflow-ers toward the dance floor. The lady responsible for this turn of events clasped her small gloved hands. As she watched the couples, her plump lips curved into a dreamy smile, and her eyes softened. Transfixed, Tristan forgot to breathe. He'd last seen that expression on a woman after a vigorous bout between the sheets.

Then Lord Broughton and his new bride approached her. All signs of the temptress disappeared as the lady faced the couple. "That's her," Tristan said.

Hawk squinted. "Who?"

"The lady I spoke to earlier. She is standing with Broughton and his wife."

"Lord help us. It's Miss Mansfield."

Miss Mansfield? She was a virtuous, unmarried lady? The devil. He'd almost made her an indecent proposition.

Hawk laughed. "You've never heard about her?"

"You're obviously itching to tell me," he grumbled.

"She makes matches for every ugly duckling in Lon-don," Hawk said, wagging his brows.

Tristan scoffed. "You're funning me."

"I'm not jesting. She's not called Miss Mantrap for nothing," Hawk said. "The woman is a menace to bach-elors. Good old Broughton is a prime example."

Good old Broughton gazed down at his pretty blond bride. The man looked as if he were suffering from unbri-dled lust, a term women euphemistically called love.

Hawk regarded Tristan with suspicion. "Why are you so interested in her?"

"Mere curiosity," he said with a shrug.

Hawk smirked. "Cut line. You thought she was available for dalliance."

He'd never admit it. No doubt she was as poor as a church mouse, without noble family connections. She probably found matchmaking preferable to taking a position as a lady's maid or governess. Most likely, she'd only received an invitation to the ball because she'd made Broughton's match.

He wished she'd not refused his offer to pay for the fan. But he understood her pride all too well, and though he thought her chosen career odd, he couldn't deny she'd made a successful match for Broughton.

Tristan's skin tingled. No, he would not stoop to hiring her to find him a bride. He could practically picture the news in the scandal rags. *The Desperate Duke has hired a matchmaker.*

He was not desperate. He was a bloody duke. With a mere crook of his finger, he could have any woman he wanted. The problem was he didn't want just any woman. He'd formulated requirements for his ideal bride.

All he needed was to find someone who met them.

He thought about spending week after week trolling for a wife in ballrooms. He thought about fetching fans, handkerchiefs, and parasols. He thought about his need for an heir. His chances of finding his perfect duchess seemed remote at best.

Tristan glanced at Miss Mansfield again and reconsidered. She needed money. He needed a bride. For the right price, Miss Mansfield would keep her involvement a secret from all but the chosen girl and her grateful family.

He frowned, realizing he was basing his decision on

one example—Broughton. Hiring Miss Mansfield meant taking a risk, but if her efforts proved unsatisfactory, he could dismiss her. Truthfully, a larger risk loomed. Marriage was for life, and as matters now stood, he was in serious danger of tying himself forever to an unsuitable wife. Or no wife at all, at this rate.

Tristan sized up the situation and realized he had two choices: continue his haphazard search or hire Miss Mansfield. After weeks of pure hell shopping at the marriage mart, the matchmaker won hands-down.

Of course, he had no intention of enlightening his friend. "I'm off to pay my respects to Broughton and his wife."

Hawk snorted. "This marriage business has addled your brain."

"I fail to understand what you find so amusing."

"Miss Mansfield is a happily-ever-after spinster." Hawk clapped him on the shoulder. "Congratulations, old boy. You've just chosen the only woman in the kingdom who won't wed you."

Tessa Mansfield wanted to kick herself.

Heaven above, she'd practically flirted with that rake, the Duke of Shelbourne. She'd never seen him before tonight, but she'd heard about his reputation. The gentleman rake, they called him. Everyone said he didn't gamble to excess. They said he never seduced innocents. Every other female, however, was apparently fair game.

She prided herself on her ability to spot a rake at twenty paces. This particular rake had fooled her with his agreeable manner. But she knew rakes used their charm to disarm their intended victims. She recalled the duke's slow smile and could not deny she'd let his handsome face turn her head.

Tessa cringed as she recalled the way she'd chattered like a monkey. He must have thought she'd dropped her fan on purpose like all those silly girls she'd read about in the scandal sheets. Oh, how lowering.

She took a deep breath, reminding herself she was unlikely to encounter him again. Thank goodness.

"I am glad to see you, Tessa. I've missed you so."

Tessa returned her attention to Anne, her former companion and dearest friend in the world. "I missed you as well."

Anne's eyes misted. "I never imagined I would make such a happy marriage. You made all my dreams come true."

For nearly a year, Tessa had promoted the match between Anne Mortland and Lord Broughton. More than once, Tessa had feared all would come to naught, but true love and a dusting of luck had culminated in this fairy-tale marriage.

Tessa glanced at Lord Broughton. "You both look well, my lord."

Broughton gazed at his bride with adoration. "I am the happiest of men."

Tessa's heart contracted with a yearning for something she could never have.

Anne clasped her arm. "Tessa, look quickly. You do not want to miss seeing Jane dance."

Tessa lifted up on her toes to see past the crowd. She caught a glimpse of her new companion, Jane Powell, but the fast approach of two fashionable and handsome gentlemen diverted her attention. As they neared, her heart thudded. She recognized the taller man with tousled black hair. It was the Duke of Shelbourne.

She turned round, hoping he'd not seen her. To her mortification, Shelbourne and the other gentleman approached Lord Broughton.

"Shelbourne, Hawk, this is an unexpected pleasure," Broughton said, rubbing his hands.

Tessa gazed up at the chandelier, wishing she could melt like the wax oozing from the candles. When she'd run away, he'd probably thought she wanted him to chase her. Belatedly, she realized her behavior only made her look guilty and a little foolish. She planted a serene smile on her face as Lord Broughton introduced her to the duke and Lord Hawkfield. Then she curtsied and rose to find Shelbourne gazing at her. In the light of the chandelier, she could see his eyes were marine blue and fringed by thick black lashes.

"Miss Mansfield and my wife are friends," Lord Broughton said. "She is the one responsible for our happy union."

Lord Hawkfield raised his brows in an exaggerated fashion. "I say, a matchmaker? If only I had known of your skills when my sisters were single, Miss Mansfield. You might have saved me the trouble of finding them husbands."

His mocking tone vexed her. She'd encountered plenty of his kind before, always quick to ridicule her avocation. "I had no idea I had a competitor. Or do you only make matches for relatives?"

Before Lord Hawkfield could reply, the duke cut in. "His self-proclaimed talent is highly overrated."

She arched her brows. "Should I be relieved?"

"He never stood a chance against you."

His distinctive baritone voice sent an exquisite shiver along her arms. She mentally shook herself. *He's a rake, he's a rake, he's a rake.*

The music ended. Lord Hawkfield excused himself and disappeared into the crowd. The duke glanced at her, and then he closed the distance between them.

She looked at him warily. Could he not see she wished him to leave her in peace?

"I apologize for detaining you so long earlier," he said. "Without a proper introduction, I fear you might have taken offense."

He'd apologized in a gentlemanly manner, even though she was equally at fault, perhaps more so, since she'd done most of the talking. "No apology is necessary. The circumstances were unusual."

He inclined his head. Though he did not smile, there was a natural curve to his full lips. His was not the pretty face of a dandy, however. Oh, no, not at all. His thick brows, angular cheekbones, and square jaw were all male. Little wonder women reportedly swooned at his perfection. No, not quite perfect, she thought, detecting a faint shadow along his jaw and above his full upper lip. His valet probably had to shave him twice a day. Her skin prickled at this evidence of the duke's masculinity.

"There is something I wish to ask you." His voice rumbled, a sound as rich and irresistible as a cup of chocolate.

Her heart thumped at the low, seductive notes in his voice. She'd thought herself unsusceptible to such tricks, but evidently her traitorous body was not.

"May I call upon you tomorrow afternoon?" he asked.

"Your grace, if this concerns my fan, I beg you to forget the matter." There, that should settle his concern once and for all.

"It is not about the fan," he said. "I have appointments early in the afternoon. May I call at four o'clock?"

She regarded him with suspicion. "Why not tell me now?"

"I prefer to discuss it in private, if you are amenable."

In private? Did he mean to make her a dishonorable proposal? Then her common sense prevailed. A handsome rake like him would have no interest in a plump spinster.

His mouth curved in the merest of smiles. "You hesitate. I can hardly blame you after I discomposed you earlier."

She lifted her chin. "I was not discomposed." What a bouncer. She'd fled as if the engraving on his card read His Grace, the Duke of Devilbourne.

"I will of course abide by your decision." Then he gazed into her eyes with such intensity, she stilled like a rabbit in the woods. He drew her in, mesmerizing her with his arresting blue eyes. She felt the pull of his will like a swift current. And everything inside her said *yes*. "Very well," she said breathlessly.

"Thank you. Until tomorrow." He sketched a formal bow and walked away.

She let out her pent-up breath. Good God, he'd seduced her into agreeing.

Anne approached, using her fan to shield her voice. "What were you and the duke discussing?"

Tessa thought it best not to reveal his intended visit until she knew his purpose. "Nothing of consequence." But he wanted something from her. She suppressed a shiver.

"He spoke to you at length," Anne said. "You must tell me what he said."

"You make too much of the matter." Why had she let him turn her head?

"He looked at you like a starving wolf. Stay away from him," Anne said. "He is well respected for his politics, but even Geoffrey admitted the duke has a notorious reputation with women. He probably has one hundred notches in his bedpost."

Tessa scoffed. "I'm sure he has no interest in carving one for an aging spinster like me."

"You are only six and twenty," Anne said. "Why must you always demean your charms?"

She ignored her friend's question. "Do not worry. I am in no danger of falling for a rake's wiles." Even if he'd persuaded her to let him call tomorrow, and she'd accepted against her better judgment.

Anne drew closer. "He has a reputation as a legendary lover. Women throw themselves in his path. I heard he can persuade a woman to do his bidding with his eyes."

Tessa gulped, knowing it was true.

Anne surveyed the crowd and grabbed Tessa's arm. "Look, there he is now by the hearth. Do you see that woman with him? That is Lady Endicott, a formerly respectable widow—until she met Shelbourne."

Tessa glanced in that direction. A tall, raven-haired beauty with jade feathers in her bandeau slid her finger along Shelbourne's lapel. Then the widow leaned against him and whispered in his ear. He turned his head and flicked her earbob.

Tessa gasped. Stars above. She'd invited that shameless rake to her drawing room.

His teeth flashed in a roguish grin. Then he winked at the lady and strode off.

"How could he engage in such brazen flirtation when his sister is present?" Anne said, her voice outraged.

Tessa swerved her gaze to Anne. "His sister?"

"Lady Julianne," Anne said. "She is dancing with Lord Holbrook."

The dark-haired young woman laughed as she skipped past her partner. Her complexion glowed with the radiance of youth, and her gold-netted gown set off her slender figure to perfection. A sliver of envy lodged in Tessa's throat. Long ago, she'd missed her own opportunity to have a season. Most of the time, she refused to dwell on the past, but once in a while, regret shadowed her heart.

Anne regarded Tessa. "Lady Julianne is purported to have declined more than a dozen marriage proposals since her come-out three years ago."

"She sounds very particular."

"Perhaps it is her brother who is particular," Anne said. "Some say the duke believes no man is good enough for his sister."

Tessa stilled. Did he mean to ask her to make a match for his sister tomorrow? No, surely he would rely on his mother's advice. Why then had he insisted on calling?

Lady Julianne Gatwick has
written a single girl's guide to
enticing unrepentant rakes.
The only problem: No one can
know she wrote it.

Please turn this page for
an excerpt from

How to Seduce

a Scoundrel.

Chapter One

*A Scoundrel's Code of Conduct: Virgins are strictly forbidden,
especially if said virgin happens to be your friend's sister.*

Richmond, England, 1817

He'd arrived late as usual.

Marc Darcett, Earl of Hawkfield, twirled his top hat
as he sauntered along the pavement toward his mother's
home. A chilly breeze ruffled his hair and stung his face.
In the dwindling evening light, Ashdown House with its
crenellated top and turrets stood stalwart near the banks
of the Thames.

Ordinarily, Hawk dreaded the obligatory weekly visits.
His mother and three married sisters had grown increasingly demanding about his lack of a bride since his oldest
friend had wed last summer. They made no secret of their

disappointment in him, but he was accustomed to being the family scapegrace.

Today, however, he looked forward to seeing that oldest friend, Tristan Gatewick, the Duke of Shelbourne.

After the butler, Jones, admitted him, Hawk stripped off his gloves and greatcoat. "Are Shelbourne and his sister here yet?"

"The duke and Lady Julianne arrived two hours ago," Jones said.

"Excellent." Hawk couldn't wait to relate his latest bawdy escapade to his friend. Last evening, he'd met Nancy and Nell, two naughty dancers who had made him an indecent proposition. Not wishing to appear too anxious, he'd promised to think over the matter, but he intended to accept their two-for-the-price-of-one offer.

The fastidious Jones eyed Hawk's head critically. "Begging your pardon, my lord, but you might wish to attend to your hair."

"You don't say?" Hawk pretended to be oblivious and peered at his windblown locks in the mirror above the foyer table. "Perfect," he said. "Mussed hair is all the rage."

"If you say so, my lord."

Hawk spun around. "I take it everyone is waiting in the gold drawing room?"

"Yes, my lord. Your mother has inquired after you several times."

Hawk glanced out at the great hall and grinned at the giant statue next to the stairwell. "Ah, my mother has taken an interest in naked statuary, has she?"

The ordinarily stoic Jones made a suspicious, muffled sound. Then he cleared his throat. "Apollo was delivered yesterday."

"Complete with his lyre and snake, I see. Well, I shall welcome him to the family." Hawk's boots clipped on the checkered marble floor as he strolled toward the cantilevered stairwell, an architectural feat that made the underside of the stone steps appear suspended in midair. At the base of the stairs, he paused to inspect the reproduction and grimaced at Apollo's minuscule genitalia. "Poor bastard."

Footsteps sounded above. Hawk looked up to find Tristan striding down the carpeted steps.

"Sizing up the competition?" Tristan said.

Hawk grinned. "The devil. It's the old married man."

"I saw your curricle from the window." Tristan stepped onto the marble floor and clapped Hawk on the shoulder. "You look as if you just tumbled out of bed."

Hawk wagged his brows and let his friend imagine what he would. "How is your duchess?"

A brief, careworn expression flitted through his friend's eyes. "The doctor says all is progressing well. She has two more months of confinement." He released a gusty sigh. "I wanted a son, but now I'm praying for a safe delivery."

Hawk nodded but said nothing.

"One day it will be your turn, and I'll be the one consoling you."

That day would never come. "And give up my bachelorhood? Never," he said.

Tristan grinned. "I'll remind you of that when I attend your wedding."

Hawk changed the subject. "I take it your sister is well?" His mother planned to sponsor Lady Julianne this season while the dowager duchess stayed in the country with her increasing daughter-in-law.

"Julianne is looking forward to the Season, but there is a problem," Tristan said. "A letter arrived from Bath half an hour ago. Your grandmother is suffering from heart palpitations again."

Hawk groaned. Grandmamma was famous for her heart palpitations. She succumbed to them at the most inconvenient times and described them in minute, loving detail to anyone unfortunate enough to be in the general vicinity. Owing to Grandmamma's diminished hearing, this meant anyone within shouting range.

"Your mother and sisters are discussing who should travel to Bath as we speak," Tristan said.

"Don't worry, old boy. We'll sort it out." No doubt his sisters meant to flee to Bath, as they always did when his grandmother invoked her favorite ailment. Usually his mother went as well, but she'd made a commitment to sponsor Julianne.

A peevish voice sounded from the landing. "Marc, you have dawdled long enough. Mama is waiting."

Hawk glanced up to find his eldest sister, Patience, beckoning him with her fingers as if he were one of her unruly brats. Poor Patience had never proven equal to her name, something he'd exploited since childhood. He never could resist provoking her then, and he certainly couldn't now. "My dear sister, I'd no idea you were so anxious for my company. It warms the cockles of my heart."

Her nostrils flared. "Our grandmother is ill, and Mama is fretting. You will not add to her vexation by tarrying."

"Pour Mama a sherry for her nerves. I'll be along momentarily," he said.

Patience pinched her lips, whirled around, and all but stomped away.

Hawk's shoulders shook with laughter as he returned his attention to his friend. "After dinner, we'll put in a brief appearance in the drawing room and make our escape to the club."

"I'd better not. I'm planning to leave at dawn tomorrow," Tristan said.

Hawk shrugged to hide his disappointment. He ought to have known the old boy meant to return to his wife immediately. Nothing would ever be quite the same now that his friend had married. "Well, then, shall we join the others?"

As they walked up the stairs, Tristan glanced at him with an enigmatic expression. "It's been too long since we last met."

"Yes, it has."

The last time was Tristan's wedding nine months ago. He'd meant to visit the newlyweds after a decent interval. Then Tristan's letter had arrived with the jubilant news of his impending fatherhood.

Hawk's feet had felt as if they were immersed in a bog.

After they entered the drawing room, Hawk halted. He was only peripherally aware of his sisters' husbands scowling at him from the sideboard. All his attention centered on a slender lady seated on the sofa between his mother and his youngest sister, Hope. The candlelight gleamed over the lady's jet curls as she gazed down at a sketchbook on her lap. Good Lord, could this delectable creature possibly be Julianne?

As if sensing his stare, she glanced at him. He took in her transformation, stunned by the subtle changes. In the past nine months, the slight fullness of her cheeks had disappeared, emphasizing her sculpted cheekbones. Even her expression had changed. Instead of her usual impish grin, she regarded him with a poised smile.

The sweet little girl he'd known all his life had become a woman. A heart-stopping, beautiful woman.

The sound of his mother's voice rattled him. "Tristan, please be seated. Marc, do not stand there gawking. Come and greet Julianne."

Patience and his other sister, Harmony, sat in a pair of chairs near the hearth, exchanging sly smiles. No doubt they were hatching a plot to snare him in the parson's mousetrap. They probably thought he was as besotted as the numerous cubs who vied for Julianne's attention every season. But he was only a little taken aback by her transformation.

Determined to take himself in hand, he strode over to her, made a leg, and swept his arm in a ridiculous bow last seen in the sixteenth century.

When he rose, his mother grimaced. "Marc, your hair is standing up. You look thoroughly disreputable."

He grinned like a jackanapes. "Why, thank you, Mama."

Julianne's husky laugh drew his attention. He set his fist on his hip and wagged his brows. "No doubt you will break a dozen hearts this season, Julie-girl."

She regarded him from beneath her long lashes. "Perhaps one will capture my affections."

Helen of Troy's face had launched a thousand ships, but Julianne's naturally raspy voice could fell a thousand men. Where the devil had that foolish thought come from? She'd grown into a stunning young woman, but he'd always thought of her as the little hoyden who climbed trees and skimmed rocks.

Hope stood. "Marc, take my seat. You must see Julianne's sketches."

He meant to make the most of the opportunity. For years, he'd teased Julianne and encouraged her in mischief. After sitting beside her, he grinned and tapped the sketch. "What have you got there, imp?"

She showed him a sketch of Stonehenge. "I drew this last summer when I traveled with Amy and her family."

"Stonehenge is awe-inspiring," the countess said.

He dutifully looked on as Julianne turned the page. "Those are some big rocks."

Julianne laughed. "Rogue."

He tweaked the curl by her ear. When she swatted his hand, he laughed. She was the same Julie-girl he'd always known.

Heavy footsteps thudded outside the drawing room doors. Everyone stood as Lady Rutledge, his great-aunt Hester, lumbered inside. Gray sausage curls peeked out from a green turban with tall feathers. She took one look at Hawk's mother and scowled. "Louisa, that statue is hideous. If you want a naked man, find yourself one who is breathing."

Hawk's mouth worked with the effort not to laugh out loud.

The countess fanned her heated face. "Hester, please mind your words."

"Bah." Hester winked at Hawk. "Come give your aunt a kiss, you rogue."

When he obliged, she muttered, "You're the only sensible one in the bunch."

Tristan bowed to her. "Lady Rutledge."

Hester eyed him appreciatively. "Shelbourne, you

handsome devil. I heard you wasted no time getting your duchess with child."

Hawk's mother and younger sisters gasped. Patience cleared her throat. "Aunt Hester, we do not speak of such indelicate matters."

Hester snorted and kept her knowing gaze on Tristan. "I heard your duchess has gumption. She'll bring your child into the world without mishap—mark my words."

Hawk considered his wily old aunt with a fond smile. Eccentric she might be, but she'd sought to reassure his old friend. And for that alone he adored her.

He led Hester over to a chair and stood beside her. Her wide rump barely fit between the arms. After adjusting her plumes, she held her quizzing glass up to her eye and inspected Julianne.

"Aunt Hester, you remember Lady Julianne," Patience said, as if speaking to a child. "She is Shelbourne's sister."

"I know who she is." Hester dropped her quizzing glass. "Why are you still unwed, gel?"

Julianne blushed. "I am waiting for the right gentleman."

"I heard you turned down a dozen proposals since your come-out. Is it true?" Hester continued.

"I've not kept count," Julianne murmured.

Hester snorted. "There were so many you cannot recall?"

Noting Julianne's disconcerted expression, Hawk intervened. "Mama, I understand we've a bit of a problem. Grandmamma is claiming illness again, is she?"

His mother and sisters protested that they must assume Grandmamma was truly ill. Finally, Aunt Hester interrupted. "Oh, hush, Louisa. You know very well my sister is only seeking attention."

"Hester, how can you say such a thing?" the countess said.

"Because she makes a habit of it." Hester sniffed. "I suppose you and your girls are planning to hare off to Bath on a fool's errand again."

"We cannot take a risk," Patience said. "If Grandmamma took a bad turn, we would never forgive ourselves."

"She ought to come to town where she can be near the family. I offered to share my home with her, but she refuses to leave her cronies in Bath," Hester said.

"She is set in her ways." Hawk grinned down at his aunt. "Few ladies are as adventurous as you."

"True," Hester said, preening.

The countess gave him a beseeching look. "Will you write William to inform him?"

"I'm not sure of his address at present," Hawk said. His younger brother had been traveling on the Continent for more than a year.

Montague, Patience's husband, lowered his newspaper. "It's past time William came home and stopped raking his way all over the Continent. He needs to choose a career and be a responsible member of the family."

Hawk regarded him as if he were an insect. "He'll come home when he tires of wandering." He'd hoped Will would return for the London season, but his brother hadn't written in over two months.

Montague folded his newspaper. "He'd come home soon enough if you cut him off without a penny."

Hawk ignored his least favorite brother-in-law and returned his attention to his mother. "What of Julianne? Her brother brought her all this way. Mama, can you not stay behind?"

"Oh, I could not ask such a thing," Julianne said. "I can stay with either Amy or Georgette. My friends' mothers would welcome me, I'm sure."

"Her friends' mothers will be too busy with their own girls," Hester said. "I will sponsor Julianne. She will be the toast of the Season."

A long silence followed. Hawk's mother and sisters regarded one another with barely concealed dismay. They thought Hester a few cards shy of a full deck, but he knew his aunt was prodigiously clever, if a bit blunt in her manners.

The countess cleared her throat. "Hester, dear, that is too kind of you, but perhaps you have not thought of how exhausting all those entertainments will be."

"I'm never tired, Louisa," she said. "I shall enjoy sponsoring the gel. She's pretty enough and seems lively. I'll have her engaged in a matter of weeks."

Hawk schooled his expression. Julianne married? It seemed so...wrong. Even though he knew it was customary for ladies to marry young, the idea didn't set well with him.

Tristan eyed Hester. "Granted, she's been out four seasons, but marriage is for life. I'll not rush her."

Hester looked at Julianne. "How old are you, gel?"

"One and twenty," she said.

"She's of age, but I agree marriage should not be undertaken lightly," Hester said.

Tristan regarded his sister. "I must approve any serious attachments."

When Julianne rolled her eyes, Hawk grinned. He didn't envy any man bold enough to ask Tristan's permission for Julianne's hand. The old boy had kept a tight rein on her for years—as well he should.

"Now that the matter is settled, let us go to dinner," Hester said. "I'm starved."

After the ladies withdrew from the dining room, Hawk brought out the port. His sisters' husbands exchanged meaningful glances. Tristan kept silent but watched them with a guarded expression.

Montague folded his small hands on the table and addressed Hawk. "Lady Julianne cannot stay with Hester. Your aunt's bold manners and rebellious ideas would be a bad influence on the girl."

Hawk met Tristan's gaze. "Join me in the study?"

Tristan nodded.

They both rose. When Hawk claimed a candle branch from the sideboard, Montague scrambled up from the table. "Patience will stay behind and look after Julianne."

"My sister is determined to go to Bath," Hawk said. "She will not rest easy unless she sees our grandmother is well." The last thing he wanted was to expose Julianne to his sister's acrimonious marriage.

"You know very well your grandmother feigns illness," Montague said. "If your mother and sisters refused to go, that would put a stop to this nonsense."

Hawk realized Montague had seized the opportunity to keep his wife at home. The man constantly queried Patience about her whereabouts and upbraided her if she even spoke to another man. "I'll discuss the matter with Shelbourne. Gentlemen, enjoy your port."

He started to turn away when Montague's voice halted him.

"Damn you, Hawk. Someone needs to take responsibility for the girl."

Hawk strode around the table and loomed over his brother-in-law. "You've no say in the matter." Then he lowered his voice. "You will remember my warning."

Montague glared but held his tongue. Hawk gave him an evil smile. At Christmas, the man had made one too many disparaging remarks about Patience. Hawk had taken him aside and threatened to beat him to a pulp if he ever treated her disrespectfully again.

As he and Tristan strode away, Hawk muttered, "Bloody brute."

"Montague resents your political influence, your fortune, and your superior height. He feels inferior and engages in pissing matches to prove he's manly."

Hawk wished Montague to the devil. The man had campaigned for his sister's hand and showered her with affection. He'd shown his true colors shortly after the wedding.

When they walked into the study, the scent of leather permeated the room. Hawk set the candle branch on the mantel and slumped into one of the cross-framed chairs before the huge mahogany desk. The grate was empty, making the room chilly. He never made use of the study. Years ago, he'd taken rooms at the Albany. His family had disapproved, but he'd needed to escape his father's stranglehold.

Tristan surveyed the surroundings and sat next to Hawk. "The study is virtually unchanged since your father's death."

He'd died suddenly of a heart seizure eight years ago, closing off any chance of reconciliation between them. A foolish thought. There was nothing he could have done to change his father's opinion of him.

"Your father was a good man," Tristan said. "His advice was invaluable to me."

"He admired you," Hawk said.

Tristan had single-handedly restored his fortune after discovering his late wastrel father had left him in monstrous debt.

"I envied your freedom," Tristan said.

"I had an easy time compared to you." Hawk's father had never let him forget it, either. Unbidden, the words his father had spoken more than a dozen years ago echoed in his brain. *Do you even know how much it will cost to satisfy Westcott's honor?*

He mentally slammed the door on the memory. "Old boy, your sister may prefer to stay with one of her friends, but I advise you to refuse if she wishes to stay with Lady Georgette. I heard a nasty rumor about her brother. Evidently, Ramsey got a maid with child." No honorable gentleman ever took advantage of servants.

Tristan's face showed his revulsion. "Good Lord. He's disgusting."

"If you prefer, take your sister to Amy Hardwick's mother."

"No, your aunt is right. Mrs. Hardwick should concentrate on her own daughter." Tristan frowned. "I cannot impose."

Tristan probably felt a bit guilty because Amy and Georgette had devoted their entire season last year to his unusual courtship. "My aunt is a cheeky old bird, but she's harmless enough. Hester will enjoy squiring Julianne about town."

Tristan glanced sideways at Hawk. "I've a favor to ask."

A strange presentiment washed over Hawk. He'd

known Tristan since they were in leading strings, because their mothers were bosom friends. At Eton, he and Tristan had banded together to evade the older boys who liked to torment the younger ones. Hawk knew his friend well, but he'd no idea what Tristan intended to ask of him.

Tristan drew in a breath. "Will you act as my sister's unofficial guardian?"

Hawk laughed. "Me, a guardian? Surely you jest."

"As soon as the fortune hunters discover I'm out of the picture, they'll hover like vultures over Julianne. I won't feel easy unless a solid man is there to protect her from rakes."

"But...but I'm a rake," he sputtered. Of course, she'd blossomed into an uncommonly lovely young woman, but she was his friend's sister. Even among rakes, it was a point of honor to avoid friends' sisters.

"You've watched my sister grow up the same way I have," Tristan said. "She's almost like a sister to you."

He'd never thought of her that way. To him, she was simply Julie-girl, always ready for a bit of mischief. He never grew tired of daring her to do something unladylike, but she'd never once backed down. "Old boy, you know I'm fond of her, but I'm not fit to be anybody's guardian."

"You've always looked out for her," Tristan said.

Guilt spurted in his chest. His own family thought him an irresponsible rogue, with good reason. He didn't even know how to locate his own brother. But clearly Tristan had complete faith in him.

Tristan pinched the bridge of his nose. "I should stay in London to watch over Julianne, but I cannot bear to leave my wife. No matter what I do, I'll feel as if I've wronged one of them."

Ah, hell. Tristan had never asked for a favor before. He was like a brother to him. Damn it all. He couldn't refuse. "Anything for you, old boy."

"Thank you," Tristan said. "There's one more thing. You're not going to like it."

He lifted his brows. "Oh?"

Tristan narrowed his eyes. "You will give up raking for the duration of the Season."

He laughed. "What?"

"You heard me. There will be no ballerinas, actresses, or courtesans. Call them what you will, but you will not associate with whores while guarding my sister."

He scoffed. "It's not as if I'd flaunt a mistress in your sister's face."

"Your liaisons are famous." Tristan tapped his thumb on the arm of the chair. "I've often suspected you delight in your bad reputation."

He made jests about his numerous mistresses. Everyone, including his friend, believed his tall tales. While he was a bona fide rake, Hawk couldn't possibly live up— or was that down?—to the exaggerated reports about his conquests. "I'll not agree to celibacy," he said.

"You don't even try to be discreet. Julianne adores you. I don't want her disillusioned."

"I'll keep my liaisons quiet," Hawk grumbled.

"Agreed," Tristan said.

He'd better forget the ménage à trois with Nell and Nancy. It rather aggrieved him, since he'd never dallied with two women at once, but he couldn't possibly keep that sort of wicked business under the proverbial covers.

Tristan tapped his thumb again. "Write periodically and let me know how my sister fares."

"I will," Hawk said. "Don't worry. Julianne will grow accustomed to my aunt's blunt manners."

"When the babe is born, bring my sister home to me." He smiled. "Tessa already asked Julianne to be godmother. Will you be godfather?"

A knot formed in his chest, but he forced a laugh. "You would trust a rogue like me with your child?"

"There is no one I trust more than you, my friend."

Hawk cut his gaze away, knowing he didn't deserve his friend's regard.

THE DISH

Where authors give you the inside scoop!

From the desk of Vicky Dreiling

Dear Reader,

HOW TO RAVISH A RAKE stars shy wallflower Amy Hardwick and charming rake William Darcett, better known as "the Devil." I thought it would be great fun to feature two characters who seem so wrong for one another on the surface but who would find love and happiness, despite their differences.

Miss Amy Hardwick is a shy belle who made her first appearance in my debut historical romance, *How to Marry a Duke*. When I first envisioned Amy, I realized that she was representative of so many young women who struggle to overcome low self-esteem. Amy doesn't fit the ideal image of the English rose in Regency Society, and, as a result, she's often overlooked by others. But as I thought back to my days in high school and college, I remembered how much it helped to have girlfriends who liked and supported you, even though you didn't have the flawless skin and perfect bodies airbrushed on the covers of teen magazines. That recollection convinced me that having friends would help Amy to grow into the woman I knew she was destined to become.

Now, during her sixth and quite possibly last London Season, Amy is determined to shed her wallflower image forever. A newfound interest in fashion leads Amy to draw designs for unique gowns that make her the fashion darling of the *ton*. All of her dreams seem to be coming true, but there's one man who could deter her from the road to transformation: Mr. William "the Devil" Darcett.

Ah, Will...*sigh*. I confess I had a penchant for charming bad boys when I was in high school and college. There's a certain mystique about them. And I'm certain that the first historical romance I ever read featured a charming bad boy. They really are my favorite type of heroes. So naturally, I decided to create the worst bad boy in the *ton* and throw him in sweet Amy's path.

William Darcett is a younger son with a passion for traveling. He's not one to put down roots—just the occupation for a bona fide rake. But Will's latest plans for another journey to the Continent go awry when he discovers his meddling family wants to curb his traveling days. Will refuses to let his family interfere with his carousing and rambling, but a chance encounter with Amy in a wine cellar leads the wallflower and the rake into more trouble than they're prepared to handle.

This very unlikely pair comes to realize that laughter, family, and honesty are the most important ingredients for everlasting love. I hope you will enjoy the adventures of Amy and Will on their journey to discover that even the unlikeliest of couples can fall madly, deeply in love.

My heartfelt thanks to all the readers who wrote to let me know they couldn't wait to read HOW TO RAVISH A RAKE. I hope you will enjoy the fun and games that finally lead to Happily Ever After for Amy and Will.

Cheers!

♥ ♥ ♥ ♥ ♥ ♥ ♥ ♥ ♥ ♥ ♥ ♥ ♥ ♥ ♥ ♥

From the desk of Amanda Scott

Dear Reader,

What happens when a freedom-loving Scotsman who's spent much of his life on the open sea meets an enticing heiress determined to make her home with a husband who will stay put and run her Highland estates? And what happens when something that they have just witnessed endangers the plans of a ruthless and powerful man who is fiercely determined to keep the details of that event secret?

HIGHLAND LOVER, the third title in my Scottish Knights trilogy, stars the fiercely independent Sir Jacob "Jake" Maxwell, who was a nine-year-old boy in *King of Storms*, the last of a six-book series beginning with *Highland Princess*. Lifting a fictional child from a series I wrote years ago to be a hero in a current trilogy is new for me.

However, the three heroes of Scottish Knights are friends who met as teenage students under Bishop Traill of St. Andrews and later accepted his invitation to join a brotherhood of highly skilled knights that he (fictionally) formed to help him protect the Scottish Crown. I realized straightaway that the grown-up Jake would be the right age in 1403 and would easily fit my requirements, for several reasons:

First, Jake has met the ruthless Duke of Albany, who was a villainous presence in Scotland for thirty-one years (in all) and is now second in line for the throne. Determined to become King of Scots, Albany habitually eliminates anyone who gets in his way. Second, Albany owes his life to Jake, a relationship that provides interesting twists in any tale. Third, Jake is captain of the *Sea Wolf*, a ship he owns because of Albany; and the initiating event in HIGHLAND LOVER takes place at sea. So Jake seemed to be a perfect choice. The cheeky youngster in *King of Storms* had stirred (and still stirs) letters from readers suggesting that an adult Jake Maxwell would make a great hero. Doubtless that also had something to do with it.

Jake's heroine in HIGHLAND LOVER is Lady Alyson MacGillivray of Perth, a beautiful cousin of Sir Ivor "Hawk" Mackintosh of *Highland Hero*. Alyson is blessed (or cursed) with a bevy of clinging relatives and the gift of Second Sight. The latter "gift" has caused as many problems for her as have her intrusive kinsmen.

Alyson also has another problem—a husband of just a few months whom she has scarcely seen and who so far seems more interested in his noble patron's affairs than in Alyson's Highland estates or Alyson herself. But Alyson is trapped in this wee wrinkle, is she not? It is, after all, 1403.

In any event, Jake sets out on a mission for the Bishop of St. Andrews, encounters a storm, and ends up plucking Alyson and an unknown lad from a ship sinking off the English coast two hundred miles from her home in Perth. The ship also happened to be carrying the young heir to Scotland's throne and Alyson's husband, who may or may not now be captive in England.

So, the fun begins. I hope you enjoy HIGHLAND LOVER.

Meantime, *Suas Alba!*

Amanda Scott

www.amandascottauthor.com

♥ ♥ ♥ ♥ ♥ ♥ ♥ ♥ ♥ ♥ ♥ ♥ ♥ ♥

From the desk of Dee Davis

Dear Reader,

I've been a storyteller all of my life. When I was a kid, my dad and I used to sit in the mall or a restaurant and make up stories about the people walking by or sitting around us. So it really wasn't much of a leap to find myself a novelist. But what was interesting to me was that no matter what kind of story I was telling, the characters all seemed to know each other.

Sometimes people from other novels were simply mentioned in another of my books in passing. Sometimes they actually had cameo appearances. And several times now, a character I had created to be a secondary figure in one story has demanded his or her own book. Such was the case with Harrison Blake of DEADLY DANCE. Harrison first showed up in my Last Chance series, working as that team's computer forensic expert. It even turned out he'd also worked for *Midnight Rain*'s John Brighton at his Phoenix organization, even though the company was created at the end of the book and never actually appeared on paper.

Interestingly enough, Harrison, although never a hero, has received more mail than any of my other characters. And almost all of those letters are from readers asking when he's going to have his day. So when A-Tac found itself in need of a technical guru, it was a no-brainer for me to bring Harrison into the fold. As he became an integral part of the team, I knew the time had come for him to have his own book.

And of course, as his story developed, he needed help from his old friends. So enter Madison Roarke and Tracy Braxton. Madison was the heroine of the first Last Chance book, *Endgame*. And like Harrison, Tracy had been placed in the role of supporting character, as a world-class forensic pathologist.

What can I say? It's a small world, and they all know and help each other. And finally, we add to the mix our heroine, Hannah Marshall. Hannah has been at the heart of all the A-Tac books. A long-time team member, she's always there with the answers when needed. And like Harrison, she made it more than clear to me that she deserved her own story. With her quirky way of expressing herself (eyeglasses and streaked hair) and her well-developed intellect, Hannah seemed perfect for Harrison. The two of them just didn't know it yet.

So I threw them together, and, as they say, the plot thickened, and DEADLY DANCE was born.

Hopefully you'll enjoy reading Harrison and Hannah's story as much as I did writing it.

For insight into both Harrison and Hannah, here are some songs I listened to while writing DEADLY DANCE:

Riverside, by Agnes Obel

Set Fire to the Rain, by Adele

Everlong, by Foo Fighters

And as always, check out www.deedavis.com for more inside info about my writing and my books.

Happy Reading!

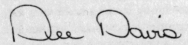

♥ ♥ ♥ ♥ ♥ ♥ ♥ ♥ ♥ ♥ ♥ ♥ ♥ ♥

From the desk of Katie Lane

Dear Reader,

Before I plot out the storyline and flesh out my characters, my books start with one basic idea. Or maybe I should say they start with one nagging, persistent thought that won't leave me alone until I put it down on paper.

Going Cowboy Crazy started with the concept of long-lost twins and what would happen if one twin took over the other twin's life and no one—save the hot football coach—was the wiser.

Make Mine a Bad Boy was the other side of that premise: What would happen if your twin, whom you didn't even know you had, married your boyfriend and left you with a good-for-nothing, low-down bad boy?

And CATCH ME A COWBOY started with a melodrama. You know the kind I'm talking about, the story of a dastardly villain taking advantage of a poor, helpless woman by tying her to the railroad tracks, or placing her on a conveyor belt headed toward the jagged blade of a saw, or evicting her from her home when she has no money to pay the rent. Of course, before any of these things happen, the hero arrives to save the day with a smile so big and bright it rivals the sun.

For days, I couldn't get the melodrama out of my mind. But no matter how much the idea stuck with me, I just didn't see it fitting into my new book. My heroine had already been chosen: a favorite secondary character from the previous novels. Shirlene is a sassy, voluptuous west Texas gal who could no more play the damsel in distress than Mae West could play the Singing Nun. If someone tied Shirlene to the train tracks, she wouldn't scream, faint, or hold the back of her hand dramatically to her forehead. She'd just ask if she had enough time for a margarita.

The more I thought of my sassy heroine dealing with a Snidely Whiplash–type, the more I laughed. The more I laughed, the more I wrote. And suddenly I had my melodrama. Except a funny thing happened on the way to Shirlene's Happily Ever After: My villain and my hero got a little mixed up. And before I knew it, Shirlene had so charmed the would-be villain that he stopped the train. Shut off the saw. Paid the rent.

And how does the hero with the bright smile fit into all of this? you might ask.

Well, let's just say I don't think you'll be disappointed. CATCH ME A COWBOY is available now.

Enjoy, y'all!

Katie Lane

Find out more about Forever Romance!

Visit us at
www.hachettebookgroup.com/publishing_forever.aspx

Find us on Facebook
http://www.facebook.com/ForeverRomance

Follow us on Twitter
http://twitter.com/ForeverRomance

NEW AND UPCOMING TITLES

Each month we feature our new titles
and reader favorites.

CONTESTS AND GIVEAWAYS

We give away galleys, autographed copies,
and all kinds of exclusive items.

AUTHOR INFO

You'll find bios, articles, and links to personal websites
for all your favorite authors—and so much more.

GET SOCIAL

Connect with your favorite authors, editors, and
other Forever fans, and share what's important to you.

THE BUZZ

Sign up for our monthly romance newsletter,
and be the first to read all about it.